Misconduct's Deadly Denial

Treachery and Fraud
in
the Research Lab

James E. Mosimann

Brightview Press
Gainesville, Virginia

Brightview Press, LLC
ISBN 978-0-9897659-0-9
July 2014

For my wife, Jean,
and her insistence on Truth.

Contents

Prologue
Summer

The recent rain had brought the desert to life. The paloverdes were in leaf, and the pungent odor of creosote bushes tickled the nostrils. Towering saguaros, bloated with water, dominated the Arizona landscape.

The walk was his idea. She was unprepared. Her shorts and sneakers did not protect her legs from the spines of the abundant cholla cacti. She could feel the sharp rocks of the bajada through her thin soles. She had to step carefully.

Still, she was deliriously happy. He had changed his mind. He had just told her that he wanted now to keep the baby, their child, and that he loved her, and that they would marry soon. At his words, the sky glowed as if with new life. The lustrous desert sunset with its brilliant red streaks, shadowed by alternating lines of violet and gray clouds, reflected her joy and peace. At last! He wanted her and the life newly-conceived within her!

Then the snake struck. She hardly felt it, but there on her leg were the tell-tale twin droplets of blood. She cried out and then froze. The somber saguaro cactus next to her also stood motionless.

Her first thought was one of relief. He was a skilled doctor. He would know what to do. But then she saw him deftly grab the rattlesnake and thrust it into a sack. *My God! It's one of the snakes from the lab! He brought it for me! No! He wouldn't! This can't be happening! Not true!* She fainted.

She awoke to an excruciating pain in her leg. *Where are you? Help me!* Her vision blurred. The pain! She tried to focus. He was gone. She cried out. There was no answer. The somber saguaro stayed silent. *God, help me!* She passed out once more.

She lost all sense of time. Dully, she realized she was walking, struggling along the trail. He was in front of her,

1

watching. *Oh God!* Her left side was on fire. Her leg burned at the hip. The lower leg was numb. For a brief second her vision cleared. She saw his eyes. They were blank, expressionless. *My God, I'm like one of his experiments!* She could not handle that! *No! Help me! Please!* She collapsed.

She awoke again. Now it was night. She was alone in his car, in the front seat. He was nowhere. She could barely move. She struggled to see her swollen leg. Vaguely she became aware of a light. It was the lab window. She was in the back parking lot.

She retched with pain. She gasped. *This is your baby! Where are you? Help us! Please!* Twisting in agony, she fumbled for the door handle. *Where is it?* Feebly she pushed. It would not yield. *Help!*

Finally, the toxin impacted the blood supply to her brain. Her thoughts slowed, and then stopped altogether. Her struggle ceased.

He peered out the window, satisfied. Deliberately, without haste, he retrieved the antivenin from the lab supply. Enough time had passed. She could not recover. It should be "safe" to inject her now. That would prove he had tried to save her. He walked out to the car.

***

It was a perfect plan, with a single flaw in its execution.

A young immunologist, Mike Hartness, had returned to the lab that evening to complete an experiment. He had seen the pair walk off into the cool desert evening. Nothing remarkable, but later he had witnessed the macabre return.

Now, from a dark window, he observed the doctor open the passenger door and begin to "aid" his victim.

***

******

Five Years Later
Chapter 1
Tuesday, November 28

Mike Hartness looked up from his desk. Dr. Lawrence stood in the doorway.

"Mike, where's my data? The talk's tomorrow."

"I'll have a thumb drive for you in a minute."

Dr. Lawrence arched his eyebrows. He did not move.

Mike shifted in his seat.

"No, wait. It's all set. I'll do it now."

It was the simplest of computer tasks. He only needed to copy seven small files from the folder *ran1* to the portable drive.

But Mike was flustered. In his haste he clicked *Select All*, and so dragged all the files in the folder. As a result, one additional file was on the thumb drive for Dr. Lawrence.

The mistake was to change Mike's life.

***

The voice came from the hallway.

"John, Dr. Lawrence wants you in the seminar room! He's having a party."

John Martin grimaced at his watch, 5:30 p.m. He was busy.

A party? There was little frivolity in the Immunology Department of Fairland University's School of Medicine, and none in Dr. Lawrence's laboratory. Curiosity overcame his irritation at stopping work. John headed down the hall.

In the usually staid seminar room, the conference table was covered with a green table cloth. On it red plastic plates were piled high with cheese, pretzels and crackers. At each end of the table was a Styrofoam ice chest. The one near the door was stocked with beer: Heineken, Samuel Adams, Killian's. John took a bottle of Killian's Red lager.

He tilted his head backwards and swallowed. The draught relaxed him. His eyes rested on a petite young woman wearing a soft gray sweater and worn jeans. Monique Laurier was from

Canada. She had come to Washington a year ago, the same time as John. Both were postdoctoral fellows under Dr. Lawrence. Both had come to the U. S. Capital to do research under his direction.

Monique caught John's stare and started towards him. She spoke with a slight accent.

"What's the party about?"

"I hoped you would know."

"Well Mike knows. Look at that grin! And he's drinking wine. He doesn't like wine!"

John looked. Dr. Mike Hartness, the senior postdoctoral fellow in the lab, stood next to Dr. Lawrence. Both were near the other ice chest. It contained several bottles of wine.

Monique saw the labels.

"C'est le ... Sorry ... It's the Beaujolais Nouveau, the new Beaujolais, chilled! Dr. Lawrence has good taste. I think I'll try some."

She slipped away.

John's eyes lingered on her longer than Jeannine Ryan would have liked. Monique was appealing. He shook himself.

Elsewhere about the room, two dozen people clinked bottles and beakers while chatting in twos or threes. High-pitched tones and laughter bounced off the walls to produce a confused clatter.

The classless scientific assembly was marked by lots of distinctions. The only tie was worn by the dapper Dr. Santini, the Chairman of Immunology. Dr. Lawrence, whose laboratory was in Santini's Department, sported a white, coffee-stained, lab coat. Both the good doctors stood erect and confident. They had permanent academic tenure.

Dr. Santini's white-haired secretary hovered nervously above the food and drinks. She wore a dress. All others in the room, like John, wore jeans or cotton slacks with sweaters or casual shirts.

The jeans of the two lab technicians from Dr. Lawrence's molecular biology section bore stains of genuine lab reagents.

John envied their relaxed attitude. They had nothing to prove, unlike the Postdocs who, like John, wanted to establish their research careers.

John drew another bottle of Killian's from the ice. Dr. Lawrence cleared his throat.

"Harrumph!"

The talking ceased. The lab chief held his glass aloft. The Beaujolais shone and wavered, rippling over the rim to add a distinctive red stain to the lab coat. Dr. Lawrence chose not to notice. Glass high, his eyes circled the room. His audience was silent, waiting. He sipped, savoring wine and moment. His eyes sparkled.

"You're all wondering why I called you here this evening on such short notice."

He sipped once more.

"Yesterday I received notice from the National Cancer Institute of their *Intent to Fund* our latest research proposal, the RO1 we put in last February."

His glass rose higher in triumph. Another red stain appeared on the lab coat.

"This new grant gives us over *seven ... million ... dollars, ...*"

His eyes circled the room.

"Over *seven million dollars* over the next five years for our fight against breast cancer!"

He paused for further effect.

"As you know, *Intent to Fund* doesn't mean anything if the National Cancer Institute doesn't have enough money. But this afternoon I called the Program Officer at NCI. She told me we're so high on the list that we're a sure thing! We will be funded! I want to celebrate now and not wait for our final notice."

The room resounded with shouts and clapping that echoed off the walls and ceiling. Most in the room, including John, were paid by Dr. Lawrence's current grants for cancer research. The increased job security was good news for all.

Dr. Lawrence put down the empty glass. He held up his hand for silence. The other hand found Dr. Hartness' shoulder. The latter gulped his wine while his chief continued.

"We owe a lot to Mike! He prepared most of the grant, and thanks to him, we are fully funded. Under his leadership, our most recent postdoctoral fellows, ..."

He looked at John and then Monique.

"... are going to pursue my work to stop breast cancer, once and for all! Our agent A-11 inhibits the activity of Dr. Johnson's oncogene, 'protein CA,' and this new grant means the NCI endorses my approach."

He retrieved his glass, refilled by a grateful technician.

"Tomorrow I'm flying to Chicago to present our research at the annual meetings. I'll acknowledge all of you in my talk."

"One more thing. Thanks to Dr. Hartness, we beat out Dr. Johnson's team at Rochester. Their application to the Cancer Institute will not be funded."

His eyes circled the room one last time.

"I'd like to stay, but it's my daughter's birthday, and I'll be in Chicago tomorrow. I'll be back Thursday. Until then Mike's in charge of the lab."

Dr. Lawrence drained his glass and headed for the door.

As if on cue, a boom box began blasting a species of synthesized rock, and the voices of those in conversation rose to surmount the elevated sound. The party began in earnest.

John left. He had work to finish.

***

The windows in the Forster Building often shone late into the night. Last night John Martin had worked until 2:00 a.m., preparing radioactively-tagged samples for the gamma counter. Today, he had come in early to check the counts and stayed. His only interruption had been the party.

Back in his lab, John felt the two Killian's. He yawned and looked out the window. The pedestrians on the sidewalk below walked hurriedly, with buttoned coats. *It must be cold.*

He heard footsteps. A white lab coat filled the doorway. It was Dr. Lawrence.

"John, I want you to check my data for tomorrow's talk."

He handed John a sheaf of papers and a thumb drive.

"These are the tables for my talk, and Mike's drive. Look them over for me. If you find any problems, call me tonight at the house. You'll get a feel for what we've done."

Dr. Lawrence smiled.

"John, I'm glad you're on my team."

John, already warmed by two Killian's, was warmed further.

Dr. Lawrence turned, lab coat swirling, and left.

After two beers John was ready to relax, but he wanted to please Dr. Lawrence. The latter, in addition to the grant just announced, had three other research grants. John added up the dollars, *in millions*. He whistled. The future was bright.

John looked at his watch. Jeannine would be waiting.

He put Mike's thumb drive in his pocket, and left. He shivered and zipped his jacket for the walk to the apartment.

✱✱✱

Far to the north, Pierre Lachance looked out the window of his apartment. Outside, the lights of Lachine, Québec shone sharply on leafless branches that twisted and tossed above empty park benches. The few well-wrapped pedestrians strode hurriedly. The temperature was below freezing.

Pierre decided to dress in layers. He put on his black woolen sweater, topped by a black half-length coat and scarf.

He had memorized André's instructions. Tonight, Pierre was to take the Styrofoam chest, packed with dry ice, to the border. He did not know the contents. André had told him, *Matériaux biologiques, c'est tout! Biological material, that's all!*

Pierre did not care. He was glad that the chest was not heavy. His code name, "Napoléon," was dumb, but the directions were clear, and his contact would understand French. Aside from the Provincial Police, the only problem was to find "le pin blanc," the White Pine, that marked the meeting place.

He looked at his watch. He had lots of time. Still he should get started. He could eat at Iberville on his way to the U. S. border. He picked up the Styrofoam chest.

***

Back at his apartment, John Martin turned on the computer. The back of his neck ached, and the whisper-whir of the computer's fan annoyed him. He rubbed his eyes and looked at Mike's data. There were no problems, but there was one more file. It was not data, but a computer program. John scanned the code.

Damn it Mike, why would you write a program like this?

John brought up a console window and typed commands from the keyboard. His eyes blinked. The computer screen blinked back. The compile was successful. He typed the name of Mike's program and struck *ENTER*.

He turned his eyes to avoid the strain of tracking the numbers that paraded in rows up the screen. After a few moments, as if in response to a military command, the numbers stopped marching and stood at attention. The run was done.

Jeannine's voice reached up the stairs.

"John, what are you doing? Aren't you coming?"

"Be down in a minute, I'm checking Dr. Lawrence's data for his lecture on breast cancer tomorrow. He's going to Chicago."

"John, you can't work like this every night."

He did not respond. He fixed his eyes on the monitor.

"Damn it! What the hell?"

The numbers on the screen were the data for the talk. Mike's program had generated them by computer. They had nothing to do with cancer. There had been no experiments. The "data" were meaningless. They were fake!

Dr. Lawrence must not give his talk. *No way!*

His stomach tightened. *This is terrible! These data are faked. Dr. Lawrence's talk is a lie, a fraud!*

John pushed through the papers on the desk to find his chief's number. His hand shook as he lifted the phone.

***

*****

Chapter 2
Tuesday, November 28

Dinner at the Lawrence household was usually a twosome. Either thirteen-year-old Sari and her mother ate together while Dr. Lawrence worked late at the lab, or equally often, Sari would eat at her friend Mattie's house, and Betty would share a late meal with Franklin. Tonight, Sari's birthday, was the exception. The three were together.

Betty liked the effect she had created for their evening. Silver candlesticks shone reflectively above the fine china brought out for the occasion. The steam from the wild rice rose and mingled with the gray wisps of smoke from the candles. Even her husband's hair, with its distinguished silvery streaks, blended into the visual composition.

The table was quiet. Sari stared at the gift next to her father. Betty broke the silence.

"Would you like more rice, Franklin?"

When first married, Betty had been afraid to interrupt her husband's silences. She had imagined that he was probing some deep scientific problem. Now she wasn't sure.

Franklin Wilson Lawrence's "deep" deduction of the moment was that his mother (and father whom he'd never known) probably had given him two "last" names to go with "Lawrence" because three "first" names would have lacked dignity.

"Do you want more rice, Franklin?"

"No thank you. I'm fine."

Sari was tired of the inactivity.

"Daddy! Wake up! It's my birthday. I want my present!"

"Daddy" twitched his daughter's hair. He turned to his wife.

"Now Betty, have you told Sari about her special present?"

"Franklin, you said we'd discuss that before we ..."

"Nonsense, look Sari, Daddy's got something for you."

Sari tore open the package. She gasped at the earrings.

"Posts! I'm getting my ears pierced! Oh Daddy!"

She threw a sideways look of triumph at her mother. Mercifully, Betty had her back turned. She was headed to the kitchen.

The phone rang. Sari ignored it.

"Thanks Daddy. You're great! Ears pierced! ... I can't wait ... It's just what I wanted. Mattie will scream."

In the kitchen, Betty picked up the phone.

"Hello?"

"Mrs. Lawrence, this is John Martin from the lab. Can I speak to Dr. Lawrence? It's very important."

"John, he'll have to call you back. He's busy."

"But, it's important. It's about his talk tomorrow in Chicago. I'm sorry to bother him, but I need to talk to him."

Betty knew John, and liked him, but she was not going to allow Franklin's work to disrupt another evening, not this night.

"I'm sorry, John he'll have to call you back."

She hung up, and then punched her own number into the phone. She heard the busy signal and put the instrument on the kitchen counter. No more interruptions!

Betty returned to the table. Franklin's eyes queried her. She stammered.

"That was John Martin from the lab. He said it was important. He wants you to call."

Surprised by her own temerity, she wheeled back to the kitchen.

Franklin started to call after her, but Sari was not to be upstaged. With her mother safe in the kitchen, Sari wanted more.

"Daddy, Mattie's mom got her a pair of designer jeans."

Before Franklin could reply, Betty arrived with Franklin's favorite cake, German Chocolate. Sari frowned, but caught herself. It was her birthday and this was not strawberry, her favorite, but things were going too well for a pout.

Betty sat to watch Franklin enjoy his first bite.

***

The whole evening was unusual. It was not often that family took precedence over profession in the life of Franklin Wilson Lawrence, Ph. D., M. D.

That night, Franklin was surprised by Betty's enthusiasm in bed. Only later, lying sexually spent and half awake with her sleeping body pressing warmly against his back, did he think of John's phone call. But his thoughts had already slowed. The phrase *I'll call him from the airport* drifted through his consciousness. Moments later he was snoring.

***

John heard the repeated buzzes. *Damn it, still busy!* Dr. Lawrence had a teen-age daughter, but how long could anyone, even a teenager, talk on the phone?

He had called repeatedly. Now it was near midnight. He gave up and went downstairs.

From the door he saw Jeannine, on the sofa, studying.

He slipped out of the apartment.

***

The Canadian sky was clear. A bright moon scattered its light on the leafless branches that Pierre Lachance pushed aside so he could locate "le pin blanc" on the summit above. The White Pine was just as André had described. It was the largest tree on the ridge. Its jagged and broken silhouette, with branches at right angles to the trunk, was easy to spot.

He climbed upwards. The dark shadows of conical evergreens, man-sized, obscured his view as he wove a path between them.

"Damn!"

He stumbled on a rock and fell into one of the dark shadows. He winced, expecting the sharp needles of an épinette, a spruce. Instead he felt the yielding leaves and twigs of a sapin, a fir tree. He righted himself and smiled. The Styrofoam container was intact.

The November cold pierced his gloves. His feet crunched on the frozen ground. He hiked higher. The trees were larger and the shadows deeper. He could no longer see the summit, nor the

11

big tree. He gained the ridge. Above him, branches rubbed and creaked with the wind. Ahead he saw a thick trunk, the White Pine.

A harsh voice stopped him.

"Qui va la? Who's there?"

The voice came from the shadow of the trunk. Pierre could see no one. He wanted to get this business over with. He replied as instructed.

"Ici Napoléon, je l'ai. Et toi, as-tu le fric? It's Napoleon, I've got it, do you have the cash?"

The voice's owner seemed satisfied.

"Over here, put it down."

The accent was American. They were near the Vermont border. Pierre drew a sharp breath. He hoped he was still in Canada.

He stepped towards the tree. Pine needles rustled and slid under his shoes. He saw a bulky envelope lying by emergent gnarled roots at the base of the trunk. Pierre balanced his container on the roots. He picked up the envelope.

Throughout, he kept his eyes lowered. He did not want to see faces. He felt his every movement was scrutinized. He thought to open the envelope and count the contents, but a slight creaking of branches behind him, and a stirring of dry needles from the same direction, revealed his vulnerability.

The "voice" from the tree trunk was not alone.

Pierre clutched the envelope and hastened down the hillside. A cloud passed in front of the moon, and he had to feel his way through the dark evergreens. He did not look back.

***

Jeannine Ryan was a graduate student in mathematical statistics at Fairland University. She and John Martin had shared their apartment for six months.

John had gone out. She welcomed the silence. She had a test tomorrow. It was the last course before her thesis research.

She leaned over her notes. The math by itself was not a problem (her Master's degree was in pure mathematics), but the study of statistics challenged her. As a statistician she wanted to use mathematics in the real world.

She shook the red hair from her forehead. *OK, let's see what this Bayesian Inference is all about.* Professor Anderson, in his lecture had seemed to imply that two different scientists, looking at the same data, *should not* reach the same conclusions. That sounded wrong. She must have misunderstood. She would ask John.

As a working biologist, John always hammered her about *data*, and not going beyond the *data*. He saw things in data. It was as if numbers spoke to him.

Maybe John and Professor Anderson would agree on how to interpret data. They both seemed to agree that Jeannine was attractive. She had worn her pink pullover and Page Premium jeans to Anderson's last lecture. She was sure he had approved.

She returned to her notebook. She plunged into the waves of equations she had written in neat rows on the page, and soon was completely immersed.

***

A cold light rain dampened John's shoulders as he walked along the sidewalk. The blacktop of the adjacent street reflected countless lights. The drivers of cars, wipers on intermittent, did not notice the lone walker in the shadows. Likewise, John noticed neither the cars, or his damp sweater.

Damn! He'd been in a good mood. Things were fine in the lab. He had at least one interesting cell line, a "hybridoma" as he had explained to Jeannine. It had properties similar to Dr. Lawrence's A-11 for treating breast cancer.

John was flattered that Dr. Lawrence had asked him to check calculations for the Chicago talk. That meant he was part of the team. Besides, how long could it take to check the data? It should have been routine. But the 'data' were not data! They were fake, from a computer. *Damn it, Mike, how could you do this? You're a scientist!*

John's uncertainty was mirrored in the glistening droplets that clung to the bare branches, as if afraid to fall, afraid to let go. He was afraid of Dr. Lawrence's reaction.

He watched as a swollen droplet did let go. It plummeted to the sidewalk, splattered and disappeared. No reassurance there.

Damn it!

Why hadn't Dr. Lawrence returned his call?

***

******

Chapter 3
Wednesday, November 29

Betty was up early. She tossed on a pale blue bathrobe, and brushed her sandy neck-length hair. Spinning about, she checked herself in the mirror. *Not bad.*

Humming, she went down to the kitchen. Her mood was as diffused and natural as the soft lighting and gentle pale shadows of the room. It was not light outside, but the large windows drew in what was available. Upstairs, Sari still slept.

Betty stood by the window and sipped her coffee. Franklin came downstairs. He looked distinguished. She handed him a steaming cup.

Franklin wanted an academic look for his talk. He'd chosen a blue gray Scottish tweed jacket over a light tan Cashmere sweater atop dark navy slacks. His tie was flannel in texture, and the shoes were cordovan wing tips. His bifocals would stay home. He had his half-frame reading glasses with horned rims.

When Franklin was a young resident, he'd been impressed by one of his mentors who would pause in the middle of a presentation, put on his reading glasses to read his notes, and stare over the half-frames. To the young Dr. Lawrence such stares signaled the superiority of the speaker.

"I'm older, smarter and wiser than you. There's a big gap between my extensive knowledge and yours. I doubt if you'll be able to bridge the gap, but on the slim chance that you might, I'll continue my presentation."

(Dr. Ohlandt, whose name Franklin had long forgotten, would have been amused at the impact of his reading glasses on the latter. A humble man, he'd been embarrassed to reveal his defective vision, and consequent proof of his age, to the general public.)

Franklin smiled at Betty as he recalled the night before. He was startled to see how attractive she looked in her robe. Betty, at forty, was still desirable.

She returned his half-smile with a full one, but then Franklin looked at his watch and picked up his briefcase. The moment was lost. She peered into her coffee, not quite sure of what to look for, but sure she didn't want him to see her hurt. A horn sounded in the street. His ride was here. He stood up.

"The flight back will be late, don't wait up for me."

Betty did not look up until she heard the taxi pull away.

The cab left Maryland and crossed the Potomac River into Virginia. Traffic on the GW Parkway was worse than usual and they arrived at Reagan National Airport with barely enough time to pass security. Carryon in hand, Franklin was the last passenger to board the flight to Chicago's O'Hare Airport. As he settled in his seat, he exclaimed.

"Blast it, I forgot to call John."

But his talk was in the afternoon, he would call before then.

***

The sun shone through the window and woke John from a night of intermittent sleep and worry. Jeannine was gone, but the coffee was made and there was a greenish yellow banana on the table. It was late, 8:30 a.m.

With half the banana in his cheeks, John went upstairs to retrieve Mike's thumb memory with the fake data. He turned to his computer, made a new directory called "Mike-fake," and copied Mike's files to it. Then he put the thumb drive into his pocket.

John's stomach was uneasy. Was it the green banana, the lack of sleep, or the unpleasant task in front of him? No matter, he stepped outside. It was cool but sunny. Like so many Washington days, by noon he would no longer need his jacket. The lab was ten blocks away. He started to walk.

***

In his Lachine apartment, Pierre's head slipped from the arm of the chair, and jerked him awake. The traffic noise from the street confirmed that it was morning. He touched the stubble on his chin and opened his eyes. He had slept in his chair.

The valuable envelope lay on the table in front of him. He counted the money. The bills were American. There were 15 packets. Each with $4,000 in hundred-dollar bills, $60,000 in all!

Pierre restored 12 packets to the envelope, folded the flap and tied the resulting package. This $48,000 he would deliver to André. The remaining three packets, $12,000, were his share. He put two of them into a sack. The other forty bills, $4,000, were for his mother. Pierre wrapped them in a plastic lunch bag.

He went to the phone and composed a familiar number. The woman on the other end of the line brightened at her son's voice.

"Maman, my boss gave me a bonus for a big sale. ... Yes, he likes my work. ... Yes Maman, I love you too. I'll put the money in the usual place. ... It's a lot of money, $4,000 American."

At his mother's gasp, Pierre felt justified in his "profession."

"Maman, pick it up this afternoon, and don't let him know."

"Him" was Pierre's father whom he detested.

Pierre's mother lived in East Montreal where Pierre was not welcome, neither by his father who was usually drunk, nor by the police who, on occasion, would drive by the mother's apartment on the chance of spotting Pierre. Today, however, he would be making two "deliveries" there, one to André, his real employer, and the other to the secret drop he and his mother had arranged to hide money from the alcoholic father.

Pierre stuffed his mother's "lunch" into his pocket and left the apartment. He walked bent forward into a cold wind.

***

At the top of the state of Vermont an unmarked and unpaved road splits off northwards and runs just south of, and parallel to, the Canadian border for several miles. To the north in Canada, an unpaved road dips south to likewise run parallel to the border. The two roads, within one mile of each other, are separated by a steep rocky ridge crowned by a mix of hardwoods and evergreens. Along this deserted stretch, no road crosses the ridge, and not even all-terrain vehicles can traverse it.

On the Vermont side, a metallic-blue Geo with Vermont plates bounced along the unpaved road. Its driver, a young, dark-haired woman, admired the sunlit hardwoods on the rocky ridge that rose high to her left. Behind it and out of sight was Canada, while to her right, a wooded hillside covered by somber spruce and fir, was shadowed from the morning sun.

The Geo's driver, Cecilia Hernandez, braked and turned onto a private roadway with a steep incline. She shifted to low gear and pressed on the accelerator. The little car spun its wheels upwards, displacing stones and rocks that rattled against its under frame. At that familiar sound, Cecilia imagined she was home in the Arizona desert, on a side road in the Tucson Mountains.

But the dark fir trees that lined the ascent forced her back to cold northern reality. The morning was bright and cold (downright freezing to Cecilia). As she neared her destination, a thin vertical wisp of smoke rose and spent its strength in a vain effort to warm the sky. The smoke was from Madame Gauthier's cabin. Cecilia smiled in anticipation of warming her hands on a cup of hot coffee. She wheeled the blue Geo in a semicircle in front of the house and stopped. The motor coughed as if puffing after the steep climb.

Tonnerre, Madame Gauthier's dog, a hulking Black-Lab-Shepherd barked furiously.

"Perro, vete!"

Tonnerre recognized Cecilia and, discomfited, retreated around the corner of the house. She pressed her jacket against her body and hurried to the door of the cabin.

Marie-Thérèse Gauthier had endured Tonnerre's thunderous barking for several minutes. He had announced Cecilia's arrival from the moment she turned onto the lane to the cabin. The dog's barking was a comfort. Madame Gauthier lived alone.

When she saw the blue car pull round the fir alley and stop, she set a stout log onto the already blazing fire. Then she shuffled to the table and poured a steaming cup of coffee to match her own. That done she went to the door.

She pulled Cecilia's jacketed arm into the room and shut the door against the cold draft that squeezed in behind her. She sat Cecilia close to the fire and handed the coffee to her.

"Ma petite, warm yourself."

This was Cecilia's first northern winter, and her hands welcomed the cup's warmth. (To herself, she thought that on her budget, hot water would do as well as coffee.)

Cecilia glanced at the Catholic crucifix on the wall and thought of a similar one in her own family home, far away in the Southwest. On the shelf by the door a framed photograph of the grandson smiled at her. He was Cecilia's age. The grandson was Madame Gauthier's single boast, the only son of her daughter Lucille who lived in Montreal.

On her first visit last Spring, Cecilia had identified herself as a special agent with the United States Customs. Then she had asked Madame Gauthier if she would mind reporting any unusual, or for that matter usual, activity along the road that she might see or hear, particularly at night. The older woman hadn't been sure that a girl so young, and with such pretty black hair, should, or could, do such work, but Madame Gauthier, a naturalized American, felt it her duty to help. She had agreed.

"Mais oui. Of course."

Duty to country soon changed to warm affection, and Madame Gauthier counted on Cecilia's visits. Her beloved Charles would have welcomed such a "daughter" into the family with pride.

This morning, Madame Gauthier was exhilarated. She had official information to report to her young friend. Madame Gauthier waved her hands. Cecilia, put down her cup and followed, as best she could, the rapidly-delivered speech. The words came fast.

"C'est le moteur qui m'a réveillé. ...matin. ... y'en avait deux, ... lumières ... The motor woke me up. ... lights, there were two of them ... colline, ... là-bas où se trouve le pin blanc."

Madame Gauthier pointed out the window. Cecilia caught up.

"About one in the morning... on the other side of the road...two lights that climbed the hill, there by that White Pine."

Cecilia looked. There was a clear line of sight towards Canada. Leaves had fallen and she could see through the once opaque forest. On the ridge across the way stood a statuesque evergreen tree whose branches shot out haphazardly at right angles from its trunk. Trees on the lower slopes blocked the view of the road.

She frowned and turned to the white-haired woman.

"You didn't turn on any lights here, did you?"

Madame Gauthier shook her head "No." Cecilia continued.

"And Tonnerre?"

Madame Gauthier again shook her head.

"Dans la cuisine. Here in the kitchen, he didn't bark."

Cecilia sighed with relief. *Thank you God for keeping that dog inside.* She spoke.

"S'il vous plaît Madame, keep Tonnerre in the house, and don't leave any lights on when you go to bed."

She was concerned for the safety of this frail woman. She was alone. Her only defense besides Tonnerre was concealment. Her house was the only dwelling for several miles, and was not visible from the road below. The entrance to her access lane was hidden by a big spruce. Casual passersby at night would not suspect its presence.

Cecilia was anxious to leave. She finished the rest of her coffee. After a warm embrace, she stepped outside into the cold.

***

Cecilia drove the Geo around the other side of the line of fir trees, and stopped on the access lane. Her car was not visible from Madame Gauthier's windows nor from the state road below. Cecilia checked her revolver, a "snubby" five-shot Smith & Wesson .38, stainless steel with a short 1-7/8 inch barrel. Loaded, everything was in order. She pointed the weapon at one of the firs. Satisfied, she put it back under her jacket.

She took the phone out of her backpack. She reached her partner's answering machine.

"Sam, I'm at Checkpoint Charley."

Cecilia had adopted the name for this location because of its association with Charles, Madame Gauthier's late husband.

"Its 10:30 a.m. I'm checking the hill opposite, with a big pine on the top. Suspicious activity last night, I'll call in by noon."

It was as cold as when she had arrived over an hour ago, but Cecilia was warm with caffeine and adrenaline. She swung her arms vigorously as she descended the rocky roadway on foot. At the bottom, on the other side of the road, she found a small stream bordered by dense thickets of alders, red osiers and other plants.

She pushed through the alders and brush and reached the stream. There was ice on the emergent rocks, but by stepping carefully she crossed without wetting her leather hikers. The summit was lost from view.

She worked her way up through the dense woods. The thick soles of her hikers protected her feet from the sharp-edged rocks underfoot. Frozen branches scratched at her jacket. She perspired under her arms while, at the same time, the cold air dried and froze her nose and cheeks. It grew colder, but in her excitement she did not care. She continued upwards in the direction she had last seen the big pine.

At the top of the ridge, Cecilia examined the ground under the White Pine. She saw trampled bracken fern where someone had waited. Moving in circles out from the tree, she found another trampled spot. At least two people had waited here.

She located a path north down the hill. A dislodged rock lay next to a fir tree with broken branches. Had someone fallen there? She shielded her face with her arms, and pushed downwards through brittle branches. Finally she broke into the open.

This was surely Canada.

At the edge of a road, a swath of plants had been pressed down, evidently by car tires, but the ground was frozen and there were no impressions.

Now the cold was bitter. She rubbed gloved hands together and climbed back up the ridge. From the top she could see the smoke from Madame Gauthier's house rise above the trees on the hill opposite. The stone walls of her house, shielded by evergreens, blended with the rocky terrain. Cecilia was reassured. If the smugglers, as she was convinced they were, worked only after dark they would not know of Madame Gauthier's presence.

Cecilia descended to the road about a quarter-mile from Madame Gauthier's entrance lane. Someone had arranged rocks to permit a dry crossing of the icy streamlet. Their wide placement confirmed that whatever packages had been carried were not heavy.

Cecilia walked the quarter mile back to Madame Gauthier's access lane. Her toes were rigid as she trudged up the frozen gravel to the Geo. She called in her status to Sam.

She drove down the hill and headed back to Rouses Point. After a long time, warm air came out of the car's heater. She could feel her toes again on the accelerator.

***

******

Chapter 4
Wednesday, November 29

Dr. Lawrence's laboratory in the Immunology Department of Fairland University's School of Medicine had two sections, Immunology and Molecular Biology. The former had three postdoctoral fellows, all paid under grants from the National Institutes of Health to Dr. Lawrence as Principal Investigator.

Mike Hartness was the most senior. He'd been in the lab for four years. He had published five papers with Dr. Lawrence. All were in respected journals.

After a year, John Martin and Monique Laurier each had a research project near completion. Neither yet had published with Dr. Lawrence, but John had found a hybridoma whose protein, like A-11, inhibited the activity of Johnson's protein CA. His paper was almost ready for Dr. Lawrence's review.

When John arrived the lab was quiet. Mike stood near the door to his "office," a former closet. Monique was at her bench. John stopped to watch her as she prepared dilutions in a "96-well plate." With fluid motions, she used a gun-shaped pipette with eight tips to produce eight wells in which her initial preparation was diluted 3-fold, another eight wells diluted 9-fold; and eight more diluted 27-fold.

He was impressed, he could not work that fast. His eyes drifted from her soft brown eyes to a trim figure. Monique was not only capable, but attractive. He nodded to her.

She looked up and nodded back.

John walked to Mike and handed him the thumb drive that Dr. Lawrence had given him to check. Mike took it and turned away.

The sound of the telephone broke the silence. Mike answered and turned to John with a puzzled expression.

"It's Dr. Lawrence in Chicago, he wants to talk to you."

At Mike's mention of the lab chief, Monique looked up. She saw John talk while Mike leaned close to try to hear the chief's words. Monique could only hear John.

"No Sir, ... You can't present the data in Tables 2 or 3. Sir, that data is bad! ... No you don't want to include that data in your talk. ... I'm sorry, but you asked me to check it. ... No, I'm not saying you're wrong ... . I can show you when you get back. ... But, it's fake! ... I'm sorry, but I tried all evening to reach you."

Monique saw that John's face was pale. Dr. Lawrence had hung up on him. Then Mike spun about and went into his office.

She gave John a quizzical look. He tossed a wan smile in her direction and left the lab. She shrugged and looked at her 96-well plate. She'd lost track of where she was. With dismay, she realized she would have to start over.

***

Dr. Lawrence smashed the phone hard into its receptacle and strode to a chair in the hotel lobby. His talk was after lunch in the "Green Room.". He pulled his notes from his briefcase.

What the hell was John talking about? The data for Table 3 couldn't be better!

Every test that was supposed to be positive had high counts, over 8000, and every control had low counts, under 800. A tenfold difference! The data admitted only one interpretation, the one he knew *had* to be true. These data were fine.

John must have a screw loose somewhere. Mike produces at least four times as much work and even Monique works faster.

He softened.

OK, I'll drop Table 2, but Table 3 stays in. It's right. I'll repeat the experiment when I get back. I can drop Table 2, but without Table 3 this talk is a bust.

Dr. Lawrence smiled at his solution. He was the "idea" man. He would keep Table 3 and drop Table 2, thereby proving that he was an understanding mentor. He stuffed the papers back into his briefcase. as a young colleague approached.

"Franklin, how are you?"

Dr. Lawrence winced at the informality, but grinned.

"Mitch, good to see you. Where are you eating lunch?"

In a booth in the hotel restaurant, Mitch and Franklin swapped complaints about deans who did not understand research, and stingy government bureaucrats who withheld money.

***

Mike was furious. When he'd heard John tell Dr. Lawrence not to present Tables 2 or 3 in his talk, he'd become disturbed. Then he had examined the thumb drive John had returned to him.

My God, my program was on that thumb drive. How? Dr. Lawrence, will know I faked those data!

Distraught, Mike slumped down before his computer. *Damn! I can't believe I did that.*

He sat up.

Wait. I can handle this!

He brought up the folder with the fake data and deleted it with all its files. Then he wiped the free space on his hard disk so that the files could not be recovered.

His misdeeds hidden, he moved to John's bench and copied the fake files from his guilty thumb drive onto John's hard drive.

"Mike, what's going on? What are you doing at John's computer?"

It was Monique. Mike assumed a serious expression.

"Monique, you heard Dr. Lawrence's call. It got me thinking, John's been acting strange lately."

"But what are you doing at his machine?"

"I've caught John cheating on our experiments. He's making up data, fabricating experiments. Look."

Mike pointed to the screen.

"These files have the data for Dr. Lawrence's talk in Chicago."

Monique squinted. There were eight files. Mike continued.

"He faked these data. They're not real."

"How do you know?"

"One of the files is a program that generates fake data."

He reached in a drawer and handed her a new thumb drive sealed in its wrapper.

"Use this new drive and copy John's files onto it for me."

Monique did as asked. At his request she also wrote a note stating what she had done. Mike put the drive and note into an envelope, sealed the flap, and signed across it. She did the same.

Her thoughts spun in confusion as Mike continued.

"His conscience must have got the better of him, that's why he told Dr. Lawrence not to present Tables 2 and 3 at the meeting today. The rat!"

At the word "rat" Monique frowned. Mike slowed.

"Hey, he must have been overworked or something. Dr. Lawrence is tough, but you can't excuse John's cheating. This could be the end of Dr. Lawrence's grants."

He smiled and pointed to the sealed envelope.

"Don't worry. I know what to do. We'll take this envelope to the Department Office. Then I'll treat you to a sandwich and a coke at the Old Goose. Dr. Lawrence will understand if all your dilutions aren't done."

Mike was good looking, was taller than John, and had published more papers, including one on protein A-11 with Dr. Lawrence. Monique was flattered. Besides, he was in charge while Dr. Lawrence was away. She couldn't say no.

"Let me finish pipetting, then I'll go with you."

She didn't want to eat though. She felt sick. She liked John.

***

The Green Room of the convention hotel was packed. Dr. Lawrence was pleased. He started with a joke. The laughter was more than he had hoped for. He continued.

"But as you all know, Breast Cancer, the subject of my talk today, is no laughing matter."

He thought. *I've got them hooked.* He was ready. He dimmed the lights and started his PowerPoint presentation.

To the audience in the darkened room, Dr. Lawrence was larger than life. His silhouette contrasted with the bright screen behind him. He was loose and in control. The large shadow of his hand pointed to the screen. His voice was resonant.

"Here in Table 3, we have conclusive proof that my protein, 'A-11' binds Johnson's protein CA. You can see the counts are all above 8000."

He clicked to the next screen.

"And here, also in Table 3, you can see that the control counts are less than 800. Recall that the experimental wells gave counts of 8000 or greater. There is a tenfold difference."

The audience hung on Dr. Lawrence's words except for two individuals. A young woman wearing a green suit in the last row and an older, disheveled, man in a gray sweater at the front. Both scribbled numbers onto their pads as Dr. Lawrence moved on.

"So you can see that A-11 binds CA. Next slide please."

The woman in green lowered her pen. *He's going too fast.*

Dr. Lawrence turned on the lights. The spectators' eyes adjusted as he concluded.

"You can see that A-11 offers hope for victims of breast cancer. I and my entire laboratory are committed to explore this possibility. Thank you for your attention."

The Chairman rose from his seat.

"We have a few minutes until the next talk. I'm sure that Dr. Lawrence would be willing to answer some questions."

Dr. Lawrence remained at the podium. He stared expectantly and wisely over his horn-rimmed half-frames. The disheveled man in the gray sweater stood up to speak. Dr. Lawrence gritted his teeth. It was that ass Johnson from Rochester.

Dr. Johnson's voice boomed through the room.

"I don't have a *question* for the speaker, but I do have a *comment*. I have a problem with the slides of Table 3 and your reported tenfold difference. In my lab we found that ..."

***

******

Chapter 5
Wednesday, November 29

The "Old Goose" was a favorite hangout of students, and since it was close to the Forster Building, was particularly frequented by biological and medical types. Several heads turned in Jeannine's direction as she stood by the door looking for John, but she gave them no notice.

She spotted John at a table in the far corner.

That can't be beer he's drinking, It's only noon!

Even one beer in the middle of the day could shoot John's work for the afternoon.

Jeannine threaded her way through the tightly-packed tables.

A grinning student pulled back a chair and asked her to take a seat. She shot one word at him.

"Jerk!"

She dropped her brown bag on John's table.

"Beer, why are you drinking with your lunch?"

Then she saw that the beer *was* his lunch. John looked up. He was unshaven and appeared exhausted.

Jeannine softened. She took a sandwich from her bag.

"Here, eat."

There was no protest. The sandwich disappeared.

He looked up.

"Jeannine, I need you to think about something with me."

She shuddered at the word "think."

After studying most of the night, and then writing that damned test for two hours, (Professor Anderson's last question had been a real nasty one) her mind was gone.

But one look convinced her of John's need.

The waiter arrived. Jeannine spoke.

"Bring me two cups of coffee, black, thanks."

John waited for the waiter to leave. Then he pushed a sheet of paper across the table.

Sample Number	Counts Per Minute	Standard Deviation	Sample Number	Counts Per Minute	Standard Deviation
1	9880	99.4	37	9654	98.3
2	9509	97.5	38	9334	96.6
3	9049	95.1	39	8996	94.9
4	9878	99.4	40	9686	98.4
5	9498	97.5	41	9530	97.6
6	8745	93.5	42	8840	94.0
7	9722	98.6	43	9790	98.9
8	9298	96.4	44	9218	96.0
9	8859	94.1	45	9069	95.2
10	9875	99.4	46	9915	99.6
11	9431	97.1	47	9380	96.9
12	8979	94.8	48	8945	94.6
13	9777	98.9	49	9819	99.1
14	9339	96.6	50	9485	97.4
15	8974	94.7	51	8970	94.7
16	9789	98.9	52	9860	99.3
17	9313	96.5	53	9439	97.2
18	9049	95.1	54	9018	95.0
19	9831	99.2	55	9888	99.4
20	9347	96.7	56	9336	96.6
21	9003	94.9	57	9036	95.1
22	10024	100.1	58	9580	97.9
23	9520	97.6	59	9521	97.6
24	8953	94.6	60	8941	94.6
25	9843	99.2	61	9881	99.4
26	9461	97.3	62	9646	98.2
27	8922	94.5	63	9034	95.1
28	9812	99.1	64	9781	98.9
29	9482	97.4	65	9333	96.6
30	8796	93.8	66	9076	95.3
31	9859	99.3	67	9685	98.4
32	9471	97.3	68	9428	97.1
33	8970	94.7	69	8864	94.2
34	9861	99.3	70	9861	99.3
35	9491	97.4	71	9554	97.7
36	9035	95.1	72	9031	95.0

"These are Dr. Lawrence's and Mike's data. They're part of the breast cancer talk he's giving today in Chicago."

His voice shook.

"What do you think of them?

Jeannine picked the sheet up and examined it. She was tired. The coffee had yet to take effect. *They're numbers anyway, some kind of stats. Maybe I can handle this.* She looked up.

"What do these numbers mean?"

John took a breath and started.

"OK, I told you about how radioimmunoassays are used to find out if one protein binds to another, right?"

At Jeannine's nod, he kept on.

"Well, these are radioactive counts, counts per minute (cpm's) from the gamma counter. Anyway they're supposed to be. And look, I've separated them in groups of three to make it easier. See how all the cpm's are greater than 8000.

Jeannine studied the counts. John was right. All the counts per minute were greater than 8000.

"OK John. What's the point?"

"Dr. Lawrence's A-11 protein was radioactively tagged, and then pipetted into wells on a plate coated with Dr. Johnson's protein CA."

"Why that protein?"

"Protein CA has to do with causing breast cancer, anyway it *might*. But let me finish."

Jeannine, was not feeling compliant, but she had already started her second cup of coffee, and the caffeine was working. Her mind was clear. John went on.

"Look, the counts are in groups of threes. The first count measures the amount of A-11, *diluted 3-fold*, that bound to the CA-coat. The second measures the amount of A-11 that bound when *diluted 9-fold*, and the third, the amount when *diluted 27-fold*. All these counts are high. They're all above 8000 whatever the dilution. They show that Dr. Lawrence's A-11 protein is binding strongly to CA."

"But John, what is 'high?' How do you know 8000 is high?"

"Because there's low radioactivity when there's no binding, and so the counts are low. See!"

John put another paper on the table. He pointed to the counts on it. They were indeed much lower.

Sample Number	Counts Per Minute	Standard Deviation
73	693	26.3
74	674	26.0
75	727	27.0
76	713	26.7
77	714	26.7
78	705	26.6
79	708	26.6
80	746	27.3
81	691	26.3
82	696	26.4
83	692	26.3
84	660	25.7
85	751	27.4
86	735	27.1
87	715	26.8
88	730	27.0
89	635	25.2
90	673	25.9
91	727	27.0
92	728	27.0
93	655	25.6
94	683	26.1
95	719	26.8
96	701	26.5

"These are the counts from the control wells. They are low. None is above 800 cpm. There's not supposed to be any binding, and there isn't. There's a tenfold increase from the control wells to the CA wells, from 800 to 8000 cpm!"

"So, what's the problem. You don't need a statistical test on results this clear."

Jeannine already had ranked the counts in her mind and mentally done a simple test. There were 96 counts and the ranks of the experimental and control counts didn't overlap. The results were "statistically significant."

John smashed the table with his fist. Jeannine's coffee washed onto the saucer, but missed her pink pullover. The beer bottle tipped, but John caught it. He blurted.

"Damn it! That is *exactly* the problem. The results are too damned significant. Look at this!"

He slammed more papers on the table, but this time Jeannine had the coffee cup safely in her hands, away from the wobble. Coffee and pink pullover were safe. John pressed onward.

"Look at this."

It was computer code. It looked like *PowerBASIC* which she knew John's lab used though she was more used to "*C*".

```
SUB rndcnt(ymean AS DOUBLE,y AS DOUBLE)
   DIM ysigma AS DOUBLE
   DIM sum AS DOUBLE
   DIM n AS INTEGER
   ysigma=SQR(ymean)
   sum=0
    FOR n=1 TO 12
      sum=sum+RND(1)
    NEXT n
   sum=sum-6
   y=ysigma*sum+ymean
END SUB
```

This was her turf. She looked at the code. Her mind raced. *Add 12 uniforms to get an approximate normal variable, OK. The variance is 12 times 1/12 so the standard deviation is 1, OK. Subtract 6 from the sum to get zero and multiply by the standard deviation. Add in the desired mean, done! Wait a minute! The standard deviation is the square root of the mean. Oh, a Poisson distribution!*

All this was to herself. She looked up at John.

"It's a procedure, a subroutine, that computes random numbers that approximate a Poisson distribution, as long as the mean you feed it is large."

"I thought that's what it did. Mike wanted the numbers to look like counts from a gamma counter, so he made them follow a Poisson distribution."

He put another sheet before her.

"This is Mike's main program. What do you think?"

```
#COMPILE EXE
FUNCTION PBMAIN () AS LONG
DIM i AS INTEGER
DIM j AS INTEGER
DIM xmean AS DOUBLE
DIM z AS DOUBLE
DIM afile AS STRING
DIM x(0,100) AS DOUBLE
afile = "c:\rand1\plate1.ra1"
OPEN afile FOR OUTPUT AS #1
PRINT# 1, afile

FOR i=1 TO 94 STEP 3
  FOR j=i TO i+2
    IF j <= 72 THEN
      IF j-i=0 THEN
        xmean=9800
      ELSEIF j-i=1 THEN
        xmean=9400
      ELSE
        xmean=9000
      END IF
    ELSE
      xmean=700
    END IF
    z=x(j)
    CALL rndcnt(xmean,z)
    PRINT#1, j;", ", ROUND(z,0); _
        ", "; ROUND(SQR(z),1)
  NEXT j
NEXT i

CLOSE #1
END
END FUNCTION
```

Jeannine scanned the lines.

"This code changes the means of the random numbers to look like dilutions. The final 24 counts (your controls) are constructed with a low mean of 700, well under the 800 limit for the controls."

At that, John's fist smashed the table once more. Both coffee cups were empty and merely rattled on the saucers.

"Jeannine, there was no experiment. The talk that Dr. Lawrence is presenting in Chicago today is based on fabricated numbers that have nothing to do with cancer. Mike didn't measure how protein A-11 binds to Johnson's CA. His 'data' are from a computer."

Jeannine raised her eyebrows.

"But how did you find out? Where'd you get this program?"

"Dr. Lawrence gave me a drive with Mike's data to check. The program was there. I ran it and got the numbers that Mike told Dr. Lawrence came from the gamma counter."

"My God, John, you've got to tell Dr. Lawrence."

"I did. That's part of the problem. I couldn't reach him last night. This morning he called from Chicago. I started to tell him and he hung up on me. He was angry, yelling."

Jeannine had met Dr. Lawrence during the obligatory dinner at his house. She had her own opinion of him. For John's sake she tried to sound hopeful.

"He'll probably listen to you."

Her voice trailed off as she saw John stare at a girl who entered the restaurant. She was with a tall man. She thought. *I know her. Oh yes, Monique, from the lab*.

John nudged her.

"The guy that just came in, that's Mike, that's *him*. He's the cheat who did this."

Mike and Monique picked a table across the room. Jeannine studied the back of Mike's neck. A shiver of dread passed down hers.

***

******

Chapter 6
Wednesday, November 29

Pierre was relieved. He'd delivered the money safely, and he'd have no more deliveries for a week. André would make tonight's trip to the White Pine tree. It would be a major delivery, many times what Pierre had carried, maybe worth a million. *Let André find that damned pine tree and deal with those bastards.*

Pierre was no coward, but he was superstitious, and those guys (there'd been at least two) had unsettled him. He did not want to go back to that spot. Besides, he had too much cash in the apartment. He needed to move it to Vermont. Lise was in Burlington and he hungered to see her.

To top it off, Pierre's mother, in an unprecedented assertion of independence from her overbearing and controlling husband, had asked Pierre to visit her mother, Marie-Thérèse Gauthier, who also lived in Burlington. Neither Pierre or his mother had seen her in recent years. Pierre was to re-establish contact.

For once, the three major forces in Pierre's life, sex, money, and filial devotion, were all pulling in the same direction. *Great!*

He had $40,000 dollars, Canadian, plus the recent $8,000, American. He divided the bills into wrinkled brown paper bags to look like trash. He flattened them on the floor of his Escort, along with old newspapers. His car was messy, like his apartment. He wasn't worried about the border inspection. He'd done this before.

He crossed the Pont Mercier, at 3:00 p.m. ahead of the rush hour. An hour later he was at Champlain, New York. The questions were perfunctory and he crossed without mishap. Forty minutes later, at St. Albans, Vermont, he stopped for groceries. To the "trash" bags on the floor were added bags of assorted chips, salsa, and cold cuts.

He called Lise.

"I'm at St. Albans. I've got food but no beer. I'm tired. I'll stop for coffee first, OK?"

It was more than OK with Lise.

"Hurry. I miss you."

***

Pierre arrived in Burlington and drove to Lise's apartment. He parked his car in the back lot. At the foyer he called through the speaker.

The door lock hummed and he pushed in. Upstairs, Lise was at the door. She embraced him, brown bags and all.

"Thank God you're here. It's been way too long. Here, let me take that."

He stepped inside. All was clean. There was no clutter, not like his apartment.

After last night, Pierre was unkempt. Lise rubbed the stubble on his chin.

"You need to freshen up."

"Right. I need a shower, but I need a beer first."

Lise handed him a can of Budweiser. Then she unpacked the salsa, chips and cold cuts. She smiled. *When we're married I'll see you get real food.*

Pierre, still unshaven, counted the money at the kitchen table. Lise helped arrange bills into piles, but tonight she had her own plans. She loved Pierre and was ready to prove it, but she wanted commitment.

For now she chatted about small things. Pierre sensed her excitement. Something was different, but he was not sure what. Lise sparkled.

He touched her arm. Desire mounted within him. He wasn't tired after all.

***

It was dark outside and Dr. Lawrence was still at O'Hare airport. Snow had delayed the flight to Reagan National. In the dimly lit cocktail lounge he sat at a round corner booth.

"Bring me a Margarita, salted rim, some of those chips, and your hottest salsa."

Dr. Lawrence reflected while he sipped and dipped. John was careful, if not fast, and he didn't want to come down too hard on him. The talk that afternoon had gone well even without Table 2. It would have been perfect if that damn Johnson from Rochester had not questioned his findings. Johnson had done the same thing at the Pittsburgh symposium. *Why the hell can't Johnson read a simple table of data, like Table 3. It's so damn clear!*

A voice interrupted his musing.

"Dr. Lawrence, excuse me, my name is Husak, Sharon Husak. I'm a science writer with the Daily Express. I wonder if I might have a word with you, Sir?"

At the sight of the slim blue-eyed reporter, dressed in a neat green suit which outlined a pleasing form, Dr. Lawrence decided that first names might be more fun.

"Sure. What's on your mind Sharon? And please call me Franklin."

He waved her to sit next to him on the circular seat. Ms. Husak smiled and sat down so that his briefcase separated them. She adjusted her skirt to reveal a bit of thigh.

"Dr. Lawrence, I was at your talk this afternoon, and I have just a few questions."

Franklin could not imagine that he had missed Ms. Husak in the audience, but the Green Room had been crowded. *Perhaps in the back?* She continued.

"In your Table 3, wouldn't you say there was good evidence that the product of your hybridoma A-11 binds strongly to Dr. Johnson's protein CA. In fact, Franklin, don't you have an agent that conclusively inhibits the action of Johnson's CA?"

Dr. Lawrence was surprised, but not displeased. *That ass Johnson! He'd been lucky to isolate Protein CA from early T-1 mammary gland tumors. Incredibly lucky, considering he couldn't analyze data. This lady reporter has it right!*

"Sharon, you've put it as clearly as I could myself. Table 3 shows exactly that."

"Then Sir, wouldn't you say that your A-11 immunoglobulin has a good chance of being an early treatment for breast cancer; that is, if Dr. Johnson's CA protein is an active causative agent, rather than just an accidental by product."

Franklin interrupted.

"Sharon, were you at the question and answer session after my talk?"

She smiled and nodded. He continued.

"Then you saw Dr. Johnson take issue with my interpretation of the data in Table 3."

What Sharon remembered was that Dr. Johnson had said the data in Table 3 were flawed, not that Dr. Lawrence's interpretation was bad. Anyway, she kept her blue eyes fixed on Dr. Lawrence, encouraging him to continue. He did.

"Sharon, about the only thing Dr. Johnson and I agree on is the biological activity of protein CA. It's a causative agent, not a mere byproduct. Today I gave proof that we can stop its activity, and if we can do that we may be able to stop tumor growth. Of course this needs to be tested and confirmed, but ..."

This time Sharon interrupted.

"Franklin, you're telling me that you've made significant strides towards the prevention and cure of at least one kind of breast cancer, and that your A-11 protein is a key find. In fact, it represents a cure. Is that correct Sir?

Sharon wore green because her blue eyes had a greenish tint. Those eyes were now focused on Franklin with her most alluring, yet professional, smile. He wasn't thinking clearly. The coincidence of the talk in the "Green Room," the green, nearly empty, margarita in front of him, and the stunning green suit and smiling eyes were all too much for him. Maybe it was fate. Whatever, he abandoned his usual caution. He smiled back.

"Yes Sharon, that's exactly correct."

Ms. Husak was on her feet immediately.

"Dr. Lawrence, I can't thank you enough. If I rush I can make my deadline. Be sure and get a copy of the Express tomorrow, Sir."

Uncharacteristically she permitted herself a genuine remark.

"Sir, thank you on behalf of women all over this country. Thanks again."

She was off. Franklin blinked and wondered. *What exactly did I agree to? Did I go too far about A-11? Why did she call me 'Sir.' Am I that old? But she called me 'Franklin' too. OK, so I'm a stupid old man. Damn it Mike, you're going to repeat that Table 3 experiment as soon as I get back!*

Franklin stared out the window of the lounge. The snow was accumulating rapidly on the runway. He ordered another margarita and thought about calling a hotel. He would not make it back to Washington tonight.

***

In Vermont, Madame Gauthier prayed her evening rosary, and retired. She awoke once when Tonnerre snuffled at something in the corner by the stove. She fell asleep again only to awake suddenly. The noise of a passing motor had stopped! She peered out the window. Snow was falling.

Through the white flakes, she saw two lights flicker up the opposite hillside. It was 1:00 a.m. Through the bedroom door she could see Tonnerre asleep by the fireplace. She looked again out the window, but the lights had disappeared. She waited for the lights to reappear, but all was dark. She dozed.

She awoke to hear Tonnerre scratching. The clock said 2:30 a.m. There were no lights on the hill. Tonnerre had to go. Remembering Cecilia's admonition, she left the lights off. She attached the chain to his choke-collar and holding tight, opened the front door.

The clearing was covered with a layer of snow, and more was falling. She stood and shivered while Tonnerre lifted his leg.   The warm urine melted yellow pockets in the white powder.

Tonnerre finished and headed back to the house.   Then it happened.   A Snowshoe rabbit went by, fast.   With a bound, Tonnerre extended the chain taut, stretching Madame Gauthier's arm to its full length.   For a moment she held, but the chain flew out of her hand and snaked after Tonnerre.   He barked his best "thunder," rounded the line of fir trees, and disappeared down the lane after the rabbit.

***

At the foot of the hill with the giant white pine, two men had just loaded Styrofoam chests in the toolbox that straddled the bed of a gray pickup.   They were in a foul mood because the Canadian contact (André) had been late for the rendezvous. And they were jittery about picking up another shipment at the same spot so soon.

One wore a red sweater.   At the thunderous barking, he jumped behind the wheel and turned on the lights.   Tonnerre's eyes reflected like two green points in the headlights.   Startled, the dog turned back up the access lane to Madame Gauthier's.

"What the hell was that?"

The second man, who had a dark mustache, answered.

"It was a dog, you dumb bastard.   Drive over that way. What's a damn dog doing here?   Where the hell did it go?"

A moment later, they spotted the access lane.

"Drive up there.   How the hell could we have missed this place?"

The gray pickup bounced up the roadway and turned at the end of the line of firs.   Standing white in the headlights, Madame Gauthier attempted to control Tonnerre.

"Tonnerre! ... Viens ici.   Come here."

But the invasion of his territory was too much for Tonnerre. When "Mustache" stepped out of the truck, Tonnerre lunged.

"Tonnere!   Non!"

Too late. Sharp canines slashed the man's arm. Blood flowed.

A shot rang out and Tonnerre thrashed on the ground. His twisting torso splattered the snow red. Then all motion ceased.

Madame Gauthier froze.

The man with the mustache commanded his partner.

"Get her in the damn house. I've got to fix this arm. That bastard chien!"

They pushed Madame Gauthier through the door.

Outside large flakes fell thick and fast.

***

By the time his arm was bandaged, snow had accumulated. The man with the mustache now knew Madame Gauthier lived alone. He spoke to "Red Sweater."

"Point the truck around so we won't have to back up in the snow. We're going to stay here awhile."

He turned to Madame Gauthier.

"Madame, would you fix us some coffee?"

It was a command. She went straight to the stove.

"Red sweater" came back in the house, settled in a chair, and dozed. Madame Gauthier served "Mustache" his coffee, and sat, shivering by the fire.

She shut her eyes, only to imagine Tonnerre, bloody, thrashing in the snow. She opened quickly. Red Sweater's eyes were fixed on her.

She looked down and prayed. *Je vous salue, Marie … Hail Mary …*

***

******

Chapter 7
Thursday, November 30

Pierre awoke at 9:00 a.m. Lise was asleep. He slipped into the kitchen and looked about. Lise's sink was shiny and clean. He thought of the scruffy mess in his.

He buttered some toast. It glistened golden, unlike the dry butterless toast of his boyhood. There never had been enough money, except for "PaPa" and his alcohol. Pierre's muscles tightened at the memories. Angry words and blows from his drunken father, followed by meaningless sober reconciliations. His mother's attempts to defend her son from the father, and once Pierre was man-sized, her husband from the son. His outrage the time he'd come home to find his mother bleeding on the floor.

He put a second slice in the toaster. Lise did not simplify his life. Last night she'd given him everything he could want from a woman, everything. Afterwards she'd whispered.

"Pierre, je t'aime, I love you. I want every night like this. I want you. I want our children. I want you near me all the time."

He had drawn her close and held her. He hadn't said no. Surprisingly, he'd wanted to say yes. He finished his toast and shook his head. Now it was morning and it should be easy to say no, but he didn't want to. Maybe he could be a father. Maybe it could be different. Maybe he could have a son. Love a son.

Lise was in the shower. She was singing "À la Claire Fontaine."

Pierre smiled. Lise did not have to be at work for several hours.

***

Betty's fingers touched Franklin's pillow. The surface was smooth and undisturbed. She forced her eyes open and stretched. The nightlight on Franklin's table was on. He had not come home. She wasn't surprised. Flights out of Chicago were either delayed or canceled due to snow.

Sari, rubbing her eyes, stumbled into the bedroom.

"Where's daddy?"

"He's stuck in Chicago, honey, he'll be back tonight."

Betty hugged her daughter. Though a mature "thirteen," Sari was not that far removed from "eleven."

"Mom, could we get my ears pierced today?"

"Why not honey, I'll pick you up after school."

Betty had no objections to Sari's ears being pierced but she did object that Franklin had made the decision alone.

"Can Mattie come with us?"

"Sure. Check with her mother."

"Thanks Mom!"

Sari kissed her mother and flew out of the room. Moments later Betty heard the water running in Sari's shower.

Betty turned on the kitchen lights and stared at the counter. She poured Sari's glass of orange juice. As Betty's fingers squeezed the glass, she thought of Sari's arms. Her daughter was thin, almost fragile.

She reacted. She mixed banana slices with Wheaties in a bowl. Then she set it and a carton of milk at Sari's place. Today her daughter would eat before school!

***

Cecilia's rooms were in Vermont, not far from her office in Rouses Point. She awoke, rested from her exertions at Checkpoint Charley.

She stepped into the shower and gasped. The cold spray felt like a shotgun load of ice pellets. She drew a deep breath and fumbled for the handles. *Chihuahua, this isn't Tucson. Cold, off. Hot, on. There, that's not too bad!*

Cecilia had been surprised by her northern assignment. After her training for the Customs Service at the Federal Law Enforcement Training Center (FLETC) in Georgia, she had

46

assumed she would return to the Mexican border where Spanish, her maternal language, would be of service. She would have preferred Nogales, because she liked the town and could visit her mother and father in Tucson.

But the logic of an assignment to the Spanish-speaking border had escaped the faceless bureaucrat in Washington who had dispatched her to Rouses Point, New York on the border with French-speaking Quebec. She was sure that the bungling bureaucrat believed that any two people who spoke English with an accent (French, Spanish or whatever) were "foreigners" who could understand each other, no matter their native language.

When Cecilia had arrived at Rouses Point, her new partner, Sam Jones, confirmed her suspicions. Sam spoke no French. Immediately he had thrust two files at her.

"These two cases have a lot of French in them. I've been waiting for you to handle them."

"Sam, I don't understand a word of French, I can't help you there."

But Sam had shrugged, and turned away. He was planning how to explain to his wife that his new partner was an attractive woman, 20 years younger.

Cecilia accepted the situation with a certain irony and good humor. At her rooms in nearby Vermont she watched French TV from Quebec. At work, she practiced French with anyone who was willing, but Madame Gauthier helped her the most. Madame spoke only French with her and made Cecilia read the newspaper, La Presse.

"Ma petite, you must learn not only the language, but the culture."

La Presse was ideal for both.

The "hot" water had lost heat. Cecilia abandoned the shower and dressed.

She left for "Checkpoint Charley" and Madame Gauthier.

***

47

Lise had gone to work. Pierre pulled out his mother's note with his grandmother's number in Burlington. He punched the phone. A woman answered. He spoke.

"Madame Marie-Thérèse Gauthier, please."

"She's not here and I don't expect her. Who's this?"

"I'm her grandson from Montreal. My mother gave me this number."

"Oh, 'Pierre,' right? Your grandmother and uncle Charles bought a camp up north before he died. She's there now and there's no phone. She'll be back in another week or two. She quits the camp after the first snow. "

The woman, the niece of Madame Gauthier's deceased husband, correctly interpreted Pierre's silence as disappointment. She volunteered.

"You know, the camp's not all that far. I could tell you how to get there."

A grateful Pierre scribbled the directions.

"North from Burlington on route 89 towards St. Albans. Start towards Richford. ... Turn towards Berkshire and Canada. ... A green barn then north on the gravel road. ... At the dead end, turn left. A big pine tree on the ridge by Canada ... Less than a mile to her cabin."

At the mention of the pine tree, Pierre shook his head. Could it be the same White Pine? He'd recognize that tree anywhere, and these directions were to the same area he had found from the Canadian side. *Maybe?*

He took Lise's car and headed north.

***

Dr. Lawrence's plane landed at Reagan National Airport at 9:30 a.m. Outside there were gray clouds, but no snow. He hailed a cab.

"Where to?"

"Fairland University Medical School. I'll show you where when we get there."

He went straight to his lab. At least, he tried to. The Department secretary stopped him in the hall. She spoke crisply.

"Dr. Lawrence, Dr. Santini would like to see you right away, Sir."

Dr. Santini was the Department Chairman. His office was dark brown and formal, with neatly polished furniture. It had a rug in contrast to the bare tiles of Franklin's lab. Dr. Santini rose when Franklin entered, but only to shut the door.

"Franklin, what's this all about?"

He handed Franklin a FAX. It was an article from the Chicago Daily Express.

RESEARCHER CLOSE TO BREAST CANCER CURE
by Sharon Husak

Women have found a new champion in Dr. Franklin Lawrence, a prominent cancer specialist who announced yesterday in an exclusive interview with the Express that he has discovered a key compound with a demonstrable effect in inhibiting the growth of early breast cancers. ...

"Franklin, what's going on? I've already had two calls from the Post, and Dean Hampton has talked to the Express. They're sticking by their story. They say they have a printed abstract of your talk yesterday plus Husak's notes from an interview at the airport. Were you out of your mind, or do you really have something? And how come I didn't know about it? If you're on to something it belongs to the University too!"

The headline, and Sharon's interpretation of their "chat" at the airport stunned Franklin. He dropped into the leather-upholstered chair that faced the desk. Sunk in the soft cushions he lost several inches of presence. Dr. Santini, in the firm chair behind his imposing desk, was higher and dominant.

Franklin did not like this office and he did not like the Chairman. Santini was a pencil pusher who had forgotten what it was like to work at the lab bench. The Chairman spoke.

"And you've got another mess too. You're keeping me and Dean Hampton busy! A Postdoc in your lab faked data! What the hell's going on?"

Franklin had not slept well in the hotel, and was tired, but the Chairman's last remark jolted him upright. His mind raced. *That sneak, John. Table 3! For John to accuse Mike of cheating, of making up data, is absurd! A jealous incompetent attacking my best Postdoc ever! What about my grant? That's it. John, you're gone, you're out of here! And my references will see you never get into any lab, anywhere!*

Gaining control, he spoke firmly.

"Mike is the best Postdoc I've ever worked with. It's a rotten thing to accuse him of making up data, and it's a lie. I personally will settle this matter."

"Franklin, you're not settling anything. It's out of your hands. We have policies and procedures in place to handle such accusations. And it's not Mike, so relax. It's your new guy, John, who's been cheating."

***

Before Franklin could react, there was a knock on the door. He did not recognize the man who entered. *Another damned suit and tie, another administrator!*

Dr. Santini did the honors.

"Franklin, this is Marshall Hanes, a lawyer in the Provost's Office. Marshall is the University Misconduct Officer and will be handling the matter we've been talking about."

Dr. Santini turned.

"Marshall, this is Dr. Lawrence, it's his lab where the data were fabricated. I've been briefing him. I was just assuring him that his best Postdoc was OK."

Marshall turned to Franklin.

"Dr. Lawrence, would you mind waiting outside while Dr. Santini and I talk. Thank you."

Franklin stepped outside and stood by the secretary. Her eyes stayed on her work. Franklin wasn't used to being slighted. His distaste changed to anger against John.

Inside the office, Dr. Santini wasn't comfortable either. Marshall Hanes wasn't about to sit in that ridiculous over-stuffed chair. He towered over the Chairman.

"You shouldn't have said anything to him. It's his lab, his grant and his data. He could be responsible. We don't know anything yet. The accusation may not be true. We've got to secure the data to see if we need a full investigation."

Dr. Santini, protested.

"But he's a colleague, and besides we were talking about the Express article."

"Oh yes, the Express article. We'll come to that later. OK, so he's a colleague, and he's in your department. The best way you can help clear this matter up, and help your department, is to let me be objective. You should not have talked to Dr. Lawrence without me. Have you got the names I asked you for?"

Dr. Santini, like Franklin, preferred situations he could control. He didn't like to be lectured, and he didn't like Mr. Hanes. He handed over the paper. Marshall spoke.

"I'll pick two of these people and we'll set up an inquiry panel. I want to act fast. Dean Hampton's working on a press release with the Provost and the President's office. If your man's Express article used fake data, the university will look like hell, and so will you."

Marshall turned and opened the office door.

"Dr. Lawrence, would you step back in here please."

***

******

Chapter 8
Thursday, November 30

Snow covered the ground to a depth of several inches, but the sky was clear and the sun was bright. Rays of light pierced the interior of Madame Gauthier's cabin. The man in the red sweater lifted himself out of the chair.

"It's almost noon. Let's get the hell out of here."

The man with the mustache shook his head.

"No. We stay. We're safe here. No one knows this place. The crews are on the roads plowing now, and the visibility's good. They'll be more snow this evening, lots of it. We'll leave then. The darkness and snow will cover us. We wait."

The man in the red sweater slumped back into the chair. His companion turned to Madame Gauthier.

"You're in luck Madame. Your breakfast was so good that we must stay for lunch. What will you fix for us? You should be nice to me after what your dog did. Something tasty please, I'm hungry. Merci!"

Madame Gauthier shuffled to the stove.

***

Cecilia sped north on route 108 towards Checkpoint Charley and Madame Gauthier's cabin.

The morning was cold, but bright. The road had been plowed of last night's snow and now dark patches of warm pavement punctuated the white surface.

Cecelia left highway 108, and turned east towards Berkshire. The earthy colors of her new Lands' End down jacket, a gift from her solicitous mother, warmed not only her arms but her thoughts. On the passenger seat, two recent copies of La Presse, each still in its plastic bag, reminded her how much French she had learned in the past six months. She was gaining familiarity with the language. *Thank God for Madame Gauthier.*

Stuffy, she adjusted the heater downwards and turned onto an unpaved road that led to Checkpoint Charley, but the snow was packed and the Geo's wheels gripped well.

On the hillside to her left, the sun shone brightly on frozen snow that clung to the branches of the trees. Underneath, the ground was powdery white with crystalline patches that had melted and re-frozen. The sparkling of those surfaces amidst the softer reflections from the powdery snow, bounced the sunlight erratically off the hillside. Coupled with the rays that scintillated from the metallic blue hood of her car, the playful reflections of winter delighted Cecilia.

Even the somber shaded hillside to her right, with its white-coated evergreens still in shadows, could not lower her spirits. Rather, the contrast heightened her appreciation of the magnificent sunlit scene on the left. The natural beauty of the wild landscape overwhelmed her. For the first time since her arrival in Vermont, Cecilia looked forward to a real winter.

Ahead on the right, she spotted the large spruce tree that signaled the opening of Madame Gauthier's access lane. She turned off the state road and stopped. The north-facing lane had not been exposed to the sun. Its snow, two inches deep, was powdery and dry. She shifted into low gear. The wheels spun as her car started the ascent.

She shifted into second. With less spinning the car climbed easily. Snow filled the holes of the roadway and the climb was quiet unlike the usual rock-rattling ascent. Cecilia, lulled by that quiet, did not feel the branches that scraped her car and shed miniature avalanches of white powder into the air.

She was completely absorbed in the climb when she realized that it was too quiet. No barking! *Where was Tonnere?*

The fieldstone house came into view, but not Tonnere! A pickup, a Ford Ranger, was parked in the clearing. The snow was smooth. No one had been out of house or truck since the snowfall. The license plate was covered in white. She could not tell the State.

Cecilia wheeled the Geo about. The maneuver was recorded by crisp semi-circular tracks in the snow. She was about to stop the car in front of Madame Gauthier's door, when a curtain moved in the window and she saw a man's face. A metallic reflection flashed from the window.

Gun!

Gun or not, the strange face in the window told Cecilia that something was wrong.

Instantly, she conceived a deception. She lowered the passenger window and flipped the plastic-wrapped newspapers towards the door. Simultaneously, she sounded the horn twice, to signal the papers' arrival. Without waiting to raise the passenger-side window, she drove the Geo away from the house.

She went down the hill fast. The Geo skidded twice, but stayed on the roadway. At the bottom, she headed east. Cold air flowed through the open window and sharpened her thoughts. She did not dare stop. Sound traveled far in the still cold woods, and ears might be listening, waiting to see if her motor stopped prematurely. She was right.

***

When the horn blew, the man in the red sweater headed for the door. He opened it only to see the rear end of a blue car disappear around the corner of the fir alley. He saw the wrapped newspapers and listened as the sound of the motor disappeared in the distance. The newspapers and the gradual disappearance of sound satisfied him. He stepped back into the house.

The man with the mustache, whom Cecilia had spotted at the window, was not convinced. He had seen a photo of that new customs agent, a girl with black hair like the girl in the car. He put his coffee on the table, and went outside. He stooped over the newspapers and checked the dates. He saw that the snow about the pickup was undisturbed. Then he followed the tracks of the Geo down the hill. He returned to the cabin, apparently satisfied.

For the first time in hours, Madame Gauthier felt hope. She realized that Cecilia knew something was wrong. She thought. *Mais oui! Of course! No barking.*

But when the man with the mustache had gone out, her hope turned into fear for Cecilia's safety. Desolate once more, she lapsed into prayer.

"Sainte Marie, Mère de Dieu, priez pour nous ... Holy Mary, Mother of God, pray for us ..."

***

A mile to the east of Madame Gauthier's entrance, an unpaved road from the south ended at the road parallel to the border. This southern road came in at a slant, so that Madame Gauthier's cabin was situated in a sharp angle between the two. Power lines along the southern road served Madame Gauthier's house with electricity.

To the south of the intersection there originally had been a house that belonged to the Scanlon family. A power line from the south had served that house. To add service for Madame Gauthier, a line had been extended from a pole in back of the Scanlon house up the hill to her dwelling. The Scanlon home had been destroyed by a fire several years ago, but Madame Gauthier was still served by the power line that followed the obscure right of way from the rear of the Scanlon property.

The two men with the Ford Ranger used the southern road to arrive at the White Pine. In scouting the location, they had assumed that the power lines, which went no farther than the foundation of Scanlon's destroyed dwelling, had stopped there. This explained their surprise when, the night before, Tonnerre's barking had revealed the presence of a second house near their nocturnal meeting place.

Cecilia knew the right of way behind the Scanlon site. She had walked it the past summer in her hikes around Madame Gauthier's property. Now she drove straight to the abandoned ruins and stopped. She called Sam, at Rouses Point. After the fourth ring she heard a click. *Chihuahua! that damned answering machine again.*

She shouted into the phone.

"Sam, pick up the damn phone and talk to me!"

She exhaled as Sam came on the line. She spoke cryptically in case others were listening.

"Sam, I'm at Checkpoint Charley. Maybe a hostage situation. I need backup, Vermont Troopers and yourself. I'll watch from Scanlon's side. Hurry! I'm off."

At Cecilia's disconnect, Sam strapped on his shoulder holster. He grabbed his jacket, and explained to the dispatcher how to find "Checkpoint Charley."

A minute later he was outside. Fresh flakes hit his face. He drove east to find Cecilia.

***

Pierre drove Lise's Toyota on route 89 North. The road had been scraped and salted. The directions to his grandmother's were on the seat beside him.

As he left route 89 for a lesser road, snow started to fall. Going downhill, the tires slipped and the car skidded. He pulled to the side. The two front tires had worn treads. *She needs new tires.* Pierre had driven on snow and ice all his life and wasn't worried for himself. But the thought of Lise crumpled over the wheel of a smashed car was too much. *As soon as I get back, I'll buy new tires for her.* Whatever Pierre's past, today he was caring and happy.

***

Cecilia stepped from the Geo. The sky above was gray and dark snow clouds had formed to the west. She tucked her jeans into her boots. Her revolver disappeared under the new down jacket, and she tightened the collar to seal in the warmth.

She needed backup, but needed also to keep Madame Gauthier's house under observation. She trudged through the snow to the pole at the rear of the Scanlon property. From there, she followed the power line, pushing through the dense mix of small firs and spruce that flourished on the right of way.

Snow, displaced from branches, fell onto her jeans and sneaked down into her boots where it melted and chilled her toes. She set her lips. She could not have "cold feet," Madame Gauthier was in trouble.

The temperature dropped. Warm breath formed miniature icy clouds and cold air stabbed her lungs. She flexed and contracted her numb fingers for circulation.

At last Cecilia reached the clearing of Madame Gauthier's cabin. Large white flakes started to fall as she studied the rear of the house. There, partly covered with snow, was the old tractor with the rusted snow plow. Next to it was the door of the enclosed shed that kept firewood dry and buffered the rear door of the cabin from the elements.

There was no sign of activity. The snow at the rear of the house was undisturbed. The rear entrance had not been used since the snowfall. *Gracias a Dios! Thank God!*

She reached inside her jacket for the revolver. She held the thirty eight in a gloved left hand, and with her teeth tugged the glove from her right. It pulled free and dropped into the snow. She switched the gun to her right and moved to the shed.

She pulled the door. It opened outward, sweeping snow from the stone step. It made no noise.

Inside the shed, gun ready, she listened at the inner door. She heard Madame Gauthier's voice, but could not make out the words. Other voices, both male, were loud and clear.

"I say kill the bitch and let's get out of here. She's seen our faces. If she hasn't already told the police about the meetings, she sure as hell will after we're gone. And the girl in the blue car, what was that all about? Driving all the way out here to deliver papers without stopping? I don't like any of this."

The other voice was calmer, but no more reassuring

"Ta guele, shut up, I'll decide what to do."

Then she heard.

"Madame, dites-moi qui était la fille dans l'auto? Madame, who was the girl in the car?"

A pause.

"Was she from American Customs?"

The last sentence surprised Cecilia. *How did he know that?*

She was unaware that the man had photographs of most of the Rouses Point Customs Agents in his apartment in Burlington. The government was not the only organization with informants, and the man's were better paid than the government's.

Madame Gauthier's reply was inaudible. Cecilia heard a loud crash followed by a horrifying moan. Then silence. She had to act. She pushed the door open and jumped to the right. With authority, she gave a clear command.

"Police! Freeze!"

Startled, the two men froze. One, with a red sweater, stood over Madame Gauthier's collapsed form. The other, the one with a mustache, opened his mouth in surprise. His hands were empty, but Cecilia saw that "Red Sweater" held a gun.

***

In a fraction of a second, a parade of images passed before Cecilia's eyes: the photograph of Madame Gauthier's grandson on the shelf, the crucifix on the wall, the overturned table, the shattered cup on the floor, the horrifying stillness of the crumpled and still-slippered form of Madame Gauthier.

Cecilia had attended parades as a child, and her father had always secured a place near the judges' reviewing stand, where each group slowed to perform its best, drawing all eyes to them while the judges scored their performance. Now it was as if each passing image slowed before Cecilia and she was the judge, evaluating each as it passed, dismissing each in turn as of no consequence.

Not so for the next image that marched into her field of vision. That was Red Sweater's gun, specifically the tip of its barrel. Cecilia's field of vision narrowed to the menacing aperture. Slowly, ever so slowly, the barrel of Red sweater's gun rose until the threatening opening pointed directly at her.

As slow as the gun's movement appeared, Cecilia's own movements were exasperatingly slower. But her training came into play in these fractions of a second. She forced her eyes from the deadly barrel, and concentrated on a small area to the right and center of Red Sweater's chest. Simultaneously and automatically, both her arms made a "V" with her revolver at its apex.

She squeezed off a shot. Nothing! Red Sweater continued to move towards her while the gun in his hand jerked slightly upwards, as if fired. Cecilia kept her focus on Red Sweater's chest and squeezed off a second shot. Again Red Sweater's gun jerked upwards as he fired once more, but Cecilia was unaware of that. She only knew that Red Sweater had collapsed and fallen, out of focus, from her line of sight.

One down! Uno mas, One to go!

She turned rapidly to her left to face "Mustache" who now had produced his own weapon and raised it in her direction.

Dios mio!

She saw that the weapon was a 9 mm semi-automatic. Again, her training came to the fore. She swept her gun around to face him. But, though her mind commanded this action, her right arm failed to obey.

Distracted, she looked down. Her arm hung limp, its fingers extending as its revolver slipped from them. Bemused, she watched the dark stain spread over the arm of the jacket. It was her blood. Red Sweater had not missed. Numb, she wondered what her mother would think about the ruined new jacket.

She did not see Mustache as he fired, but she felt her whole body pushed involuntarily a step backwards.

Señor ten piedad, Lord have mercy.

Those were her last words as she fell.

***

******

Chapter 9
Thursday, November 30

Snow was falling heavily as Pierre left the paved road and turned north. The gravel surface was completely covered with white flakes. He was alone. There were no other cars. He strained to discern the edge of the road while his wipers struggled to clear semi-circles in the snow on the windshield. Still, Pierre was not anxious. He knew winter driving.

After some time, he saw a blue Geo, partly covered with snow, parked off to his left. A short distance farther, the road ended. He turned left.

Even through the falling snow he made out the large tree on top of the hill. It was the White Pine! *Damn!* André had been there last night.

Pierre recalled his directions. *OK, now where's the big spruce?* He passed it before he recognized the entrance. He turned the car around and stopped. The access lane was buried in fresh snow. His experienced eye gauged the steep slope. *I'd better not try that with these tires.* He trudged up the roadway.

He rounded the fir alley, and saw the cabin with smoke rising from the chimney. He approached, but something was wrong. From inside he heard curses, a man's voice.

Pierre pushed the door ajar and peered in.

A woman, her neck at a horrible angle, lay on the floor. *Grandmère!* To the right was a man, his back turned. He held a gun.

Pierre jumped back outside, but the door did not close.

Quoi faire? What to do? The snow gusted in his eyes. Sightless, Pierre pressed his body against the cold stone of the cabin. His hand reached a trimmed branch that leaned there. It was thick, solid. He grasped it like a club and held his breath.

***

Mustache leaned over Red Sweater and felt his carotid. No pulse, nothing. He retrieved the keys to the truck from the dead man's pocket.

As he turned to check Cecilia's body, a surge of cold air struck his back. *Who?*

He spun to face the intruder. The door was open, but there was no one.

The wind?

Gun ready, he pulled the door wide and peered out into the falling snow. He saw only large flakes amid a gray mist. *OK, so it was just the wind.*

But an icy gust hit his face and he lowered his eyes. He looked down and saw trampled snow in front of the doorway.

That's no wind!

He raised his gun and looked to the right.

This was his last conscious act.

"Whomp!"

Pierre swung the branch full force. The impact smashed the bridge of Mustache's nose. Delicate facial bones crushed and splintered brainwards. He toppled backwards into the house.

Pierre took a deep breath and stepped inside. Mustache lay on the floor, legs quivering. One gurgle, and breathing stopped. His fingers twitched and the semi-automatic slid off his palm.

Pierre kicked the weapon across the room. Then he stooped and retched.

Je l'ai descendu, I killed him.

He stood and surveyed the scene. First, his grandmother. She resembled his mother. But *Mon Dieu*, her neck! He turned away.

He went to the man in the red sweater, and examined his wallet. Only a few dollars, but a paper with a phone number, area code 514, that Pierre knew well. It was André's number in Montreal. So these were those bastards at the pine tree! He pocketed the paper but replaced the wallet along with the money.

Next he checked Mustache's wallet, there were no notes, but several hundred dollars American. Pierre left the money and the wallet.

Finally he turned to the woman with black hair. She was alive, but barely. He saw the Smith & Wesson .38 by the fireplace. Then he saw her badge. He drew back. She was a cop! Une femme flic! He hated cops, "la flicaille." He turned to leave.

But a scene from his boyhood flashed before him. He saw his mother prostrate and bleeding on the floor. He saw his father leave the room and heard his mother's weak voice, *À moi, Pierre, aides-moi! Help, Pierre, help me!*

It was too much. He turned and bent over Cecilia. One look was enough. She couldn't last. He ripped a strip from the tablecloth, and tied it tightly about her upper arm, down jacket and all. Not tight enough. The bleeding continued. He tightened until the flow stopped. Then he knotted the cloth. That was the best he could do.

He had to get out of there. Away from the blood, from his grandmother's body, from the smashed face of his victim. He burst from the house. He slipped and stumbled down the roadway through the falling snow.

At Lise's car, he brushed the accumulated snow from the windshield and rear window. He fumbled with the ignition. The wrong key. He tried another. It worked.

The wheels spun in the snow. Too much power! He shifted to second and gradually pressed the accelerator. The car eased forward and regained the road. The wheels spun as he pressed the gas. He passed the ridge with the big pine and turned south. A few minutes later he passed the lonely blue Geo. It was now completely white. His hands shook on the wheel.

Farther down the road they shook again. A state police car, lights flashing, approached from the other direction. Pierre was glad his license plates were covered with snow. The police car passed without slowing down.

When Pierre reached the paved route, he turned the way he had come. The windshield wipers struggled to sweep the snow aside. He skidded several times. At last he reached route 89 where crews were scraping and salting the surface.

He headed south to Burlington.

***

Sam Jones and Mac, a State Trooper, climbed the road to Madame Gauthier's. They had worked together before. A second trooper's car was at the Scanlon site, and had notified them that Cecilia's Geo was there, covered by snow. Sam had not heard from Cecilia.

Guns drawn, they approached the fieldstone house under cover of the falling flakes. The front door was open. Neither man was prepared for the scene inside.

"Oh my God!"

Sam shuddered and shut his eyes. Then he forced himself to study the scene. The old woman by the table was dead. That was apparent from the angle of her neck with her body. He pointed.

"That's Madame Gauthier."

Stepping over the man in the red sweater, he noted two entrance holes in the man's chest, about six inches apart. One was through the heart. He'd died instantly. Then Sam reached Cecilia's still form near the rear door. *My God, what blood, it's like "Nam."*

He'd seen his share of hopeless cases in Viet Nam, but this! He forced himself to recall Cecilia's natural vivacity. He could not believe that this gray face, ashen skin set off by black hair, had once been hers.

He leaned over her body. Startled, he yelled.

"Mac, she's breathing. Call for help!"

The wound in Cecilia's chest was high and he couldn't tell what damage it had done. But her arm! That blood! Was any blood still in her body?

Then he noticed the tourniquet around her arm.

"How did that get there?"

Sam was puzzled. He did not believe in angels, not the good kind anyway, but without that tourniquet his partner would be dead.

Mac had his own puzzle, the body near the door. Face up, the nose and facial bones crushed by a massive blow. *Who did this? It couldn't have been Cecilia! Could it?*

The tree branch lying just inside the doorway was damp with melted snow. Mac looked at the circumference of the branch, and turned to Sam.

"Sam this took somebody big. And strong!"

There was not much they could do for Cecilia. They were afraid to move her. They covered her with blankets. Sam added logs to the fire.

***

The paramedics found Mac's police cruiser with the flashing lights at the bottom of the access road. They came up on foot.

Mac called to them.

"Over here. She's still breathing. The others are dead."

There was no question of a helicopter, the snow was heavier than ever. They carried Cecilia down the access road to their Emergency vehicle.

Sam doubted she'd make it. He knew he'd have to call Cecilia's mother. *God, what can I tell her?*

It was Mac who searched the toolbox in the back of the Ranger pickup and found the Styrofoam containers with the dry ice.

Sam looked up at him.

"Mac, what the hell kind of drugs could be worth three dead and an officer dying. A beautiful girl like Cecilia, just starting out. My God, what am I doing on this job? Life's got to make more sense than this."

Mac gripped his arm. The house was now filled with supervisors and other types used to giving orders.

65

Sam tonelessly answered the questions posed to him. He heard Mac tell one of the interrogators.

"She was his partner."

After some time, he felt a hand. It was Mac again.

"Come on Old Buddy, they don't need us here anymore. I'm driving you to Rouses Point. Bill will take your car back there for you."

"Damn it Mac, I should have stopped her. I knew better. I should have made her wait!"

Mac pushed him out the door. The snow was still falling.

***

******

Chapter 10
Thursday, November 30

John had worked at the library most of the day. He copied several articles of interest for his paper with Dr. Lawrence. By the time he finished, it was after five. Hungry, he went to the Old Goose.

There were lots of empty tables. He chose one by a window.

While he ate, he studied a chapter on clinical immunology in a new compendium. Figure 4 displayed a curve with a mathematical equation. He'd save that for Jeannine. He kept reading.

An hour had gone by when he felt a touch on his shoulder. He looked up. It was Monique. Her voice was soft.

"May I sit?"

"Of course. What's up?"

John had never been alone with Monique. He studied her eyes. They were moist with concern and affection. Whatever the feelings behind this combination, John was hooked. Jeannine had never looked at him this way.

Monique found her voice.

"John, where have you been?"

Her tone was serious, even for Monique. Before he could answer, she pushed on.

"John, if you're in trouble, I want you to know I'd like to help."

"What do you mean?"

Monique swallowed hard. This was not easy for her.

"I know about the Table 3 data. Mike showed me."

"He did?"

"Yes, and now they've come and taken your computer away."

"*My* computer? Who's 'they?' Monique, what are you talking about?"

"Dr. Lawrence, Dr. Santini, and someone in a dark suit whom I don't know. They came just before lunch. Mike gave them his lab notebook for the A-11 project, and they took your computer."

"*My* computer?"

John was totally disoriented. Monique plunged further.

"John, I'm sorry. I helped Mike copy the programs off your computer myself. I didn't realize what he'd do. He's not going to stop until you're kicked out of the lab. He's mean, real mean. I came to warn you. I would have helped you with those experiments if I'd known you couldn't keep up. I mean I'm sorry, really sorry."

John was completely confused. What programs could she be talking about. He was upset, but Monique was more so. Her eyes flooded with tears. He reached towards her, but she pushed away from the table and fled the restaurant.

A minute after her departure, his confused thoughts arranged themselves with an awful clarity. He exclaimed.

"That bastard Mike, he's saying I did it!"

***

Sari admired the gold posts in her ear lobes. She tilted her head at various angles before the mirror and laughed. Her friend Mattie laughed too. Passing shoppers turned their heads. Sari and Mattie didn't care. They were a pair. Sari looked at her mother.

"Mom, why don't you come to the movies with us?"

Betty was flattered that the girls wanted to spend time with her.

"All right girls, but let's get something to eat first. We have time before the movie."

They ate at the mall food court. Betty chose a meatball sandwich and the girls, pizza. Sari wolfed her pepperoni down. Mattie hardly touched her slice. Betty made a mental note to ask Helen, Mattie's mother, about Mattie's eating.

The movie was fun. When the credits rolled by at the end of the film, Betty realized that she had thoroughly enjoyed her night out with "the girls."

***

Franklin felt for his key. The house was dark.

"Sari? Betty?"

There was no answer. He dropped his briefcase and stepped into the kitchen. There was cold coffee leftover in the pot.

He was embarrassed and angry. He had thought that Mike had done the counts for Table 3. When Mike told him that was John's work he'd been displeased, and more so because Dr. Santini and Hanes had been present. It made him look like he wasn't in charge, as if he did not know his own lab.

Not good. Not good Franklin, you've got to stay more on top of things.

Mike had made a bad error in trusting John to do that work. He would speak to Mike about that. Mike must learn to judge character. John could not be trusted.

The phone rang. Franklin answered.

"Betty?"

"Not exactly. Larry, It's 'Mackie,' How're you doing?"

"Mackie, I don't believe it. How are you?"

Mackie's real name was Dr. William McElroy. He and "Larry" had been friends in Medical School and residents at the same hospital afterwards. They owed each other. As residents, Mackie had stopped Franklin from giving a patient mislabeled medicine. Four years ago, Franklin had hired Mike Hartness based on Mackie's recommendation.

"Larry, my clinic in Arizona has taken off. It's not like the old hamburger days. It's Mercedes time! But you? I saw the Daily Express. You're big! Tell me about this cancer thing. It sounds hot."

After Santini and Hanes, Franklin did not want to talk about protein CA or breast cancer.

"I've got a good protein, from a hybridoma, but it's too early to say."

"Come on Larry, I can read. I saw the newspaper, and I got a copy of your abstract too."

Franklin tried to switch the subject.

"Are you still interested in homeopathic medicine? How about acupuncture?"

"Don't knock acupuncture. Even the NIH gives grants in alternative medicine these days. Get with it, Larry. You molecular guys aren't alone. There's gold in them thar hills."

Mackie switched back.

"Maybe your A-11 will work with human subjects. Let me know if you want to try."

Franklin was aghast.

"You know the rules for human subjects, plus FDA regulations for new drugs. What are you talking about?"

"Don't get technical on me Larry. I'm talking about saving lives. There's another country just across the border, Mexico, you've heard of it. I'm not talking about anything wrong. Listen, I'll be in Washington soon. We can get together for dinner."

"Why not. Call when you're here."

"You bet I'll call you. And we'll talk about your A-11. Don't wimp out on me!"

There was a click, and Mackie was gone.

Franklin looked at his watch, 8:30. Damn A-11. He went to the den and retrieved the TV remote. He sank in his chair, and surfed the channels.

***

Jeannine sat down on the sofa, and dumped her tennis shoes on the floor. She threw her socks at the shoes, extended her legs, and stretched. She was home and her feet were free.

She heard steps on the stairs. It was John. He looked terrible.

"Jeannine, where have you been? They think *I* did it. Mike told Dr. Lawrence those were *my* counts in Table 3. They think *I* made up the data. They've locked up my computer."

"John, how could they? That's crazy."

It *was* crazy. John was incapable of falsifying observations. How could Dr. Lawrence be so blind?

"I'm not crazy. Dr. Santini and Dr. Lawrence think I faked the counts. Monique too."

"John, I didn't mean you were crazy, I meant Dr. Lawrence was, or anyone who would think that, including your 'friend.'"

She avoided naming "Monique." This was not going well.

John wanted sympathy. Hell, he knew he hadn't faked the counts. He stood a moment longer. Jeannine was looking at her feet again. *I've got a real problem. Can't you forget your feet?* He responded.

"Monique's OK, she believed Mike. That's all."

Jeannine wanted to say, "*Look, you're a good scientist. This will all work out.*"

But she was honest. She didn't know if it *would*. John misinterpreted her silence.

"You don't understand, and you don't care."

Without thinking, he added.

"Monique cares more than you do."

As soon said, he was sorry. Too late!

"Monique! What do you mean, John!"

He averted his eyes.

"Nothing. It's nothing. It's just that lately you don't smile much. And now I'm not sure of anything, about *Mike*, about the *lab*, about *Dr. Lawrence*, about *us*."

All Jeannine heard were the words "about *us*."

"I'm not sure about *us* either. Maybe we need to be apart. Starting tonight!"

John spun on his heels.

"To hell with it. I've had it. You do whatever you want. I'm going to bed. Good night."

He went upstairs. She heard his shoes crash against the wall and fall to the bedroom floor.

***

Jeannine stayed on the sofa with her books, but she could not concentrate. She was furious with Dr. Lawrence, with Dr. Santini, and especially with Mike, and she was concerned for John. He was in serious trouble and she had not helped him.

She did not like herself. She did not like herself at all.

She wrapped her arms about her knees and bowed her head. Hurt pride. She knew John was bored with her. Not a good feeling. But worse, burned out. *He doesn't love me. We don't love each other.* Different schedules had made it easy for her to hide her feelings. Her new habit of studying late was not just dedication to learning. *I've been waiting for him to fall asleep before going up.*

For Jeannine, sex and love were inseparable. She could give all of herself, or nothing. She'd given everything to John but it had not worked. *I've tried, but this is not love.*

Painful honesty didn't soothe her guilt. Tonight, John was needy and she'd blown up at him. *I'm an uncommitted louse. He needs me. I don't love him. I can't fake it.*

She picked up her Probability book and tried to lose herself in "Sigma additive measures." Math had always worked before, but not this night. She dropped the book. *Damn!*

She extended her legs and stared vacantly at her bare feet.

***

Upstairs, John's thoughts raced from Mike to Dr. Lawrence to Dr. Santini and back. Finally, he dozed off.

In front of him stood Dr. Lawrence. John stretched his hand towards him.

"You know that I didn't do this."

But Dr. Lawrence turned his face away. When he turned back he wore a black executioner's hood.

***

******

Chapter 11
Friday, December 1

The university's inquiry panel met in the morning to determine if an investigation was needed. Of the two members, one was a molecular biologist from the biology department (outside the Medical School to avoid the possibility of conflict) while the other was an immunologist from a nearby university. They met in Marshall Hanes' office and studied the signed statements of Mike and Monique, along with the files from John's computer. Clearly the entries in Table 3 were not real data.

An investigation was called for. Both scientists agreed to serve further on the investigation committee.

Marshal immediately wrote to the Public Health Service.

CONFIDENTIAL/SENSITIVE
Office of Research Integrity, PHS, Address ?????
Dear Sir/Madame,
As required and in accordance with Fairland University's Assurance, this letter is to notify you of an investigation into alleged research misconduct under grant R01 CA26B12-01 from the National Cancer Institute, Franklin Wilson Lawrence, M.D., Ph.D., Principal Investigator. The respondent, John Martin, Ph. D., is alleged to have fabricated data. Dr. Martin is employed full time under the above grant. The complainant, Michael Hartness, Ph.D., is employed half time under the above-named grant and half-time under grant R01 CA13C20-04 also from the Cancer Institute.
Please note that the enclosed Daily Express article refers to data questioned in the allegation. Because of this publicity, I respectfully request you take extra steps to maintain confidentiality.
A report will be sent to you upon completion of the investigation.
Sincerely,
Marshall Hanes, Esq.
Research Integrity Officer
Office of the Provost

He added the following note for his secretary.

Sarah, Fill in the address and get me a final on this will you. Copies to the President, the Provost, Dean Hampton and Dr. Santini. And check the grant numbers. They're in my "Santini" file. Thanks.

Marshall sat back. He needed a third scientist for the investigation, one with no connection to Fairland University, but preferably with government experience. On Dr. Santini's list was a Dr. Sadler. She was on sabbatical from a prominent university to serve with the National Science Foundation. Marshall dialed her number. An answering machine responded. He left a message.

Next, he composed a letter to John

CONFIDENTIAL/SENSITIVE
John Martin Ph. D. Box ???
Department of Immunology
Fairland School of Medicine
Dear Dr. Martin:
In accordance with university policy this is to notify you that the university is investigating an allegation that you committed research misconduct by fabricating data in connection with grant R01 CA26B12-01 from the National Cancer Institute.
As a university employee it is expected that you will cooperate fully with this office which is administering the investigation. This investigation will be objective, thorough and fair. There is no presumption of either "guilt" or "innocence" on your part. You have the right to counsel.
The university will treat this matter with strict confidentiality and expects you to do likewise. The Office of Research Integrity of the Public Health Service has been notified of this investigation.
If you would like further information please call me at the above number.
Sincerely,
Marshall Hanes, Esq.
Research Integrity Officer
Office of the Provost

Marshall was determined to push this investigation. He threw on his coat and spoke over his shoulder.

"Sarah, I'm meeting Dr. Santini at the Faculty Club to discuss the Martin case. I'll be back by two. Could you have both letters ready by then?"

He was gone before she could answer.

***

John awoke from a fitful sleep. He dressed and went downstairs. The usual banana was on the table. Jeannine was gone. They had not seen each other since last night's debacle.

He avoided the lab. He went straight to the library to finish the references for his paper with Dr. Lawrence. Maybe that would please his mentor. Alone in the stacks, he did not have to talk with anyone. He worked through the lunch hour. He felt better, but still had no appetite.

At three in the afternoon he finished. He organized the photocopies with his notes into a folder. His literature search demonstrated that his research results were new and should be published. That would please Dr. Lawrence. John headed to the Forster Building.

The department secretary stopped him in the hallway. Her face was grim with authority. He followed her to her desk. She was unsmiling.

"John, here's a letter for you from the Provost's office. I need you to sign this receipt."

John took the letter and scratched his name on the paper she offered. She continued.

"And here's a note from Dr. Lawrence. He can't see you right now but he wanted you to have this right away."

Still no smile. John unfolded the note and read.

John,

Due to an unexpected demand on the funds of my grant, I am sorry to tell you that there is no money available for your salary after this semester (December 15). You should look for a position elsewhere.

(signed) F. W. Lawrence Ph. D., M.D.

John saw red. This couldn't be happening. Damn it, this wasn't real. Even without the new grant there was plenty of money! John felt he was in some kind of "wonderland." The words of the Queen of Hearts formed in his mind, *"Sentence first - verdict afterward."*

He turned to leave. His research folder was still on the desk. The secretary called.

"John, your folder!"

He paused and stared with glazed eyes. The secretary dropped her gaze. When she looked up, John was gone. The folder was still there.

***

Monique was working face down at the bench when a sudden gust peppered the window with sleet. She looked up. The sidewalk trees waved wildly, branches swirling with the shifting gusts. A second sheet of icy particles rattled the panes. Below, on the street, she spied John. He was bent into the wind, hair awry and jacket blown open. He glanced up towards the lab windows. The look on his face frightened her. She jumped up, grabbed her jacket, and rushed after him.

Mike saw her leave. He was curious. It wasn't like Monique to leave without saying where she was going. He stepped out of his office into the lab. Through the window, he watched her, hood up and jacket buttoned against the sleet, headed in the direction of the Old Goose. He decided to follow. Frowning, he put on his jacket.

Monique caught John at the door to the Old Goose. She spoke above the wind.

"John, what's up? Where were you today? Your cell samples came back. I put them in the freezer next to my desk."

John looked at her with dull eyes.

"I was at the library checking references. I was going to stop by the lab later."

He stood motionless, unaware of the pelting sleet and cold. His jacket was still open. The wind gusted and puffed it away from his body. Monique took the initiative.

"Let's go inside. It's miserable out here."

She opened the door and pulled John inside. He did not resist.

The restaurant was not crowded. It was mid afternoon, and there were lots of empty tables. She selected a table away from the door and steered him to it. Monique had never seen John so passive, so docile. She took a seat and waved him into the opposite chair. He sat.

The waiter came.

"I'll have a cup of hot chocolate. Bring him a cup of coffee. Thanks."

Her eyes questioned John to see if coffee was OK. He nodded. When the drinks arrived, she paid.

Monique sipped her hot chocolate and waited. John stared at his coffee. Abruptly he shoved Dr. Lawrence's dismissal note at her. She read it and shuddered. Tearful, she looked up. Still silent, John took out the letter from the Provost's office, and handed it to her. She read it too.

Now the tears flowed.

"Oh John!"

She swallowed a mix of tears and chocolate. John still had not touched the coffee.

"Oh John! I shouldn't have listened to Mike, but when he found those awful files on your computer, I didn't know *what* to think. I copied them from your machine onto a drive for him. Then he wanted me to go to the office with him. We gave the drive to Dr. Santini and I signed a statement. I'm so sorry."

In spite of his disordered state, John saw what had happened.

"Monique, Mike put those files on my computer. They're his files. He's the cheat."

She knew it was true.

"You're right. I caught him at your computer. He seemed confused. He must have just put them there. Then he said that you had faked data. John, I can straighten this out with Dr. Santini. And I can tell the investigation committee too. I'm sorry."

She continued.

"But what about Dr. Lawrence. I've never seen him change his mind about anything. You're here until December 15. You've only got a couple of weeks."

Monique swallowed hard.

"He's got to change his mind about you. He has to!"

John reached for his coffee. He swallowed half the cup in a single pass. He saw that Monique wanted to help. He reached for her hand.

"Monique, thanks for trying, but ... ."

Her moist eyes filled with affection.

"John, I'll do anything ... ."

But John's eyes remained vacant. He did not respond. He drained the coffee cup, and stood.

"I've got to go. Thanks for the coffee."

He wove through the tables and left the restaurant.

***

Mike was waiting in the bookstore across the street. When he saw John leave the Old Goose, he stepped out into a misty rain, crossed over and looked in the door.

Monique was at a far table. He backed outside, thoughts racing. *So she did meet him. What are they up to? OK, I can't trust her! But Santini already has her statement!* He turned to see John disappear around a distant corner.

Mike hunched his head against his collar, and took a side street. He stopped at a pay phone and fed coins to the hungry instrument. A familiar voice answered.

"Hello."

"It's Mike Hartness. I'm in some trouble here at the university. I need help."

"So!"

"I said I need help. There's this girl Monique and this guy John Martin. If they get together, I'm screwed. I'll be fried."

"So, why the hell are you calling me. We're even. I set you up four years ago. Take care of it yourself. Good bye."

Mike's hand tightened on the phone. His voice grew higher.

"Have you forgot what I know? If I go down, I'll take you with me. You've got contacts. I need to shut this Martin up."

"All right! All right! Stop whining. Where are you?"

"I'm at the usual pay phone. You know the number."

"OK. Stay there I'll call back in 15 minutes. Be there!"

Mike waited at the phone, pretending to talk. His hand trembled as he brushed his wet forehead. He shivered and shuffled his feet. Finally the phone rang. He picked up.

"Shut up and listen. I called Burlington for you. My contact has a man in Washington for a few days. Call this number. Ask for Kurt. He's expecting your call. Tell him 'Explorer' said to call him. Don't mention my name or yours."

Before he could reply, the phone went dead. Mike wrote down the number and walked through the cold rain to the Forster Building. Monique was in the lab, working, pipette in hand. Without speaking he went into his office and shut the door.

***

It was Friday evening. Sari was at Mattie Morton's house for the night. Franklin should have been home an hour ago. Betty sat staring at two empty place settings. *Typical Franklin, working late and not calling.*

The phone rang. Betty was tired of Franklin's explanations about how important his work was. She forced herself to pick up. It was not her husband.

"Mrs. Lawrence, this is Marshall Hanes, I'm an attorney with the Provost's Office at the university. Is Dr. Lawrence there?"

"No, he's not home yet."

There was silence on the other end of the line. Then Marshall Hanes spoke. His voice was strained.

"Mrs. Lawrence, I just heard that Dr. Lawrence terminated a Postdoc, Dr. John Martin, today. Did you know that?"

"No, I did not."

She inhaled. *John? Why?* He was her favorite Postdoc.

Marshall continued.

"I don't know what your husband has told you but there's a problem with Martin's data in his lab.

He went on as if talking to himself.

"He shouldn't have fired him without checking with me. He must not know the regulations about whistle blower protection."

Marshall caught himself.

"Anyway, ask your husband to call me as soon as he gets in. I don't want Martin making trouble for him or the university."

"Franklin's probably still at the lab."

"Thanks. I'll try there. Good bye Mrs. Lawrence."

Betty stared at her empty plate. *Why was John dismissed, and what trouble could he make for Franklin?*

***

Jeannine returned to the apartment at midnight. There was no sign of John. He was gone, truly gone, his closet was empty. There was only a note, no address or phone number.

> **Jeannine,**
> *I need to be alone for a while. Dr. Lawrence canned me. If you want to know what happened ask Monique Laurier at the lab. I need to be alone. You can have my share of our computer. I'll get in touch later. Thanks for everything.*
> **John**

Numb, Jeannine collapsed on the sofa. What could she do? Her feet were compressed in her sneakers. She took off her shoes and socks, extended her legs, and stretched. Her bare feet stuck out. They felt better, but she was miserable.

***

******

Chapter 12
Wednesday, December 6

Sam Jones located the small Catholic church outside of Burlington. The rural setting communicated peace. The gray stone building topped by a shining cross reminded him of his vacation last summer north of the St. Lawrence. He had seen a number of churches like this in the Quebec countryside.

Sam pulled his car, an aging Ford Taurus, into the church parking lot. To the left of the church was the cemetery followed by open fields. The cemetery ground was covered by a thin layer of week-old snow, but was not frozen. A large mound of freshly-turned earth was piled next to a gaping hole. Madame Gauthier would be buried right after the funeral.

Sam was late for the funeral, but he had planned to be. He wanted to check the parking lot before going into the church. There were few cars. One was from Quebec. He assumed Madame Gauthier's daughter had come in that one. The rest of the cars had Vermont plates, except of course, his Taurus from New York. He took a small notebook from his pocket and jotted down the license numbers.

One car in particular drew his attention. It was a late-model Toyota, brown with new tires. He drew a breath. That fatal day, the state trooper responding to the call from the southern road had seen a brown car pass in the opposite direction. It had been snowing, but the trooper thought it was a Toyota. It wasn't much, but it was all they had.

Sam scratched an asterisk next to the Toyota's license number.

***

Lise sat in a back pew. She tried to concentrate on the funeral service, but she was scared. She could not forget Pierre's wild eyes when he had come back to her apartment. His eyes had been black and cutting, like obsidian.

And he was different. For four days he had stayed, silent and morose, in the apartment. Only yesterday had he ventured out. He had bought new tires for her Toyota, but had returned immediately to the apartment. They had ordered Pizza.

Today, he had forbidden her to come to the funeral. His words still echoed in her head.

"You can't go. The cops, les flics, will be there, and maybe the guys who killed my grandmother. Tu ne dois pas aller! It's too dangerous. You can't go. I won't let you!"

But she had come nonetheless. She had to. She had to pray for, and honor, his grandmother. She was frightened, but she was here.

There were no police at the service. *Thank God.* She lowered her head and prayed. To the front she recognized Pierre's mother, weeping quietly.

A middle-aged man came in and sat behind and across from her. She turned to look. He could be a detective, but he appeared harmless. She turned back to the altar.

***

Sam put the notebook in his pocket. He was in the last pew on the left. In front of him, also to the left, were three women in the first row. One was surely Madame Gauthier's daughter. *Her name's Lucille Lachance.* To the right of the aisle were four men. Their clothes were rough and rural. They appeared to be local and Sam guessed, rightly, that they were volunteer pall-bearers. *OK, nothing there.*

Sam was most interested in the girl with dark hair seated, like him, well to the back, across the aisle. She was two rows in front of him. Her looks were ordinary, but she had a good figure. Her eyes were red with tears. *I'll bet she goes with the brown Toyota.*

Sam turned his attention to the priest who started to speak.

"Marie-Thérèse Gauthier was a good woman, a gentle woman. She missed her husband Charles very much. Now at last they are both united in Christ. But her death was a terrible tragedy, and today I want to say a few words to her daughter, here from Montreal, and to her niece, ..."

Sam settled into his seat.

***

Outside, on a hillside above the church, a white Ford Explorer paused by the side of a road. The driver waited while the man on the passenger side stepped out. The driver spoke.

"Don't screw up. We've lost two men and $300,000 on this deal already."

Boots on and camera in hand the man strode into the frozen field. The telephoto lens brought the cars in the church parking lot into sharp focus.

"Click, Click, Click."

There! He had the photos he wanted. The only car whose plate he couldn't read through the lens was the one from New York. That one belonged to that damned customs investigator. They knew about him anyway.

He pulled out a notebook and focused his camera once more. There. He copied the Toyota's number into a notebook.

Back in the car his companion queried.

"Did you get them?"

"Yeh."

"You sure you got the Toyota? That may be Lachance's girl. If it is, we can track the bastard."

"I got it. You want a picture of her?"

"You mean wait?"

"Yeah."

"Screw it! Sam Jones is down there. We're out of here."

The White Explorer turned towards Burlington. The men rode in silence.

***

The Mass was over. Lise genuflected in the general direction of the altar and left. She could not talk with anyone. She rushed to her car. Her new tires crunched on the crushed rock surface as she pulled onto the country road.

Back in Burlington, she drove aimlessly. She needed to be alone, to think. Ahead and to her right was a shopping mall. She pulled into the parking lot and cut the engine.

***

The funeral done, Sam drove into Burlington to the hospital. Mounds of dirty snow about the perimeter reduced the available space and the lot was full. Sam saw back-up lights go on. He signaled, and waited as the car backed out. He swung into the open space. Another driver, circling like Sam, shouted in disappointment, but Sam ignored him. He had bigger worries. He headed for the hospital entrance.

At the reception desk, a neatly-dressed woman smiled at him.

"I'd like the room number of Miss Cecilia Hernandez, please."

"Are you family?"

"Not exactly. I'm a co-worker."

Her smile disappeared.

"I'm sorry Sir, only family are allowed in that ward."

"But her family is miles away."

"I'm sorry Sir."

The woman turned from Sam to a young woman waiting behind him.

"May I help you Miss?"

Sam stood fuming. When the receptionist had finished, he started again. He flashed his ID.

"Look, I've driven here from Rouses Point. My name is 'Jones', 'Sam Jones.' It's official business. I'm her partner."

The receptionist frowned.

"I'm sorry Sir. I'll have to ask the physician in charge."

She stepped away from the desk to a phone behind a glass partition, out of earshot. He could see her talking, hands waving. He could not hear her voice. She came back.

"Dr. Madison says you have five minutes. Report to the nurses' station on 5A. They'll let you in. The elevator is straight ahead."

She turned to a young man waiting behind Sam. Her smile returned.

"May I help you, please."

Sam headed for the elevator.

***

At the nurses' station on 5A, Sam identified himself.

"I'm here to see Miss Hernandez. Dr. Madison said it was OK."

The nurse stared at Sam from behind the counter. She'd had enough of these "police-types." Cecilia's quiet will to survive touched her, and she was concerned for her patient.

"Look, the police were here yesterday, twice. Thirty minutes each time. Do you want this woman to live or die? What are you trying to do?"

"I got their reports, but Miss, this visit's personal. I drove down from Rouses Point to see her. She's my partner. I won't upset her or ask her anything. I just want to see her. I promise. Five minutes, no more, but if you don't think I should."

The nurse softened.

"OK, but two minutes, not five. She's very weak."

She led Sam to room 511. He waited while she went in to speak to Cecilia. The nurse came out.

"She wants to see you. Remember, two minutes."

Cecilia was lying on her back. Her face was pale, but not ashen as he had last seen her. Her black hair, clean, shone against the white pillow and surroundings. There were bouquets of flowers on the window sill and on the dresser. Sam checked the cards. One was from her parents, another from his office. He turned to Cecilia. She smiled, but her head remained on the pillow. She spoke with effort.

"Sam, you came."

"Cecilia, you look real good."

"Chihuahua! You're a lousy liar, Sam. I look terrible and you know it."

"I just wanted to see you. They say you're getting better."

"Sam, tell me what happened. They got my story, but nobody would tell me anything."

Sam had studied the transcripts of Cecilia's statements. He was not here to ask her anything.

"Take it easy. I just wanted to see how you're doing."

Cecilia would not be denied.

"How's Madame Gauthier. She's dead isn't she?"

At Sam's nod, Cecilia turned her head sideways, away from him. He waited. When she spoke her voice was a whisper.

"My God, it was my fault. Dios mio!"

Her voice trailed off. Sam worried that this visit was a bad idea, but Cecilia's next question was determined.

"Did you get the one with the mustache?"

Sam nodded.

"He's dead. Someone smashed him with a log or something after you went down. ... Guess what? That was Karl Mason. He's the 'Mason' in our last report. That was him."

"Sam, Mason smuggled drugs, cigarettes, illegals, anything. What was it this time? Did you seize it?"

"We think we got it all. It's the damnedest thing!"

"What do you mean?"

Cecilia seemed to gain strength as she talked. Her face was almost its natural color. Sam was relieved.

"We got Styrofoam chests, packed with dry ice out of the pickup. The report came back from the DEA lab in Montpelier yesterday. Most of it was biological stuff, frozen cells they say. But there were also a number of small sealed plastic tubes. Each had a reddish fluid in it."

Her head still lay on the pillow, but Cecilia's eyes were alert. "So?"

"So the DEA lab guys say the tubes are filled with *water. Ordinary water with a little red food coloring added.* The same kind of red coloring you have in Easter Egg dye!

One of the lab guys has kids, and when all the usual tests were negative, he compared the spectra of one of the tubes with a sample of red Easter egg dye. They were the *same.* The damned stuff is *water.* Can you imagine that, smuggling *water* with a *little food coloring.*"

Sam lapsed into thought. *Colored water!* His mind went back to the carnage at Madame Gauthier's house. The blood! *Cecilia could have died because of colored water!*

But her mind was working too. She was struggling to remember the name of a fellow class mate at FLETC, a guy from the Public Health Service's Office of Research Integrity. What had he told her? This *water* had a familiar ring to it. Where had she heard something like this? But she was too exhausted. She shut her eyes. Sam continued.

"Look 'C,' someone else was in the cabin. There was a tourniquet on your arm. Someone helped you, and it couldn't have been Madame Gauthier."

Cecilia flushed. Her head shifted on the pillow.

"The grandson!"

"What?"

"It *wasn't* a dream. Madame Gauthier's grandson! I know his face from the photograph. I dreamt he was leaning over me as I was lying there. I thought it was a dream, but maybe it wasn't!"

She was about to continue when the nurse appeared.

"Mr. Jones, I've already let you run over time. You've had five minutes. You must go."

"OK, thanks."

He turned to Cecilia. Already, her eyes were shut.

***

Sam left, mind racing. He knew Madame Gauthier had a grandson named Pierre. Maybe Pierre had downed Karl Mason, put the tourniquet on Cecilia, and then fled. But why had he run, and how? Maybe the brown car. And if the brown car was the one he had seen this morning, then it could have been Pierre's girl at the funeral. It was worth checking.

Sam stepped out of the elevator, and punched his cell. A familiar voice answered.

"Vermont State Police."

"Mac, it's Sam Jones. I'm here in Burlington."

"Quick, Sam, how's your partner?"

"She's OK, Thank God. I'm at the hospital now. I'll fill you in later. Right now I need a favor. Could you run a license plate for me? I'm in a hurry."

In a minute Sam had a name, Miss Lise Jordan, along with her phone and address.

Sam continued.

"And Mac, is there a Vermont Driver's permit for someone named Pierre Lachance?"

"Sam, you've got a hit. He's listed at the same address!"

Bingo!

Sam checked his Burlington Map. Lise Jordan's apartment was across town.

***

In Lise's apartment, Pierre answered the phone. He expected to hear her voice. Instead he heard a man.

"Pierre Lachance?"

Pierre froze. The voice continued.

"Don't worry. We know you're there. You've got something that's ours."

Pierre's English was in good shape. He'd been in Vermont all week. Still the words wouldn't come. The man continued with a lie.

"Your pal André told us where to find you."

At the mention of André's name, Pierre nearly dropped the phone. *André, what have you done. I trusted you.* Pierre found his voice.

"I don't know what you're talking about."

"Right. André's got our money or you do. You guys aren't as smart as you thought. Don't try and leave. We just want our money back, that's all. We need to talk."

Pierre calmed himself. He enunciated each word.

"Look! I've got some information for you. Hold the line, I'll get it."

Pierre laid the phone down and headed for the kitchen. He grabbed his coat and stuffed a paper bag with money under it. Cautiously he opened the door to the apartment. There was no one in the corridor. He took the stairwell.

He went out the back door of the apartment building. He passed his car. It was plowed in. There was no time to dig out. Too bad, he liked that Escort. He climbed a mound of snow, dropped over the fence, and went down an alley to the street behind Lise's apartment. He walked fast.

He was ten blocks from Lise's apartment when he stopped at a pay phone. He punched André's number in Montreal. A voice answered. Pierre shouted.

"Sale cochon! Dirty Pig! You sold me out. You pig."

He slammed the receiver down and hurried away. He was breathing heavily. His hand felt the brown bag under his jacket. At least he had lots of cash.

Too bad about Lise. He had to take care of himself.

***

The man in the White Explorer was on his cellular phone. He couldn't believe the caller.

"You called Lachance? You *warned him* you dumb ass!"

The caller continued. The man in the Explorer exploded.

You *think* he's still in the apartment. You *think*! You *don't think*. That's the problem. Stay there and keep watch. I'm coming now. I'll be there in five minutes. Don't move."

***

Sam parked the Taurus in front of Lise's apartment. He didn't notice the van parked across the street, some distance away. He

89

went to the front door of the building and scanned the list of names. There she was, "Lise Jordan," Apartment 3B. He buzzed, but there was no answer. He buzzed the manager's apartment. A man answered. He had a slight accent.

"Yes"

"U.S. Customs, official business."

"I'll be right there, Sir."

The man was from India. His English was clipped and melodious. Sam queried.

"Has there been a man living with Miss Jordan in 3B."

"*Living with* her? I don't know, but there's been a man *staying* in her apartment."

"Do you think he's there now?"

"No, I saw him leave ten minutes ago, out my rear window. He was by his car in the rear lot. Then he climbed the snow pile in the back and jumped over the fence."

"Show me."

The manager led Sam through a back hallway and out a rear door.

"That's his car over there. There's where he went over."

The snow was piled against the fence. Anyone could scramble over. The Escort was sealed by frozen snow. Sam scraped the snow and saw the Quebec motto, "Je me souviens" on the plate. He jotted the number.

Sam called Mac and asked him to put out an APB for one "Pierre Lachance," for questioning. Then he called his contact in the DEA and told him to get over to the apartment, fast.

***

The white Explorer drove by the apartment. The driver spotted the Taurus. The same car they had seen earlier at the church.

"That's Jones car. Get us the hell out of here!"

They drove by the parked van and signaled. The van too pulled away from the curve.

***

******

90

Chapter 13
Wednesday, December 6

Marshall Hanes had assembled a solid investigative panel for the misconduct allegation against John Martin, Ph. D. He had hired a court reporter to tape and transcribe the proceedings. The conference room, with its dark stained table and large leather-upholstered seats appeared suitably "judicial." He arranged a bank of four chairs on one side of the table. A single chair on the other side was for the interviewee. At the end of the long table he placed a chair for the court reporter. He was satisfied.

The secretary had arranged a tray of bagels with cream cheese and other spreads and the coffee was ready. Marshall poured himself a cup.

The first to arrive was the court reporter who busied himself with an elaborate array of wires and microphones which he arranged in front of each chair. Marshall gave him a list of the panel to verify the spelling of their names.

The next to arrive was a panel member, Dr. Lester Barker, the molecular biologist from the biology department. Barker was a pure-science type whose work involved animals, not humans. But his credentials were impeccable.

Marshall extended his hand.

"We met at the Inquiry, remember? Marshall Hanes, Counsel from the Provost's Office. Thanks for agreeing to do this."

Barker's eyes roamed the room, including the portraits of past deans of the Fairland School of Medicine. He shook Marshall's hand casually.

"You medical types have it pretty plush over here. Good thing I wore a tie. Ah, you've got something to eat."

Barker headed to a tray and spread a gob of cream cheese on half of an onion bagel. His first bite extended his cheek. Barker was speechless while he poured himself a cup of coffee. It didn't matter, Marshall had turned to the next arrival, an immunologist from a sister university.

Dr. Lewis, good to see you again. Thanks for helping us out."

Dr. Lewis had gray hair, and a distinguished look. He nodded to Marshall and headed over to the coffee pot. He spoke to Dr. Barker.

"Les, good to see you so soon. Did you get that DNA sequence from that roundworm?"

Dr. Lewis had served with Dr. Barker on the previous Inquiry Committee.

A woman entered the room. Marshall Hanes rushed towards her.

"Marsha, good to see you. Thanks for coming."

He turned to Barker and Lewis.

"Gentlemen, this is Dr. Sadler. Marsha's on detail to the National Science Foundation for a few months while on sabbatical. She has agreed to help us. I'm sure you've heard of her work. She is going to chair the committee."

***

Monique waited outside the conference room. She sat in a straight chair. Normally this wouldn't bother her, but today, instead of jeans, she wore a skirt. This was for John. She needed to make a good impression on the panel. However, Mike was seated across the hallway, leering at her. She shifted her legs awkwardly, crossing and re-crossing them. Mike disturbed her. She had come to detest him. He was a fraud. Now she was physically afraid. She looked down into her lap.

The door to the conference room opened. Looking upwards, she recognized the man who had seized John's computer. It was Marshall Hanes. He pointed to Mike.

"Dr. Hartness, would you come in please."

92

As he rose from his chair, Mike threw a look at Monique that was a combination of hatred, scorn and controlled rage. Stunned, she lowered her head.

Mike disappeared through the large double doors to the conference room. Monique looked at her watch. It was 9:15 a.m.

***

At 9:30 a.m., Franklin and Betty were in the kitchen. He sipped his coffee and tried to distract himself with the newspaper. Betty, opposite, sipped her coffee. She wore her pale blue bathrobe, and her hair was brushed. Franklin did not notice.

Betty broke the silence.

"Franklin, don't you think you should have waited until the investigation to fire John? What if he didn't do it? That man Hanes said that whistleblowers are protected."

Franklin drummed his fingers on the table.

"John's not a whistleblower, he's a cheat. I don't need your help to run my lab."

Betty looked into her coffee. She knew he was worried about his interview with the committee at 10:30 a. m. When he looked at his watch, she spoke.

"You have an hour to get there."

He replied without looking.

"I'll take the metro. Drop me at the Bethesda station. We leave in fifteen minutes."

"All right. I'll throw something on. I'll be right back."

She headed up the stairs. From the bathroom she heard the phone ring.

Franklin picked up. He did not recognize the voice.

"Dr. Lawrence, this is Jeannine Ryan. I met you at your house. I'm a friend of John Martin."

Franklin was cautious. He certainly remembered the stunning redhead.

"Yes I remember you, 'Miss Ryan,' right? What can I do for you?"

"Dr. Lawrence, I know the investigation committee is meeting today, and I wanted to speak with you."

"That's not possible, I'm about to leave right now."

"But John, showed the computer output to me. He didn't fake the data. He is sure Mike Hartness did it."

"Miss Ryan, if you have information about this case you should present it to the investigation committee. Not to me."

"Yes Sir, but I spoke to Mr. Hanes, and he said I had nothing to offer."

"Mr. Hanes is a competent lawyer. If he told you that, I'm sure he's right."

"But Dr. Lawrence. ..."

"Look, Miss Ryan if John is innocent, why did he run away. Where is he?"

Jeannine grimaced and squeezed the phone. She wished she knew where John was herself. She shot back.

"You fired him! He didn't run away."

By this time, Betty was standing next to Franklin. She saw his face redden.

"Goodbye Miss Ryan."

He slammed the phone down.

Betty reached into her purse for the car keys, and headed for the front door.

The phone rang again. Franklin frowned, stepped back and picked up.

"Look Miss Ryan ..."

He heard a laugh. It was his friend Dr. McElroy, "Mackie."

"Larry, you always expect it to be a woman."

Franklin was silent. Mackie continued.

"Look, I know you're in a hurry, and I know you're talking to the investigation committee this morning, so I won't take much of your time."

Franklin wondered how his friend knew these facts. Mackie continued.

"Just remember, Mike Hartness is a damned fine researcher and I won't have anybody smearing his reputation. Don't mess him up."

The tone irritated Franklin. Mike did not need defending.

"Mackie, I know that. There's no problem. I know Mike's a fine young man."

It was Mackie's turn to pause and think. Evidently, Franklin didn't suspect Mike. He shifted gears.

"Don't mind me, Larry. I was just worried about Mike's career. I didn't want to see it ruined. That mustn't happen. He's a fine young researcher. But you and I are on the same wave length. I'll let you go. I'm heading back to Tucson tonight. I'll call later about your protein A-11. Thanks buddy!"

Franklin put the phone down. *What the hell was that all about?* He looked at his watch. He was late. He turned to his wife.

"Betty, you'll have to drive me downtown. It's too late for the metro."

Betty was dressed for the outdoors with a gray jacket, blue sweater, casual slacks and sneakers. She looked younger, but Dr. Lawrence paid no attention. She followed him out the house.

***

Opposite Monique, the double doors swung wide. Mike emerged holding his head high. Before turning down the corridor he smirked. She lowered her eyes. Then she heard a voice from within the room. It was Marshall Hanes. His tone was stiff and unpleasant.

"Miss Laurier, would you come in now."

Monique rose and went through the doors. Inside, a long dark table filled much of the space. On the far side sat several people. Near her was an empty chair. She sat down and looked across the table.

She recognized Dr. Barker. She had audited his Molecular Genetics lectures. She did not recognize the other two. At the far end of the table a man fiddled with a tape recorder. He spoke to Monique.

"Would you say something into the microphone please, so I can adjust it."

Monique leaned forward.

"Hello."

"Could you speak louder?"

Monique spoke again. The reporter adjusted his machine and nodded to Monique.

"That's fine."

Then he turned to Marshall Hanes.

"I'm ready."

Monique shifted in her seat.

***

Jeannine heard the click. Dr. Lawrence had hung up. Jerk! *John how did you put up with that guy? But damn it. Where are you? John, what are you doing?*

There had been no word from John. It was days since he had moved out. She had called the immunology department. He hadn't been back at the lab. No one knew where he was.

Would he defend himself before the committee? They were meeting this morning in the main conference room of the Fairland Medical School. The conference room was in the Medical Center Building, known as "Main Med". Perhaps John would show up. It was worth a try.

Jeannine left the apartment. She and John often had walked this way. Thanks to him she knew that the trees lining the sidewalk were Gingkoes, and that they were male trees. She also knew that the species, *Gingko biloba*, was a "living fossil," known as a fossil from the Triassic (older than "Jurassic" as in the "Park") and found in China today. John knew a lot. She respected him.

But she knew now that respect was not love. She was confused, and disappointed with hurt pride, but she was relieved to no longer live with him. She could stop pretending to herself

and to him. *John, we need to talk. You and I need closure …
Are you all right? Where are you?*

She reached the Main Med building and entered the spacious
foyer. It was semicircular and lined with potted plants; some fig
trees, some Norfolk pines, but no Gingkoes. She smiled.
You've still got me thinking about plants! She spotted the
corridor that led to the conference room.

She turned into the corridor and saw Monique disappear
between two large doors. Then she saw Mike, headed her way.
He was coming fast. Jeannine stepped back around the corner.
She didn't think Mike knew her, but she wasn't sure. He might
have seen her photo at the lab. She moved near a potted fig and
stood there studying the leaves.

Mike rounded the corner and strode to the main door. He
paid no attention to Jeannine nor to anyone else. Something
about his haste made her follow him. He left the building. She
stayed inside. Mike crossed the street and went into "Le
Papillon," a French restaurant. Jeannine had seen the posted
menu. It was expensive.

She glanced at her watch. Le Papillon was not open yet.
There's nothing to do there.

In answer to her thoughts, Mike re-emerged. With him was
a man in an expensive suit. They appeared to argue. She could
not hear, but Mike raised his fist. The man turned and got into a
cab. Mike tried to follow, but the door slammed and the cab
pulled away. Mike, fists clenched, stood in the street. Then he
shrugged and walked in the direction of the Forster Building.
Jeannine watched him go.

Who was that guy? What was Mike up to?

***

Jeannine stayed at the doorway. A blue car stopped at the curb.
The driver, a woman, looked familiar. *Mrs. Lawrence?*

Dr. Lawrence stepped from the car. He wore a blue tweed
jacket and dark blue slacks. The car pulled away and Jeannine

saw a vanity license plate, "LAB-DOC." She smiled. *Maybe he's got some flair after all.*

Dr. Lawrence strode to the entrance. Jeannine ducked back and leaned over a potted Norfolk pine. She was getting used to leaves. With a stiff stride, Dr. Lawrence disappeared down the corridor.

Jeannine looked down the hall. Dr. Lawrence sat stiffly in a chair by double doors. No one else was there. Specifically, there was no sign of John.

She sat by a potted fig tree. Its twisted gray-green leaves were dry, like her mouth. She waited.

***

Betty pulled away from the curb. She was free for the afternoon and evening. Sari was to spend the night at Mattie's house, and as for Franklin, why wait for him at home when he never came.

She checked the fuel gauge. She had a full gas tank, and lots of time. She was dressed for the outdoors.

She headed across the Roosevelt Bridge to Route 66. The day was clear and cool. *Hello world!* She turned up the radio and tapped the wheel to the beat.

For once, Franklin would not know where she was. *Too bad. Franklin, I don't care! I can manage on my own!*

She surprised herself. She felt good.

***

The conference room was quiet except for the sound of shuffling papers. The woman opposite Monique arranged her notes. Monique waited. The unsmiling white-haired Doctor in the large portrait stared down at her. She tried to read the name on the small brass plaque on the frame, but could not. It was too small. Her mouth was dry.

The woman in charge addressed Monique.

"Good morning Dr. Laurier. I'm Dr. Sadler the chairperson of this committee. This is Dr. Lewis, and I believe you already know Dr. Barker. To my right is Mr. Hanes, counsel for the university. Would you state your name for the record please?"

98

Monique leaned into the microphone. She swallowed.

"Monique Laurier."

Dr. Sadler read from a sheet of paper.

"This is an investigation into alleged research misconduct on the part of Dr. John Martin. As part of this investigation we are interviewing you. We expect your answers to be truthful and complete. For your protection as well as ours we are recording this interview. You will be offered a copy of the transcript of this interview for correction. If you wish, you may have counsel with you at this time."

Dr. Sadler raised her eyes and spoke.

"Dr. Laurier, you are alone. You choose not to have counsel present, is that correct?"

Monique nodded. Marshall Hanes frowned.

"Monique, could you speak louder for the reporter and the tape recorder. Thank you."

Monique did not like Mr. Hanes. She spoke each word singly.

"Yes ... I ... do ... not ... need ... counsel ... here."

Instantly, Dr. Sadler liked Monique. She was not going to let a male panel intimidate this young female researcher. Her tone softened.

"Thank you Dr. Laurier. You are a postdoctoral fellow in Dr. Lawrence's laboratory, is that correct?"

"Yes, in the Immunology Section."

"Are there other workers in that section?"

"Yes, Dr. John Martin and Dr. Mike Hartness."

"Could you describe the workspace in the section, whose computer is where, and so forth?"

"Our lab is on the third floor, at the front of the Forster Building. We're all in the same space except for Mike, Dr. Hartness. His desk is in a small office, a closet really. His computer is in there. My desk is by a front window, my work bench is too. I don't have a computer of my own. I use a shared computer on the bench by the window. It has our gamma counter software on it, and a printer, a LaserJet."

"Where is Dr. Martin's computer?"

Monique looked across the room.

"Well I see right now you have it here on that table in the corner. That's it with the photo taped on the side."

The photo was of Jeannine. Monique could recognize, and dislike, that photo from twenty feet away. Dr. Sadler smiled.

"You're right of course. But where is it normally?"

"On his desk, next to his bench. He faces the wall opposite Mike's closet."

Dr. Sadler continued with her scripted questions. She had done her homework for this interview.

"Were you in the lab on the morning of November 29th?"

"Yes."

"Was there a phone call?"

Monique described Dr. Lawrence's call from Chicago, and John's efforts to get him to drop Tables 2 and 3. She described Mike's anger and John's departure. Dr. Sadler continued.

"What did you do then?"

"I continued working on my plates. Then I left the lab to get the mail from the department box. I stopped at the machine in the hall for a coke. I was gone twenty minutes. When I got back I found Mike Hartness at John's computer. And ..."

Dr. Sadler interrupted. She placed a sheet of paper and a computer thumb drive in front of Monique.

"Dr. Laurier, is this your statement, signed November 29, about what happened when you found Dr. Hartness at Dr. Martin's computer?"

Monique started to nod, but saw the microphone. She spoke into it.

"Yes, but ..."

Dr. Sadler continued.

"And is that the thumb drive referred to by you in your signed statement."

This time Monique could only nod. Marshall Hanes spoke. "Answer out loud please."

Monique's voice was a whisper.

"Yes."

Dr. Sadler continued.

"Dr. Laurier, is everything in your signed statement true to the best of your recollection today?"

Monique started to nod, but remembered to speak.

"Yes, but ..."

Dr. Sadler smiled at Monique. The dead Doctor in the large portrait remained unsmiling.

"Thank you Dr. Laurier. You've been most helpful."

Monique squirmed in her seat and opened her mouth, but before the words could form, Dr. Sadler smiled.

"Dr. Laurier, have you anything you wish to add at this time?"

Monique took a deep breath. Her face flushed.

"Yes, I would like to say that I believe that John, Dr. Martin, did not fabricate those data. I believe that Dr. Hartness did."

Dr. Barker stared at her. He did not smile. Next to him, Dr. Lewis broke in.

"Monique, .. uh, ... Dr. Laurier, we've been told that you have a personal relationship with Dr. Martin, is that true?"

Monique was flustered. *Damn you Mike, what did you tell them.* How she wished the answer was "Yes."

"Not really, I mean no, but ..."

Dr. Sadler frowned.

"Dr. Laurier, the committee understands that you believe that Dr. Martin could not have fabricated the data. Is there anything else you wish to add."

Monique's answer was barely audible.

"No."

Dr. Lewis raised his eyebrows and whispered something to Dr. Barker. Neither looked at Monique. Dr. Sadler spoke.

"Thank you for your cooperation Dr. Laurier. You will be sent a copy of the transcript. Oh, one more thing. Do you know where Dr. Martin is at this time?"

Another question she wished she could answer "Yes." *Where was John?* Monique shook her head and looked down.

"No."

Marshall stood up and escorted Monique out of the room. In the hallway, Dr. Lawrence sat waiting in the same chair she had used. He rose, but did not acknowledge her. She heard Marshall apologize to him because they were running late.

She stumbled down the corridor. John was destroyed. Her signed statement had damned him. She stepped erratically through the foyer. Her eyes misted. Potted plants and people became blurs. Where was the rest room? There, by the reception. She struggled through a group of visitors.

"Excuse me, …, Pardon, … I'm sorry."

Shoulder against the door, she pushed into the rest room.

Inside, Monique slumped over the sink. She wept.

***

Monique bent, sobbing, over the sink. Minutes passed. The door opened. Someone had come in.

She felt a touch on her shoulder. She looked up. In the mirror, through her tears, she saw reflected red hair. It was Jeannine. *No!*

Monique scooped water onto her face and rubbed. *Non … Non … pas possible! …Not possible! … Not her! …She can't see me like this. …It's not right. What a mess! … my eyes, my makeup, my hair. Anybody but her!*

She looked again in the mirror. Through her tears she saw Jeannine's eyes. They were moist and kind. No coldness, only softness and warmth.

Behind her, she heard Jeannine's voice.

"I think you need a friend. I know I do. We need to talk."

***

******

Chapter 14
Thursday, December 7

Daylight! At last! Cecilia's good hand felt for the button on the side of the bed. *There!* The motor hummed and cranked the bed to a sitting position. She tugged a pad of paper onto her lap. *OK!* She fumbled for the pencil. *Good!* She pressed the pad against her thigh and tried to write. *Ouch!* The pad wobbled. *Where's my right arm when I need it?* Sweat beaded her forehead. She studied the characters she had printed.

BOB DELANEY ORI.

"Honey, what are you doing? Why aren't you resting?"

Cecilia started. It was Norma, the morning nurse.

"I have to write things down. I don't want to forget, and I need you to help me make a phone call."

Norma's brow furrowed. She pointed at the pad.

"Is that for work?"

Cecilia shook her head no. Norma took the paper and put the pad to the side, out of reach.

"Whoever 'Bob' is can wait. You *need* your rest. No use fooling me honey, I've seen your type before. Here, lie back down."

Norma was fond of her patient. She lowered the bed and adjusted the angle of the headrest. She fluffed the pillow, maneuvering it for comfort. Then she stuck a thermometer under Cecilia's tongue.

"There, let's see how you're doing?"

Norma chatted nonstop while checking Cecilia's pressure and pulse. Cecilia could not retort. The nurse made notations on a chart, paused and wrote some more. Finally she drew the thermometer out.

"How can I talk with that thing in my mouth?"

"That's the idea honey. Any pain when I do this?"

Norma touched Cecilia's right shoulder. The latter grimaced.

"No!"

"A little honesty would help, honey. Do you want Demerol?"

Cecilia shook her head no.

"OK, Dr. Madison says you start physical therapy for the arm tomorrow. How about your chest? Did you sleep well?"

Cecilia shifted her head away. *You guys wake me up all night and I'm supposed to sleep?* She turned back.

"Fine."

"Honey, you *are* doing fine, but you have to *rest* now. I'll be back in a half hour for your breathing exercises."

Norma left.

***

Cecilia struggled to reach the phone. She did not have much time. With one hand she wedged it against the pillow. She punched the number at Rouses Point. A familiar voice answered. Cecilia exclaimed.

"Bueno, Sam. It's you, not the stupid machine!"

A startled Sam stammered.

"Cecilia! You're OK!"

"Sam, I've got to talk fast. If Norma comes back she'll kill me. Worse, she'll disconnect the phone. She's already stopped all incoming. I need a phone number."

Sam waited. Cecilia continued.

"This colored water. ... When I was at FLETC the guy next to me was from the Office of Research Integrity. A scientific type. Anyway he told me about homeopathic medicine."

"What?"

"Sam, don't make me repeat. The idea is to give people weak doses of medicine. As weak as you can, so the medicine doesn't hurt you more than the disease."

Sam thought this was odd. Cecilia spoke again.

"Anyway, it's got supporters, some real scientific types. The National Institutes of Health has a program for something called 'Alternative Sources of Medicine,' and ..."

"Have they got you on pain killers, 'C.' You're not making sense."

"Hang on. The guy is Bob Delaney, *D E L A N E Y.* He's a Ph. D., a real brain. I taught him to shoot, small arms. You remember the pistols with the red-handles."

The only weapons allowed at FLETC were the Training Center's. They had red handles.

"So. What are you getting at?"

"He told me about this fraud case where someone wanted a grant of two million dollars to study medicine that was diluted all the way, so there was just water left."

Cecilia caught her breath. She was tiring fast.

"They started with some real medicine. ... I don't know. ... They'd dilute 'til you couldn't tell whether anything was left or not. So they got a very dilute medicine, so dilute *you couldn't tell it from water.* So afterwards, *they added food coloring* so they could tell their stuff from ordinary water."

Sam thought of the seized vials. She made sense.

"So what happened to the two million dollars?"

"The NIH never gave them the grant. Some of their data looked funny! The reviewers canned it."

"OK. How do I get a hold of this Delaney?"

Cecilia had strength for one final burst.

"*You* don't Sam. *I* do. Give me a break, it's my idea, and I kind of like him! Just get me his number. He's in Maryland, Bethesda or maybe Rockville. Leave it with the nurse. Tell her it's my brother."

Cecilia didn't have a brother. Sam started to protest.

"Chihuahua! She's coming. I gotta go or she'll take the phone out."

A sharp click resounded in Sam's ear.

***

105

An exhausted Cecilia shut her eyes and laid her head back. Norma checked the still figure in the bed and smiled. At last she had made Cecilia rest, if only for a few minutes. Norma touched her on the shoulder. The patient opened her eyes.

"Time for breathing exercises, honey. I need some deep breaths today!"

Cecilia tried to smile. Norma had a big heart, but Cecilia was really tired.

***

By afternoon Sam had the information. Bob Delaney was an investigator in the Office of Research Integrity of the Public Health Service in Rockville, Maryland. He called the hospital in Burlington. He did not reach Cecilia. He got the nurses' station on 5A.

"No, you can't talk to Ms. Hernandez right now. The doctor is with her. ... Yes, I'll give her the message with her brother's number. ... No, Norma's off now. She'll be on again tomorrow morning. ... Yes, I'll be sure she gets it. You're welcome, Good-bye."

Sam sighed. He wanted to push this lead right away, but he deferred to his partner. He could wait a day. Besides, he had the Mortimer case. He picked up that folder and headed for the copier. Thank God! Cecilia seemed better.

***

Dr. Bob Delaney was a virologist. At least he had been a virologist. Now he was a scientist-investigator with the Office of Research Integrity, the "ORI," in Rockville, Maryland.

The phone sounded.

"Dr. Delaney, there's a 'Mr. Hanes' from the Provost's Office of the Fairland Medical Center on the line."

"Thanks Sherry. Tell him I'll be with him in a second."

Marshall Hanes' letter had been assigned to Bob yesterday. He scanned it quickly. Mike Hartness alleged that John Martin had fabricated data. Both were paid by Public Health Service funds. The press was already interested in the study.

Bob looked at Sharon Husak's article. There was no sign the press knew of the alleged misconduct. *Damn, another case about breast cancer.* He picked up the phone.

"Marshall, this is Bob Delaney. How can I help you?"

Marshall informed Bob about the meeting of the panel.

"… We should have transcripts of the interviews back in a day or so. The investigation is almost complete. The committee is drafting the report now. The whole thing should be wrapped up soon."

"OK, Mr. Hanes, but be thorough. It's good that you sequestered the computer right away. Take what time you need. We'll review the report when it arrives."

"Dr. Delaney, has anyone from the press called you on this?"

"No. You're the only contact I've had."

"Good. The Medical School wants to wrap this up fast."

"That's understandable."

Bob hung up. Then he ran an IMPAC search of the research grants data base. The information provided by Hanes was correct. The ORI had the authority to review the matter. The research involved Public Health Service funds, and data fabrication was research misconduct under the PHS definition, as well as anybody's.

Over the past two years Bob had worked on two 'breast cancer' cases. Both had generated Congressional Hearings, and a lot of press coverage. He did not want another.

His eyes drifted to a photograph on his wall. It was a class at the Federal Law Enforcement Center in Georgia. Bob stood on the back row. In front of him was a dark-haired woman from Tucson. He remembered "Cecilia" well. They'd had beers together at Pam's, the unofficial FLETC watering hole. He'd heard she was somewhere up north.

It was late. The office was empty. Bob liked it that way. He could get work done.

***

107

In Burlington, the man parked the white Explorer at the side of the road. He awaited a call from Kurt, the younger brother of Karl Mason, the dead man with the mustache.

The phone vibrated. The man listened and exploded.

"Shut up Kurt. I don't give a damn about what you did in Washington and I don't give a damn about Hernandez either."

The man continued.

"Find that SOB Lachance. He's the one that killed your brother, not the Hernandez girl. It's in the police report. She was already down. Forget her. The whole operation's at stake. I got no room for your personal crap."

At Kurt's protests he reddened.

"Forget Karl, and leave the Hernandez bitch alone. Stay away from that hospital, and stay away from her, or you'll feed the fishes in Lake Champlain. If you want blood, find that bastard Lachance."

He jammed the accelerator and squealed the tires. He drove away "speaking" to a dead man. *Karl, you were a good man, family, but I can't control your brother. Once he gets Lachance, I'm gonna have to put him away. Understand me, it's nothing personal against you.*

Call it superstition, call it what you will, he had to clear the matter with Karl.

***

Kurt Mason stood at the phone in the hospital lobby and fumed. *Screw you boss!*

Two doctors, stethoscopes bulging in their lab coats, walked past. One had a mustache, like his brother. Karl's face flashed before him. He too spoke to his dead brother. *Karl, what are you trying to tell me? You know I can't forget you.*

Kurt saw his brother's eyes sad and full of reproach. *Karl, what do you want me to do?* He found the men's room and splashed his forehead. He needed a shave. More, he needed a drink. Somewhere on the fifth floor was the woman who had killed his brother, and he needed a drink, bad. *Karl, if you want me to get Hernandez, you gotta help. I don't know where she is. They won't tell me!*

His stomach cramped. He opened a stall, dropped his pants and sat down. The stall door swung shut. As he sat there miserable he heard two men enter the room. Beneath the stall door he saw white shoes and pants, hospital attendants. They sounded relaxed. It was the end of their day. He listened to the banter.

One spoke.

"I think I win this week. The blond on 3B is a clear winner. Pay me five bucks."

The other laughed.

"Not yet, buddy. Not yet! You haven't seen Hernandez. Jet black hair. She'll top your blond any day. She's sick and she still looks good. Wait 'til she's well. There'll be no contest. Get your money ready."

"OK, I'll give you one more chance. Where is she?"

"Fifth floor, 5A, room 511."

"I'll take a look tomorrow, but get ready to pay up. She won't beat 3B. See you in the morning."

"Take care."

Kurt heard the door shut. Water still splashed in the sink. The splashing stopped and the dryer whirred. Then the door shut a second time.

His body shook. Karl had found Hernandez for him!

He left the stall, steadied himself on the sink, and stared into the mirror.

OK Karl. I got your message. Thanks. Room 511. I'll get her.

He left the rest room and walked to the elevators. He passed a mother and her little girl, but no one else.

Alone at the elevator, he pushed the button.

Why didn't it come? Where was it? He shifted his feet.

He pushed the button again. The light went on. The doors opened and he stepped in. He pushed five.

The elevator rose. The light blinked in succession: 2, ... 3, ... 4, ... 5, nonstop.

The doors parted. He stepped out. To his right was the nurses' station, 5A. To his left was the door to the stairwell. *Good.* He would take the stairs when finished.

His fingers closed, opened, and closed again on the 9 mm semi-automatic in his jacket pocket. His mouth was dry, and there was rhythmic throbbing in his head.

He tightened the grip on his gun and turned towards the nurses' station. He saw a tall nurse. He drew a deep breath and paused, but she rose and hurried down the corridor. *Good.* She disappeared at the far end of the hall.

He moved forward. The throbbing increased.

He stepped past the station and looked to his left.

Room 505.

He took five more steps, Room 507. *Good.* He was headed right. He kept on.

Room 509.

Five more steps and he stood by the door of 511 itself.

His lips were cracked. He swiped them with his tongue and took a breath. He peered into the room.

The near bed was empty, but there were flowers on the windowsill.

A curtain shielded most of the far bed, but he saw the sheet move. She was there!

Hernandez!

The throbbing ceased. His mind soared. There was no hearing, no feeling, only sight. He saw every detail in the room, but he was not in it. He was above it. He was in control. Power flowed from the gun through his fingers and arm to his chest.

Triumph!

OK, Karl. What do you think of your little brother now?

He would spray his shots through the curtain.

***

"Excuse me Sir, you can't go in there. Who are you looking for?"

The voice crashed through Kurt's consciousness. His suspended sense of hearing, affronted, registered sound again. He turned in anger. It was the tall nurse. She had come back. Her eyes were steady, at a level with his. He stared. Her eyes wavered. She glanced sideways. She was scared. *Good.* He gripped the gun in his pocket.

Then he heard running. The nurse had signaled someone. A man in a white coat appeared behind her. He was bigger than Kurt and was not afraid. Yet he was polite.

"Can I help you Sir?"

One too many. *Damn.* Kurt's fingers loosened their grip on the semi-automatic. His mouth and throat were dry once more, and his head started to throb. He heard other voices approaching. This wasn't working. He needed a drink more than ever. His eyes fell. He looked at his feet and heard himself mumble.

"I must be on the wrong floor. I thought this was 3A."

Then he turned and walked down the corridor towards the stairwell.

The nurse looked at the orderly. He was on the phone to security.

"We've got a real weirdo here on 5A. Blue jacket, blonde hair, about 5-11. Went into the stairwell by elevator 11. Watch out, he's probably on drugs."

The orderly headed for the stairwell.

In the stairwell, Kurt ran down to the main floor. He slowed to walk through the lobby and out the main entrance. Outside, he sprinted to his car. Panting, he opened the door.

The car started. He spun out of the lot.

***

Later, on a stool in the bar near his apartment, Kurt filled himself with alcoholic resolve. He thought of his brother. *Karl, I won't let you down. Tomorrow, first thing, you'll be able to rest. I'll get her for you, brother. First thing tomorrow. The boss can't stop me. Nobody can. I'll get her for you. She's dead.*

He swallowed half the draft in one gulp. His eyes glazed. He'd lost count of the beers. No matter, he'd be ready tomorrow. His head slumped sideways on the bar. Vaguely, he realized that someone had come and sat next to him.

He felt himself lifted to his feet. The voice in his ear was familiar. Stumbling he went along. Outside the cold air woke him and through a mist, he saw the waiting van. He told his feet not to get in, but they wouldn't listen to him. He was half pushed, half pulled inside. A flash of fear cleared his thoughts, and he exclaimed.

"Wait ..."

But a crushing blow stopped him.

The driver of the van spoke.

"Get his gun. Where'll we dump him?"

"Next block, at the intersection. It'll be a hit-and-run."

In the darkness, the van slowed. Kurt's body hit the icy pavement.

The van sped away.

***

******

Chapter 15
Friday, December 8

The van was on its way to Albany. The driver and his companion had stripped Karl's apartment of its photographs and papers. They would meet their boss, Tony, later.

Tony Diorio, the man of the white Explorer, had abandoned that stolen vehicle on the outskirts of Burlington. He now drove an inconspicuous dark-colored Honda Accord. He had one more thing to do. Outside the city, he stopped at a mini mall. He pulled out his pre paid cell phone and punched Arizona. The conversation was one-sided and short.

"No more screwed up deals with your damned medicines. It's too damned hot. I've lost three men, and got a cop shot. Shut up! Don't talk. We know where you are. Shut your mouth or your clinic will fry, with your ass inside."

He hung up and checked the minute hand on his watch. At half past the hour, he called Rouses Point, an extension in the same building that housed Sam Jones' office. He let the phone ring two times and then hung up. He called again. This time he let the phone ring once. The pre-arranged time and signal told the listener, *No more contacts. Lay low.*

Finally, he called New York, the city. He spoke.

"We're shut down. Secure here. I'm coming in."

He got back into the Accord and headed for New York. He spoke aloud to his windshield.

"That smart-ass doctor. I'm screwed because of this medicine crap."

Crack cocaine and heroin were his line. He was scared to go back to New York, but more scared not to. Karl's medical deals were crap. Burlington was shut down. If he started that operation again it would be for regular business.

Tonight he'd be back in the Bronx where he knew the rules.

***

Seated in his Clinic on the outskirts of Tucson, Dr. William McElroy, Mackie, was stunned. His hand still gripped the phone. He looked at his white lab coat half-expecting to see it smudged and soiled from the call. He put the phone down and shook himself to regain his composure. He had never met any of the Burlington crowd. They were dirty and dangerous. He was better off without them, but he'd better call André in Montreal. Something else would have to be worked out.

He leaned towards his intercom.

"Paula, hold all my calls. I'll be back in a couple of hours."

He slipped out of his office by the rear door. He strode past a towering Saguaro cactus behind which one could see the foothills of Mount Lemmon. His cream-colored Mercedes shone in the desert sun. He got in and backed out of the parking spot, careful not to brush the car against the stick-like Ocotillos that lined the drive. He drove into Tucson.

***

Sam was back in Burlington. The interview with the tearful Lise Jordan had produced nothing, *nada,* as Cecilia would have said. And Kurt, Karl Mason's brother, was dead, beyond interrogation! Sam knew the death was no accident, but knowledge and proof were two different things. No one had seen anything. Witnesses at the bar knew Kurt was drunk, that was all. Another blank. There was no news on Pierre's whereabouts.

There was nothing more to do here. He called Cecilia. Instead, he reached an orderly.

"I'm sorry Sir, Ms. Hernandez is in therapy.

"This is Sam Jones. Can you tell her I called?"

"Of course, Sir."

At least Cecilia was on her feet. That was good news. Sam headed back to Rouses Point

***

In Rockville, Maryland, Dr. Clay Hayman, Ph. D., sat in a government-gray office and looked out at an equally gray sky.

On the desk top were three packets arranged in a neat row, three proposals for review and evaluation by the Assistant Secretary for Health, Department of Health and Human Services. The intercom buzzed.

"Dr. Hayman, on your call to Mr. Hanes at Fairland University, I have him on the line for you."

Clay picked up.

"Marshall! I've been wanting to talk to you. Guess what. I'm here in Washington, well Rockville actually. It's been a long time. How do you like Fairland?"

For the next few minutes Marshall and Clay exchanged reminiscences about their past work together in the offices of a Midwestern university, then Clay explained his presence.

"The university gave me a leave of absence to come to Health and Human Services. I'm a consultant in the Office of the Assistant Secretary for Health."

Marshall was intrigued.

"No kidding. You're in HHS. Anything to do with the Office of Research Integrity?"

"The ORI, I'm reviewing them. Why? What are you doing with them?"

Marshall detected disdain in Clay's tone.

"We have a research misconduct case, a Public Health Service grant, cancer research. I'm in charge. We report to ORI. Anything wrong with that?"

Clay snorted.

"Nothing, except they don't know what the hell they're doing!"

"What do you mean?"

"Marshall, you remember that case with Dr. 'G,' one of our best medical researchers. He got tons of grant money for his department. Some dipsy grad student, 'Sarah something,' said he hadn't done some experiment. Of course he had! The matter was cleared up right away. I chaired the meeting. He produced a summary of the data, in his own handwriting. An acid spill in the lab had destroyed the original printouts, but he had a summary he had written."

Clay cleared his throat before continuing.

"The student still wasn't satisfied. She still claimed he hadn't done the experiment. Hell, she went to the ORI. They were a real pain in the ass! Believe me. They tried to check my investigation. It was all settled, but they couldn't see the obvious. Imagine! They listened to a grad student!"

Marshall hesitated.

"Clay, I haven't had any problems so far."

"You will! The ORI is dangerous. What about academic freedom? It has no business impeding progress. Science is too important."

"Are you saying I can ignore the HHS regulations, that I don't need to report to them?"

"I'm not saying that."

"What are you saying then?"

"Nothing, except that there are a lot of us in the academic community who don't want that damn office to exist. We want the universities to "police" themselves, with *no* government oversight."

"But your leave from the university? You've only got a year as a consultant."

"So what. I've already completed my proposals."

Dr. Hayman's secretary signaled him from the doorway.

"Marshall, I've got to run to a meeting. It was good to talk to you. Let's keep in touch."

The conversation was over.

***

That conversation with Clay unsettled Marshal. He punched Dr. Sadler's number and spoke.

"Dr. Sadler, Marshall Hanes at Fairland University. I'm calling about the misconduct investigation of Dr. Martin. Can you tell me when the committee's report will be finished?"

Dr. Sadler's response was crisp and unemotional.

"We'll be done in another few days. The first part is being typed. We're meeting again on Monday to wrap up part two, but that's just details."

Marshall was pleased.

"Can you tell me your results."

"Yes. It is research misconduct. Dr. Martin fabricated data."

Dr. Sadler paused, then continued.

"We would have liked to have Dr. Martin's testimony, however."

"He can't be found. He's run away."

"I understand that."

To herself, Dr. Sadler thought how sad this affair was for Monique Laurier. The young Dr. Laurier reminded her of herself at that age. Monique's signed note indicating John's guilt had impressed the committee. Unfortunately, her evident feelings for Martin had only strengthened the weight of her statement. Martin was guilty.

Dr. Sadler sighed.

"We think we have enough evidence to support our conclusion. You should have our report by next Friday. That's the 15th. We want to finish before Christmas vacation."

Marshall Hanes was pleased. He rubbed his hands together. His tone was ingratiating.

"Thanks very much for all you've done Dr. Sadler."

"Of course. Good bye."

Marshall leaned back in his chair, satisfied.

***

Mike Hartness sat in his closet-office. He put his feet on his desk and tilted his chair. Scuttlebutt was that Hanes' committee had found John Martin guilty of scientific fraud, of faking data. Mike laughed.

Just over a week ago he had sat at this desk, head in hands, career finished, because John had discovered his cheating. Now John was discredited. Gone. *Goodbye Martin!*

His thoughts turned to Monique. She had avoided him since the Hanes-committee. Mike was challenged. That stimulated him. If he could get her to bed, life in the lab would be much less dull!

He knew Monique was afraid. He could use that to his advantage. And she was naive. He could use that too. *She's lucky! She just doesn't know it yet.*

The phone interrupted his reverie.

"Mike, this is Dr. Santini's office, could you stop by right away."

Mike wished that the secretary had addressed him as, "Dr. Hartness," but he suppressed his irritation.

"I'm on my way."

The secretary was alone.

"Mike, John Martin left his folder here last Friday. Would you see that he gets it."

The secretary extended the folder. Mike frowned. *I'm no damned messenger boy, send it to him.* But he did not voice that thought. He feared the "borrowed" power that she wielded. He took the folder.

The secretary disappeared into the inner office. Mike stood alone.

***

Monique sat at her workbench. She punched the number of the Mathematics Department and asked for Jeannine who came on the line.

"This is Jeannine."

"This is Monique Laurier, I was hoping you would have some time to talk this morning. If you're not busy or anything."

Jeannine calculated the time to walk from Dr. Anderson's class to the Old Goose.

"11:25 at the Old Goose?"

"Thanks, thanks a lot."

Monique hung up. Mike entered the lab and smiled. She ignored him.

The door to his office slammed shut.

***

Mike exhaled and sat down. Monique was stimulating!

He opened John's folder. He had no intention of giving it to John, wherever he was. He examined its contents. The articles John had copied covered several topics: Protein CA, T-1 tumors, tumor growth inhibition, Estrogen receptors and some special cell-fusion techniques. There were two of Mike's and Dr. Lawrence's articles on A-11, as well as papers by Mike and Dr. McElroy. Mike was intrigued.

Under the journal articles he found John's lab notes, dated sheets of numbers, graphs, even text, all organized and annotated. Mike examined them.

A half hour later, he pushed his chair back from the desk. He mopped the perspiration from his forehead. *My God, John's got it! He's got a protein that does what I've faked A-11 to do for three years. He's done it! The bastard's got it*!

He shuffled his feet and looked once more at the papers. The data were there, the RIA's, the ELISA's, the controlled inhibition experiments. *This protein's better than the fake A-11. Protein CA is inhibited! He did it*!" He whistled.

A knock on his door startled him. He threw John's papers into his briefcase.

It was Monique. Her face was blank.

"Dr. Lawrence just went by. He wants to see you."

"Sure, thanks. You look great today Monique."

He headed out the lab.

***

Dr. Lawrence had on his coffee-and-wine-stained lab coat. He sat on a stool.

"Mike. Good to see you. I wanted to say I'm sorry about this mess. You know I had to make John leave."

Uncharacteristically, Mike interrupted his mentor. Whatever Mike's faults, indecisiveness was not one of them.

119

"Dr. Lawrence, I've got to tell you something. You know how I've been helping John and Monique with their work, and doing your A-11 experiments."

Dr. Lawrence wanted no more surprises. His lips tightened. Mike plunged on.

"I didn't tell you this before because I wanted to see how it worked, but I've been running some experiments on my own, all year, on another protein I've isolated... and ..."

Mike stammered.

"It's got better properties than A-11!"

For Mike, the die was cast. John's work was now his. Dr. Lawrence was stunned. Mike continued.

"Sir, I've been following this lead for a year. I knew you wouldn't mind my using the reagents. They're the same as we use for the A-11 experiments. The bottom line is that we have something better than A-11 here."

Mike had chosen "We" in the last sentence. Dr. Lawrence hesitated. He did not want A-11 to be surpassed. But Mike was enthusiastic, and the work was done in Dr. Lawrence's lab so it was "We" who had done this.

"What is it *we've* got Mike?"

Mike had foreseen this question.

"Let me get my notes and everything together this weekend. I'll go over the whole thing with you next week."

Dr. Lawrence checked his schedule.

"I'm busy Monday. I'll see you Tuesday at ten o'clock."

"That'll be fine, Sir."

Dr. Lawrence clapped his hand on Mike's shoulder.

"Mike, it's great having you in my lab."

Mike smiled. John's work was now Mike's.

***

Monique was bent over the computer when Mike returned. He went to his office and shifted through John's notes. There, on the last sheet, was a list of John's cell samples.

"Damn!"

Mike gasped. John had sent his cells to a friend's lab to have them grown up. He had to have those cells, or there was no point in talking to Dr. Lawrence.

He stepped out of his office. He kept his voice from shaking.

"Monique. You know those cells that came last week. You signed for them. Do you know where they are?"

"You mean John's?"

"Yes. What did you do with them?"

Mike tried to look nonchalant. This disturbed Monique. John was gone and there was no reason not to tell Mike where the cultures were, but she did not trust him.

There were two liquid nitrogen freezers used by the lab, a small unit next to Monique's workspace and a large unit down the hall. Monique was the most organized person in the lab. She knew where the samples were, but she feigned incompetence.

"I'm not sure. I think they're in the big freezer down the hall. You could look there."

Mike left. Monique picked up the phone and dialed. She spoke.

"Anne, can I keep some cells in your freezer for a while?"

"Sure."

"Good, I'll be right down."

Monique turned to the small freezer next to her, removed John's vials from a rack, and put them in a Styrofoam bucket with powdered dry ice. She grabbed her jacket and stepped into the corridor. Mike called from down the hall.

"Monique. I don't see them, and they're not on the log."

"Check the freezer by my workspace. They must be there."

And she was gone, her hands clutching the Styrofoam bucket with John's cells.

***

Mike checked the small freezer. The samples were logged in with Monique's handwriting. They were the last entries on the log, but the rack was empty. *Strange. Where are they? Could John have sneaked back into the lab and stolen them?*"

Mike was outraged by the possibility that John had taken his own samples. *Damn it, Martin. You have no rights. You're a thief. I can't claim your experiments without those cells.*

The phone rang and he grabbed it.

"Mike, this is Anne Simmons in Embryology. Has Monique left yet?"

"I guess so. She's not here."

"Then she's on her way. She has some cells to put in my freezer. Something's come up and I have to leave. I don't want to miss her. Oh! Here she is. Sorry to bother you."

Mike gritted his teeth. He was furious, and afraid. *Monique, you little bitch. You almost fooled me. What are you up to?*

He ran to the stairwell. Two flights of stairs, two at a time. At the far end of the corridor was the embryology laboratory. There was no one in sight. He slipped inside. The air smelled of paraffin and preservative. On the left was the freezer. The last entries in the log were Monique's. There on the top rack were John's vials. Mike reached for them.

Damn. He hadn't brought a container!

He saw a Styrofoam bucket on the floor. Monique's initials were scratched on the top. It was half full of dry ice. *Thanks, Monique.* He placed the vials in the cold bucket.

No one was in the corridor. He walked to the stairwell and climbed the steps.

Back in the lab, he hid the precious vials in a rack with his own samples. He put Monique's container by the door. Relief and jubilation swelled his chest. *What a morning! I've got the weekend to prepare for Dr. Lawrence. Tuesday. I can do it!*

He felt damned good. He was hungry and decided to go for a beer and sandwich at the Old Goose. He might even see Monique. Her duplicity had increased his estimation of her.

***

******

Chapter 16
Friday, December 8

Monique entered the Old Goose. Jeannine waved. Monique wove her way through the tables and chairs to sit down.

Monique's brown eyes encountered Jeannine's blue. They reflected the same question. Brown and blue eyes dulled simultaneously. Neither had heard from John. Monique's shoulders drooped.

Jeannine regarded Monique. She was attractive and her vulnerable femininity, which Jeannine felt she lacked, was appealing. Monique possessed just what men, like John, seemed to want and need.

Monique for her part had to admit that Jeannine was more striking in life than in her photograph. Jeannine in vivo was better than Jeannine in vitro. Monique was sure that no man would look at her after seeing the red head.

Jeannine spoke first.

"I'm sorry there's no news. It's not like John not to ..."

Monique slumped more. Any news would have helped. She murmured.

"I can't imagine he wouldn't call you. I mean you're ... ."

But Mike broke into her thoughts and she blurted.

"Mike's trying to steal John's experiments."

Jeannine's face flushed. Her hair appeared redder.

"What!"

Scientific caution tempered Monique's words.

"I'm not sure, but this morning Mike asked me for John's cell lines. He was gloating."

The waiter took their order and repeated.

"Two Tuna sandwiches and a coffee."

He looked at Monique.

"And a hot chocolate for you."

He disappeared. Monique continued.

"I haven't seen John's lab notes, his folder, anywhere in the lab. I'm sure Mike has them. Today he wanted to know where John's cells were."

"What did you do?"

"I hid them with a friend in Embryology. Mike disturbs me. I can't concentrate. I can't be near him. I'm afraid. He looks at me like I have no clothes on. He's disgusting."

Jeannine nodded. She had no experience with scientists' cheating with data. That notion was contradictory. But she had lots of experience with lecherous looks. Her response was pure Jeannine.

"You're absolutely right. The bastard's framed John, wants to steal his work, and wants your body as a bonus. We've got to stop him."

Her bluntness reassured Monique. She wasn't imagining things.

"But what can we do?"

"Can he steal John's work without those cells?"

"Not really, even with John's data and results, sooner or later he'll have to produce the cells. The hybridoma arose from a random experiment. No, he has to have the cells."

"OK, then don't let him have them. Wait for his next step."

Their order arrived. Jeannine finished and sipped her coffee. She spoke softly.

"I think you should know that it's all over between John and me."

Jeannine paused. The words did not follow easily.

"And, I think, I'm pretty sure that John cares for you. A lot."

There, she had said it. It wasn't closure with John, but it was close. Jeannine studied the look of disbelief and hope that illuminated those moist brown eyes.

Monique quivered. Before she could respond, Mike appeared, loud and confident.

"Monique! Here you are. You know *my* cells that we were looking for. You put them in the Embryology freezer. It's OK. I've got them now."

He sneered.

"Dr. Lawrence doesn't like cells kept outside the lab. Don't worry, I won't tell him, but be more careful next time."

He looked past Monique at her companion. He wanted to say "Who's the babe?" but Jeannine's crystalline stare froze him.

He turned and left.

Jeannine sat silent. After seeing Mike, she understood Monique's disgust.

Monique reached across the table, squeezed Jeannine's hand, and fled.

***

Jeannine kept her seat. She drained the last of the coffee and put four one-dollar bills on the table. It was a generous tip by Old Goose standards.

The waiter appeared at once.

"More coffee?"

"Thanks."

The rich aroma stimulated her. She sipped thoughtfully. *Damn it John! Where are you? How could you leave without telling me?*

The Old Goose filled further. Students and professors jostled among themselves for the now-crowded tables and chairs.

Jeannine wore a faded gray sweatshirt with the letters *SKYLAND* still visible. Old clothes couldn't hide her attractiveness. She appeared alone and in distress.

The apparent distress appealed to a tall blond male nearby.

"Do you mind if I sit down? Maybe I can help?"

Jeannine raised her eyes. The speaker was familiar. *The class last spring in Time Series Analysis. He had been in the second row.*

She surveyed the cropped blond hair, the field jacket and the backpack which hung from his shoulder. She looked down at the heavy hiking boots. She stood up. *The boots! Of course! Damn it Jeannine, wake up! That's it!* She exclaimed.

"Thanks. Thanks a lot. You've been a big help!"

She dashed to the door, leaving the puzzled student alone and staring.

***

Jeannine ran all the way to the apartment and dashed up the stairs to John's former study.

There was the computer, its lifeless dark screen, surrounded by scraps of paper at odd angles. Taped to the wall was the paper she sought, a phone number. Amid various folders on the desk, she located the phone, and punched 1-703- ... .

A cheery voice answered.

"Shenandoah National Park, Thornton Gap"

"This is Jeannine Ryan. My friend is backpacking on the trail, coming out near Stony Man Mountain."

Jeannine followed up her guess with a falsehood.

"I'm supposed to meet him, and I lost directions about when and where."

"What is your friend's name?"

"Martin. John Martin. Would you mind checking?"

The next thirty seconds appeared as fifteen minutes.

"Yes, we have a John Martin. He's making a loop. He started last Monday."

The cheery voice paused. When it resumed, it was no longer cheery.

"He was supposed to come out yesterday morning. At Little Stony Man trailhead at mile 39. But we haven't signed him out yet."

Jeannine's guess about Stony Man Mountain was confirmed. She knew John. He was late and that was typical, but no matter. She queried.

"What's the weather been like up there."

"It's been sunny and clear during the day. A little rain around Stony Man, but it's been freezing every night here at the station, and Stony Man is colder."

The Ranger hung up abruptly. She had to act. She had been derelict in not checking the log. She signaled her partner to go to the trailhead and look for John's vehicle.

Jeannine was both vexed and relieved. John was damned inconsiderate. Still, she might be able to intercept him at the trailhead before he went elsewhere.

Her watch said 12:30. She could beat the Friday traffic on Route 66 and get to Thornton Gap by 5:00 o'clock.

She picked up the phone again.

***

Monique returned to the Forster Building. Mike was not there. *Thank God.* She shut down the computer and grabbed her tennis shoes. She wanted to get away.

Her Styrofoam bucket was by the door. Then she saw the incubator running. Inside were two T25 flasks filled with medium. They were dark purplish red rather than bright cherry. The flasks hadn't been "cooking" long, maybe only 10 minutes.

Mike was growing cultures from John's frozen cells. By Monday, he would have enough antibodies for experiments. She felt sick. She had wild thoughts. *I'll spill the flasks or maybe pull the plug of the incubator. Better yet, I'll turn off the Carbon Dioxide and the cells will die. But what if they're no more cells, then John's cell-lines would be lost. I can't do it. They're still John's.*

She could not sabotage John's work, even if Mike stole it. She turned and kicked the Styrofoam bucket. It flew across the floor, spilling dry ice.

The phone rang.

"Ici Monique ... eh ... pardon, Monique here."

On the other end of the line, Jeannine jumped. Monique spoke perfect English and it was easy to forget that French was her native tongue.

"Monique, John is in Shenandoah Park. Do you want to go there with me? I can pick you up at Forster in five minutes."

"Mais oui, I mean sure. I'll be outside."

She dashed down the stairs, tennis shoes in hand.

***

A Gingko tree had been inserted into a square patch of earth in the concrete sidewalk. Monique waited nearby. Her spirits soared. John was found, and her former enemy, Jeannine, was not only an ally, but incredibly, a friend. Moreover, it was Friday. She was free of the lab until Monday.

She loosened the top of her jacket and threw back the hood. Cold air flowed around her neck. Invigorated, she turned to face the sun. She liked the mild Washington "winter."

A blue Mazda swung to the curb. Jeannine was behind the wheel. Monique hopped in. Blue and brown eyes met for the second time that day. This time they sparkled with rays of relief and hope.

"Jeannine, thanks for letting me go with you."

Jeannine shrugged and smiled. The Mazda jumped from the curb in front of an incoming taxi and raced to the traffic signal.

"I should have thought of the trail sooner. John thinks better away from the city and people. Stony Man Mountain is one of …, one of *his*, … favorite spots."

Jeannine had been about to say "our favorite spots," but caught herself. It wasn't just sensitivity for Monique's feelings. Jeannine couldn't say "our" anymore.

"I hope we can catch him before he leaves the trail."

Jeannine's "his" instead of "our" thrilled Monique. Her hopes rose that John might care for her. She changed the subject.

"How did you get into statistics?"

Jeannine glanced sideways and smiled.

"My father was a physicist, and I always liked mathematics. When I did my Masters in math I took a course in statistical methods. Then I started helping biology students look at their data. It grew from there. Of course, there was John. He knows a lot of statistics, a real lot. One time John had ..."

Monique pretended not to notice that the topic had returned to John. Monique understood her friend. She was happy to pick up the theme.

"Last summer in the lab John was ..."

Jeannine laughed at the surprise ending. She kept the topic alive.

"You should have seen John in the kitchen when he ..."

The two highly-trained professional women were soon lost in "John trivia." Smiles, laughter and relief filled the little Mazda. Neither had talked like this since High School.

From the Beltway, the blue Mazda sped onto Interstate 66 headed for Route 81. Jeannine wanted to enter the park via Luray and Thornton Gap.

***

At 4:00 the Mazda exited Interstate 81 and headed past Luray towards Shenandoah Park. The road narrowed, and the small motor strained to climb the steep ascent to Thornton Gap. The conversation slowed, and then ceased altogether as Jeannine swung the wheel from left to right and back to master the twisted roadway.

Monique stared through the windshield, oblivious to the silent beauty of the empty leafless hardwoods punctuated with green pines and an occasional dark hemlock.

Both women remained silent. Words were not needed. Each knew the question in the other's mind.

What if we don't find him?

Reality had returned to the little world inside the Mazda.

***

At 4:30 the Mazda entered the Park and stopped at Skyline Drive. The road sign indicated *SKYLAND* to the left. Jeannine turned the Mazda in that direction and the car resumed its climb.

Ahead of them was a dark tunnel which had been blasted through the rock. Monique looked at Jeannine's sweatshirt with the faded letters *SKYLAND*. *She and John were here together. Maybe he bought it for her.* The soft and ample folds of the pullover collapsed on Jeannine's breasts and enhanced her feminine form. Feelings of jealousy and inadequacy overcame Monique. *She's so beautiful. How could he choose me over her?*

Ahead was the tunnel. Lights on, the Mazda entered as fleeting shadows flickered across Monique's face. Jeannine spoke.

"Don't worry. Whatever John and I thought we had, we didn't. It's over. I mean really. And I know John likes you. I know more how he feels than he does. Listen to me. He likes you a lot. He does."

Monique brightened as the Mazda emerged from the tunnel into the light. Ahead the sun's rays slanted sideways through the trees, throwing their shadows eastwards.

The car continued to climb. To the left, the hillside dropped precipitously. On the right, to the west, the sharp slope was populated with stark oaks whose brittle brown leaves clung desperately to dry twisted branches. Some leaves, despairing, fell to the stiff breeze while others, already fallen, rustled across the road in front of the blue car.

They were high above Thornton Gap. Jeannine broke the silence.

"Up ahead on the right. That's Stony Man Mountain. Do you see it?"

Ahead, the mountain top had an emergent rock outline that resembled a face, half-reclined, that faced west. The "nose" was aquiline. Jeannine continued.

"It's the highest point on Skyline Drive. It's not far to the trailhead. We're almost there."

The Mazda accelerated.

The trailhead was a cleared space to park cars, with a paved surface that was covered by a layer of dead leaves. Jeannine strained forward. A brown van was parked in the shade.

"Thank God. That's John's van."

Monique clutched Jeannine's arm.

"You did it. You found him!"

Jeannine ran to the van. The accumulation of leaves and twigs on top of the vehicle showed that it had not moved recently. She peered inside. John's clothes and possessions were crammed into the available space.

Jeannine knew John, and his love of backpacking. She turned to Monique.

"He started from here and he'll end up here. He loves Stony Man Mountain, and I know just where he'll be at sunset."

The sun was low in the western sky. Evening was coming. Jeannine wrote a note.

We're here, looking for you up top.
If we miss you, wait here for us.
Jeannine and Monique.

She stuck the note under the windshield wiper.

"Get in the car, there's a shorter way up."

Jeannine fastened her seat belt. The Mazda was rolling as Monique jumped in.

Twigs and leaves flew behind the spinning wheels. They spun onto Skyline Drive and headed farther south.

***

It was more than a mile to the turn off for Skyland Lodge. Jeannine parked the Mazda in an isolated parking area surrounded by leafless trees. There were no other cars. No buildings were visible, only the winter woods. Jeannine buttoned up against the cold.

"We climb to the top from here."

Jeannine dashed up a worn path that wound through the forest. White streaks on the trunks of widely spaced trees marked the trail. Jeannine ran ahead. Monique, slower, followed the blazed trunks. By the time the trail turned westwards to ascend steeply, Jeannine was no longer in sight.

Monique increased her pace. She could see clearly. The leaves of the forest floor were lit by slanted rays from the West.

Stony Man Mountain was the highest point on the Drive, and Monique was captivated by the cold-tolerant plants, familiar to her from her youth in the Laurentians. At one point the trail was embraced by Moosewood, l'érable à bois barré, whose bare branches exposed a bark with alternate pale and green vertical stripes. She passed a fir tree and smiled, un sapin. Up to the left was a whole grove of firs, une véritable sapinière. Climbing further she brushed a needled branch, a red spruce, l'épinette rouge. Even the increasing cold warmed her Canadian heart.

The last ascent was the steepest. In a dark hollow, shaded from the western rays, was a large hemlock, une pruche du Canada. Monique emerged into the sunlight where bright red berries of le cormier, the Mountain Ash, greeted her. There, waiting, sat Jeannine.

They sortied onto bare rock. Monique realized she was treading on Stony Man's face.

Jeannine scrambled from rock to rock until she reached a large boulder. Then she disappeared from view. Monique followed. She held on with both hands while her feet felt for sure footing. Cautiously she rotated herself around the boulder and found herself on a narrow ledge. There stood Jeannine, motionless.

Jeannine's confidence was gone. Her arms hung listlessly.

"I was sure he'd be here. This is his spot. You can see why."

She pointed. Monique's eyes followed. The whole Shenandoah Valley lay stretched before them. Far to the west, the sun hung above a dark blue ridge on the horizon. Closer in, the lights of Luray sparkled in the evening shadows. Below, but still well above the tree tops, a lone raven soared on the wind. On the ledge, a gentle breeze sifted strands of Jeannine's hair, reddened further by the western rays of the sunset.

"Careful!"

Monique froze.   A loose stone, dislodged by her foot, disappeared over the edge. She waited to hear it hit. There was no sound, and then it cracked distantly against the rocks below. She was on the edge of a cliff with a major vertical drop.

Jeannine continued.

"Where is he? We couldn't have missed him. The sun hasn't gone down yet. If he was anywhere nearby, he'd be here for the sunset. God, where can he be?"

Her evident despair alarmed Monique.   She glanced westwards. The soaring raven had broken its glide and was flapping towards the cliff. It disappeared from view beneath her. She tightened her handhold and looked over the edge to see where it had gone.

"Sainte Mère! Jeannine, look!"

"Oh my God!"

Both women recognized the blue color on the talus far below. Each knew that color well. John's jacket! They focused and saw his motionless outline, screened by the branches of a pine. Jeannine started to her left.

"Monique!   Over here! You can't go down the rocks. There's a way down on this side. Don't slip. Come on!"

Monique followed Jeannine's voice. She left Stony Man's chin and climbed down through a dense mix of pines, spruce and Mountain Ash. Her feet slipped on loose talus, but she pressed on.   Now she was in a thicket.   Brittle branches scratched her cheeks. In spite of her rapid descent, it took minutes to find the scrubby pine.

John was motionless. His eyes were closed and dried blood caked his forehead. The hair at the base of his neck was not matted. Monique was relieved. If his head had bled, the blood would have flowed there. She felt for John's pulse. *Thank you God!*

Monique called out.

"Jeannine, over here, he's breathing!"

Jeannine clambered down. She spoke.

"He's hypothermic and in shock. We need help fast."

They covered him with Monique's coat. They didn't dare move him. His leg and back were at an unusual angle. Jeannine removed her jacket.

"Here. Use my jacket too. Don't move. Stay here. I'll run to the lodge for help."

Jeannine left. Her silhouette merged with the shadows of the trees below.

The emotional peaks and valleys of Monique's day flattened into a level, unchanging, numbness. She stared at John's drained face. She arranged Jeannine's jacket over his motionless legs. About her the individual shadows of the plants merged into a formless gloom. Nothing could be distinguished. She shivered, and clasped her arms together. She waited in the darkness.

***

The park rescue team lashed John to a stretcher and carried him to the lot where the Mazda was parked. There a helicopter waited, lights flashing in the darkness. A blast of swirling leaves and dust forced Monique and Jeannine to shut their eyes. The helicopter rose straight up, hovered for a moment, and then turned in the direction of Front Royal.

Jeannine and Monique gave brief statements for the ranger's report. They could detail more later. Dismissed, they headed for the Mazda. Jeannine breathed heavily and leaned against the car. The long run had taken its toll. Monique volunteered.

"Would it help if I drove? You drove all day."

Jeannine shoved the keys into her hand.

Monique steered the Mazda onto Skyline Drive. She glanced at Jeannine. Her eyes had closed. The Mazda headed for the hospital at Front Royal.

***

******

Chapter 17
Monday, December 11

Jeannine rubbed her eyes and focused upwards at the ceiling.

Where am I?

The crown molding above was familiar. She was in her own apartment, downstairs on the sofa with bare feet protruding from wrinkled jeans. She struggled to lift her head.

How? Saturday, the wait with Monique at the hospital in Front Royal. John's persistent coma with IV tubes dripping and machines clicking. A drab Front Royal motel Saturday night. That listless drive home Sunday.

Home! Right, I'm on the couch!

She focused on the clock. It was past 11:00. *It's Monday, Dr, Anderson's class! I missed it!* But she was tired. Her eyes closed and her breathing became regular. She dozed.

John! He was standing on the ledge at Stony Man. Watch out! Don't fall.

Suddenly, he flexed his knees and jumped. Seconds later she heard broken branches and a horrifying thud.

She bolted upright. *My God! What have I done? Did he jump because we broke up? I can't think about this!*

She buried her head into the cushion. She dozed again.

Dr. Anderson was lecturing, but the class was in the Old Goose. No. It was Mike who was lecturing. He leered at her, but she kept taking notes. He grabbed her!

Mike disappeared. She was back at Stony Man, at the bottom of the cliff. John?

She awoke and lifted her head. Her forehead was damp.

My God, what have I done?

She went to the window. Outside the sun shone on the passing cars. A couple paused before crossing unhurriedly in front of a slowly cruising taxi. A young mother calmly took off her gloves to wipe her toddlers face. All was normal.

The normality of that scene cleared her thoughts.

OK! I don't know what happened, and *OK, I know John, and we both knew that it was over between us. It didn't work out. But John would never jump. He loves nature. He wouldn't do anything to despoil Stony Man.*

She voiced that thought.

"OK, he wouldn't jump, and he didn't!"

Rightly or not, it comforted her to "objectively" decide that John had not jumped.

Maybe he fell? But John knew that spot well, and he's sure-footed. It just isn't likely.

Then she spied a piece of paper on the table. It was John's farewell note.

He had printed it from the computer. For the first time she noticed that the paper was torn. Was there more to the message?

She went up the steps the office. It was a mess. Not much had changed since John's departure. She sat at the computer and clicked on John's most recent file.

His note appeared.

Jeannine,
I need to be alone for a while. Dr. Lawrence canned me. If you want to know what happened ask Monique Laurier at the lab. I need to be alone. You can have my share of our computer. I'll get in touch later. Thanks for everything.
John

She scrolled downward. John had added a postscript.

I'm sorry about us. It's not working, but it's me, not you. Sorry. Just got a call about Dr. Lawrence and Mike. It won't do any good, but I said I would be at Stony Man next Wednesday evening and could talk then. I'm off to hike the Appalachian Trail near there.
Sorry, John

Jeannine gaped. John had met someone at Stony Man!

136

The floor went cold under her bare feet. Her shoulders shook. *My God! He didn't jump and he didn't fall. John was pushed!*

John knew Stony Man. He knew the ledge. He'd been there often, and he was sure-footed. She shouted.

"He was pushed. Damn it. Pushed!"

But who? John had not identified the caller. Perhaps he didn't know the person. He had torn off the footnote. *Why? No matter.* He was pushed!

She grabbed the phone. Through the receiver she heard Monique's phone ring.

***

At Thornton Gap, the weary park policeman reached for the phone. Agent Turner managed to sound professional.

"Agent Turner."

"The operator said I should talk to you."

"Yes?"

"It's about the accident at Stony Man Mountain that was in the paper yesterday. It may be nothing, but my wife and I were hiking on the mountain last Wednesday afternoon."

Agent Turner pulled out his pen and reached for his note pad.

"Keep going."

"It was late afternoon, and we were on a trail near the rocks, up top. We couldn't see them, but we heard two people above us, they were arguing. We couldn't make out the words. One of them had a high voice, like a woman. Anyway, we're retired. We live in Madison County, and we like to walk. It's real good for my wife's health. She's got high blood pressure and ..."

Due to the digression, agent Turner caught up with his note taking.

"About what time did you hear the voices?"

"Like I said, late afternoon. The sun was going down, about 5 o'clock. We were heading back to our car. We wanted to get off the mountain before dark. There was nobody else on the trail. Anyway we didn't see anybody."

"Where was your car parked?"

"At Little Stony Man trailhead, on Skyline Drive."

"When you got to your car, what time was it?"

"Maybe 5:15. It was pretty dark by then."

"Any other cars parked there?"

"Well there was this brown van, and there was our Plymouth of course, and let's see. There was one other car parked on the other side of the van. It was blue I recall. Yes, it was blue."

"And that's all?"

"Only the three cars."

Agent Turner wrote the caller's name, phone number, and address on his pad. He glanced over his notes. He didn't want to miss anything.

"Sir, you said you couldn't make out the words. What made you think they were arguing?"

"There were trees, pines I guess, green anyway, between us and the cliff. What with the wind and all and my hearing. I couldn't tell what they said, but the woman, anyway the high voice, was upset."

"Were there more than two people?"

"We only heard the two voices."

Agent Turner reviewed his notes one more time.

"Sir. The blue car. Could you tell what kind of car it was?"

"No. But I don't know cars much anyway."

Agent Turner decided to check the caller's memory.

"What was the weather like?"

"It was a little cold. There was a light drizzle on the mountain but it was on and off."

That checked. There had been sporadic light cold rain at Stony Man and Skyland last Wednesday. Agent Turner thanked the caller and hung up. He looked at the scattered papers on his desk. He picked up the phone and buzzed.

"Yes?"

"Liz, could you call the Front Royal Hospital and find out how John Martin is doing and if and when I can talk with him. Buzz me right back, OK?"

Agent Turner looked at the reports on the incident. He filed two names in his memory: Jeannine Ryan, Monique Laurier. They had found John Martin, last Friday night. If the caller was right Martin had been exposed on the mountain for 48 hours. The phone buzzed. It was Liz.

"John Martin is in stable condition. He's still unconscious. He was hypothermic and dehydrated, shock, exposure, the works. Head injury. A broken leg with a cast below the knee. No other broken bones. Doctors think it's safe to move him. They're sending him to Fairland University Hospital in Washington. He worked in a lab there. But there's no sign of his coming out of the coma. You'll have to check with Fairland tomorrow if you still want to talk to him."

"Thanks Liz. I'm going to Washington tomorrow. Find out who he worked for at Fairland, will you, and see if you can get me an appointment with whomever. And Liz, call the university hospital tomorrow. I need to talk to Martin as soon as he's able."

Agent Turner was over-worked. He did not need this "accident" to turn into something more serious.

***

When Monique heard about John's note, she shouted into the phone.

"Mike! Mike pushed him!"

Jeannine held the receiver from her ear. She hesitated.

"Would Mike know Stony Man Mountain?"

"The lab had a department picnic there the year before I came. It was all anyone ever talked about. Both Dr. Santini and Dr. Lawrence had too much to drink. Everybody said it was great."

"Was Mike there?"

139

"I'm sure he was there. He told us about Santini and Dr. Lawrence."

This satisfied Jeannine. Monique spoke again.

"I'm scared of Mike. I can't face him. There's no way I'm going to the lab this afternoon. Anyway, they're bringing John to the university hospital today. I'll go over there. Maybe I can see him."

"Monique stay away from the lab. I'll come pick you up. We'll get away from campus. We can drive to Tenley to eat. On the way back, we'll stop at the hospital."

"That's fine. I'd like that!"

***

Mike Hartness worked steadily. One set of tubes was already in the gamma counter. His hands shook as he separated the wells of a second 96-well plate for counting. He wanted to finish one of John's experiments for himself before meeting Dr. Lawrence. If necessary he would work all night.

***

******

Chapter 18
Tuesday, December 12

Mike studied his face in the mirror. He shuddered at the gray stubble. He reached for his razor.

Since Friday, Mike had worked continuously to make John's work his own. He had copied John's notes before destroying the originals, but he had kept a few pages written in John's hand. These he would represent as work John had done under Mike's direction. Dr. Lawrence would appreciate that Mike had mentored the lab newcomer, John.

Yesterday, Monday, Mike had been alone in the lab. Monique had not shown up, so his work with John's cells had been uninterrupted and unobserved. He had repeated one of John's assays and obtained the same results. *Thanks, John. It's my work now.*

Mike felt entitled to John's work. *Hell, I'm smarter, so it's just a question of natural selection. I can't argue with evolution.* Added to this musing, was some professor's statement that selection reflected relative reproductive success. *Hell, I'll prove that too with Monique's help. So Darwin was obsessed with sex. That's OK with me.* Mike did not question his rationalization.

He decided to name John's monoclonal antibody "L-12." The "L" was for Lawrence. Mike rehearsed.

"It's called 'L-12.' I named it for you Dr. Lawrence."

He finished shaving and slapped his face with aftershave. He slipped into clean jeans and a fresh blue shirt. He collected *his* L-12 notes, *his* graphs and *his* text and headed for the Forster building to meet Dr. Lawrence.

***

Mike paused at the door. Inside the office, Dr. Lawrence was reading a scientific journal. Mike cleared his throat.

"Dr. Lawrence ..."

Dr. Lawrence glanced at the clock, 10:00 o'clock. He liked punctuality. Mike, with his blue shirt, open collar, and clean jeans, had the look of a successful lab scientist. Dr. Lawrence smiled because he, Dr. Lawrence, was the cause of Mike's success.

Mike was clean-shaven, but he had shadows under his eyes, and his cheeks were pinched. His arms cradled a bulky pile of notes. Dr. Lawrence smiled a third time, but with a tinge of concern.

"Mike, on time as usual! You've been working hard. Are you getting enough to eat? What about sleep? You know you should relax a little. Why not take Monique out somewhere. I'm sure she'd like to know you better."

It was Mike's turn to smile.

"You're right Sir, but I've been so wrapped up in this work that I just haven't had time. It's been a heavy weekend."

Mike gestured at the stack of papers he had placed on a corner of the desk.

Dr. Lawrence gauged the pile of papers, reprints and graphs.

"Let's go to the seminar room so you'll have space to spread out. There's nobody there until this afternoon. You can take your time. I have all morning."

They set out. The long table in the seminar room was empty. Mike's notes and graphs used the entire length.

"To start with, Dr. Lawrence, our antibody is called L-12, and the "L" stands for 'Lawrence.'"

Dr. Lawrence warmed to the presentation. Mike continued.

"I want to show you the sandwich assay first. The coating protein is Johnson's CA. Look at this table."

Mike talked for over an hour with an occasional nod or grunt from Dr. Lawrence in affirmation. At the finish, Mike's throat was dry and his voice scratchy. He ended.

"And that's the story of L-12."

Dr. Lawrence was speechless. He stood up and leaned across the table to examine the last graph. In reality he was just collecting his thoughts. Finally he spoke.

"Mike, I didn't think A-11 could be topped, but you've done it. L-12 is incredible."

He added.

"We have to publish our results right away."

Mike was ready. He thrust a sheaf of typed papers, all copied from John's notes, into Dr. Lawrence's hands.

"I've thought of that Sir, and here's a first draft that we can work on."

Dr. Lawrence was overwhelmed. He was amazed that Mike had done all this work in his "spare" time. "L-12" was the real thing. Dr. Lawrence would be assured of continuation grants for the next five years. maybe more.

"Mike, er Dr. Hartness, I'm going to have lunch at Le Papillon. Would you like to come with me. My treat. How about some snails and a nice red Bordeaux?"

Snails? Still, Mike liked the title, "Dr."

"Sounds good, Sir. Thank you."

Together, they left the building. Mike reveled in his newfound status of equality. At the restaurant, he hesitated before opening the door for his mentor.

***

Dr. Lawrence returned to his office. The lunch had gone well. The tournedo with béarnaise sauce had been delicious, very tender. He was pleased with Mike, and of course, with himself. Mike had been thorough and his presentation clear. Dr. Lawrence repeated. *L-12 ... L-12 ... L-12 ... . Yes "L" for "Lawrence" had a ring of quality, a good choice.*

The phone disturbed his thoughts.

"Hello"

"Dr. Lawrence?"

The voice sounded familiar.

"Yes. This is Dr. Lawrence."

"Dr. Lawrence. This is Jeannine Ryan."

"Miss Ryan, I already know about John's accident."

"Dr. Lawrence, it's not that. I need to talk to you about something else. I was hoping I could see you today sometime? It's very important."

"Miss Ryan, I had an appointment this morning that took up a great deal of time. I can't spare any time this afternoon."

"But Sir, It's very important that I see you. It's about John Martin's experiments, and Mike Hartness."

"I'm sorry Miss Ryan."

He hung up.

***

Dr. Lawrence reached for the current issue of the New England Journal of Medicine, and started to read. He was deep into an article when his phone sounded.

"Hello"

"Larry, this is Joe Santini."

Dr. Lawrence winced at the "Larry." He had no intention of calling the Department Head "Joe."

"What can I do for you Dr. Santini?"

"Larry, there's a young woman in my office, a Miss Ryan from Statistics. I think you should hear what she has to say."

Dr. Lawrence spluttered.

"I talked to her earlier."

Dr. Santini was adamant.

"Yes, she told me. She also said you hung up on her. Look, she thinks Mike Hartness may have ... 'appropriated' some of John Martin's work. I think you better talk to her. Use my office. It's private and I have to leave for a meeting. She'll wait here."

Dr. Lawrence started to protest, but Dr. Santini had already hung up.

***

Dr. Lawrence was furious. He reached Dr. Santini's office. Neither the secretary nor Dr. Santini was there. Jeannine sat by

144

the secretary's desk. He strode into the inner office and motioned her to follow. He took a position behind Dr. Santini's massive desk. He gestured her to sit in the stuffed chair.

Jeannine remained standing. Dr. Lawrence decided to conduct an interview.

"Do you have a degree Miss Ryan?"

"I have a Masters in math. I'm working on my Doctorate in statistics."

"So you're a ... student."

Having established Jeannine as an inferior species, he continued.

"Just what do you have to say to me?"

"It's pretty simple. Mike Hartness is stealing John's experiments."

Dr. Lawrence was aware that Jeannine's blue eyes were gauging his.

"That's outrageous. Besides, John Martin doesn't work for me anymore."

Seeing those blue eyes harden, he shifted to the attack.

"Theft of intellectual property is a very serious charge, Miss Ryan."

He added.

"You should know better than to make accusations without any basis in fact."

He lowered his tone in condescension.

"But I don't think you understand just how a biomedical laboratory works."

Dr. Lawrence assumed an expansive stance. He leaned forward benevolently. He smiled.

"There's a lot of expensive equipment in my laboratory that I've accumulated over the years. No young researcher could hope to do the work I do here without my help. They wouldn't have the means. You see, it's a privilege to work in my laboratory. In my lab a worker gets my experience and my expertise, my research ideas and proposals, not only all my facilities, but me too."

His words inspired him. He continued.

"To an uninitiated person, like yourself, it appears that someone like John Martin is doing his own work, but the reality is far from that. That work is an extension of my work. Also, an experienced worker like Mike Hartness *is expected* to give a junior member like John assignments and work to do. Mike's had the benefit of working for me for several years. He knows what I want. That gives him more than enough knowledge to direct a novice like John."

His smirk changed to a tolerant smile.

"So you see what might look to you like John's notes and data are actually Mike's, and ultimately, mine."

He shifted sternly.

"For you to accuse Mike Hartness of stealing John's work is uncalled for … "

His final tone was triumphant.

"… and represents an invalid *unscientific* conclusion based on your own, I'm afraid, *ignorance.*"

Dr. Lawrence was quite pleased with his lecture, particularly the conclusion that Jeannine was *unscientific* and *ignorant*. To emphasize the latter points, he delivered the last conclusion with eyes staring over his half frame reading glasses.

Jeannine wanted to shout "You're a horse's ass," but instead she replied with restraint.

"Dr. Lawrence, I accept your contribution in making your laboratory and experience available to younger researchers, but you depend on their work and ideas as much as they depend on you. If you accept the credit for all the good work done in your laboratory, don't you have to accept the responsibility for any bad work, including cheating."

Dr. Lawrence bristled, but Jeannine went on.

"I mean, if someone fakes data in your laboratory, aren't you responsible? If you get the credit when the work is good, then you should get the 'credit' when the work is bad too. You, Sir, are responsible. You signed as Principal Investigator on your grant, and you are responsible for all the work done under the grant. In fact, isn't that what you've been telling me?"

Dr. Lawrence's face grew red.

"If someone faked data in *my* lab it would be a violation of *my* trust. Your John Martin faked data, and he'll get no mercy from me. I resent your accusations against me and Dr. Hartness. Do not spread your lies to anyone on campus or I'll take legal action against you. Miss Ryan, I could forgive your ignorance, but I will not forgive malicious gossip. I don't believe you should represent this University at any level, much less the doctoral."

The threat was not lost on Jeannine, but she remained calm.

"But Dr. Lawrence, suppose it was Mike Hartness who violated your trust. Then shouldn't you be mad at him?"

His fist slammed on the polished desk.

"Miss Ryan, if you persist in spreading your damnable lies you will be sorry. This interview is over. I'm a busy man."

Jeannine saw no further reason for restraint.

"You mean you're a busy horse's ass!"

Swinging about, red hair flying, she left the office and headed for the stairs.

***

Outside the Forster building, Jeannine leaned against the cold wall. She felt like retching. *Jeannine, you screwed things good with that pompous jerk. Some help you are.*

She walked in the direction of her apartment. She was tired and her feet hurt.

She headed straight for the sofa, without a glance at her course notes scattered about the floor. She was behind by a couple of lectures, but it did not matter. *Sit in a corner and be quiet? No Way!* She yelled to the empty room.

"John! How could you work for that ass?"

She threw her sneakers across the floor. Poor tired feet. She stretched to relax.

***

Florid faced, Dr. Lawrence strode out of Santini's office. The secretary had returned, but her eyes were lowered on her work. She might have been smiling, but her face was turned away from him. A student stood, silent, in the doorway.

Dr. Lawrence pushed by without a word. Back in his own office, he stood motionless. *To hell with that red-headed twit, only a student, not even in biology. What nerve. Maybe the secretary didn't hear her.*

That was little comfort. He was sure that Jeannine's voice had carried through the outer office and into the hallway.

He resented Jeannine's good looks. He denied that she appealed to him. *It's damned clear what she's in school for! John, you fool, she's using you.*

He realized that he might be jealous of John. His anger increased. The memory of Jeannine's words fueled it further. *No one can call me a "horse's ass."*

A voice broke into his musing.

"Dr. Lawrence?"

The speaker stood at the door. He wore a tie and jacket. He was not "university."

"I'm Dr. Lawrence."

"Agent Turner, National Park Service."

Agent Turner waved a badge and photo ID, at Dr. Lawrence.

"I believe we have an appointment."

Dr. Lawrence glanced at his watch.

"Oh yes, right. Here let me clear this stool for you."

The stack of papers and books was taken from the top of the stool and deposited on the floor. Agent Turner balanced himself on the vacated top.

"Dr. Lawrence, I'm here about John Martin's, uh, accident. I understand he works for you."

"He used to work for me."

"I see. Was there trouble?"

"Yes."

"What sort of trouble?"

Dr. Lawrence chose his words carefully.

"He didn't do an experiment he was supposed to do."

"So you fired him?"

"I asked him to leave, ...Yes."

"Do you know anyone who might want to harm Dr. Martin?"

"I couldn't say."

"Did he have a girl friend?"

"Yes, Jeannine Ryan. They shared an apartment."

Agent Turner knew that name from the report. He followed up.

"Know anything about her?"

Dr. Lawrence grimaced. *A "horse's ass" am I.*

"She's arrogant and has a vile temper. They weren't getting along too well. She had her hooks into John, and, frankly she has a dangerous temper. She's a violent woman."

Agent Turner scribbled to keep up.

"Sir, would you know if she has a car?"

"No."

Dr. Lawrence glared over his half-frame reading glasses. For practical purposes the interview was over. The remaining questions were answered with a curt "yes" or "no."

***

Monique deposited the groceries on the kitchen table. John was still in a coma. There must be good news somewhere. She clicked on the TV.

"In local news this afternoon, an apparent murder-suicide in Silver Spring. ..."

Enough! She turned the TV off and heard a knock on the door. With the chain latched, she cracked the door open.

"Miss Laurier, I'm Agent Turner from the National Park Service. I would like to talk to you about John Martin's accident."

149

The agent held his credentials up to the crack. Monique unlatched the chain.

"Come in. The place is a mess."

"Thank you Miss Laurier. I'm sorry to come without notice, but I just finished another interview and have time before I go back to Front Royal. How is John?"

"He's still in a coma. The doctors say he's OK otherwise, but ..."

"I'm sorry to hear that. I won't take long. Do you mind if I sit down?"

"Help yourself."

Agent Turner pulled out his notepad. The first question was a surprise.

"Miss Laurier, how long have you known Miss Ryan, Miss Jeannine Ryan?"

"Well, I've known *about* her since I've been in Dr. Lawrence's laboratory, through John, for about a year. I've known her personally this past week. She's a good person."

"So you met her about a week ago?"

"Yes, it was last Wednesday."

Monique recalled weeping in the restroom at Main Med, and Jeannine's touch on her shoulder.

"That was late morning?"

"Yes."

"Did you see her later that day?"

"No."

"By any chance did she tell you where she was going later that day?"

"No."

"Miss Laurier, could you tell me how you and Miss Ryan came to be in the Park last Friday evening, and how you found John Martin at Stony Man Mountain?"

Monique recounted Jeannine's phone call and the subsequent ride to the park.

"Did it seem strange to you that Miss Ryan knew just where Martin's van would be?"

"Not really. Jeannine had called the park and they told her Stony Man trailhead?"

"If Miss Ryan told the park officer that she was supposed to meet John Martin in the park would that surprise you?"

"Yes."

"When you and Miss Ryan found the van, did you wonder where John might be?"

"No. She knew where. She left a note on the windshield. She knew a shorter way up, so we drove there."

"Miss Laurier, is this the note?

He held out a copy of Jeannine's note. Monique nodded.

"And this note was written by Miss Ryan?"

Monique nodded again.

"Miss Laurier were you aware that Miss Ryan and Mr. Martin were breaking off their relationship?"

Monique nodded a third time. Where was this going?

"Miss Laurier, when you started up the mountain, who went first, you or Miss Ryan?"

Monique recalled how she tried to keep up with Jeannine.

"She was first."

"Did you think it odd that she knew exactly where to go?"

"No. I think she and John knew the spot together. You would have to know Jeannine. She makes decisions and follows up on them."

"So she knew that John Martin liked that spot?"

Monique felt uneasy. What did agent Turner want?

"Miss Laurier, do you think John fell off that ledge, or do you think he was pushed?"

At last! Monique exhaled with relief.

"I think he was pushed, and Mike Hartness pushed him."

"Miss Laurier, suppose I told you that Mike Hartness was nowhere near Stony Man the night of the, uh, 'accident.' Suppose I told you that a witness says that there was a woman on the mountain arguing with John Martin before he fell. Suppose further that same woman pushed Martin and that's why he fell. Suppose that woman panicked and left him on the mountain. Suppose after a while that same woman couldn't bear the thought of Martin, someone she once loved, dead or dying alone on the mountain."

The agent cleared his throat. He looked straight at Monique.

"Suppose that same woman arranged to take someone with her, someone innocent, up that mountain to find the body or maybe a nearly-dead body. She would make sure the innocent person found the 'body.' Miss Laurier, wouldn't that woman behave just like Miss Ryan behaved that evening? She didn't hesitate. She knew where to go. And you found the body! Think about it Miss Laurier. That woman would do the same things Jeannine Ryan did, just as you described them, out of your own mouth."

Monique's eyes glazed with horror. *Mon Dieu, My God. Spare me this. First my statement damned John and now my words damn Jeannine. God have mercy. Ce n'est pas possible! This can't be happening.*

She forced the words out.

"My friends are my friends. John is innocent of faking data, and Jeannine would never harm John. Never. For God's sake, open your eyes. Find out where Mike Hartness *really* was that night. Now, please leave my apartment."

Agent Turner flipped the cover on his notepad.

"Thank you very much Miss Laurier. Please think about what I said. I know it's hard, but think about it. What you recall may be a real help. Oh by the way, ..."

"Yes?"

"Miss Ryan's car is blue isn't it?"

Monique stared. The agent did not wait for an answer, but turned and left the apartment.

***

******

Chapter 19
Friday, December 15

Cecilia stood by the window of her room. The hospital parking lot was almost empty. Everything was gray, the sky, the scattered cars with splotches of dried salt, the border of pushed ice and dirty snow. In contrast, Cecilia wore a red wool sweater, and had a new blue down jacket in her arms. (The latter, from Lands' End, was a replacement sent by her mother.)

Cecilia smiled when she saw Sam's Taurus pull into the lot. He must have washed it, because it shone brightly in the dull light that diffused through the low clouds.

A few minutes later, Norma appeared at the door. Her eyes were moist, but she beamed at her charge.

"My goodness honey. You're all ready to go! You must want to leave us! Your ride's downstairs, and I've got your wheelchair."

"Norma, you know I'll miss you, but ..."

"No matter honey. Come on. Into the chair. One last ride."

"I'm fine. I can walk."

"Get in. Hospital regulations say you ride. Besides look *who* came to push you."

"Thanks, Norma."

Cecilia hopped into the wheelchair.

"Watch out for that arm, honey!"

Norma plopped Cecilia's new jacket onto her lap and handed her the vase of flowers from the windowsill.

They headed for the elevator. Once in the lobby, Cecilia could see Sam outside. He stood by the Taurus.

The emotion of the moment, seeing Cecilia alive and whole again, was too much for Sam. He only managed two words.

"Hi 'C.'"

"Hi Sam."

Cecilia handed him the flowers, stepped from the wheel chair, and turned to hug Norma. The latter squeezed back. Cecilia's eyes strayed to the windows on the fifth floor. She located her room. A final wave to Norma was followed by a brief nod to her partner.

"Let's go Sam, get me out of here."

Sam steered out of the hospital lot. He was exhilarated. Cecilia had her normal color.

"The wife and I want you to stay at our place for a few days. Until you're on your feet and all that."

"Sam, that's sweet. Thanks. But I'm fine. I'd rather be at my own place, if you guys don't mind."

Sam was about to protest when Cecilia spoke.

"Look Sam, you know where I've got to stop before we head back?"

Eyebrows lifted, he looked at Cecilia, but only for a moment. He turned at the next intersection and headed back the way he had come.

***

The gray stone of the small Catholic Church and its peaceful rural setting were the same. Sam drove into the parking lot. To the left of the church was the cemetery followed by open fields, just as he remembered. Where he had seen a gaping hole nine days ago, there now was an earthen mound, Madame Gauthier's grave.

Without a word Cecilia stepped out of the car. She walked to the grave and placed her hospital flowers on the freshly-turned earth. Then she stood motionless with her head bowed. Moments passed before she turned, waved to Sam, and disappeared into the church.

Some minutes later, she emerged and came back to the car.

"Thanks, Sam."

They drove out of the lot in silence.

***

They were past St. Albans when Cecilia broke the silence.

"You know Sam, I'm responsible for what happened to her. I'm the one that asked her to help ..."

"'C,' I know you feel that way, but ..."

"No Sam, let me finish. Words won't help. I know what I think. I've got to do something. It's not good for me to stew about this. Tell me everything that's happened, and what you found."

Sam was more than willing to talk. Anything was better than the silence.

"OK. Here's what I've got. You remember the Mason report you worked on? About a group in Burlington with connections in New York that was moving cocaine, heroin, cigarettes, illegals, anything in from Canada. Well your man with the mustache, the one the grandson leveled, he was Karl Mason, the scum bag himself. The man in the red sweater, the scuz ball that you dropped, was his right hand man. An enforcer, a killer."

Sam thought of Cecilia, ashen on the floor, and the inert form of "Red Sweater." He caught his breath.

You remember a week ago, when they changed your room at the hospital?

"Sure."

That was because there was an 'incident,' an orderly chased a weirdo from your room. So I got worried, and ..."

Cecilia interposed.

"I noticed a policeman hanging around."

"Right, I told him not to be conspicuous. Anyway, the guy that was in your room matched the description of Karl's younger brother, Kurt Mason. A cheap hood. He was in Washington when you got shot. Kurt was found dead on the street the morning after he was in your room, an apparent hit and run. His blood alcohol was off the wall."

"What do you think?"

"I think New York cleaned up loose ends, and Tony Diorio, the liaison, shows up in New York City a few days later. It means Burlington is shut down. And 'C,' I know it's not much help, but it's because of you and Mme. Gauthier."

Cecilia did not reply. Sam continued. He had saved the choicest news for last.

"One thing more. The kid brother Kurt wasn't too smart. He used the same hotel room once too often, and DEA had a line on his activities before your fireworks at Checkpoint Charlie. Thanks to them we've got a lead for a medical connection which you might want to check on."

"Chihuahua, Sam! Spill it."

"There's a possible connection with a clinic in your home town, Tucson. It's the *AMAH Clinic*, run by a 'Dr. McElroy.'"

"I know where that is. It's up north, in the Mt. Lemmon foothills. What do you have on the doctor?"

"Not much, just the phone calls. But there's also a possible Washington connection. In the past couple of weeks there were several calls from the clinic to a pay phone near the Fairland University Medical complex, and a call from the same pay phone to the hotel where Kurt Mason stayed."

"You've been busy, Sam."

Cecilia thought of Bob Delaney in Rockville and her family in Tucson. She smiled to herself.

"I think you've justified my trip to Washington and to home too. Thanks."

"Hey. *De nada*! And one more thing. The gang at the office got together and got you this. We bought it. It's yours to keep. It's not the government's."

Sam passed Cecilia a shiny new object. It was a .38 revolver, a "snubby" Smith & Wesson, just like her old one.

"It's not loaded. We figured the evidence guys would keep yours out of circulation for a long time. Anyway, you'll have to 'sight' it yourself. We didn't want you to be without protection."

Before he could finish, Sam felt Cecilia's arm around him. Her kiss brushed his cheek.

"Thanks, Sam."

Disconcerted, he concentrated on the road ahead. A few minutes later, when he glanced at Cecilia, she was sound asleep. Her breathing was normal, and her face, flushed with excitement, shone from under her black hair. Sam sighed. His young partner was back!

***

Marshall Hanes was seated in his office at the Fairland Medical School. He was pleased. The Provost had approved the report from Dr. Sadler's committee. John Martin was guilty of research misconduct and Marshall was confident the ORI review would confirm that decision. He finished a cover letter to Dr. Delaney at the Office of Research Integrity. He filled out the Federal Express slip for delivery Monday morning.

Marshall was glad Martin no longer worked for Dr. Lawrence, and grateful that the case had been simple. He liked neat cases. He looked at his watch. Why not leave early? He could meet his wife at their favorite restaurant in Rockville.

***

Jeannine was in her apartment, surrounded by papers with mathematical equations. She had to catch up in Bayesian analysis. She had missed two classes, and the exam was next Monday. This was her last formal course before her thesis research. She had to do well.

The phone rang. Jeannine picked up.

"Miss Ryan, this is Dr. Santini. You spoke to me several days ago about your concerns regarding Mike Hartness and John Martin's work."

"Yes."

"Was Dr. Lawrence able to satisfy your questions?"

"No he wasn't."

"I thought that might be the case. Do you have any more news about John?"

"There's no change. He's still in a coma."

157

"Miss Ryan, have you spoken to Marshall Hanes in the provost's office?"

"He doesn't return my calls."

"Look, I don't know what to think about your complaint, but I would like to make sure that John gets a fair shake. There's someone you can call to talk to about it. Do you have a pencil?"

Jeannine had just worn out two pencils scribbling equations. She reached for a third.

"OK."

"His name is Dr. Delaney, at the Office of Research Integrity. Tell him that I suggested you call. His number is 301-..."

"Thank you Dr. Santini."

Jeannine shook her head. Dr. Santini sounded open-minded. Maybe all biology professors weren't bad.

She looked at her watch. It was 5:00 o'clock. In fifteen minutes Monique would be at the Old Goose. She donned her jacket and headed for the door.

***

Mike, writing furiously, hunched over his desk.

He had written his own set of laboratory notebooks detailing what had been John's experiments and copied John's data, with a few alterations, into them. Moreover, he had reproduced the results for a few crucial experiments himself and produced fresh notes and data. Elsewhere he had kept John's notes, in the latter's handwriting, and annotated these as work that he, Mike, had ordered John to do.

As a final touch, he constructed a new manila folder that looked like the one that John had left with Dr. Santini's secretary. The new one was innocuous. In it were copies of journal articles along with some notes from Mike that directed John to look up certain references for the project.

Mike was pleased. His deception was complete. He wasn't afraid of a confrontation should John recover. Mike's story was

158

well prepared and documented. Besides, John was already discredited. No one would believe him.

Mike thought of his panicked call to Dr. McElroy, and the subsequent conversation with that hood Kurt. He recalled Kurt's high-pitched curses and his scornful refusal to help. But maybe he had come through after all, or maybe John *had* fallen.

It didn't matter. John had been gone when it mattered the most.

Now Mike was concerned about Monique. She had called in sick all week. Clearly she was upset, but potentially she could cause trouble. Her ruse with John's cells proved that.

In the midst of these musings, Monique entered the lab.

"Monique, where have you been? Dr. Lawrence has been asking for you. I told him you were still sick."

Monique's face was drawn. She avoided his eyes.

"Like you said, I was sick."

"Well you look pretty good to me."

Mike's eyes roamed the length of her body. He smiled.

"How about a beer and sandwich at the Old Goose?"

"I've got to meet someone."

"That's OK. I'll join you."

Monique shuddered.

Mike did not notice. He handed her John's sanitized folder.

"John left this folder in Dr. Santini's office. Put it with his things for me."

Without a word she took the folder to a stack of books and papers that awaited removal. John's desk was already cleaned out.

Mike started for the door and smirked.

"I've got to take these notebooks to Dr. Lawrence for him to study this weekend. We're writing a paper together. I'll see you and your friend at the Old Goose."

He disappeared down the hall. Monique dashed out the lab and down the stairway.

Outside, the wind was rising, and fresh flakes of snow melted as they hit the sidewalk. She raised her collar against the chill.

***

The Old Goose was not crowded. Jeannine was at "their" table. Monique slumped into the opposite chair.

"We're going to have a visitor."

"Who?"

"Mike Hartness. I haven't been at the lab all week. Just five minutes with him and I'm sick already. He wants to eat with us."

Jeannine's blue eyes became hazel. Her voice was cutting.

"He's harassing you. He's playing mind games. He must be afraid of you."

"I don't think so."

Jeannine shrugged. She knew Monique had spent most of the afternoon at the hospital.

"Any change in John?"

Monique shook her head.

"He's still the same."

Jeannine reached across the table and grabbed a limp hand.

"Look. We can't count on John. If he regains consciousness we don't know what he'll remember or how soon. My final exam is Monday morning. Monday afternoon, we'll call someone who might help us. Believe it or not, Dr. Santini gave me a name, a Dr. Delaney with the Office of Research Integrity."

"All right, but did that agent Turner talk to you yet? I told you he's crazy. How could he think you would push John off the ledge?"

"No, he hasn't called. What can I say? Anybody can think anything. Everybody has an angle. Nobody seems to care about the truth anymore."

"But he can make trouble!"

Jeannine squeezed.

"Monique, I don't care about Turner, but thanks for defending me. At least one good thing has come out of this mess. We can count on each other. But you're beat, and you shouldn't be alone. Come spend the night at my place. I'll clear the couch and you can sleep there. I'll study upstairs."

"I'd like that. Thanks. And I'd like to go there now, before Mike comes."

They left together.

There was no sign of Mike.

***

The windows in Monique's apartment were dark. Mike stood in the doorway across the street. The silhouetted branches of a nearby tree dripped wet snow that glowed in the glare of the street lamp.

He shivered in the damp cold. All he could think of was the shapely Monique. Her aversion for him made her more desirable than ever. He had missed her at the Old Goose. Dr. Lawrence had kept him to go over the L-12 notebooks.

Mike's plan was simple. Monique lived alone. When she arrived he would invite himself in, and not take "no" for an answer. After that, Monique would be too ashamed to talk. If she dared to talk, he would say she had invited him in. No one would believe she hadn't consented.

A gust of wind shook the tree in front of him, splattering icy drops everywhere. It grew colder. Mike rubbed his face.

He looked at his watch. It was 11:00 p.m. *Damn. The little bitch has got to come home sometime.*

He huddled in the dark doorway.

Sometime later, Mike shivered and cursed one final time. He abandoned his vigil and left for his own apartment. For the first time in weeks he had fallen short of his goal.

Still, for him and Monique it was only a matter of time.

***

Dr. Lawrence studied the notebooks and Mike's suggested text. Their paper was almost done. Tomorrow he would write up the methods section, but that would be easy. Mike could check the references. By Monday they would have a complete draft.

He looked at his watch. *11:30 p.m. Oh no! It's Friday.* He had forgotten again. Fridays, Sari would spend the night with her friend Mattie, and he and Betty would eat supper together. *Damn.*

He arrived home to an abandoned cold supper. There was no note.

Upstairs, he undressed in the dark. Betty moaned and tossed as if disturbed by an unpleasant dream. He eased into the bed so as not to touch her. She turned her head on the pillow. A groan escaped her lips. Then she lay still.

His mind churned. *I'll get that graph drawn up on Monday. They'll rush it for me. This L-12 paper will blow them all away!* He couldn't wait to drop a copy on Dr. Santini's desk. Maybe he'd call that reporter in the green suit. *What was her name?*

Rolling on his side, he repeated to himself, *L-12, L-12, L-12. It has a nice ring to it. Lawrence-12. L-12, L-12...*

A final *L-12*, and he slept.

***

In Vermont, Cecilia awoke. Her arm ached. She struggled to the bathroom and grabbed two Advil. She turned on the tap.

"Chihuahua!"

Icy water splashed from the sink. She swallowed the Advil, and turned back to bed. Shrinking under the warm comforter, she smiled. No nurse would wake her to ask how she was sleeping. She shut her eyes. Her lips formed a desperate prayer.

Dios mio, help me. I can't handle this. Tell Madame Gauthier I'm sorry and ask her to forgive me. Por favor!

Mercifully her sleep was dreamless.

***

******

Chapter 20
Tuesday, December 19

Jack Anderson bent over his desk. The young statistics professor had worked quickly to correct yesterday's exam. The papers were in three piles. The leftmost pile had the poorest papers. He marked each with a C, failure for a graduate course. The middle pile contained eleven papers. He variously wrote B or $B+$ on the exam books.

The last pile had the two best papers, Jeannine Ryan's and Paul Pagé's. They alone had completed the last question on the estimation of scale in the "exponential family". Jack marked each paper A. He reflected. Paul exhibited mathematical maturity, but lacked statistical insight. Jeannine knew why the statistical assumptions were appropriate.

Which of these two students would he accept for doctoral research? Jeannine Ryan's insight offset the slightly superior skill of Paul Pagé. He chose Jeannine.

His decision had consequences. The medical school sponsored a "quantitative biology" fellowship to be awarded to a doctoral student in the mathematical sciences. The fellowship paid more than a teaching fellowship, and had no assigned responsibilities like teaching or consulting. The recipient could devote full time to research.

The fellowship was vacant this year, and the head of the Mathematics Department had agreed that the student Jack accepted would be nominated. This pleased Jack. He would be up for tenure soon and he needed the publications a doctoral student would generate.

Jack smiled as he wrote Jeannine's name on the nomination form. She had not worn her pink pullover to the final exam, but she had been stunning, even in that faded sweatshirt and jeans. He surmised (correctly) that she had studied all night to prepare.

His smile disappeared. He was not oblivious to her looks, but the real reason for his choice was that she was the best student in the department! Jack kept a responsible distance from his students.

He sealed the envelope with the nomination form, and personally carried it to the office.

***

Jeannine's vision, blurred by sleep, cleared. Monique leaned over her.

"Monique. How long did I sleep?"

"You were exhausted from the exam. You collapsed on the couch. You've been there since. You slept through."

Jeannine held her head. She was dizzy.

"That's the last time I'll stay up all night studying. That damned exam. That last question took me two hours! What day is this?"

"Tuesday."

Jeannine sat up on the sofa. She looked down at bare feet.

"Thanks for taking the shoes off."

Monique nodded. She held a steaming cup of black coffee.

"Drink this. How *was* that exam?"

"It was OK, except maybe the last question. Anyway, I put down all I knew."

Jeannine sipped. Monique stepped into the kitchen and returned with a butter croissant and jam.

"Try this too."

Half the croissant disappeared into Jeannine's mouth. Cheek distended, she spread jam on the remainder. It too disappeared. When her tongue was free, she spoke.

"Thanks. Did you go into the lab yesterday?"

"I called in sick, but I'll have to go in soon. At least long enough to tell them I'm going to Montreal for Christmas."

"Are you?"

"No, but I am not going back to the lab until I have to."

***

Jeannine struggled off the couch. She located the phone number Dr, Santini had given her, and punched it.

"Dr. Delaney please."

"This is Dr. Delaney."

"Dr. Delaney, this is Jeannine Ryan. Dr. Santini of the Fairland University Medical School suggested that I call you."

The report from Fairland University was on his desk. He found Dr. Santini's name. He was the head of the department. The respondent was a Dr. John Martin, a Postdoc. Delaney's tone was noncommittal.

"Miss Ryan, what is this in reference to?"

"Dr. Mike Hartness stole work done by Dr. John Martin and is claiming it as his own."

Delaney started to take notes.

"How do you know this?"

Jeannine detailed Monique's suspicions, the appropriation of John's cells by Mike, and subsequent events. He took notes until she stopped.

Delaney reflected. That issue was authorship, not data fabrication. The Sadler committee had determined that Martin had fabricated data. From the transcript of Monique's testimony, he knew of her doubts. But the incriminating files had been found on Martin's computer. Still, Miss Ryan might have relevant information.

"Miss Ryan, what can you tell me about the fabrication of data by Dr. Martin?"

"Dr. Martin didn't fabricate data. He showed me the data for Table 3 and explained to me how Mike Hartness had produced fake data. I'm a statistician. I helped him understand the random number program."

"When exactly was that?"

"Let's see, it was at the Old Goose, that's a university hangout. It was after my inference class, so it had to be Monday, Wednesday or Friday. Yes. It was Wednesday, the 29th, lunch time."

Bob Delaney checked the report again. Mike Hartness and Monique Laurier had copied the programs and bad data from John Martin's computer before noon on the 29th.

"Miss Ryan, was that before noon?"

"I don't think so. My class was over at eleven o'clock. But I stayed afterwards to talk to the professor, and it takes time to get to the Old Goose. I think I got to the Old Goose a little after noon."

Delaney quickly scanned Monique's testimony, and Mike's. Miss Ryan did not add much. The files already had been discovered on Martin's computer when Ryan and Martin were at the Old Goose. Still, her timing could be off. He should hear her story.

"Miss Ryan, I could meet you tomorrow afternoon at four."

He added.

"But I have to tell you that if Dr. Hartness takes credit for Dr. Martin's experiments that is a different issue. It's a matter of intellectual property, of authorship. That's not in our definition of research misconduct. We don't handle coauthorship disputes.

He continued.

"From what you told me, all the work that Dr. Hartness appropriated was done in Dr. Lawrence's laboratory, right?"

"Yes, but the work was done by Dr. Martin."

"Right, but under Dr. Lawrence's grant, and under his auspices."

"So Dr. Hartness can steal the work?"

"He works for Dr. Lawrence doesn't he?"

"Yes, but it's not his work!"

"But Martin worked for Dr. Lawrence too. I'm not saying it's right, or good. But we don't deal with problems of authorship. You're not talking about plagiarism of a submitted or published manuscript, are you?"

"I guess not. No."

"Well then it's Dr. Lawrence's lab and his grant. It's up to him. I won't be much help there, but we can still meet tomorrow at four o'clock. Any information you have on data fabrication in the lab would be helpful."

"I'll be there."

She hung up and turned to Monique.

"I'll see him tomorrow, but they're not going to do a damn thing about Mike and Dr. Lawrence stealing John's work. They want faked data, not stolen real data!"

Monique pursed her lips.

"But what about the truth? Don't they care?"

Jeannine grimaced.

"Care! Nobody loves the truth. Nobody gives a damn about it!"

***

Drs. Hartness and Lawrence checked their manuscript. Dr. Lawrence had inserted apparently flattering references to the work of Dr. Johnson at Rochester and to his protein CA. To insiders, however, those references proved that Johnson did not understand his own results. Dr. Lawrence was pleased, very pleased. The manuscript was ready for publication.

Mike Hartness had another thought. He swallowed and addressed his co-author.

"Dr. Lawrence, I think that the entire immunology section should be authors of this paper. I mean Monique Laurier has contributed here, so she should be an author too. Do you agree Sir?"

"Mike that's a generous thing for you to say. You are right! All section members should be on the paper, but don't include John. He's a cheat and is no longer with us. And he accused you! Sure. Add Monique's name on the title page."

He peered over his half-frames.

"Let's send this paper out tomorrow. We both can give it a final read tonight. You've done a terrific job, Mike. I am very pleased!"

Mike relaxed. As an author of John's work, Monique would be compromised. She would be "stealing" his work as much as anyone else. Any criticism by her would be neutralized. She should even be grateful!

"Thank you Sir. I'll check the paper tonight, and I'll type a new title page with Monique as an author right away."

Mike turned and left the office.

***

Monique left Jeannine's apartment. She walked briskly towards the lab. Her lips compressed against the cold, but the sun was shining and the air was clear. *Don't let Mike be there!* As she neared the Forster building, Jeannine's words echoed in her mind.

"They want faked data, not stolen data."

There was no one in the corridor, but Dr. Santini's office door was open. She looked into the lab. *Thank God!* No Mike!

John's belongings were stacked in the corner. On top was the manila folder she had put there at Mike's request. She examined it. There wasn't much. In addition to photocopies there were several reprints of articles by M. J. Hartness and W. D. McElroy, and by McElroy alone. She recalled that Mike had worked with a Dr. McElroy at some clinic in Arizona. The papers had been published before Mike came to Fairland.

Monique put the manila folder under her arm. She went to her desk.

She froze.

On her desk was a draft manuscript. The authors were: "M. J. Hartness, M. Laurier, and F. W. Lawrence." Her head reeled. The manuscript described John's experiments. *My God, I don't believe this! How could he do this?*

Mike had made her an author of John's work, his cell lines, his experiments, and his analyses. If she allowed her name on the paper, she would be a thief!

She retched, but nothing came up. She sat down with her head in her hands. After a moment, she raised her eyes. There was a note attached to the manuscript.

Monique,

Dr. Lawrence and I think the whole immunology section should share in this success. This manuscript is being submitted tomorrow. Please read it tonight and let me know if you have any changes. Congratulations!

Mike

P.S. I hope you are feeling better. I miss you.

Her stomach churned. Her mind spun. She shoved the manuscript into the manila folder and rushed into the corridor. She nearly collided with Dr. Santini's secretary.

"Monique. Are you all right. You don't look good."

"Pardon. No I'm not well."

"You better take care of yourself. Mike has been asking about you. He's concerned, Dr. Lawrence too."

Monique tried to smile, but could not.

She ducked down the stairs. Outside, the cold air cleared her mind. She headed to her apartment to pick up extra clothes for her stay with Jeannine.

***

Jeannine, already showered and dressed, was downstairs when the phone rang.

"Miss Ryan, this is Professor Anderson from statistics."

"Oh. Hi."

"Miss Ryan, congratulations. Yours was the best test paper. You did well!"

"Thank you."

"I wanted you to know that I placed your name in nomination for the Quantitative Biology Fellowship. The department is sending just one name, so I am sure you will have it."

Jeannine was delighted.

"Thanks very much for your confidence Dr. Anderson. I look forward to working with you. You know I read the papers on the Gibbs sampler you gave me, but I have some mathematical results beyond the computer simulation. I'd like to show you."

"Could you meet me in my office tomorrow afternoon."

Jeannine started to say "yes," but remembered Dr. Delaney.

"Could we make it Thursday morning. I'm going to be off-campus tomorrow."

"Ten o'clock Thursday, then."

He wanted to add, "And wear your pink pullover," but he caught himself. This was not going to be easy, but he resolved that emotion would not complicate their work.

***

The sun was high in the sky when Monique arrived at her apartment. She had not been here in four days. Since Friday, she had slept at Jeannine's.

She checked the mailbox. Besides the mail, there was a copy of La Presse from her mother in Montreal. Once in her apartment, she fastened the chain on the door.

She was sorting clothes into an overnight bag, when the apartment door opened.

"Qui va là? ... Who's there?"

There was no answer. The door rasped harshly against the security chain. The taut links held firm. She heard a muttered oath, followed by footsteps departing down the hallway.

She rushed to the door and turned the dead bolt. Through the window she caught a glimpse of a man's back as he turned the corner. She was sure it was Mike.

***

Monique called Jeannine. The latter did not mince words.

"It had to be Mike. The bastard has 'date rape' down to an art. He counts on messing up your emotions. He's counting on your fear, and afterwards your shame."

Jeannine continued.

"Wait there. I'm on my way. Keep the door locked 'til I get there. We'll pack all your stuff. You're staying with me until this mess blows over."

Monique did not protest. She went into her bedroom to fold clothes. Her hands shook. She stared out the window and watched for the blue Mazda.

***

In her cubicle in Chicago, Sharon Husak, science reporter, answered the phone.

"This is Sharon."

"Miss Husak, my name is Joan Wilson, I'm a temp in the provost's office at the Fairland University Medical School."

"I know. We talked on the phone a week ago. What's up?"

"You remember the article that you did on breast cancer and Dr. Lawrence?"

Sharon searched and brought the piece up on her computer.

RESEARCHER CLOSE TO BREAST CANCER CURE
by Sharon Husak
Women have found a new champion in Dr. Franklin Lawrence, a prominent cancer specialist who announced yesterday in an exclusive interview with the Express that he has discovered a key compound with a demonstrable effect in inhibiting the growth of early breast cancers. ...

Joan continued.

"The provost just forwarded a university report on research misconduct to the ORI. The misconduct was in his lab."

"The same 'Dr. Lawrence' as in my article?"

"The same. And I think the public has the right to know."

"Right, but I need to digest this. I'll call you back. OK?"

Sharon hung up. The news about Dr. Lawrence's lab disturbed her, but before she could think, the phone rang again.

"Sharon, this is Dr. Lawrence at Fairland University Medical School in Washington. Breast cancer. Remember?"

"Of course."

"You should know what's happening here at the university."

Sharon braced for a defensive discourse about Dr. Lawrence's lab and research fraud. She was surprised.

"Sharon, remember your article on A-11 and breast cancer."

Remember it? She was staring at it on the computer screen.

"Sharon, I'm submitting for publication a manuscript on a powerful new agent, L-12, superior even to A-11. I thought you might like a copy."

Sharon was nonplused. Dr. Lawrence had not mentioned research misconduct, and there was no trace of concern in his voice. His enthusiasm was real.

"Dr. Lawrence, I'd be honored to see the article, Sir."

"Call me 'Franklin.' It's 'Franklin,' Sharon. I'll Fed-Ex the paper to you this afternoon. You'll have it tomorrow morning.

"Thank you for remembering me, Sir, ... I mean, Franklin."

"Good, but please don't write about it until I give you the OK."

"Of course, and thanks again, Franklin."

Sharon hung up, perplexed. Her two phone conversations exhibited no relationship. What was happening at Fairland?

She called her science editor. He listened to her proposal and responded.

"OK. Maybe you should go to Washington for a few days. But not before you finish your project on lead in paint and its effect on children. Finish that first and then we'll talk."

Sharon returned to her computer, but her thoughts were in Washington. How could two phone calls about the same lab be so disconnected? She was perplexed.

***

Jeannine found Monique's apartment without incident. The two of them packed and loaded the Mazda with Monique's belongings. Neither of them noticed the lone figure standing in the dark foyer across from Monique's building.

***

******

Chapter 21
Wednesday, December 20

The messenger arrived at 10 a.m. Dr. Lawrence looked up.

"Excuse me. Are you Dr. Franklin Lawrence?"

"Yes. Do you have something for me?"

The messenger handed him a brown envelope and left. It was from the head of the Mathematics Department, addressed to Dr. Lawrence, Chair, Quantitative Biology Fellowship Committee.

Dr. Lawrence opened the envelope. It was time to make the fellowship award. There was only one individual proposed, a "J. Ryan." *Good*. He could handle this matter with two phone calls and avoid a meeting.

The committee trusted the nominations of the Mathematics Department. With only one nominee for the fellowship, approval would be automatic.

Mike Hartness appeared in the open doorway.

"Sir, I read our manuscript last night and checked the figures and tables. I found these changes and some typos. If you agree, I'll finish the manuscript."

Dr. Lawrence took the papers and examined the changes, nodding assent.

"Did Monique have any changes?"

"I left the manuscript for her yesterday afternoon. She picked it up. I haven't seen her yet, but the secretary saw her. She said Monique looked ill. I think we'd better send the manuscript off today. We can catch any changes she might have later."

"All right, but I wish she were more responsible."

"She will be. I'm working to help her on that."

"Thanks Mike. When you get the final copies, we'll toast the manuscript together."

Dr. Lawrence returned to the nomination forms. He read the paragraph of proposed research. *Why can't mathematicians talk English? ... This guy Bayes is dead for 200 years? Oh well, maybe we'll get something useful out of the fellowship.*

Abruptly his face reddened. *Could "J." Ryan be "Jeannine" Ryan?* He checked the forms. There was no indication of gender. He called the Mathematics Department.

"This is Dr. Lawrence in Immunology. How many graduate students do you have named 'Ryan,' either in math or statistics?"

"We have two, Jeannine Ryan in statistics and William Ryan in algebra."

"Is William Ryan's middle initial 'J' by any chance?"

"No Sir, it's 'F.'"

"Thank you."

His face reddened further. His chest constricted and his pulse rate rose. "J. Ryan" was Jeannine. *Calm yourself Franklin. Don't let that twit affect your health.*

He took a breath. His face lightened and his abdominal muscles relaxed.

The phone rang. It was Marshall Hanes.

"I don't know if I told you Franklin, but the provost forwarded the Sadler Committee report to the Office of Research Integrity last Friday. They found that John Martin committed misconduct. It's a good report. I think the ORI will confirm it."

Aloud, Dr. Lawrence was all sweetness.

"Thanks very much for the information Marshall. I agree with the report, of course."

But his thoughts were less accommodating. *Hanes, you SOB, It's Wednesday already and you're only calling now. It's a damn good thing I spoke to Sadler last Thursday. Thanks for nothing.*

He returned to the fellowship problem. His face reddened once more as he thought of Jeannine. *"Horse's ass" am I. We'll see.*

***

Dr. Lawrence called the Mathematics Department.

"May I speak to Dr. Anderson, please?"

"Hello. This is Jack Anderson."

"Dr. Anderson, this is Dr. Lawrence in the Medical School. I'm the chair of the Fellowship Committee. I understand that you will be directing Miss Ryan's work if she receives the Quantitative Biology Fellowship."

"That's correct."

"Dr. Anderson, I believe that you understand that one purpose of this fellowship is to promote good applications of statistics in biomedical studies."

"Of course!"

"Dr. Anderson, the committee takes its task seriously. One of our jobs is to evaluate the potential for an individual to be a good statistical consultant to biomedical scientists."

"Jeannine Ryan has an excellent consulting record. Better than any student in the department. I'm sure that ..."

Dr. Lawrence interrupted.

"Of course you believe that since you nominated her. But some members of my committee know individuals who were offended by Miss Ryan as a consultant, and concerned about her lack of understanding of how labs work."

It was Jack's turn to interrupt.

"Dr. Lawrence, that's difficult to believe. Jeannine has made a special effort to collaborate with other researchers. She is especially effective with research biologists. Who is it that's not pleased with her work? I'm sure things can be worked out."

"Dr. Anderson, I'm sure you realize that the committee receives these opinions in strict confidence."

"But ..."

"Dr. Anderson, I just don't believe that I can, in conscience, get the committee to approve the fellowship for this individual."

"But she's the only one nominated!"

"I understand that, and I'm sorry. Maybe I shouldn't tell you this, but the Computer Science department feels they should have access to this fellowship too. They are willing to submit a suitable individual."

"Dr. Lawrence, don't you think you could persuade your committee members to reconsider Jeannine. She's the best student in the department. She would not disappoint you. And she is an excellent consultant. I'm sure. ..."

"Dr. Anderson, I'm sure I cannot change the committee's opinion."

"But, there must be some mistake."

"There's no mistake in my information. I thought I was doing you a favor by calling you, and I expect you to keep this call confidential, except for your Chairman of course. I'm sure neither of you wants Computer Science to have the fellowship."

"But ..."

"Go talk to your department head. I'll wait until this afternoon for a different nomination. If not, I'm sure Computer Science will be happy to fill the fellowship."

Dr. Lawrence paused.

"I'll wait until three o'clock. If your messenger hasn't arrived by then I'll assume that your department is not interested in cooperating with us. I hope we can keep the collegial approach we've had in the past."

He hung up.

Dr. Anderson could not believe what he had just heard. He left his office to find the department head.

***

At the Office of Research Integrity, Bob Delaney was at his desk when the phone rang. He recognized the caller.

"Cecilia? Cecilia Hernandez! You're in Washington. Where are you staying?"

"In Bethesda, with my cousins."

"That's great! I'd like to see you."

"I'm going to Mass at Our Lady of Lourdes church at noon. Could you pick me up there at one o'clock? Do you know where that is?"

"I do. But why Mass? When did you get religion?"

"Never mind Bob, I've always 'got' religion. I need to pray for a friend who died. … Because of me."

"Look. I'm sorry. About your friend, I mean."

"What time do you have to get back to work?"

"I have an appointment at four. We've got until then."

"Good. Mass should be over by 12:45. I have a lot to tell you."

"I'll be there."

Cecilia being here was the best news Bob had had in weeks.

***

Monique and Jeannine stopped by the hospital. There was no change. John was still in a coma. They left for Rockville

Jeannine's appointment at the Office of Research Integrity was not until 4:00 p.m. They stopped at the Cheesecake Factory in the White Flint Mall.

The restaurant was crowded. They waited twenty minutes before being seated. Their table was by a window. Through it they saw a pulsating flow of shoppers rushing to make holiday purchases. Jeannine was in a holiday mood herself.

"You know Paul Pagé is a *real* mathematician."

"Jeannine, I told you I'm impressed. You beat the *Sorbonne*. You got the fellowship!"

"That's why I'm buying. Order whatever you want!"

For desert they shared Blueberry and Chocolate Mousse cheesecakes. Jeannine had black coffee. In a spirit of togetherness, Monique drank coffee instead of hot chocolate.

Some time later, all that remained were two empty plates.

Monique put John's folder on the table and took out the L-12 manuscript.

"They've made me an author. Mike wants me to steal John's work too."

"Monique. How can they do that? What will you do?"

Monique stared outside at the bustling shoppers. She turned back.

"They have to take my name off. I left a note on Mike's door."

"You know Mike won't say anything. You've got to tell Dr. Lawrence yourself!"

Monique nodded and pursed her lips.

"You're right. I'll call him now."

***

Bob Delaney and Cecilia arrived at the Cheesecake Factory at two o'clock. Bob was all smiles. Cecilia took her seat. She favored her right arm. She had waited a long time for this conversation.

"Bob, you remember that time at FLETC when you told me about homeopathic medicine, and an NIH grant to study dilute medicines."

"I remember. The 'funny water' project."

"But it wasn't funny."

"No. Only 'funny' as in 'peculiar.'"

She shifted her gaze. Her voice was low.

"Bob I was in the hospital? Did you know I was shot?"

"No?"

"And Bob, I killed a man."

He was silent. She added.

"... and I as good as killed my friend."

"Bob, before I ask you about 'funny water,' I'd better tell you about Madame Gauthier and Checkpoint Charley. But it's a long story. Have you got time?"

"Cecilia, I'm here. Take all you need."

***

Cecilia finished her story. Bob looked at her with new respect.

"Cecilia, I don't know what to say."

178

"It's OK, Bob, what about the 'colored water.'"

"It looks like you're dealing with homeopathic remedies. That's what the colored water must be, but there's no reason to smuggle homeopathic medicine, unless you believe in it, and ..."

"And what?"

"And you were *stealing* someone else's preparations. There's no restrictions on bringing homeopathic medicine into the country. Water's not restricted. You said there were frozen cells too. They sound important. The colored vials must be an extra, an afterthought."

"What about the frozen cells?"

"They're probably stolen cell lines. They could mean real money for pharmaceutical houses and the like. That's where the money is."

"But Bob, the 'funny water' could be a clue. Whoever wanted the shipment must use homeopathic remedies, right?"

She continued.

"When we were at FLETC, you told me about a grant for diluted medicines. You didn't think even a molecule of the original compound would be left after the last dilution. You remember that? How could I get a copy of that grant?"

Bob frowned.

"The grant was turned down, and the NIH doesn't keep rejected applications. I used to have a copy, but I threw out a lot of stuff when we moved to Rockville. Still, it might be around."

"Who was the Principal Investigator? Do you remember?"

"Some guy from Arizona. Phoenix. Maybe, Tucson. I can't recall."

"But who was this guy?"

"I think his name was 'Mc' something. ..."

"McElroy?"

"That could be it."

"Bob, I have a link between the contraband at Checkpoint Charley and a Dr. McElroy at a clinic in Tucson. That's why I'm here."

"I hope there's another reason too."

Finally Cecilia smiled.

"Could be!"

"Let's go to my office and check my files."

Bob and Cecilia left.

***

At a table near the one vacated by Bob and Cecilia, Monique picked up her cell phone and called Dr. Lawrence. After a brief exchange, Monique asserted herself.

"Dr. Lawrence, I cannot have my name on that paper!"

Jeannine could not hear Dr. Lawrence's reply, but Monique's response was clear.

"Acceptable or not, I will *not* be an author of that paper."

Monique fell silent. Moments later Jeannine heard her stammer.

"I hope it doesn't come to that, Sir."

Monique hung up. Her face was pale.

Jeannine touched her wrist.

"What did he say?"

"First he talked about my lack of loyalty to the lab. Then he said that it was not 'acceptable' that I take my name off the paper. Then he said that if I did, he would have to reevaluate my position in the lab."

"Meaning?"

"He'll stop my Postdoc. He'll kick me out! Like John."

Moisture accumulated in Monique's eyes.

"But there's no way he can make me steal John's work. *No way*. I will *not* be an author on that paper. I will not. ... *pas possible!* No way!"

Jeannine stood up.

"You'd better not wait here alone. Come to the ORI with me. Delaney said there's a small cafe in the lobby. You can sit there while I talk to him."

Monique nodded her agreement.

***

180

The building that housed the Office of Research Integrity had a small cafe on the ground floor. Jeannine left Monique there and went to the elevator to go up to Delaney's office.

Monique sat. She had a copy of La Presse her mother had sent. Maybe Montreal news would distract her. A moment later the sound of her native tongue surprised her.

"Excusez moi. That's La Presse. Are you Canadienne?"

Monique looked up at the speaker, a young woman with jet black hair and a warm smile.

"Oui. Je suis Québécoise, et vous? Yes, I'm a Quebecer. And you?"

"I'm American, from Arizona. But I work on the Québec border. My name is Cecilia Hernandez. You?"

"Monique Laurier. So you know Montréal?"

"A little. I had a friend, a dear lady, who was originally from Montreal. She used La Presse to teach me French."

"You said 'Mon-tree-all!' Don't you mean 'Mon-ray-al?'"

Cecilia laughed. Monique handed the newspaper to her.

"Sit down with me. Look at La Presse if you like."

"Thanks."

Monique opened John's folder. She started reading an article by a William McElroy, but something was wrong with Figure 4. *But what?* Monique looked up at a wide-eyed Cecilia.

"Monique, that article, is the author's name 'McElroy?'"

"Yes. Why?"

"Is he at the *AMAH Clinic* in Tucson?"

Monique checked. It was her turn to stare wide-eyed.

"That's it! How did you know?"

Cecilia wanted to say "It's a small world," but she resisted.

"Monique, tell me all you know about this McElroy."

***

Jeannine's meeting with Dr. Delaney had been uneventful. Throughout, he had appeared distracted. Discouraged, she took the elevator to the street level. As she stepped into the lobby, Monique appeared with a dark-haired woman in tow.

"Jeannine, this is Cecilia Hernandez. She's a U. S. Customs Agent from New York. She's pursuing a lead on Mike's old mentor, Dr. McElroy. She may be able to help us. She'd like to visit the university."

Jeannine tried to smile.

"Cecilia, I'm driving back there now. How about it?"

"Thanks, but I'm meeting a friend, Bob Delaney, in a few minutes. Tomorrow would be better."

Now Jeannine understood why Delaney had been distracted, Cecilia was very attractive.

"All right, Cecilia, call us tomorrow."

Jeannine wrote her phone number on a scrap of paper and handed it to Cecilia who went back into the cafe. Monique turned to Jeannine and raised her eyebrows.

"Well? How was Dr. Delaney?"

"Nothing! Unless Cecilia can help us, we are on our own."

***

The new article was on its way to a prestigious journal. Its authors, Dr. Lawrence and Mike, sat at a table in Le Papillon. Each held a glass of wine to toast their achievement.

Dr. Lawrence spoke.

"Mike, we need to consider a replacement for Monique. Her heart is not in our work. I took her name off our paper. I have several applications in my office. I have to replace her"

Mike had his own plans for Monique. He would convince Dr. Lawrence to keep her, but not now. He raised his glass.

"I'll look at them, Sir, but first, a toast to the future of L-12."

Dr. Lawrence refilled his glass. He gave a toast of his own.

"To the best damn Postdoc on the East coast!"

Mike grinned.

***

******

Chapter 22
Thursday, December 21

Monique was still asleep when Jeannine showered and dressed for her meeting with Dr. Anderson.

Jeannine gathered her notes on a solution for a problem that Dr. Anderson believed could only be solved by simulation. She laid the pages on the kitchen table, peeled a banana, and checked the proof. Fubini's theorem could be invoked, and then? Yes, the proof was sound. Anderson would be pleased.

She finished the banana and thought of Monique. How dumb could Dr. Lawrence be? He had two first rate Postdocs, John and Monique, and appreciated neither. Yet he admired that slime, Mike. Was Mike that clever, or did Dr. Lawrence *want* to believe him?

She looked at her watch. She wanted to be on time. At least something good had occurred. She had the Quantitative Biology Fellowship!

She slipped out.

***

Jeannine was on time. Dr. Anderson sat at his desk. He spoke without rising.

"Miss Ryan, I tried to reach you at your apartment, but you had already left. I have bad news I'm afraid."

He almost choked.

"I'm sorry, but the Quantitative Biology fellowship was awarded to Paul Pagé. It was out of my control. I can't tell you how bad I feel."

Jeannine struggled to understand. His words were unreal. She stared. He continued.

"Paul will be working under my direction. I already am directing two Masters students, and, counting Paul, two doctoral candidates. I am sorry that I can't take on any more students."

He glanced up at Jeannine before lowering his eyes.

"You will have to find another advisor for your doctoral research. I can't have more than four students. I'm sorry."

"You're sorry? Two days ago you told me I had the fellowship."

Dr. Anderson broke in.

"I spoke out of turn. I was wrong"

"You were wrong? Dr. Anderson, is that all you can say!"

He looked down. She could not see his eyes.

"There still might be a teaching fellowship available. You need to ask Dr. Carson. You should do that right away before it's too late."

She started to speak, but stopped. She stumbled from the office and stood outside, out of his sight. She shook with shock and shame.

Dr. Anderson was on the phone. His voice was audible through the open door.

"All right! So Dr. Lawrence gets his way, and you save the Quantitative Biology fellowship for mathematics. I still feel like hell!"

Jeannine thought. *You feel like hell! How do you think I feel? And Dr. Lawrence gets his way?*

Dr. Anderson hung up on his chairman, and stared at his desk. He was ashamed of the department's capitulation to Dr. Lawrence.

Ruefully, Jack observed that Jeannine had worn her pink pullover for the appointment. Ironically, now that he no longer was her professor, he was free to relate to her in a personal way. The difficulty was that she would never speak to him again.

***

Jeannine's usually ordered mind was in chaos. So this is how John felt! Dr. Lawrence, you son of a bitch.

She walked aimlessly for several blocks. She could not return to the apartment in this state. She needed time to settle down. *Think, Jeannine, Think!*

Calmed, she returned to the Mathematics Department. She went to Dr. Carson's office to inquire about a teaching fellowship.

Dr. Carson was a kind white-haired man, an algebraist whose specialty was lattice theory. He remembered Jeannine. She had gotten the highest grade in his seminar.

"I'm sorry Jeannine, we had more applicants than teaching fellowships for next semester. I thought you were getting the QB fellowship."

Dr. Carson leaned over his list. He wanted to help.

"I can get you some hours in the Math Tutoring Lab."

Jeannine shook her head. Dr. Carson was a kind man, but her anger was rising. It would be wrong to explode at him.

"No thank you Dr. Carson."

She turned and left. Without a fellowship, she would have to leave school for at least a semester. There was no money to pay her tuition, much less food and the apartment.

At the math library, she picked up the latest issue of the American Mathematical Monthly. She did not open it. She stared at the cover.

Outside, a light snow began to fall.

***

Cecilia slept late and awoke to an empty house. Her cousins had gone to work, and she was alone. She chuckled. It had been a good evening with Bob! But she had work to do.

She called Monique.

"Monique, Cecilia Hernandez. Is there any chance you could take me around the university today?"

"Why not? I won't go near the lab, but you can come over now."

"I don't need to see the lab. I really need to check that pay phone I told you about."

"I'm free. Jeannine's gone to arrange her fellowship."

"Great. I'm in Bethesda. I have my cousin's car. I'll leave in a few minutes."

Monique looked at the clock. It was nearly noon. She had time for a shower before Cecilia came.

***

Monique was ready and waiting when Cecilia arrived.

"All right, Cecilia, what would you like to see first?"

Cecilia unfolded a piece of paper and handed it to Monique.

"This is a DEA sketch that shows the location of the phone that was used to call a hood named Kurt Mason, and McElroy too. I'd like to check it out."

Monique looked.

"That's near the lab. It's not far."

A light powder sprinkled the cars white as they started out. After a few minutes, Monique touched Cecilia.

"The Forster building is up ahead on the right, but we turn here."

They turned, went one block, and turned again. Monique pointed.

"That's your phone over there, across the street."

The pay phone was attached to a brick wall. There was no enclosure, only two side 'wings' and a small roof that projected from the wall. Cecilia checked the phone number and scanned the surroundings. She looked at Monique.

"Monique, someone used this phone to call McElroy in Tucson and Kurt Mason's hotel when he was in Washington. I'm willing to bet it was your guy, Hartness. How close are we to your lab?"

Monique went to the corner and pointed.

"That's the Forster building over there and that's the entrance I use. Up on the third floor, those windows are the lab."

Monique jumped back as a man stepped out of the building.

"That's Mike. He's coming this way!"

"Get behind that van across the street. He doesn't know me. I'll stay here."

Monique disappeared. Cecilia waited between two cars as Mike passed her and went to the phone. He made a call.

Cecilia walked towards him, shuffling the contents of her purse, as if searching for change.

Mike saw her. He lowered his voice, but she heard his words.

"The L-12 is on the way, I'm shipping it tomorrow."

Cecilia stopped to sort her coins. Mike lowered his voice further. A second later he hung up. He frowned and headed back to the Forster building.

Cecilia recorded the time of the call. The DEA would have the number Mike had called. She was sure it was McElroy. She crossed back to Monique.

"Monique. What does 'L-12' mean?"

Monique explained Mike's theft of L-12. Cecilia frowned.

"Monique, Mike is sending L-12 cells to Dr. McElroy."

Monique frowned. Would Mike cheat Dr. Lawrence too?

***

Dr. Lawrence sat in front of the computer. At his side were Mike's lab notebooks. He clicked on the printer icon and produced his text. He examined his note.

> **To: Dr. J. Santini, Chair**
> **From: Dr. F. W. Lawrence, Graham Professor of Immunology**
> **Re: Your query concerning Dr. Hartness' laboratory notebooks**
> **In answer to your query concerning a question raised by Ms. Jeannine Ryan, I fully explained to her the laboratory's position on authorship and laboratory note-keeping.**
> **With respect to Dr. Hartness' notebooks I wish to state that these notebooks fully comply with standard record keeping in my laboratory and are clearly the product of Dr. Hartness. In those instances where work was performed by Dr. Martin, it is clear that such work was performed under the direction of Dr. Hartness.**

To Dr. Lawrence this memo was a waste of time. He detested administrative trivia. Dr. Santini loved to generate paperwork.

On a whim, he went to his bookshelf and grabbed the last several annual reports of the department. He thumbed the pages for several minutes. His facial muscles relaxed and he grinned and spoke aloud.

"Just as I thought. That SOB Santini hasn't published a single article in the last two years."

Then he thought. *I should tell Dean Hampton that Santini isn't publishing any more.*

Returning to his desk, he sipped his coffee and buzzed the department secretary.

"I have some memos for Dr. Santini. Could you come get them please."

While he waited, he looked at his second memo of the day. It said:

To: Dr. J. Santini, Chair
From: Dr. F. W. Lawrence, Graham Professor of Immunology
Re: Award of Quantitative Biology Fellowship to Mr. Paul Pagé
The committee met by conference call and unanimously approved the award of the QB Fellowship to the nominee of the Department of Mathematics, Mr. Paul Pagé.
Please notify Dean Hampton of this award, and please forward our thanks to the Mathematics Department for an excellent nominee.

There, these memos should get rid of Miss Ryan, once and for all. Satisfied, he leaned back in his chair.

***

Bob Delaney stared out the window. Scattered white flakes floated downwards. Several ring-billed gulls flapped in erratic patterns. The birds appeared disturbed. Bob frowned. *We're due for some weather.*

He turned to his notes from the interview with Jeannine. There wasn't much there. John Martin had told her about the fabricated data *after* they had been discovered on his computer, *not before*. Her information added nothing.

And the authorship of the paper was an internal lab matter. Dr. Lawrence was the Principal Investigator and the lab chief. He had the final say.

Bob sympathized with Dr. Lawrence. The university had found Martin guilty of misconduct. Why would anyone want Martin as an author?

Next, Bob turned his attention to Marshall Hanes' report itself. There was no doubt the data were fabricated. Monique Laurier thought that Mike Hartness was the fabricator, but she herself had downloaded the programs from John's computer. The committee had established that Monique liked John Martin. From his talk with Jeannine yesterday, it was clear that Jeannine liked him too. Apparently Martin appealed to women.

Martin had not testified on his own behalf. That fact did not help his case. The fabricated numbers were from his computer. He was guilty.

A face appeared in his doorway. It was his Chief.

"Bob. What case are you reviewing?"

"The Fairland Medical School report."

"Any problems?"

"I don't think so. It seems straightforward, but there's one more thing I'd like to check."

"Forget it. The fabricated data weren't published were they?"

"No."

"Then there's no scientific literature to correct. Wrap it up. Martin's guilty."

He continued.

"I need you downtown with me this afternoon. There's all hell breaking loose with a new case, a major multi-center clinical trial. A congressional hearing is scheduled for next week. I'll get the car and meet you downstairs in 10 minutes."

Bob Delaney stopped by the paralegals' office

"Charlene, I've got to go. Could you help me with the Fairland oversight case."

He put on his jacket as he talked.

"Dr. Martin is guilty of research misconduct. We concur with the university's decision. We recommend that Martin be debarred from Federal funds for three years... Not allowed to work on *any* grant. ... The usual. ... Thanks."

He handed her the file.

"And Charlene, do me another favor, please. Call this number and leave a message for 'Cecilia.' Tell her I'm sorry, but I can't meet her tonight. ... I'll call her later. ... Thanks."

Through the window he could see large snowflakes. *Damn this snow and damn this meeting. We won't be done by eight, if then.* He hoped Cecilia would get the message.

***

Jeannine left the library. A gust of cold air lifted the hood on her jacket. She shivered, and pulled the hood strap tight. After a few blocks, large white flakes had settled on the tree branches. The sidewalk was patched with snow. The warmth of her shoes melted it leaving wet footprints on the sidewalk.

Her spirits sank. She had counted on the QB fellowship.

Nature apparently shared her mood. Icy flakes flecked her cheeks and chilled her skin. The wind whipped stinging white particles into her eyes. She looked down. The flakes no longer disappeared where she stepped. Instead her shoes crunched dry impressions in the deepening snow. It grew colder.

She was near the apartment when a heavy hand gripped her shoulder.

Mike Hartness!

He wore no hat. White flakes clung to his hair and eyebrows and gave him an eerie look. She tried to pull away, but could not. He fixed her with his eyes.

"You're Monique's friend so get this message. Dr. Lawrence wants to fire her, but I can stop him. I'm her only chance. Look at you. You found out what Dr. Lawrence can do! You lost your fellowship. Unless you want your friend to

190

lose her job too, tell her to be nice to me. I'm not so bad if you're on my side."

Jeannine swung her fist, but Mike caught her arm and held it. He was strong.

She tried to pull away. He kept his grip on her shoulder. Then he shoved. She dropped to one knee on the slippery sidewalk, wrenching her hip. Somehow, she retained her balance. Her right hand felt for and grasped a rock. Mike paid no attention.

"And tell your friend I know she's staying with you. She can't hide. I know where to find her! And you too!"

Jeannine straightened herself, the rock in her hand. She stood her ground.

"You bastard!"

Mike grinned.

"You're right, but I'm a sexy bastard."

He strode away. Jeannine shouted after him.

"Leave her alone."

Mike turned his head and grinned. He walked off and disappeared in a swirling cloud of snow.

***

Monique's feet were sore from touring the campus and she was hungry. She led Cecilia through the snow to the Old Goose for supper.

The casual dress of the students and professors appealed to Cecilia. She was reminded of the cafeteria at FLETC. She and Monique ate, but mostly talked.

They trudged back to the apartment. By the time they arrived, snow had covered both street and sidewalk. Monique pointed.

"This is Washington. This snow is already enough to stop traffic. You'd better not drive. Come up with me, we'll check the weather."

"Really? It doesn't seem that bad."

"Yes, really. I insist."

They found Jeannine asleep on the sofa, shoes off. She stirred, but did not wake up.

Monique went to the window.

"Spend the night with us. The snow is too deep and it's sticking."

Cecilia looked. Outside, traffic was snarled. A car was abandoned in the middle of the whitened street. Drivers struggled to pass. Wheels spun. One man, out of his car, was gesticulating wildly.

"I'll call my cousins and see how it is in Bethesda."

After the call, Cecilia was convinced.

"OK, you win. My date is canceled anyway. And they don't want me to drive their car in this stuff. It's safer here. They say to stay with you if I can."

"I'll find some sheets.

We won't wake Jeannine, she doesn't mind the couch."

***

Upstairs, Monique set up the roll-away bed. She turned to Cecilia.

"I know Mike pushed John off the cliff, but they say Mike was at a lecture that afternoon."

"Monique, maybe someone else did it for Mike."

Cecilia took a notebook out of her handbag.

"That phone Mike used today was used to call Kurt Mason's hotel in Washington on Friday, December 1."

"That's the night John moved out of his apartment. Someone called him just before he left. It must have been Mike. But Agent Turner ..."

"Who?"

"Agent Turner. He's with the National Park Police. He has a witness who says John was arguing with a woman when he fell. Turner thinks it was Jeannine."

"Monique, Kurt Mason had a high-pitched voice."

Monique jumped from the bed.

"That's it! It was Kurt. I knew Jeannine couldn't have done it! Where is he now?"

"He's dead. You don't want to mess with his friends, they're the mob."

"Cecilia, John left a note that he was to meet someone at Stony Man."

"You say John fell on the evening of the 6th?"

"Right, and that evening Mike was with Dr. Lawrence at the Hayes Memorial Lectures, afternoon and evening. Mike must have had Kurt do it for him."

Cecilia frowned and consulted her notebook.

"Kurt returned to Burlington on December 5. He was there all day Wednesday, December 6. He and his cronies were hunting Pierre Lachance, the man that saved my life."

Cecilia recalled Pierre's face staring down at her as she lay bleeding. She continued.

"And the next day Kurt tried to kill me in the hospital. He died later that night. Kurt wasn't at Stony Man. He didn't push John."

It was Monique's turn to frown.

"Well if it wasn't Kurt or Mike, who was it?

Cecilia was silent.

***

Agent Jack Turner of the Park Service hung up the phone. The hospital reported no change in John Martin's condition. He was still in a coma.

He thought of calling Monique Laurier. Perhaps now she would talk about Jeannine's activities at Stony Man. He was convinced that Jeannine had been there with John.

He shrugged. He had plenty of work without the John Martin "accident." That case could wait another day.

His phone rang. It was Beth, one of the employees at Skyland Lodge.

"Jack, are you still working on the Martin accident?"

"Yes. What's up?"

"There's been a screw-up here. I have a message that the desk clerk took back on December 6. Isn't that when John Martin fell?"

"Yes. What's the message?"

"A woman called to report an accident on Stony Man Mountain, at the cliffs."

"Why didn't we get the report?"

"I don't know. The clerk says he was going off duty and left it for the next clerk to call in. I'm sure he was drinking. We've always had a problem with him. Anyway, he says he left a note on the desk. I just found it on the floor, and called him."

"Did he get the woman's name? Was it Ryan?"

"She didn't leave a name."

"How does he know it was a woman?"

"He remembers that much."

"Where is he now?

"Home. He left early to avoid the snow."

"All right, I'll talk to him tomorrow."

Turner looked out at the snow-covered hillside. *All right Miss Ryan. This proves you have some conscience, but not enough. You left him on that mountain! You are not going to get away with this!*

***

******

Chapter 23
Friday, December 22

Jeannine awoke to a dark room. Chilled, her hands groped for the bed covers. She felt only a loose blanket and coarse upholstery. She was on the couch downstairs.

She struggled to focus on her watch, 3:00 a. m. She shivered. Her fellowship was gone. Mike's words reverberated in her ears. *"You found out what Dr. Lawrence can do."*

She was helpless. She had no money, and she could not ask her mother for help, not with her stepfather in control. She would have to quit school, but she wanted to stay in Washington.

StatFind Consultants had tried to hire her. Their work was computer programming. Dull, but at least it was statistical.

Maybe Monique could move in and they could share expenses. But what about Mike? How could Monique work in that lab while he was there?

Jeannine turned on her side, faced the back of the couch, and pulled the blanket tight about her. Darkness settled her thoughts and her eyes closed.

Monique lay on her back. A man was on top of her, fumbling with her jeans. It was Mike!

Jeannine tried to yell. No sound! She picked up a rock to smash him, but someone grabbed her arm. It was Mike. ... No, it was Dr. Lawrence. He disappeared.

Meanwhile Mike pulled at Monique's jeans. Jeannine reached for her rock, but her fingers froze. She could not move. Mike turned from Monique and glared at Jeannine. He came towards her.

She awoke sweating. She lay still, shaking in the shadows, afraid to close her eyes.

Finally she dozed.

***

Jeannine awoke again, but this time bright morning light filled the room. In the distance she heard Monique on the phone.

"She's here, I'll get her."

Someone else is here? Then Jeannine heard a cheery voice.

"Bob! You tracked me down."

Jeannine forced herself alert. She knew that voice. *Oh, it's Cecilia.*

"Bob, of course, I want to see you. My flight for Tucson leaves this afternoon. Great, but what about the snow?"

Jeannine struggled to the window. Outside, the sun was out. The sky was bright, with only a few clouds. Dark streaks of asphalt, exposed by the tires of passing cars, signaled the departure of the snow. Melting was underway. The streets were passable.

She heard Cecilia finish her call.

"Bob, I'll be in Bethesda at two o'clock. Pick me up then. The flight leaves at six."

Jeannine struggled into the kitchen. Monique and Cecilia were at the table.

Jeannine's hip hurt from Mike's shove. She sat down gingerly and recounted her encounter with Mike. Then she told them about Dr. Lawrence and the lost fellowship.

Monique jumped up, scratching her chair across the floor.

"I can't work for that man, and I can't be around Mike. I quit."

Jeannine raised her hand.

"Monique wait. Don't do that. You need Dr. Lawrence's recommendation for another position. You can't quit without a reference. You have to ride it out."

"But what about Mike?"

"Maybe you could work with the molecular biologists in the other section long enough to get Dr. Lawrence to write a good letter."

"But I'm an immunologist, and ..."

Cecilia shook her head at both of them.

"Look, if Mike is connected with McElroy, then he's dangerous. Neither of you are safe."

Monique's shoulders drooped.

"Then I can't go back. That's it. My career is over. I'll never get another research job. Dr. Lawrence will see to that."

She stared at the floor.

***

It was noon when Cecilia left the apartment. Monique went to the car with her. The snow on the windshield had melted and the road was clear.

Cecilia handed Monique a slip of paper.

"I'll be in Tucson tonight and over Christmas. Here's my mother's phone number. If something comes up, call me."

Cecilia drove away. She smiled as she turned onto K Street. She would have an hour with Bob at the airport before her flight.

***

When Monique returned, Jeannine was on the phone.

"No, there's no change in his condition. Monique Laurier, from the lab, stops by every day. The doctors say his leg is healing fine, but there's no telling when he'll come out of the coma."

Jeannine paused and listened for a few seconds. She spoke again.

"The doctors are optimistic, there's nothing we can do but hope."

Jeannine hung up. Monique queried.

"Who was that on the phone."

"You're not going to believe this. It was Mrs. Lawrence."

"What did she want?"

"To know how John was doing."

"That's all?"

"That's all. What do you think?"

Monique grew thoughtful.

"I think it's curious. She's snooty to us Postdocs."

197

"Well, look who she's married to!"

Monique jumped suddenly, agitated.

"Jeannine, is the phone listed under your name or John's?"

"Our number is unlisted."

"Right, but at the lab, we had your number. And Dr. Lawrence has the number at his house. And ... ."

Monique was excited. She grabbed John's note from the table.

"Look at it!"

Together they examined the postscript.

I'm sorry about us. It's not working, but it's me, not you. Sorry. Just got a call about Dr. Lawrence/Mike. It won't do any good, but said I would be at Stony Man next Wednesday evening and could talk then. I'm off to hike the Appalachian trail near there.

Sorry, John

Jeannine broke the silence.

"Of course, whoever called John had this number!"

Monique stared at her friend.

"I always thought it was Mike, but it could have been ... Someone who wanted to talk John out of hurting the lab. ... Someone who had this phone number.

Jeannine broke in.

"Someone who did not want to see her husband hurt."

Monique's brow furrowed.

"Exactly! ... Mrs. Lawrence!"

***

Betty sat in her kitchen, looking out the window. Wet branches dripped and glistened in the warm sun. In the shade, the ground was white except for tips of grass that pierced the thin covering of snow. Elsewhere, the turf, matted in spots under damp leaves, was dark green from the sun.

The thaw did not comfort Betty. She had an acid taste from her stomach, and stuffed sinuses. She was tired and afraid.

For two weeks she had not slept, not that Franklin had noticed. He'd been lost in one of his "great discoveries." If he told her one more time that the "L" in L-12 stood for "Lawrence" she would scream.

Her initial relief at learning that John was alive and safe at Fairland Medical Center had given way to trepidation. When would he regain consciousness? What would he remember? What would he say?

Sari's voice brought her back to her whereabouts.

"Mom, would you drive Mattie and me to the Mall?"

Schools in the area closed at the slightest sign of snow, and Sari had been home all morning, with Mattie. Betty looked at her watch. It was 12:30 p.m.

"OK girls, get your coats."

Sari's arms went around her mother's neck.

"Thanks, Mom!"

Mattie and Sari navigated the slush on the driveway and hopped into the back seat. Betty noted that even with a winter coat, Mattie appeared thin. Sari was less delicate. For several weeks now Betty had made her eat breakfast.

The trip to the mall was uneventful. Betty dropped the girls at the entrance near the movie theater.

"I'll pick you girls up here at five o'clock. Be here. Stick together, and don't talk to strangers. Mattie, do you have enough money?"

Mattie nodded.

"OK, five o'clock. Have fun girls."

They disappeared into the crowd of late Christmas shoppers.

Betty turned the car onto 270-South, and headed downtown to the University. She needed to talk to Franklin.

***

Mike Hartness was in the lab. Next Monday was Christmas, and today was Friday before the holiday. Support staff were gone, either to the rollicking party at Main Med, or home to shop. Mike, Dr. Lawrence, and one or two others were the only ones in the building.

199

Monique was absent. She had neglected her work. This made it harder to defend her. No matter. He would convince Dr. Lawrence to keep her and gain her gratitude.

His desire for Monique was now an obsession. His plan was simple. The next time she appeared in the lab he would lock the door and "introduce" himself to her.

Mike was lost in this fantasy, when he heard light footsteps in the hall. Monique! He moved near the door, out of sight, ready to close it after she entered. He was thrilled.

The steps approached. Mike smiled. He would be gentle at first.

The steps went past the doorway. His smile changed to a scowl. He looked out in the hall, only to see Mrs. Lawrence disappear into her husband's office. *Damn, what's she doing here?* Mrs. Lawrence rarely came to the lab.

Mike was curious. He tiptoed down the hall to the hall cabinet next to Dr. Lawrence's door. The door was open. He could hear everything.

***

Dr. Lawrence was deep in a journal. His back was to the door. He heard someone enter.

"Mike is that you? I've got something here you need to see."

He looked up and saw Betty.

"You? What are you doing here? Where's Sari?"

"She's with Mattie, at the Mall. I'm picking them up in two hours. Franklin, I need to talk to you."

"I'm busy."

He turned back to the his article. He underlined several sentences and continued to read.

"Franklin, this won't wait. I should have told you earlier but I was ..."

Dr. Lawrence sighed, marked his place and put the journal on the table. He turned towards Betty, his eyebrows lifted. She continued.

"It's about John Martin ..."

Franklin picked up the journal again.

"I have no intention of discussing John Martin with you or anyone else. There's nothing to talk about."

He reopened the journal, but Betty pushed ahead.

"But there is. I'm trying to tell you. I was at Stony Man with John when he fell. We argued!"

For once, Franklin had no response. He stared, first at the Human Genome poster on the wall, then at the floor, finally at her. All the while his mouth was open. Betty kept on.

"I wanted to see him, to tell him not to tell anyone about the cheating in your lab, about the bad data. I was afraid he would make trouble for you, as a whistleblower, firing him like you did. I told him I wanted you to give him his job back."

Franklin's mouth stayed open.

"What?"

"Marshall Hanes told me John could make trouble, that you had fired him without cause."

Franklin stood and smashed the desk with his fist.

"So you met John on the mountain. What a crazy stupid thing to do!"

He addressed the Genome poster rather than her.

"Stupid ... Stupid! ... Stupid!"

Fury overtook him.

"And you threw him off the cliff!"

Betty stared at him in horror.

"How could you think that? When he said you would never take him back, that you were too stubborn, I got mad and struck at him. It was wet. I slipped. He pulled me back, and then, I don't know, I grabbed a branch, and he fell. It was an accident. I looked over the edge. It was a long way down. He didn't move."

Franklin stared.

"I was afraid for your reputation, Franklin. What would happen to you. I was scared. I ran."

Betty covered her face.

"My God! I called the park from Luray. Told them someone had fallen. Then I drove home. You were at a lecture. I cried myself to sleep. You were late as usual. You didn't notice, and you haven't noticed since. You're always busy."

Franklin found his voice.

"Stupid. This is stupid. How can I put up with this. Go home. Don't tell anyone about it. I'll pick up Sari at the Mall. You go home and wait. You're ruining me!"

He added.

"And stop trying to think. I'll think of something. Just go. Leave."

Betty took her hands from her face and stood erect.

"I've a right to think!"

"As much right as pigs have to fly!"

Betty stepped towards him, fist raised. She looked into his eyes.

"I'll pick up Sari, for God's sake! You haven't seen her in two weeks. You wouldn't even recognize her. Leave *my* daughter out of this. I'll be home, you can come or not."

She dropped her arms and lowered her eyes. They filled with tears. She turned to hide them.

"I'm sorry, sorry. I thought I could help. God, Franklin, I'm in trouble. Can't you see? God help me!"

She sobbed and rushed out. She did not see Mike Hartness, silent behind the hall cabinet.

***

Bob Delaney pulled his car into the lot at Reagan National Airport. He switched off the engine and reached for Cecilia.

Cecilia sat back against the passenger door. Bob stared.

"Damn, you're beautiful!"

Cecilia backed away and frowned. Something was on her mind.

"Bob, you've worked a lot of investigations, right?"

Bob was nonplused. *What does this have to do with us?*

"Quite a few, why?"

"Have you ever hated anybody you were investigating?"

"What do you mean?"

"I mean, I told you about this 'funny water' case, and Madame Gauthier's death, and ..."

"Cecilia, you're not responsible for her death."

"I wish I could agree with you, but anyway, that's not what I'm talking about."

Her brow furrowed. She stared at the car seat.

"I mean, my father worked hard all his life. He has an accent, Bob, and his hands are rough. He has dirt under his fingernails. He came home dusty and tired. He worked hard for me and my mother. Two jobs! He always had two jobs so I could go to college."

Bob waited.

"Bob, what would you think of somebody rich, in a clean lab coat, a doctor with a big car, clean fingernails and a big desk. Somebody who wouldn't invite any 'accents,' like me to his parties. A rich Anglo who could kill three people and me too, almost, ... anyway *cause* them to die. And not give a *damn!* Not even want to know if they died or not."

Cecilia lifted her eyes and engaged Bob's. He reached for her. She added.

"Because his own damned nose was stuck so high in the air he couldn't see the bodies on the floor. All he worries about is getting his own fingernails dirty!"

"So?"

"So I hate this man, at least I hate who I think he is!"

"Cecilia, maybe you should step back. You're pretty involved."

"Of course I'm involved, whether I like it or not!"

"So what are you telling me?"

"I'm telling you that when I get to Tucson, I'm going to see this McElroy, and I'm not sure what I will do."

"Cecilia, he may not be guilty of anything. You're a pro. You'll stay objective, and keep control. Now come back here."

Bob drew Cecilia to him. She started to protest, but he drew her head to his shoulder. She felt the strength of his arm and started to relax.

"But Bob, I might ..."

Bob was done talking. He silenced her with his lips.

"Cecilia, I think we could ..."

She pulled away abruptly.

"Chihuahua! It's time. I can't miss my flight. I gotta go!"

She touched his lips with her fingers and opened the car door. Bob grabbed her bag. Cecilia was grateful for that. Her right arm tired easily.

They walked towards the terminal.

***

******

Chapter 24
Saturday, December 23

At home in Tucson, Cecilia arose at 11:00 a. m. After a slow shower, she heard her mother on the phone, planning the Christmas meal. Her father was in his chair.

Cecilia slipped out. Instantly the desert dust assaulted her. Startled, she realized that she had become accustomed to the humid air of the lush green East.

Her parent's "lawn" consisted of graded rocks, interspersed with several species of cacti, including a saguaro that was now taller than Cecilia. In its sparse shade grew a cluster of prickly pear. Two paloverdes shielded the family car from the overhead sun. Their green branches and stems were leafless, awaiting rain.

Across the street a tortilla stand beckoned. She wasn't hungry, but the thought of a green corn tamale, leaf-wrapped corn mush that enclosed a hidden pepper, tempted her. She decided to postpone the treat. Her resolve was tested when two Hispanic boys, tamales in hand, walked, munching, down the street.

She drove rapidly east and north to the Santa Catalina foothills. Unsure of her direction, she drove slowly. She was on target. Ahead and on her left was the *AMAH Clinic*.

The clinic was larger than she remembered. To the left of the main entrance an ocotillo-lined driveway led to a rear parking lot. The front lot had space for several dozen cars. The building had a new façade, a pleasing desert stucco.

Cecilia was not on official duty, but she wanted to see the clinic. Just inside the main door, a female in nurse's white stopped her.

"May I help you Miss?"

"I hope so. Is Dr. William McElroy the Director of this clinic."

The nurse-receptionist was not convinced that Cecilia's black hair and tannish skin belonged here.

"Yes, he is, but you would need an appointment to see him, and he's very busy. All of our patients are referrals. Who is your doctor?"

Cecilia improvised.

"It's not for me. It's for my mother. Is that Dr. McElroy?"

She pointed to the large gilt-framed portrait that dominated the foyer.

"Yes it is. Excuse me, but ..."

Cecilia quickly memorized the face in the portrait.

"Do you have a brochure for the clinic?"

Frowning, the receptionist indicated the exit.

"Your mother would have to get that from her doctor, if he's affiliated with us. I'm sorry but I have to ask you to ..."

Cecilia didn't wait for the ending.

"Thank you for your help."

The doors parted automatically and she stepped outside.

***

Across the road was a group of tall saguaros whose arms reached skyward at erratic angles. Other stands of these tall thick cacti dominated the rocky slopes of the surrounding foothills. Cecilia paused. She had forgotten the beauty of the desert. And not just the desert, for as her gaze lifted towards Mount Lemmon, she recalled the shaded spruce forest on its summit. That had been her only experience with northern forest before her assignment to Vermont.

She smiled to herself and relaxed. The clinic was forgotten. She was home.

The peace was disrupted by the sound of a motor. A cream-colored Mercedes appeared from behind the clinic, roared out the ocotillo-lined driveway, and turned towards the city. For a brief moment the driver was visible. His was the face in the portrait, Dr. McElroy.

The bastard! Cecilia jumped into her car.

He drove too fast for her. After several long blocks, he turned right. In his path was a bicycle. The rider swerved to avoid being hit, but the movement was too sharp. Bicycle and boy fell to the pavement. The Mercedes, unscraped, did not pause. By the time Cecilia arrived the boy, a Latino, had struggled to his feet, trousers torn and knees scraped. She pulled over.

"Are you OK muchacho?"

"Si Señora, OK."

Cecilia would have preferred "Señorita." *Am I that old?*

"Seguro? Are you sure? What's your name?"

"It's Pedro, Señora, and si, OK."

He pedaled away in the direction he had come.

She looked down the roadway. The cream-colored Mercedes was nowhere in sight.

***

Cecilia turned the car around and headed east. She drove with her left hand, while she flexed her right arm. It was still not normal, but it was much better. Her new destination was the firing range. She wanted to "sight" her new revolver.

At the range, she exercised her arm for some minutes. Then she found a station, arranged mufflers over her ears, and loaded five rounds into her Smith & Wesson. In front of her was a dull-black, man-shaped, target set at a "close" distance for her short-barreled gun. The revolver's shiny barrel reflected the sun's rays.

Cecilia made a "V" with her arms and pointed her weapon. She squeezed off two rounds.

"Crack, ... Crack."

The sounds had an unexpected effect. In an instant she was back inside Madame Gauthier's cabin firing at "Red Sweater." Then, Cecilia had been unaware of sound. Here and now, her two practice rounds, though muffled, brought back those suppressed "Cracks" that had dropped Red Sweater.

Disturbed, she aimed at the body of the target and squeezed off three more shots in rapid succession.

"Crack, ... Crack, ... Crack."

She examined the target. All the shots were high and left. Also, they were too scattered. Her "sight" was off, and she was not concentrating. Still, her arm felt good.

She shook herself, and reloaded five rounds. She squeezed them off in rapid succession.

"Crack, ... Crack, ... Crack, ... Crack, ... Crack."

This time the holes were centered where she had aimed, but they were even more dispersed than before. *Chihuahua, 'C!' Concentrate!*

She removed the mufflers from her ears, and loaded five fresh rounds. She stood silent while the man at the next station examined his results. They were way off the mark. His groan of disappointment was low, but audible.

Señor mio, Dios mio! His groan brought back Madame Gauthier's horrifying moan. *Dios!* She grimaced and replaced the muffler on her ears. She again made a "V" with her arms and aimed at the target's head.

"Crack."

That was for "mustache."

Cecilia was not smiling now. She clamped her jaws. She saw the broken form of Madame Gauthier on the floor, slippers still on. Anger flashed. She saw Dr. McElroy, the cause of everything, in his cream-colored Mercedes that her father could never afford. She saw the fallen Pedro, his bicycle on the ground. That rich snob doctor was above everyone. Suddenly she was back in Vermont.

He killed her, just as surely as if he was there!

The target in front of her appeared alive. It *was* McElroy. A black bitterness that had hidden unsuspected in her heart surged forth and overwhelmed her. Dr. McElroy was sneering at her.

You bastard!

Cecilia did not waver. Now Dr. McElroy sneered at Madame Gauthier's twisted body.

Too much. She focused on the sneer and fired the remaining rounds in quick succession.

"Crack, ... Crack, ... Crack, ... Crack."

Then she dropped her arms, breathing rapidly. Where was she? What had she done? Slowly she exhaled. The explosion of grief transmuted to rage left her shaking and confused. What had happened?

Chihuahua!

She checked the target. This time all five shots were within a radius of a few inches. The center of the paper head was shredded. Thank God, the target was only a target.

Dios mio! Am I capable of Murder?

Cecilia had met herself, and found a stranger. She leaned on the rail, cold and shivering under the hot desert sun.

***

Pierre Lachance, newly named "Pierre Lejeune," arrived at the target range just in time to see the dark-haired Hispanic girl blow away the head of the target. *Damned impressive.* Then he recognized her.

Mon Dieu! That's the policewoman, bleeding, dying on the floor at my grandmother's camp. *La femme flic! What is she doing here?*

He pocketed his own 9 mm semi-automatic. He could practice later.

He rushed to his car and headed back towards the clinic. He had to tell Dr. McElroy that Hernandez was in Tucson. André would want to know too. He pressed on the accelerator.

Back at the clinic, Pierre was disturbed further. The receptionist's description of the female visitor that morning matched Hernandez. She even had asked for Dr. McElroy by name!

What the hell was Hernandez doing in Tucson?

***

Back home, Cecilia parked under the paloverdes and crossed the street to the tortilla stand. She paid for her tamale. Then she peeled the corn leaves back, and bit into the soft corn mush. Her teeth hit the pepper. *Chihuahua!*

She hugged her mother and went to her bedroom. It was three hours later back East, but she could still catch Sam at the office. He worked Saturdays. She punched his number.

"Sam?"

He was taken aback.

"'C,' Where are you?"

"Home, Tucson. I stopped by McElroy's clinic."

"You're supposed to be on vacation."

"I know, but I was just driving around."

"How's the arm?"

"Pretty good. Can you get the DEA to check some phone records for me?"

Cecilia gave Sam the time that Mike Hartness had called from the pay phone by the Forster building. She continued.

"Sam, I saw Delaney in Washington. It *was* McElroy's funny water grant, but, the real reason I called is I'm afraid. Sam, I'm scared of what I might do."

She recounted her emotions at the firing range.

"I blew him away, just as if he'd been there ... four rounds! ... I pumped four rounds into him. I just kept going. ... Maybe I shouldn't work this case anymore. No! I've got to see that the bastard gets what's coming to him."

"'C,' you're scaring me. Look, you've been through a lot. You're on vacation. You'll be back soon. Meanwhile, relax. Don't go near that clinic. We'll talk when you get back. Stay away!"

"But!"

"No 'buts.' Just stay away from McElroy. Break a piñata or something and have a merry Christmas with your family."

"Feliz Navidad to you and your wife too, Sam. Thanks."

She hung up and went to her father. She threw her arms around his neck.

"Yo te amo, Papa."

It was good to be a little girl again, even for a few seconds.

***

Pierre sat at his desk in the clinic. The bare walls about him were devoid of decoration. There were no windows. The phone buzzed.

"Security, Pierre."

It was the receptionist.

"Dr. McElroy called. He won't be back. He'll call you from his car."

"Did you tell him anything?"

"No. He was in a hurry. I left that for you."

"OK. Thanks Paula."

Pierre stared at the bare plaster walls. The sight of Cecilia shook him. She brought back the vision of his grandmother's body, and "those guys" that had killed her. In Pierre's mind, he, André and Dr. McElroy had nothing to do with his grandmother's death. "Those Burlington guys" had killed her.

He had nothing personal against Hernandez. He himself had saved her and she had tried to save his grandmother. Though anonymous, his actions were public knowledge. Newspaper accounts of the "massacre" stated that the unknown visitor (Pierre) had saved the young agent's life.

But how had she connected Dr. McElroy to the massacre? This rattled him. He had known neither the *AMAH Clinic* nor its Director until he had reconciled with André after fleeing Burlington. How had she found McElroy? Pierre disliked the arrogant doctor, but he was grateful for this job far from Vermont.

Pierre "Lejeune" fingered the safety on his 9 mm semiautomatic. He was not a hood. He hoped he would not have to use this weapon.

***

Cecilia was in her bedroom when she heard the phone ring. Moments later, her mother called.

"Cecilia. It's for you."

She picked up. It was Sam.

"Cecilia, I want you to do me a favor."

"What's that?"

"Leave the gun at home. Don't carry it. You're on vacation. And for God's sake stay away from that doctor and the clinic. OK?"

"Don't worry, Sam."

"But I do worry. Promise me."

"OK, Sam"

Sam was relieved.

"Good. Now relax. I'll see you after Christmas."

"OK, Sam. Feliz Navidad."

Cecilia took the revolver from her backpack. She had promised Sam. But! Her lips hardened in a slim grim line. *You have no right to ask that, Sam. I'm fine. No slimeball like McElroy is going to make me do anything! I can handle myself.*

The revolver dropped back into the pack. She strode to the living room.

"Papa, can I borrow the car for about an hour."

"Your mother's fixing dinner. Don't stay any longer."

"Gracias, Papa."

Cecilia tossed her backpack onto the passenger seat, backed out of the driveway, and headed towards the *AMAH Clinic.*

***

A brown United Parcel Service van was stopped in front of the clinic. Cecilia pulled alongside. She met the driver as he returned to his truck and flashed her ID.

"U. S. Customs. Could I see the slip on the package you just delivered?"

"Sure Miss."

He handed Cecilia the clipboard. The shipment had originated in Washington, D. C. It was addressed to Dr. McElroy.

"Was there anything special about the package?"

"It says there 'frozen biological material.'"

"Did Dr. McElroy sign for it?"

"No. I gave it to the receptionist. She called someone to come get it right away."

"And?"

"I think she said, 'Dr, Hermann, the L-12 cells are here. Come get them.'"

Bingo!

She took the driver's name and number.

"Thanks for your help."

The driver left hurriedly. Now he was behind schedule.

***

Backpack in hand, Cecilia entered the clinic. The receptionist recognized her.

"Miss, you do not have an appointment. I must ask you to leave."

Cecilia flashed her badge. She could be cold too.

"U. S. Customs. I'm here to see Dr. McElroy."

The receptionist was undaunted.

"He's not here, and he hasn't been here since you came this morning. Leave your name and number and he will call you."

"Is Dr. Hermann here?"

"He just left for the day."

"I'll stop back tomorrow. Tell the good doctors that Cecilia Hernandez needs to talk with them."

She stepped to the door without waiting for the reply.

For the second time that day she paused before the scenic desert. The arms of the tall saguaros across the road pointed in different directions. Likewise, Cecilia's thoughts led to different options. She decided. Spinning about she returned to the receptionist.

Cecilia did not know Dr. Hermann or his car. She took a chance.

"Dr. Hermann hasn't left yet. His car is still in the lot. Please buzz him."

The receptionist, off guard, picked up the phone.

"Dr. Hermann?"

"Yes"

"This is Paula, at the desk. I'm sorry to bother you but there is a Ms. Hernandez, a U. S. Customs Agent, who insists on seeing you."

Dr. Hermann had just logged in the vials of L-12 in the freezer. On his bench, in a row, were eight T-25 flasks that contained media for cell growth. Dr. McElroy wanted lots of L-12 cells right away. Tomorrow was Christmas Eve, and he had to start the cells growing. They'd be ready the day after Christmas.

"Tell Ms. Hernandez I can't see her now. If she works Sundays I can see her tomorrow morning at ten. Otherwise, she can see me after Christmas."

Paula relayed the message.

Cecilia smiled.

"Ten o'clock tomorrow will be fine. I'll be here."

She stepped out in time to see a brown Honda leaving the lot. She had a clear view. Another driver, another face recognized!

Dios mio! The grandson! Lachance!

She flung her backpack on the seat and pulled out after him.

***

Pierre drove slowly. He needed to think. Ahead, the low jagged peaks of the Tucson Mountains pointed to a flaming red sky streaked with broad gray bands layered with light pink clouds. The natural beauty was lost on Pierre. Somehow, the U. S. Agents had traced him to Tucson. Somehow, Hernandez knew about Dr. McElroy's dealings. What else did she know?

He left the valley, and drove upwards towards Gates Pass. The Honda climbed with effort. Then he noticed the gray car with Arizona plates behind him. Was it his imagination, or had that car been parked at the clinic?

He drove higher and left the valley's desert dust. Now the ground was rocky and spotted with tall ribbed saguaros. The dry beds of occasional streams were outlined by strips of paloverde and mesquite. He accelerated, but the gray car kept pace.

Pierre turned north onto a gravel road. His eyes went from the lonely road ahead to the rear view mirror and back. It was dusk, and visibility had diminished. He switched on his headlights. Car lights appeared in his mirror. He was sure they belonged to the gray car.

Ahead was a stop sign. He stopped and then turned east onto a paved roadway, headed back towards Tucson. Ahead and below in the river valley, the lights of the city shimmered and sparkled. He pulled off the roadway behind a grove of mesquite. He extinguished his lights and waited.

Behind him, car lights stopped and then turned east on the pavement as he had done. The lights approached and passed, headed towards Tucson. It was the gray car.

The road behind Pierre was empty. Ahead, the tail lights of the gray car were dim red spots, just visible in the dusk. He left his own lights off and followed the dim red spots.

***

The road was deserted. Cecilia shrugged. Lachance had disappeared. She was "0 for 2" in trailing cars this day. There was nothing for her but to continue back to Tucson.

She gasped when she realized that she had been gone two hours. Her mother was holding dinner. And she had promised her father she'd be back! She reached in her pack for her cell phone. Then she remembered that she had left it in Bethesda with her cousin. Ahead was a shopping center and a phone.

The lot was filled with cars of Christmas shoppers and she had to park a distance away and walk. At the mall entrance, she found a pay phone.

"Papa, I'm sorry I'm late. I'm west of the city, coming from Gates Pass. ... I'm really sorry ..."

"OK, Querida mia, but hurry. Mama t'espera."

Cecilia walked back to her car. A paper advertisement flapped under the wiper on her windshield. Irritated, she grabbed it to throw away, but it was no advertisement. It was a note.

I know who you are Hernandez. If you make me a deal, I may be able to help you get your man. Be alone at that pay phone at 10:15 a. m. tomorrow. Don't talk to Sam Jones or anyone or no deal.   *Napoleon.*

She scanned the lot. A family loaded their van with gifts. A teen and his girl were arguing. There were people, coming and going, but there was no brown Honda.

Still the note must be from Lachance! It had to be! Somehow, he had spotted her. Cecilia frowned and clenched her fist. Maybe he could help break this case wide open. Maybe she could nail that snob McElroy!

***

******

Chapter 25
Sunday, December 24

Mike Hartness opened his eyes and stretched. He struggled to the bathroom and waited for the water to warm. He shaved quickly. Not a scratch! He was in the shower when the phone rang.

Wet and irritated, he left a trail of moist footprints on the hardwood floor.

"Yes?"

"Mike, is that you?"

It was his mentor. He changed tone.

"Dr. Lawrence?"

"Mike, I was wondering if you would like to celebrate Christmas Eve with us. Betty is fixing turkey and the trimmings. Sari and a friend will be here."

"What time, Sir?"

"We'll be eating at seven o'clock. If you come early, we could do some work together. I have ideas for our next L-12 paper."

Dr. Lawrence wanted Mike to accept. Betty would hesitate to argue with him in front of his Postdoc.

"I'd be happy to come! I'll bring a gift."

"It's not necessary, but do what you want."

"I'll bring something. Sir, should I invite Monique?"

"No, Mike. I know you defend her, but she may not be with us long."

This was not the time to press Monique's case.

"All right Dr. Lawrence. I'll be there at five."

"Good. And Mike, bring that graphic calculator of yours. I have some figures I want to check."

"I will, and thanks."

Mike hummed and stepped back into the shower.

***

Dr. Lawrence called downstairs to Betty.

"Mike Hartness is coming to dinner with us tonight. We'll need one more setting."

He did not hear her reply, but turned and flipped the pages of a scientific journal. This article was by Johnson. He had to understand it by five o'clock.

Betty appeared at the door.

"Franklin, you said you would do the thinking. Have you?"

"About what?"

The color rose in Betty's cheeks.

"About me, your wife, about John Martin and Stony Man?"

Franklin's eyes returned to the Johnson article. He had lost his place. Eyes down, he mumbled.

"Not now. I'll talk to you later."

He waved his hand in dismissal and tried to concentrate.

Betty's face hardened.

She started to speak but Sari appeared.

"Mom, Mattie says she's not hungry, but she will eat cereal with me. Could you make us hot chocolate?"

Betty turned to her daughter and left.

***

At her apartment, Jeannine, loaded with bags for Christmas pies, stepped into the kitchen.

A waiting Monique jumped up and exclaimed.

"Mike's not the only cheat, McElroy is too. And he was Mike's mentor. It looks like he taught him well!"

She waved her arms in a wide arc. Jeannine jumped back and one of the bags split. Apples rolled on the floor.

Jeannine stooped to retrieve them, but Monique pulled her upright.

The apples kept rolling.

Monique ignored them and shoved a journal in front of Jeannine.

"This is McElroy's article. Look at Figure 4. It's wrong. It can't be right."

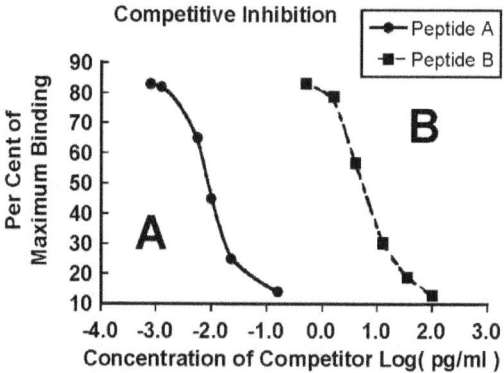

"I'm not a biologist. What's wrong with it?"

"I'll tell you. This is a competition assay. We do them all the time in the lab. They show how much of a 'competitor reagent' is needed to inhibit binding by a radioactive 'probe.'"

"I don't follow you."

"It doesn't matter. All you need to see is that the horizontal axis shows the concentration of the reagents, and that the concentrations increase from left to right. So smaller concentrations are to the left. See, A's circles are to the left of B's squares. It takes smaller amounts of A to inhibit binding than B."

Jeannine was hesitant.

"I heard what you said, but I don't follow it."

"You don't have to. All you need to know is that the circles for Peptide A aren't threefold dilutions. That means they've been faked!"

"Why do you say that?"

"They're not spaced right. I made a new graph with horizontal lines between the points. With threefold dilutions, the spaces should all be the same length."

She added.

"Look at the concentrations for Peptide A. They should have equal step widths, but they don't."

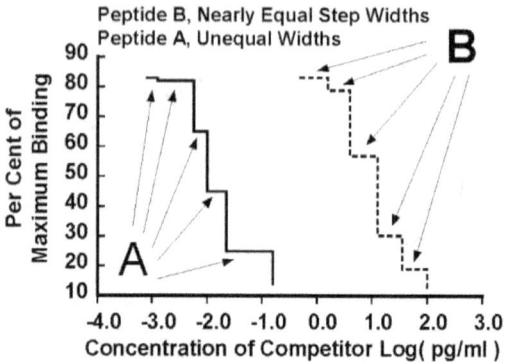

Monique kept on.

"Peptide B looks OK. The spaces (step widths) between the lines are all close to the same length. They *must* be, because when we *dilute* the concentration of peptide, we do it by *fixed* factors. In this experiment the dilution was by *three's*."

She continued.

"But Peptide A's points aren't evenly spaced. They are not threefold dilutions. When McElroy plotted Peptide A, he made up the points but he forgot that the points had to be evenly spaced."

Jeannine stooped to recover two of the apples and bagged them. She whistled.

"Monique, you'd make a damn good detective."

"It's biology. Each concentration *HAS* to have a ratio *three* times the previous one!"

"*HAS* to? But what about error? The dilutions can't be exact."

"That's true, we don't know how well we dilute, but we plot the ratios *as if the dilutions are exact*. There's nothing else to do. The only error in the *horizontal distances* should be from plotting."

The last errant apple went into the sack.

"I see. Let's go upstairs to the computer. You can measure the distances between the lines, and read them to me."

Jeannine bounced up the stairs. Monique found a magnifying glass. She measured the distances and read the numbers to Jeannine. Together they examined the results.

	Monique's Measured Widths. Should be Log(3) = 0.48	Calculated Dilution Value. Should be 3
Peptide A	.20	1.6
	.65	4.5
	.25	1.8
	.35	2.2
	.85	7.1
Peptide B	.50	3.2
	.40	2.5
	.50	3.2
	.45	2.8
	.45	2.8

The dilution values for Peptide B ranged from 2.5 to 3.2. All would round to 3, the dilution value. The points for B reflected the correct dilution.

Not so the values for Peptide A. They ranged from 1.6 to 7.1. None was close to three. These were not dilution values. When McElroy plotted the fake points, he had forgotten that the *horizontal* distances between the points *had to be the same.*

Jeannine frowned and tossed her head.

"Monique, you've got to get into statistics! You're a natural, like John!"

But Monique said nothing. She stared at the graphs. Her face was pale. After a minute, she looked up to see Jeannine biting her lip. Their thoughts were the same.

Is there no end to the cheating?

***

Monique and Jeannine stared at each other, the jangling ring of the phone pierced the somber silence. Monique picked up.

"Hello."

"Monique, it's Cecilia, I'm in Tucson."

Monique looked at the clock. It was eleven. In Tucson it would be 8:00 a.m.

Cecilia continued.

"I want you to do me a favor."

"Yes?"

"These are my partner's phone numbers, home and office. His name is Sam Jones. He's at Rouses Point, New York."

Monique wrote down the numbers. Cecilia continued breathlessly.

"I've got a break on the McElroy case. I'm meeting someone in a couple of hours. I wanted to tell someone, so that's you."

"Why not call your partner?"

"Because he wouldn't approve. He'd want me to check things first, have backup, but there's no time. I want to fry this creep."

That scared Monique.

"Can't you wait? You're on vacation."

"No. Look, I wanted someone to know. If I haven't called you back by four this afternoon, seven your time, call Sam for me. He could be at the office or home. Tell him that Lachance is at the clinic in Tucson. Tell him that Lachance wants to roll over, and that I went to meet him. Will you do that for me?"

"Yes, but ..."

"Gracias, hermana!"

The line went dead.

***

There had been no time to tell Cecilia about McElroy's faked research. Monique recounted the call to Jeannine. Jeannine jumped up.

"My God! She's already been shot once, damn it. Call Sam Jones right now!"

But it was Christmas Eve. At Sam's home there was no answer, and at work, they only reached his message machine.

They left a message and their number. It was all they could do, except call Cecilia back.

They reached her mother.

"Cecilia's gone out for the morning. She won't be back before this afternoon. Can I have her call you?"

"Yes, Mrs. Hernandez, please have her call us as soon as she gets back."

Jeannine hung up. Monique stared.

***

The firing range was on the other side of town from her destination, but Cecilia needed to calm her nerves and build her confidence. She had the target set at "close" range. She placed a box of ammo on the stand, and loaded five rounds into her revolver. She took aim.

"Crack, ... Crack, ... Crack, ... Crack, ... "

She squeezed off the shots in succession. When she examined the target, she was pleased. All holes were within a radius of six inches, centered in the middle of the body. She was not trying any fancy "head" shots as on the previous day. She reloaded.

"Crack, ... Crack, ... Crack, ... Crack, ... Crack."

Cecilia liked the feel of her new Smith & Wesson. If anything, the grip felt better than her former weapon. She relaxed and reloaded.

"Crack, ... Crack, ... Crack, ... Crack, ... Crack."

She had a rhythm. It felt good. She was calm and in control. The target was just a target, there was no flashback to the image of Dr. McElroy. Everything was fine. She reloaded the chambers and flipped the cylinder shut. She left the firing range.

***

Cecilia arrived at the Mall at 9:30. The stores opened at 10, and few cars were parked in the lot. The Christmas decorations cheered her. It was Sunday and also Christmas Eve.

The "rendezvous" phone was on an exterior wall. From it she could see inside the Mall. A window display of bright cotton sweaters caught her eye. She still needed a present for her father.

Chihuahua!

She had forgotten Dr. Hermann! She stepped to the phone and called the *AMAH Clinic*. There was no answer. After six buzzes, the message machine clicked on. She spoke.

"Dr. Hermann, this is Cecilia Hernandez. I'm sorry I can't be there today at 10 o'clock. I would like to reschedule. Thank you."

She scanned the parking lot. Cars were arriving, but there was no trace of Pierre's brown Honda. She checked her watch. Seven minutes to go, not enough time to buy the sweater for her father.

Cecilia stared at the phone.

***

The holiday spirit had left the apartment. Monique stood listlessly as Jeannine peeled the Granny Smith apples. She stopped and put the knife down.

"I can't make these pies now. We need to do something!"

"We could visit the hospital. We may not get there tomorrow."

The hospital was not a cheerful prospect, but it was better than staying in the apartment. They walked slowly under a bright sun. The air was cold, but there was no wind. Over the sidewalk, the motionless branches of the Gingkoes stretched stiff and bare. Monique had memorized those intricate forked patterns. She knew this route by heart. She could have walked it blindfolded. Every day she had visited John with the same result. No change.

Jeannine, too, knew the route well. She had strolled under these same Gingkoes with John. How their lives had changed in just a few weeks. She put her arm around Monique.

"We'll see this through. At least we're in this together."

For the first time on that dreary walk Monique smiled.

***

Monique and Jeannine entered the hospital. They took the near elevator to the third floor. The nurse on duty knew them both.

"Any change?"

The nurse shook her head.

They started down the hallway towards John's room, but as they turned the corner, their path was blocked. Monique gasped.

"Mike!"

"Well, well. Both of you at the same time! You gals look good today."

Monique was silent. Jeannine spoke.

"What the devil are you doing here?"

"Just seeing how my friend John is doing. Did you give Monique my message?"

Jeannine's eyes flashed. Mike grinned.

"Don't worry. I'm leaving. You know you're a real babe when you're mad. I like that."

He turned and sauntered down the hallway. Monique stood shaking. Jeannine gritted her teeth and embraced her.

***

Agent Turner shuffled his papers. He looked at his file on the John Martin case. Damn it, if Martin died, it could be manslaughter, or worse.

He put the file away and closed his desk. It was Christmas Eve. He had a long drive to Maryland, and he needed to buy gifts for his wife and her mother.

***

225

******

Chapter 26
Sunday, December 24

Cecilia waited by the pay phone. Activity at the mall picked up as new shoppers arrived. As she stared at the mute instrument, a well-dressed woman stopped and spoke.

"Excuse me, are you using that phone?"

Cecilia started to panic.

"Rrring, ..."

Relieved, she grabbed the phone and waved the woman away.

"Hernandez."

"Good. Listen. Get in your car, leave the lot by the palm tree. Turn right. Drive five blocks. Wait by the phone next to the motel with the Flamingo sign. You have ten minutes."

The phone went dead.

Cecilia ran to her car.

***

Cecilia took five minutes to reach the motel and locate the phone. This neighborhood was dramatically different from the upscale shopping mall. Pieces of broken bottles lay unswept on the sidewalk, and the motel appeared abandoned. Its faded pink stucco was shaded by several mesquite trees, and the grounds were not attended. Against one fence, dried pale tumbleweed had accumulated.

Across the street, the nearest house had windows nailed and boarded. Next to its darkened entrance, several male Latinos leaned against the wall. Their impassive stares made her uncomfortable.

She stepped to the phone, but it had been vandalized. The coin return had been jimmied, and there was nothing to pick up, except a wasted wire that drooped from the side of the box. What had been a phone was a useless artifact. Apprehensive Cecilia turned back towards her car. At the same time she slipped her hand into her pack and groped for her weapon. She felt a tug at her arm.

"Excuse me, Señorita Hernandez?"

She looked down at a boy, no more than 10 years old.

"Yes, that's me."

The boy thrust an envelope at her.

"The Señor said to give you this."

He fled behind the motel fence before Cecilia could speak. She looked around her. One of the men across the way stared at her. He grinned.

Cecilia looked down at the envelope. It was empty. She turned it over. On the back, printed in block letters was "ROOM 14." *Is this a trap?* She looked up. Across the street, the man still stared.

She strode to the entrance of the motel. The once pink adobe-like surface was faded and discolored, but the entranceway was clean. There was no one behind the desk. She entered the dimly-lit corridor. Cecilia's conscience screamed. She was violating every safety rule she could think of. She knew Sam would have stopped her, but she pushed forward. *He's her grandson. I know he won't harm me.*

The door to room 14 was closed. Nearby in the hallway was a fixture with a dim bulb. Cecilia knew that when she opened the door she would be framed, a silhouette in a luminous rectangle. Less confident, she gripped the revolver, but kept it in her pack. With her left hand she tried the knob. It turned easily. She pushed the door, and spoke into the darkness.

"Pierre. Are you there? It's Cecilia Hernandez."

"Ne bouges pas! Stop. Stay right where you are. Don't move!"

The interior of the room was all shadows. The dim light from the hallway illuminated the space directly in front of her, but Cecilia could distinguish nothing in the far corner. She herself was outlined in the doorway, like the target at the firing range. She thought of jumping to one side, but did not.

"Pierre, it's OK. You can trust me. I know you saved my life."

"Don't move, I've got a gun. Take your hand out of that pack. Slowly! And leave your gun in it!"

Pierre's voice quavered as he spoke, and was high-pitched. Cecilia realized his fear constituted a real danger. She spoke.

"OK. OK. There. It's OK. You can trust me. I knew your grandmother."

Her voice caught.

"I know you loved her. I did too. She talked about you a lot."

She withdrew her hand, empty, from the pack, but kept a grip on the pack itself. Her eyes became accustomed to the dim light. She distinguished the dark curtains over the window and a large chair in the corner. Pierre's voice, she was sure it was he, came from behind that chair.

"Look, I went to see my grandmother, that's all. So I killed that mec, Mason, but it was him or me. He would have got me, and he sure as hell would've finished you."

"Pierre, if you turn yourself in, nobody will hold that against you. God knows I thank you! But you're not telling me everything. If you're not involved, why are you here at the clinic? You've got to be straight with me."

Once again Cecilia thought of stepping away from the door frame, but again thought better of it. She stood there, a target, still convinced that Pierre would not harm her. She persisted.

"Look, you're not the guy we want. We're not after you. We want McElroy. Help us get him and we'll see what we can do."

Pierre was relieved. Cecilia appeared unaware of André and the Montreal side of things.

"I want to stay in the U. S. I did you and Jones a big favor. I need to know if I can stay. There's nothing on me here except this mess."

"As far as we know that's right. But I can't promise anything. You know that. Sam Jones would say the same thing if he was here. I *can* tell you that Lise Jordan is clean. Nobody's investigating her."

Cecilia felt his sigh of relief. She continued.

"Look, we already know you're here in Tucson. Help us get McElroy. It's your best bet. Believe me, it's your only option."

As she spoke, Cecilia's eyes, more accustomed to the darkness, made out Pierre's hand on the back of the stuffed chair. Against the lighter upholstery, she could see an ominous outline, a semi-automatic 9 mm! She stiffened. Pierre *did* have another option. Her muscles bunched, ready to spring sideways, but she stayed still and kept talking.

"What's McElroy up to?"

"I haven't been here that long. I guess he's collecting fake Medicare payments, inventing patients that don't exist, and he's probably treating people with untested drugs here and in Mexico."

"You guess? Probably?"

"I can find out."

"How did you get to know McElroy?"

Pierre lied. He would not mention André.

"That man at my grandmother's cabin had the phone number in his pocket."

"Is McElroy moving illegal drugs from Mexico."

"Not that I know."

"Pierre, if you're not straight with me I won't be able to help you."

"I don't know if he is or not. I don't think so."

"Then what can you give us?"

"I can work for you on the inside, and I know where he keeps the records. You'll never find them. They're not in Tucson."

"When do you think you might have something?"

"Be at the pay phone at the mall next Wednesday. Alone. Same time. Wait for my call, 'Napoleon.' And don't look for me at the clinic or you'll screw us both. He knows you're here."

Cecilia heard rustling behind the chair. She still had not seen Pierre's face. There was an increasing tightness in his voice.

"Keep your hand out of that pack. Now back outside and shut the door, ... slowly. Stand still. Count to twenty before you move."

Cecilia did as she was told. At the count of "eight" she heard a car motor. She pushed into the room. The formerly dark unit was flooded with shafts of light that streamed through the open back door. Desert dust and pollen outlined the edges of the beams. She dashed to the door and peered out. She blinked and tried to focus in the bright sunlight. Except for dust the back alley was empty.

***

The motel desk was still unoccupied when Cecilia left. Outside, one of the Latinos had crossed to her side of the street and now stood, leaning against the vandalized phone. His eyes dropped to Cecilia's ankles and then reached up the length of her body. She paid him no heed.

She was relieved when the car started right away. She accelerated from the curb.

Cecilia relaxed. She could buy the sweater for her father and make it home in time to help her mother.

Meanwhile her mind raced. The Health and Human Services Office of the Inspector General would be interested in Medicare fraud, and the Department of Justice too. They might use the FBI to investigate. It would be possible to prosecute McElroy under the False Claims Act, and if he used unauthorized drugs on human subjects the FDA could jump in. The DEA was already interested in McElroy because of the Mason gang's narcotics connection. The jurisdictional problems spun Cecilia's head.

Damn it, the Customs Service had to be involved. It had to be. *It's my case, Damn it! That scuz McElroy has got to go down! I have Lachance. No one else can talk to him. Chihuahua. He saved me once. He won't hurt me!*

At the mall, "Silent Night" played through the loudspeakers. Cecilia saw the sweater she wanted in the window. She decided to buy it. It would look good on her father.

***

When Cecilia returned home her mother came running. Breathless, she held her daughter at arm's length, and examined her.

"Niña, are you all right? Where have you been? Everyone's worried for you. Sam Jones called. And that girl from Washington too. They want you to call them back right away. What were you doing? Where were you?"

"Don't worry Mama. I'm fine. It's nothing."

Her father looked up from the television.

"I'm OK Papa, go back to your football game."

Her father returned to the TV. His team was losing.

Cecilia hugged her mother.

"You know I love you Mama. Let me go upstairs and call Sam and the girls. Don't worry! Go back to the kitchen. I'll be down to help you in a few minutes."

She bounced up the stairs to the bedroom. She checked her watch. It was three o'clock - six o'clock back east. She punched Sam's home number first.

***

The clock on the kitchen wall said six. Jeannine's hands were white with flour. She pursed her lips and blew upwards. The reddish hair over her eyes wafted off her forehead. She could see again. She continued to roll the dough, while Monique peeled the apples. They were both laughing.

They laughed by design. The "sorrowful circuits" of their respective brains were overloaded by recent events, Jeannine's loss of her fellowship, Monique's likely loss of her Postdoc,

232

John's coma, Mrs. Lawrence's push, McElroy's fraudulent data, Cecilia's danger, and most disturbing of all, Mike's sudden interest in John's condition!

The cumulative effect was overwhelming. They could either cry or laugh. They chose to laugh and lose themselves in preparing a feast!

When she heard that Jeannine was making her own dough for apple pies, Monique decided to add the traditional Quebec meat pie, tourtière, to the holiday menu. On the way home from the hospital, she bought chopped meat and spices.

As Monique peeled the green-tinted apples, she began to sing.

"Il est né le divine enfant, jouez haut bois, ..."

Jeannine knew the French carol, but not the words. She hummed along as Monique continued.

"Depuis plus de quatre mils ans, nous le promettaient les prophètes."

Their reverie was interrupted by the sound of the phone.

Jeannine could only hear Monique's side of the conversation.

"That's wonderful! Thank God! ... Should we come over there right now? ... No? ... OK ... Thanks very much. ... Yes, Thank you. ... We'll be here all day. Tomorrow too. ... Yes! ... Thanks again. ... Thanks, Bye."

Monique collapsed, breathless, back on her chair. Jeannine raised her eyebrows in anticipation. Monique smiled at her, brown eyes overflowing.

"That was the nurse at the hospital, the one with blond hair. It's John. He's started to respond. He gripped the doctor's hand and he blinked his eyes. He's coming out of the coma. She'll keep us informed."

"Should we go over there?"

"She said no. The doctor is with him now. If there are further developments, she'll call us. I told her we'd be here."

Jeannine's moist blue pupils met Monique's wet brown eyes. For a full five seconds they were silent. Then without releasing her gaze, Monique intoned the next line of her Christmas carol.

" ... nous attendions cet heureux temps."

She smiled at Jeannine as she translated.

" ... we were awaiting this happy time!"

Laughter filled the kitchen with hope. Jeannine blew the hair from her eyes and resumed rolling the pie dough. Monique, humming, arose and set the temperature on the oven. Then she turned and embraced Jeannine, flour and all.

"Joyeux Noël, Jeannine!"

"Merry Christmas, Monique!"

***

Mike Hartness was not happy he had been seen at the hospital. He had wanted to scout John's room undetected. Moreover he did not like to see Jeannine and Monique together. Either woman by herself could be dangerous, but together they posed a real threat.

He was due at the Lawrence's before seven. He had said he would bring something, but had decided against a gift for Mrs. Lawrence. Dr. Lawrence was furious with her for pushing John, but a gift for Sarah would please Mrs. Lawrence without offending his mentor. He stopped at the local mall and bought a set of stretch gloves and scarf, "one size fits all." For Mrs. Lawrence's sake, he paid extra for gold wrapping.

It was mid afternoon, the Lawrence house was only minutes away. He had lots of time, so he walked to the Food Court and bought a slice of Pizza. While he ate, a heavily-laden man arrived at the next table. Mike watched him deposit his packages on the floor. The face was familiar.

Of course! The agent who had done the interviews about John's fall at Stony Man.

Mike stood and spoke.

"Agent Turner, you don't remember me, but I'm at Fairland University. You interviewed me about John Martin's fall at Stony Man Mountain."

Agent Turner did recall Mike Hartness, and he did not like him. Further, Turner was weary from last-minute shopping and he was due at his wife's mother's in Rockville. He did not want to spend Christmas Eve with his wife's mother, and he damned well didn't want to spend time talking to Mike. He growled.

"I'm not working now."

"I understand, but it will just take a moment. There's something you should know."

Turner's professionalism asserted itself.

"What's that?"

"You implied there was a woman with John Martin when he fell. I know who she was."

Agent Turner studied Mike's face. Mike continued to lie.

"It was Jeannine Ryan, I overheard Monique talking to her."

"What did she say?"

"She said, 'Jeannine, you're my friend, I would never tell anyone that you pushed him!'"

"Are those her exact words?"

"Pretty much, yes. I was shocked. I couldn't forget."

"Where were you?"

"I was in my office at the lab. The door was cracked. Monique was outside in the lab, on the phone."

"When was this?"

"Maybe a day after you interviewed me and Dr. Lawrence."

"Maybe?"

"No. It was late the same day."

"Which is it?"

"Late the same day. I'm sure now."

"Why didn't you call me?"

"I didn't want to get involved. I like Monique."

Agent Turner looked at his tray. *You ingratiating bastard, you only like yourself, but even a rat like you can be right.*

"OK. Don't tell anyone what you told me. I'll get your statement after Christmas."

Mike was no fool. Agent Turner disliked him, but he was sure Turner believed him.

Agent Turner grappled with his packages and left.

***

Mike congratulated himself. He would "rescue" Mrs. Lawrence, and earn Dr. Lawrence's gratitude. Accused, Jeannine would be too busy defending herself to protect Monique. And Agent Turner would be happy that his intuition had proved correct. The only possible hitch to Mike's plan was John Martin. He knew the truth, but he was in a coma. All Mike needed was for the coma to last a few more days.

He arrived at Dr. Lawrence's house and knocked on the door framed by red and green lights. Dr. Lawrence answered and called over his shoulder.

"Betty, Mike's here."

If there was a response, it was inaudible to Mike. He held out the gold-wrapped box.

"Here's something for Sarah."

Dr. Lawrence called out again.

"Sari, there's a present for you!"

Sari emerged from the kitchen and took the present. Through the kitchen door, Mike saw Mrs. Lawrence. She did not look up. Dr. Lawrence grabbed Mike's arm and pulled him towards the study. He looked back.

"Betty, Mike's thirsty. Will you fix us some drinks."

Back in the kitchen, Sari heard her mother mutter.

"Merry Christmas?"

"Mom, are you all right?"

Betty shook her head. Her hands quivered as she filled two glasses with ice.

***

******

Chapter 27
Tuesday, December 26

She was an actress, forty years old and still very beautiful. The vanity lights around her mirror were unforgiving, and most women, even in their youth, could not have tolerated their utter honesty. Every line, every blemish in the skin, was revealed in their bright reflection. For years she had faced her image unafraid and confident. That particular day, vividly recorded in her memory, she had looked in the mirror as usual. Her skin was fine, and her perfectly shaped breasts stood revealed, as ever, flawless even to her critical eye. But when she had placed her hand under the left breast to elevate it, she had felt the small lump. It was so small, it couldn't be a matter for concern. She was sure it would go away. She willed it to disappear. *Go away!* But the next day it was still there, and the next.

Then she realized that it must be a harmless cyst, and she willed that too. It had to be harmless. A week later she had seen her physician-friend in Los Angeles to have it aspirated. His brow had furrowed and she had known right away that he was concerned. When the test results came back, he had driven to her home to talk with her face to face. He recommended surgery, which he explained using unfamiliar terms like estrogen receptors and Tamoxifen and positive nodes, as well as other words that she neither understood nor cared to.

The bottom line was that if she were lucky and the "margins" were negative (whatever that meant), only a portion of her breast, a "lump" would be removed, but otherwise she would lose her breast and have a "total" mastectomy not a lumpectomy. She would not find out which until she awoke from the anesthesia. *Dear God!* It was only a question of the degree of mutilation!

Her physician-friend had stressed that her life was important to her admirers as well as herself, and that she could continue her career. She had always used a double to do the nude scenes anyway. Only *she* would know the difference. Even her director need know nothing. As her physician, and friend, he wanted to schedule the surgery as soon as possible.

Never before had she thought of him as lacking understanding. He did not realize that in the past, no matter how well-formed the nude double, she had always *known* that she was more beautiful. She shuddered. Now she would know the opposite. She would be a fraud, a misshapen fraud. She had asked for time to settle on a day for the operation. He had told her not to delay.

When he left, she had retreated to her bedroom in a deep depressive mood. Then a fellow actress and confidante had called, and she had shared her misery. What hope that call had brought! Her friend had been anorexic, and this wonderful doctor at this wonderful private clinic in Arizona had cured her. Yes, he treated breast cancer too, and he was wonderfully open-minded! He used wonderful drugs that the medical establishment did not want anyone using because then surgeons would not make any money. And wasn't the courage of this doctor wonderful! And the clinic was wonderfully confidential. With the hope that phone call brought her, she hadn't minded her friend's "wonderful" enthusiasm, although as soon as she hung up she questioned how any medicine could be so "wonderful."

Nonetheless, she had called the *AMAH Clinic*, and here she was, the day after Christmas, traveling incognito, with her bodyguard driving the car. In particular, her Los Angeles physician-friend was unaware of her whereabouts or intentions. She would preserve her beauty at all costs.

Her bodyguard turned the car into the ocotillo-lined driveway, and brought it to a halt at the rear of the clinic building. It was not yet 5:00 a.m. and still dark. The shadowy forms of the sentinel-like saguaros stood mute and motionless as she stepped out of the vehicle. They did not applaud, but they were old friends. One of her favorite films had been shot at Old Tucson, to the west of the city, and well to the west of the clinic.

She processed towards the light that shone through the aperture of the door that opened to welcome her. She stepped inside. In spite of her apprehension, she rose to the occasion. Her entrance was grand. She knew she was beautiful.

Dr. McElroy was overwhelmed by her presence. He gave his speech with aplomb.

"Your name while you are here is 'Miss Jones.' The only people allowed in your room will be myself, Dr. Hermann, and nurse Hudson. Your bodyguard will have the room next to yours. He's carrying in your belongings. Let me assure you that every possible convenience, consistent with your medical treatment, will be yours. We at the clinic are here to serve you, and we are very grateful for the amount of your initial contribution. Your generosity in support of our research will benefit not only yourself, but others."

Then he smiled with a bow.

"Miss Jones, if I may be permitted an observation, although I would not have thought it possible, you are much more beautiful than in your films."

He turned away.

"Nurse Hudson, please see that Miss Jones is comfortable. I'm sure she's tired."

Looking once again at Miss Jones, he added.

"Dr. Hermann and I will do our initial medical examination at 10:00 a.m., if you are sufficiently rested."

Miss Jones nodded. She followed the nurse down the empty hallway.

***

Dr. McElroy walked to the other wing of the clinic. The lights were on in the laboratory where Dr. Hermann was already up and working. A cot with rumpled bedding was in the far corner. He had not left the building for two days. Dr. Hermann needed a shave.

"How's the L-12 going?"

"Good. I've tried our preparation in the sensitive mouse strain, and found no allergic effects so far. I need more time though."

"We haven't got more time."

"Then why don't we use preparations with the A-11 cells that you conned out of Dr. Lawrence?"

"Because Hartness says that A-11 is a bust. He faked the data."

"Hell, what was he trying to prove by that?"

"Using it to impress Lawrence I guess, and buying time to find something else."

"Well, who says L-12 is any good."

"Hartness does, and he wouldn't dare lie to me."

"Then damn it, let's take our time and check L-12 on some Mexicans first."

"Can't. She's here already."

"Look, Mackie, this is no psychological crap like anorexia, this is cancer. There's no imagination here! We don't have any idea of what this will do. We're not even close to doing a Phase I trial!"

"Don't get technical on me. We've managed before. Besides, she's donated a million to the foundation, and that's just the start."

"We should wait."

"We can't wait, damn it!"

"All right, All right, if you say so. I'll have some cell preparations for you tomorrow."

"Fine. Meanwhile, we'll examine Miss Jones at 10:00 a.m. today."

"Who?"

"That's her name while she's here."

"Oh."

Dr. Hermann changed the subject.

"What will I do if that agent Hernandez calls again."

"Put her off until after tomorrow. I've already got Pierre working on that problem."

Dr. Hermann nodded.

"One more thing, the homeopathic preparations you wanted are ready."

"Good. Get a shower and shave, and put on a suit. No lab outfit. We see Miss Jones at 10:00. I'm going to the office for a nap."

Dr. McElroy yawned, and head lowered, headed out the lab. Dr. Hermann rubbed his rough chin. Then he turned back to his L-12 cell suspensions.

***

Pierre arrived at work later that morning. Dr. McElroy briefed him. Pierre was to keep the door to A-corridor locked at all times. No strangers were to be allowed there, and room A100 was off-limits to all personnel except nurse Hudson and Drs. Hermann and McElroy. Even Pierre was not allowed in A100. The occupant, Miss Jones, must not be disturbed.

One other person was allowed in Miss Jones' room. He was the bulky man staying in room A101 across the hall. Pierre could call him "Rob." Rob had a permit to carry a weapon. Pierre was not to worry about Rob, but should cooperate with him on any reasonable request. Notwithstanding, any unusual activity by Rob was to be reported immediately to Dr. McElroy.

The only additional detail was that nurse Hudson would be living at the clinic for a while, in room A98. There was a connecting door to A100 which Miss Jones might choose to leave unlocked if she wished. A98 was off-limits to all but nurse Hudson.

That briefing accomplished, Dr. McElroy looked down and shuffled some papers on his desk.

***

Pierre stood by the desk and waited. Dr. McElroy broke the silence.

"Now, tell me about the Hernandez woman."

241

"I made contact with her like you said."

"So soon?"

"Sooner than I wanted. She came back to the clinic in the afternoon. She must have spotted me leave. She followed me."

"And?"

"I ditched her and then followed her. I left a note on her car that I would call her."

"Did you?"

"Yes. She thinks I'm going to help her. I should be able to keep her away for a while, but she's damned clever."

"Not clever enough. You're doing good. Maybe André was right about you."

For the first time that morning Pierre smiled. McElroy was an arrogant bastard.

Dr. McElroy waved his hand in dismissal. It was 9:30 a.m. He had to take Miss Jones' medical history in a half hour.

"Tell Dr. Hermann I want him here and ready in fifteen minutes. And Pierre, keep a close eye on A-corridor, and check with me every day about Hernandez."

Pierre nodded and left the office.

***

At Fairland University hospital, the doctor attending John Martin turned to see two young women in the doorway. He waved them in and turned back to the patient. He spoke with a cheery condescending tone that might be used to train a parrot.

"Mr. Martin, how are you feeling? We're glad you're back with us. Do you know where you are?"

John's eyes had a pained expression.

"My leg hurts. ... What happened?"

"You don't remember your fall?"

"What fall? Where?"

Monique approached the side of the bed. John turned towards her. Her voice was soft.

"John, you were climbing at Stony Man. Don't you remember?"

"Monique? No. What am I doing here? Where's Jeannine?"

Jeannine stepped alongside.

"I'm here. Don't you remember your fall?"

John strained and lifted his head from the pillow. Then he laid back and shut his eyes.

"I remember being fired. And I remember seeing Monique at the Old Goose, but ..."

His forehead furrowed. He was exhausted.

The doctor stepped in and leaned over him.

"Mr. Martin, You've been unconscious. You're in the hospital. You fell at Stony Man Mountain. Remember?"

John shook his head no. His eyes focused on the doctor.

"Dry."

The doctor soaked a washcloth and put it on his lips.

"Here, bite on this."

The doctor turned to Jeannine and Monique. His tone was professional.

"Would you mind stepping outside. He's going to be fine. It will take time."

Jeannine and Monique left the room.

***

Agent Turner stopped at the hospital information desk. A neatly-dressed receptionist smiled up at him.

"May I help you?"

"I'm looking for John Martin."

"He's in B326. It's the third floor. You can take one of the elevators over there."

At the third floor, Agent Turner found corridor B. He approached room 326. Two women were seated nearby. One had red hair. The other he recognized.

"Miss Laurier, I'm Agent Turner, remember me? And this must be Miss Ryan."

His eyes locked onto Jeannine with a penetrating stare. She stared back.

"You're the jerk who thinks I pushed John."

Agent Turner was nonplused, but only for a second.

"Why yes, Miss Ryan. I do think that."

"Then you are wrong. Why don't you ask John?"

"Thank you. I intend to. Have you had time to coach him yet?"

The words slipped out. Agent Turner regretted them immediately. The redhead had provoked him to act unprofessionally. Before he could apologize, Jeannine struck.

"You're just like Delaney. I'm sick of guys who don't give a damn about the truth. If you *wanted* to find the truth you could. Monique and I know what happened. You don't! What's more, you'd rather not open your eyes and find out because then you'd be wrong! What do they pay you for? Do your damn job *right* and leave *me* alone!"

There was honest anger in that response. Jeannine's flushed face, surpassed by flaming hair that waved as she shook, shocked Turner. He gaped at the fury he had unleashed. He admired her spunk. At that moment he wanted to believe Jeannine was innocent.

"Miss Ryan, I'm sorry. Forgive me. I misspoke. I would like to hear your side of this."

Before she could answer, the nurse from B326 appeared. She smiled.

"Dr. Martin's doing well, but he has no memory of the accident. We are working on his leg. We'll be about an hour. Maybe more. Perhaps you should come back later?"

Agent Turner turned to Monique and Jeannine.

"We could talk in the cafeteria on the second floor, if you don't mind waiting there?"

Monique and Jeannine exchanged looks. To them, Turner's apology was meaningless. Still, they had to wait for John. They both nodded yes.

"Fine. Let's find a table and let the doctor do what he has to do."

To himself, Agent Turner wondered. *Damn it, why are the "guilty" ones more likable than that "innocent" bastard, Hartness.*

***

Agent Turner was a good listener. He let Monique and Jeannine do the talking. By the end of their discourse, he wanted to believe them.

But he had seen too many cases where the convincing story of one individual was later contradicted by the equally convincing account of a second individual. As an investigator he had to suspend judgment until he had all information.

He stayed objective. Monique's support for Jeannine was the support of a loyal friend. Jeannine could have typed John's note herself, as well as the postscript. If she had done that, then all this talk about unlisted numbers and Dr. Lawrence's wife was meaningless.

Monique spoke.

"Mr. Turner, why did you tell me that Jeannine's car was blue?"

Agent Turner paused. He asked questions, he did not answer them. But Monique's eyes disarmed him. He relaxed his rules.

"A witness saw a blue car parked next to John's van that evening."

As he said this, he glanced sidewise at Jeannine. She did not react. Monique continued her interrogation.

"Was it large or small? Jeannine has a blue Mazda. It's not big."

Agent Turner had answered enough questions. He waited for Monique to continue. It was a standard interviewing trick. It was surprising how people could not tolerate silences. Monique was no exception. She spoke.

"I mean, isn't there some way you could know it wasn't her Mazda?"

Jeannine interrupted.

"Dr. Lawrence has a blue car, I saw his wife drop him off at Main Med."

Agent Turner prodded.

"When?"

"It was Wednesday, the day John was supposed to meet somebody at Stony Man."

"Do you remember anything else?"

"The car had a vanity plate. Something like 'DOC-MAN' or 'something-DOC'."

Agent Turner scribbled onto his pad.

"What time did you see the car?"

"In the morning, before I met Monique."

Agent Turner closed his notepad and thanked them both.

"OK. I'm going up to see Mr. Martin. Would you mind waiting a few minutes before you come up?"

He left the table. Upstairs, his visit with John was short and fruitless. John did not recall falling.

The doctor assured him that John's memory loss was temporary. Turner thanked him and left. His next stop was the Lawrence home in Bethesda.

***

Betty grabbed the car keys and headed out of the house to the car. The color, blue, was her choice, but that ridiculous vanity plate, "LAB-DOC" annoyed her. Her hands fumbled with the ignition key. She backed out of the driveway.

Helen Morton, Mattie's mother, had called. At her voice, Betty had dropped everything. She had never heard her friend so agitated, stressed out. Kensington was a short drive away. Betty drove fast.

Helen stood at the front door, waiting.

"God! I didn't think this could happen to me!"

"Helen, what's the matter? What is it?"

The slender Helen, whom Betty had only seen fashionably dressed and meticulously groomed, appeared to be another person. Her hair was at odd angles and her dress rumpled. Betty pushed her into the living room and into a chair.

"It's Mattie!"

Betty waited. Helen continued.

"You know how you've been telling me that Mattie doesn't eat when she's at your house. Well she doesn't eat here either. She went to the school this morning to work on decorations for the New Year's dance. I got a call from the nurse. Mattie had collapsed in the hall. I drove over and picked her up and took her to the doctor's office. He saw her right away. It's real bad."

"Where's Mattie now?"

"She's in Suburban hospital. She's being fed with an IV. I just got back from there and called you. The doctor says Mattie's anorexic. She's past the point where her body can recover on its own, even if she starts to eat. She's got to be treated. My God! I've been so stupid, always talking about my being overweight in front of Mattie."

Betty saw Helen's slenderness in a new light. Helen wasn't just slender, she was thin. Mattie was thinner. Betty thanked God that she had forced Sari to eat.

"Helen. Don't blame yourself. That won't help Mattie. Have you called the ex?"

"He's gone for the holidays, probably skiing with his girlfriend, the bimbo. I don't know where they are. It's just like him. He was never around when I needed him. Anyway, his next visit with Mattie isn't 'til next week."

There would be no help from the ex-husband. Betty grasped Helen's hands. She stopped shaking. Betty spoke.

"Look, Franklin has a friend who has a clinic in Arizona. He's treated eating disorders. He's not cheap, but ..."

Helen rose from her chair. Her eyes lit with hope.

"Money doesn't matter! How can we find him. Could we call? We can at least get advice."

The clinic had an odd name. Betty did not want Franklin's help. She called 411 for the phone number.

Momentarily, she forgot her own problems.

***

Agent Turner stood at the door of the Lawrence home. He had no appointment. He wanted a spontaneous, unprepared encounter with Mrs. Lawrence. If "the girls" were right, she might admit her role in John's fall. It was worth a try.

The brass knocker was covered by an evergreen Christmas decoration attached to the door. He used his fist. No answer, and no car in the driveway. The attempt at a spontaneous interview had failed. He walked back to his car.

***

Mike Hartness was at work in the lab when the phone rang. It was Monique's friend, Anne, in Embryology.

"Hi Mike, is Monique there?"

"I haven't seen her."

"She must have called me from the hospital then. Isn't that great news!"

"What news?"

"John Martin's out of his coma. He's talking!"

"Anne, that's great. Great!"

"Ask Monique to call me when she comes in will you?"

"Of course."

Mike ground his teeth. *Damn! OK, Mike! Think!*

He wasn't worried about John's claiming L-12. John was disgraced, guilty of research misconduct. Mike had covered that possibility. No one would believe John about L-12. *Damn it! I shouldn't have told that agent that Jeannine pushed John!* But it was a minor slip. It had been Christmas Eve. He could say he'd had too much to drink. He spoke to himself.

"Damn it, Mike. This is just a detail. Tell them you heard wrong that's all. Besides, maybe John doesn't remember?"

He donned his jacket and left for the hospital. What *did* John remember?

***

******

Chapter 28
Wednesday, December 27

At her home in Bethesda, Betty regarded the dirty dishes in the kitchen sink. She reached around them and filled a glass with water. Dr. Lawrence noticed her manicured nails as she drank.

Without looking at Franklin, she smoothed her navy blue dress and adjusted a bright silk scarf. The variegated colors contrasted nicely with the blue outfit. She looked in the mirror. The hairdresser had done well, her hair had a light teased effect. She turned to leave.

Dr. Lawrence reddened. Florid-faced and furious, he raised his voice.

"Didn't you hear me? I'm busy. You can't go to Tucson."

"I heard you."

"Then why are you going? Who'll take care of Sari?"

"Helen's my friend and she needs me. Mattie's sick. Sari's a big girl. All you have to do is come home at a decent hour and eat supper with her. She's your daughter too."

"You can't go! My project with Dr. Hartness is important."

"Franklin, you always have a project. Have Mike come here to work, to your *home*. It *is* your home you know."

"You're not rational! What about John Martin? He's conscious. Any day his memory will come back. And then I'll be embarrassed! My own wife. Don't you think?"

"You told me not to think remember!"

"You cannot fly to Tucson. Period!"

"Franklin, listen. I'll be back Sunday."

"Didn't you hear me. I'll be at the lab. I cannot watch Sari."

"*Watch* her? Try *being* with her sometime! All right, forget it. School's out. If that's what you want, Sari can fly with me."

"You pushed John! It will look like you're running away."

"Franklin, it was an accident, and I made up my mind. I'm going to Tucson. I'll call Agent Turner when I get back."

"What will you tell him?"

"I'll tell him the truth."

Betty had had enough. She took her key chain out of her purse. Its ornament was a pink plastic pig. She shook it.

"See this pig Franklin. It's going to fly! It has a *right* to, and *I* have a right to *think*! Go to the lab, and forget your 'Wonderland' quotations about pigs not flying."

She caught her breath.

"The Limo for Dulles Airport is picking us up in an hour."

Betty lifted the phone and arranged a seat for Sari. Franklin stared at his wife, his mouth open. He started to leave, but Betty's voice stopped him.

"Franklin."

"What now?"

"You'll need the car keys. They're in the kitchen."

He went and grabbed them. She spoke again.

"Don't forget. The car needs gas. It's low."

He slammed the door. The wreath's ribbon caught in the crack.

***

Mike arrived late at the lab. He was surprised that Dr. Lawrence was not there. He unlocked the door to his office and sat down. It was time to think.

John remembered neither the accident nor his research project. Though this was temporary, when he did remember he would find his work belonged to Dr. Lawrence.

Mike fingered a copy of Dr. Lawrence's memo to Santini. He particularly liked the last paragraph.

To: Dr. J. Santini, Chair
From: Dr. F. W. Lawrence, Graham Professor of Immunology
Re: Your query concerning Dr. Hartness' laboratory notebooks
With respect to Dr. Hartness' notebooks I wish to state that these notebooks fully comply with standard record keeping in my laboratory and are clearly the product of Dr. Hartness. In those instances where work was performed by Dr. Martin, it is clear that such work was performed under the direction of Dr. Hartness.

250

He laughed. Not only was John guilty of research misconduct, he could not claim his work. The research grant was designated to the University, and Dr. Lawrence was the Principal Investigator. Mike knew the rules!

He heard footsteps enter the lab. He looked through the crack of his door.

It was Monique!

Her back was turned and she was as attractive as ever. She wore a soft gray sweater that hung in loose folds and came to rest on her round hips. He stepped from his office and grabbed her about the waist. His hands groped through the sweater's folds. He felt firm flesh. She had nice abs. She must work out. He pulled her backwards against him.

She went taut. He whispered.

"Monique, I've been waiting for this."

"Let her go!"

The voice came from the doorway. Startled, he turned. The redhead, Jeannine, stood glaring at him. He dropped his hands and released Monique. He grimaced.

"Just welcoming our friend back to the lab. She's been gone too long. What are you doing here?"

Monique straightened her sweater. Mike focused on Jeannine.

"You can't protect Monique, so get lost. You have no business here. Dr. Lawrence does not want you in the lab."

Jeannine glared at Mike and put her arms around Monique. Mike drew back, uncertain.

Dr. Lawrence, collar askew and shirt miss-buttoned, appeared in the doorway and took over.

"That's right Miss Ryan. You're not welcome here. What are you doing?"

"I came to help Monique pick up her notes, and it's a good thing I did. You should control Dr. Hartness and his damn hormones."

"Miss Ryan, You will not insult my assistant. You have no business here. I insist that you leave."

Monique found her voice.

"Dr. Lawrence. It's true. Jeannine came in case Mike ..."

Dr. Lawrence appeared to notice Monique for the first time.

"Miss Laurier. How nice of you finally to come to work. I'm sorry to tell you, but January 15 will be your last day with us. That gives you two weeks to clear out your belongings. Turn your lab notebooks and supplies over to Mike now."

Even Mike was not prepared for Dr. Lawrence's decision.

"Excuse me Sir, don't you think that we should wait?"

Dr. Lawrence stared. Mike shut up.

"I'll be in my office. Bring me Miss Laurier's notebooks, and don't let her on the lab computer. I don't want any data deleted out of spite, and she better not have any personal files there. You have thirty minutes to bring me the notebooks, all of them."

He turned back to Monique.

"I'm sorry Miss Laurier. It hasn't worked out. You don't work hard enough."

Then he addressed Jeannine.

"As for you Miss Ryan, if you don't leave now, security will escort you out."

He thrust past her and left. He slammed the door, but the anti-slam device thwarted him and his hand absorbed a painful shock. He glowered, held his wrist, and headed down the corridor to his office. Mike spun about into his office and shut the door. The lock clicked.

Jeannine's stomach churned.

"Monique, I'm sorry. If I hadn't been here Dr. Lawrence might not have ..."

"Not at all! If you hadn't been here, that animal Mike would have, ... *Mon Dieu!* And Dr. Lawrence already had his mind made up. Thank God you *were* here."

Monique's hands shook as she collected a number of bound lab notebooks and put them in sequence by month.

"Here's a year of my life. A year's worth of experiments."

She stacked the notebooks into a pile outside Mike's door

From a drawer she retrieved sneakers and a torn lab coat. A few minutes more, and the contents of her desk were dumped into a cardboard box. Monique loaded it on a rolling cart and pushed it towards the door.

John's belongings were in a corner, unclaimed. She looked at Jeannine who shook her head.

"You have enough for one load. We can get John's stuff later."

Monique nodded. She started to push the cart, but turned and went to the window by her former bench. A spray of sleet slammed against the glass. Outside, gusts twisted the branches of the trees lining the street. From this same window a month before she had seen John, jacket open, make his way to the Old Goose through a similar storm. He had just been fired

Now it was her turn.

She surveyed the lab. Of the three of them, John, Monique and Mike, only Mike remained. She stared at his door. No sound came from within. She reflected.

I'm saying good-bye to immunology.

Never again would she do research in this field. Even if she wanted to, it wouldn't be allowed, not if she needed a reference from Dr. Lawrence.

She nodded to Jeannine. They pushed the cart into the corridor.

***

Dr. Lawrence stormed into his office, spluttering. Betty's insubordination and the insolence of that redhead unsettled him, Monique and John too. *Damn you Betty. Damn your stubbornness, and damn that stupid girl Mattie. Sari's got to pick better friends. And damn you Martin. You wasted a whole year of mine, and Monique too.*

Red hair flashed into these thoughts.

You damn redhead. Stay out of my lab!

He called security and warned them about Jeannine. That done, he saw the large envelope on his desk. Inside was a note from Sharon Husak, the reporter.

Dear Franklin,

Thanks for the 'heads-up' and manuscript of your research paper. Enclosed is my draft of an article I plan to publish in the Science section. I'm shooting for a Sunday edition. It's kind of rough. Please correct any errors of fact or make any suggestions you want.

Thanks, Sharon

Franklin dropped the note and started to read her copy.

SCIENCE FROM A WOMAN'S PERSPECTIVE:
BREAST CANCER, A NEW HOPE
by Sharon Husak

<u>You have cancer.</u>

No phrase is more dreaded in this country today! There are many different kinds of cancer, and probably as many different causes, but cancer cells share a common characteristic. They multiply too much and spread themselves throughout the body. If they spread ("metastasize") from the original colony ("primary tumor") to form multiple colonies in other organs, there is often little hope for survival. Early detection of any cancer, before this spreading or metastasis, is very important. Then medical treatment can focus on the single location of the primary tumor.

<u>You have breast cancer.</u>

As women, we particularly fear "breast cancer," that starts when glandular cells in the breast begin to multiply uncontrollably. (Cancers originating in glandular-tissue are called "carcinomas".) Incredibly, in our modern society, one out of every fourteen women may expect to develop "carcinoma of the breast." The dreaded words, "You have breast cancer." are all too frequently heard. Like others, I too fear these words.

Dr. Lawrence finished the first two paragraphs. So far the article was boring. His name was not mentioned. He turned to the next paragraph. It was more to his liking.

But there is hope.

A prominent cancer researcher, Dr. Franklin Wilson Lawrence of the Medical School of Fairland University in Washington D. C. has overcome not only faulty funding, but fraud in his laboratory to bring hope to women all over America. Dr. Lawrence and his laboratory coworker, Dr. Michael Hartness, have just completed research that soon will be published in the prestigious journal ...

Sharon showed discernment and promise, but the mention of 'fraud' was unnecessary. And he was not ready to recognize Mike as an equal "Coworker." *I'll tell her to change those items.*

He read on. His name occurred only twice in the next paragraphs, and he scanned them quickly. Sharon had overestimated the contribution of Dr. Johnson at Rochester. *I'll help her correct that!*

But he smiled at the last paragraphs.

We can stop Johnson's CA.

Dr. Lawrence and his coworkers have discovered two protein products that are effective in stopping the deadly behavior of protein CA. Dr. Lawrence has named these protein products A-11 and L-12. Not only do treatments with A-11 and L-12 offer a potential defense against the formation of breast tumors, but, they offer a possible way to attack existing carcinomas of the breast.

... By means of clever experimentation, Dr. Lawrence has established not only that protein L-12 binds to CA and disables it, but further that this occurs even when protein CA is incorporated into cell membranes. In other words Dr. Lawrence's protein can stop growth in an existing cancer. Exciting? Yes it is!

Thank you Dr. Lawrence.

We women may soon be thanking Dr. Lawrence and those in his Laboratory for our lives!

Dr. Lawrence penciled in his changes and some corrections to obvious errors. He sat back and reflected. *Not bad! This woman understands me. She's smart.*

He recalled Sharon's green-tinted blue eyes, her trim figure, and remembered that night in the airport lounge in Chicago. All thoughts of Betty, Monique, and Jeannine slipped away at the memory of Sharon's green suit and her exposed thigh. Here was an attractive woman that understood him and his science!

For the first time this day, he relaxed. He straightened his collar, and re-buttoned his shirt. Someday soon he might see Sharon again. He hoped so.

He felt much better.

***

The flight to Tucson by way of Dallas left Dulles Airport on time. Helen Morton sat next to a subdued Mattie. Betty had the aisle seat across the way. Sari, next to the window, was not happy. She did not understand why Mattie ignored her.

Helen leaned across the aisle.

"Could I see that brochure on the *AMAH Clinic* again."

Betty handed it to her. Helen scanned it and spoke.

"Betty, how do you know the clinic's Director."

"Mackie, that's Dr. McElroy, and Franklin were residents together in Boston. They went through hard times together."

"Did you know him yourself?"

"Yes, but I was with Franklin. Mackie liked to play the field."

"This says, the clinic is good at treating eating disorders."

"Helen, I'm sure you're doing the right thing for Mattie."

"And 'Mackie' sounds like 'Mattie.' Maybe it's an omen!"

At that point the stewardess came by with drinks.

***

Agent Turner left Thornton Gap and drove east towards Madison to meet the elderly couple that had reported John's argument at Stony Man Mountain. The weather was damp and depressing. The temperature was at the freezing point and warm air from the defroster melted the icy raindrops upon impact.

But the highway was clear, though the shoulders were edged by monotonous dirty gray lines of plowed snow now ice. Leafless trees bordered the barren fields. A turkey vulture soared in the distance.

Agent Turner drove in silence. Ahead was a frame house with a woman standing on the porch. He stopped the car and got out.

"Mrs. Henderson?"

"Yes."

"I'm Agent Turner. We talked on the phone."

"We were waiting for you, Mr. Turner. Come on in the house. I've made tea."

Mrs. Henderson led Turner into the parlor and poured him a cup. Her husband, Bill, sat bundled in an easy chair. She adjusted his blanket and turned back to Turner.

"My husband has a cough. He's not himself"

Agent Turner took several sips before speaking.

"Mrs. Henderson, do you remember anything more about that day at Stony Man Mountain."

"More?"

"Yes. Anything at all. For example, when you got back to the parking area. It was getting dark wasn't it?"

Bill Henderson stayed silent. Mrs. Henderson responded.

"Yes, we were on the shadow side of the mountain."

"But you saw a van, and a car?"

"There was, our car, the brown van, and one other."

"You told me the other car was blue. Wasn't it too dark?"

"There was still some light, and Bill had a flashlight."

Agent Turner turned towards Mr. Henderson.

"Mr. Henderson, do you recall anything?"

Mrs. Henderson intervened.

"Bill's not well. We're waiting on Doc Gordon now."

At the word "Doc," Bill's fevered eyes lit up and he gestured.

"I do remember. That car's plate had the letters 'DOC.'"

"Are you sure? It's important!"

"Of course I'm sure. It was 'DOC,' like all caps, 'DOC.'"

Mrs. Henderson nodded in agreement.

"I remember that too."

Agent Turner was elated! All objectivity departed. Dr. Lawrence's plate was "LAB-DOC." Mrs. Lawrence had been on the mountain with John! The girls were right and Jeannine was in the clear. The good "guys" were "good" after all.

He chatted with the Henderson's while he finished his tea.

***

In Tucson, Cecilia stood by the pay phone at the mall. Pierre's call was overdue. She shifted her feet.

"Rrring."

She picked up immediately. Before she could speak, she heard a rasping voice.

"Hernandez?"

"Yes."

"McElroy is still worried about you. I told him not to. I can't get to the records today. Stay away from the clinic and McElroy or you'll spook him. The records aren't in Tucson."

His tone became harsher.

"Leave Sam Jones out of this or no records."

After a pause, he whispered.

"I can't talk. Someone's coming. I've got to go. I'll call you tomorrow, at 10:30. Be there."

Before Cecilia could reply the phone clicked off.

***

******

Chapter 29
Thursday, December 28

There was something 'up front' and tough about Pierre, like a saguaro cactus, strong, straight with visible spines and thick needles that threaten to pierce any would-be aggressor. In contrast, Cecilia's toughness lay beneath the surface. She was more subtle, like a creosote bush, whose leaves, filled with unpalatable oily resin, repel the attacker after first bite. In the desert, the creosote bush is as protected by its resin, as the cactus by its spines. To the wise, the musty scent of the creosote bush is sufficient warning of its indigestibility. Leave it alone.

Dr. McElroy was not wise about Cecilia. He knew that the prickly Pierre needed to be handled with care, but he had no discernment regarding the attractive customs agent whose photo he studied. He translated attractiveness as softness. Moreover she was a 'Fed' and therefore an intellectual 'zero.' Only her official status worried him. She could engage a higher and wiser authority to expose him.

Dr. McElroy was a physician, and a scientific cheat as Monique and Jeannine had discovered, but he was subject to the mores of his intellectual class. The unfortunate use of the Burlington border gang was an aberration. That distasteful outcome convinced him. He never again would allow his hands to be dirtied. He saw no need for overt violence. Although he kept his contact with Montreal, and had agreed to hire Pierre, there would be no more shipments from André. That business was over. He did not need it.

The current influx of celebrity patients like "Miss Jones" assured him an early retirement to his hacienda in the state of Sonora, but he could not bear investigation. Snoops like Hernandez must be deterred. He turned to his desk.

He read Dr. Hermann's notes on the suggested dosage for L-12. A voice came through the speaker.

"Dr. McElroy, that private investigator you hired is on the line."

Dr. McElroy pushed a switch.

"Steve, what did you find out?"

"Hernandez works out of Rouses Point. Her partner is named Jones, Sam Jones. He's pretty well known. She was involved in an old fashioned shoot-out a month ago. She nearly died."

Steve narrated the details to his employer. Most of them were new to Dr. McElroy, except for a few that Pierre had provided when he was hired. Steve kept speaking.

"This next item could be good news for you. She's not officially on the case anymore, on any case for that matter."

"You're sure? Then what's she doing here?"

"I'm positive. She was on sick leave, then administrative leave. Now she's on vacation. Her folks live here in Tucson."

Steve gave him the address of Cecilia's parents.

"You mean she's not officially investigating me or the clinic?"

"Don't make me tell you how I found out, but since the shooting, she's not assigned to any case. Period! Right now she's on leave. It's Christmas. Fact is, she's on her own."

"Steve, you're a whiz. Thanks. You've been a big help."

"How do you want to be billed?"

"I'll settle it personally. I'll stop by your office in a few days.

"All right. But bring the cash soon. I'm short."

***

Dr. McElroy grew thoughtful. If Cecilia was acting on her own, without proper authority, he might be able to neutralize her without repercussions. Perhaps he could arrange an accident. He buzzed the receptionist.

"Paula, what time does Pierre come in today?"

"He's here now Dr. McElroy."

"Good. Send him to my office. I need to talk to him."

Considering its importance, Dr. McElroy's conversation with Pierre was brief and to the point. At its conclusion, Pierre left the clinic to drive to the dilapidated motel where he had met Cecilia several days before.

Pierre was worried. Unlike McElroy, he did not underestimate Cecilia. He had seen Red Sweater's body at his grandmother's cabin, and he had seen Cecilia blast that target at the firing range. She was dangerous. Dr. McElroy might be the boss, but he was not smart.

Pierre parked his car in the alley behind room 14. He entered and stood in the room by the phone. He looked at his watch. It was 10:30. Time to call. He dialed and was relieved to hear Cecilia's voice. She was there. Good. The message was short.

"Same motel, same room."

He arranged a large brown envelope on the table. Then he stepped out into the alley and drove away.

***

Cecilia steered through the mall parking lot towards the large palm tree that marked the exit. It was five blocks to the motel. She parked. The same broken bottles lay, unswept, on the sidewalk. More dry tumbleweed had accumulated against the fence.

This time, there were no idle men across the street. There was no one at all. Cecilia gripped the revolver inside her pack, keeping it out of sight. There was no external indication that she had a gun.

She went to room 14 and knocked. No answer. She opened the door, standing to one side as she did. The room was empty, but a brown envelope leaned against the lamp on the table. She grabbed the envelope and left. No one was near her car.

She started the motor. The envelope contained photocopies of documents along with a sheet that had a message.

Hernandez. If these papers interest you, be alone at the
phone marked on the map at 11:15. There's lots more. Don't
call Jones or anyone or no deal.
Napoleon

She looked at the location of the phone. It was still in
Tucson, but far to the east. She had to hurry.

Nonetheless, she paused to examine the documents. The
first was a Medicare reimbursement form for treatment
performed at the *AMAH Clinic*, for Mrs. Delores Gomez, age
66. The social security number was circled. The second
document was a newspaper obituary notice for a Mrs. Delores
Gomez, dated *a year prior* to the date of the treatment on the
reimbursement form! Mrs. Gomez was dead at the time of the
alleged treatment.

The third document was a page of a journal article by Dr.
McElroy. A sentence was circled. Patient Number 342 was a
66 year-old Hispanic female. The article acknowledged the
support of a drug company, and described a small clinical trial
that tested the effect of a new drug. The date of the research
was circled. If patient 342 was Mrs. Gomez, then she was dead
at the time of the purported research.

The fourth document was a copy of a letter to Dr. McElroy
from a drug company that had supported his research. The letter
cited Dr. McElroy's journal article based on that research and
ended with an unflattering paragraph.

Because of discrepancies between our records and yours, as
reported in your journal article, and because our repeated
efforts to clarify these discrepancies with you have met with
no satisfactory explanation, we regret that we are unable to
continue our support of your studies.
Sincerely,

Both the letterhead and the signature on the photocopy had
been cut away, but the drug company was doubtless the one
referred to in the journal article.

Cecilia whistled. More records like this, and she could nail McElroy. Inventing patients for clinical studies and stealing social security numbers from the dead to commit Medicare fraud. She looked at her watch. She had lost precious minutes. She dashed to her car.

She must arrive at that phone on time.

***

Dr. McElroy stood up behind his desk to welcome his visitors. Mackie was at his most charming.

"Betty, how good to see you! How's that old scoundrel Franklin. Well, I hope. And this must be Sarah. How are you?"

He stepped from behind his desk and kissed Betty on both cheeks. He turned to Helen.

"And you must be Mrs. Morton, and this must be our newest patient, Mattie. Welcome to the *AMAH Clinic*."

Mattie felt the warmth of Mackie's welcome. For the first time that day she smiled. Dr. McElroy turned back to Betty.

"I'm sure you know that Mrs. Morton and I have some things to discuss. I have appointments at noon and all afternoon, but I've arranged for a car and driver to show you the city. Maybe Sari would like to see Old Tucson, or the Desert Museum. I won't be free until tomorrow morning. We could talk then."

Betty smiled. It was the same flattering, and terribly busy, Mackie. He had not changed.

"Thanks, Sari and I would like that."

***

Cecilia arrived at the location of the second phone with three minutes to spare. It rang on schedule. The voice appeared different. Perhaps it was disguised.

"There's a trash bin over to your right. Take out the McDonald's bag on top. Put any phone you still have in the bin. You're being watched. Don't call anyone, or it's off. You have five minutes to get to the next phone. You have to drive fast."

Cecilia went to the trash. She had no phone to dump, but the bag was there. In it was a map. The next phone was six blocks away. She dashed back to the car.

***

The phone stood at the edge of a concrete apron, the remains of a former service station. The pumps had long since been removed, and the building was boarded. To the east was a desert field of low-lying shrubs, mostly creosote bush. Cecilia stood by the phone and waited. She checked her watch. She had arrived on time. The call was past due. Had she blown it? She had followed instructions to the letter.

From across the street, Pierre watched. Satisfied that Cecilia had not been followed, he dialed the number on his cell phone. He saw her answer. His mouth was dry. He took a deep breath. This was the critical part of the meeting. If she did not cooperate, there would be trouble. He hissed into the phone.

"Don't look behind you. Leave the backpack at the phone and keep your hands in sight. Come across the street and step in the open doorway. You won't be hurt."

Cecilia turned and peered across the street. She saw the doorway. She stopped.

Pierre clamped his jaw. What would she do?

Cecilia shrugged and put the backpack on the ground. She held her palms open and started across the street.

***

It was a deviation from McElroy's plan, but Pierre took the chance. Cecilia's calm as she crossed into a possible trap impressed him. Also, he was attracted by her vulnerability. He was sure no one had followed her. He stepped out of the doorway into the sunlight. He stretched out his hand.

"Lachance."

Cecilia, whose stomach churned in spite of her apparent calm, took his hand.

"Hernandez."

"We'll take your car."

Pierre directed Cecilia to the passenger seat and tossed a dark hood at her.

"Put this over your head."

"My backpack's under the phone."

"OK, I'll get it for you."

Pierre stepped around the car and retrieved the pack. He felt the revolver inside. He tensed, but only momentarily. Hernandez owed him. He shut her pack in the trunk.

Back in the driver's seat he adjusted the hood about Cecilia's head. Nervous, he lapsed into his native tongue.

"Tu ne vois rien, non? You see nothing, right?"

"Rien, nada, nothing."

"Bon. That's good"

Pierre drove east, away from Tucson.

***

At the clinic, Dr. Hermann was agitated.

"Mackie, damn it. Miss Jones is OK. There's nothing wrong with her!

Dr. McElroy gaped at his colleague.

But it's a T-1 tumor, it's under two centimeters."

Dr. Hermann continued.

"It's under two centimeters all right, but it's not malignant! Somebody screwed up. Maybe the lab samples got mixed. It's just a damned cyst. She can be out of here this afternoon."

"You're sure?"

"Of course, I'm sure. Look for yourself."

Dr. McElroy did not need to look. He was visualizing the bill.

"All right. You know it and I know it, but she doesn't. We've got to treat her. I want our second payment."

Dr. Hermann feigned shock, but he wasn't surprised. Mackie was no stranger to him.

"Look, this gives me time to run animal tests with L-12. You're not going to stick L-12 into her are you?"

"Hell no. You can run your dumb trials, but we've got to treat her for at least two weeks. Give her Tamoxifen as a prophylactic, and we'll try some of that French homeopathic junk that André stole. We paid for it, and it can't hurt her."

"What about nurse Hudson?"

"I pay her to go along with such protocols. She'll be fine."

Mackie smacked his lips.

"This is *great*. We have a *guaranteed breast cancer cure* for Miss Jones, and we'll soon have another million in the bank. Plus, she'll get us more rich patients."

Dr. Hermann wondered what would happen when those rich patients weren't cured, but he shrugged and turned away. Mackie looked at his watch. It was 2:00. He addressed his associate.

"You handle things here. I've got to meet Pierre. I won't be back today."

Dr. Hermann was relieved. L-12 scared him. He was not ready to try it on a human being.

***

Dr. McElroy left the clinic. He carried a canvas bag tied at the neck. He chose his Jeep Cherokee. He expected rough roads.

He deposited the sack on the back seat. It moved. Something inside the sack was alive. He smiled. This was his surprise for the Hernandez woman.

He drove out of the city to the east.

***

It was a twisting road, and it was not paved. Cecilia could not see through the dark hood. She did not know that the car had ascended past rocky hillsides with scattered scrubby piñons and junipers into a higher woodland of graceful spreading Emory Oaks.

The wheels spun as Pierre forced the car higher. The sound of loose rocks hitting the underside of the car reminded Cecilia of the climb up Madame Gauthier's hill. She imagined herself on the fir-lined lane that led to Madame Gauthier's cabin. She half-expected to hear Tonnerre's welcoming bark.

A deep sadness, enhanced by the black hood, set upon her.

The sadness was accompanied by physical discomfort. Blinded, she was unable to anticipate the twists in the road. Consequently, she was tossed about as the car swerved from side to side. Finally Pierre braked the car to a stop.

Still, Pierre did not remove the hood. From the branches rustling in the wind and the cool freshness of the air, Cecilia knew that she was high in the mountains, but she was not aware they were surrounded by a forest of tall Apache Pines.

Pierre assisted Cecilia out the car and pulled her along on foot. The ground sloped downwards. Harsh stems of grass scratched her ankles. She heard an unknown birdcall. She stumbled, but Pierre caught her. He was strong.

She stood helpless. Metallic squeaks of a padlock and latch were followed by the rubbing of rusty hinges. Pierre spoke.

"Step up. Watch the rise."

She stepped up and forward and was assaulted by warm stale air that smelled of old paper and boxes. Behind her the padlock clicked. She was locked in. Through the door she heard Pierre.

"You can take off the hood now. There's a lantern and matches in the corner if you need light. I'll be back."

***

Cecilia lifted the hood and surveyed her surroundings. She was in an old wooden storage shed. Against one wall, stacked five-high, were about twenty cardboard storage boxes. The outside light came through a small transom above the door. There was a Coleman lantern in the corner, full of fuel. On the floor was a box of matches.

She pushed three of the cartons to the door and climbed to the top to see through the transom. Nearby were tall Apache pines. Back up the hill stood a cabin in a cleared area with a few scattered oaks and piñon pines. Elsewhere, more large pines filled the landscape.

She was well above the desert zone.

There was no sign of Pierre or of her car. Perhaps it was on the other side of the cabin. She looked at her watch. It was 4:00 p.m. If Pierre had not backtracked, they were at least two hours away from Tucson.

Cecilia was concerned, but there was nothing to do but examine the boxes. If these were the clinic records she wanted, then Pierre had fulfilled his promise. The cartons to her left were dated more than six years ago. She ignored these. Under the False Claims Act, the statute of limitations would apply. To the right, the records were only two years old. She pulled the top box from the pile. She sat on the concrete slab that served as the shed's floor and spread the folders around her.

"Bingo!"

The very first folder had newspaper clippings and obituary notices, each attached to a sheet of papers. Penciled in under the clippings were social security numbers and addresses. She wondered what ruse had been used to obtain those numbers. One of the first clippings was for Mrs. Gomez, the one she had seen in the brown envelope. She estimated there were about 150 obituaries in the folder.

The next several folders were thicker. They contained Medicare claim forms. She gave them a cursory examination. Those names she checked were all listed in the obituaries. All of the treatment dates were after the date of death.

Another folder contained correspondence between the *AMAH* clinic and a drug company. At the end of the file she saw the letter that Pierre had copied. Also in the file was a reprint of Dr. McElroy's clinical study. She read the abstract. There were 150 patients, all 65 or older, that had been studied. The patients were all from the obituaries.

There never had been any study! All the supposed subjects were dead at the time!

***

******

Chapter 30
Thursday, December 28

Dr. McElroy pulled the Cherokee to a stop on the cleared grassland in front of the cabin. Cecilia's car was parked next to the door. He lifted the canvas bag from the back seat. The bag twisted back and forth as he carried it into the cabin where Pierre waited. Dr. McElroy spoke first.

"Have you got the woman?"

"She's locked in the shed."

"The shed! With all my records?"

"What do you care? She's here. I did my job."

"You're not done yet. I've got a surprise for you, for her I mean."

Mackie hefted the canvas bag as he spoke. Pierre was puzzled.

"What's that?"

"A little something from the lab. It will make the perfect accident for Ms. Hernandez."

Pierre stared at the canvas sack. He did not like the way the sack was twisting. Something inside was very much alive.

"You said there wouldn't be any violence. What's that?"

"It's not violent. It's an 'accident' for Hernandez. It will be perfect. She drove into the country, and took a walk, and got bitten. She couldn't get to the hospital for help. She died. They'll find her body, not here of course, but some miles away. No violence, just a tragic accident. No one will know."

As he spoke, he untied the sack and put it on the tile floor of the cabin. At first the bag was still. Then a scaly triangular head with two vertical-striped eyes appeared at the mouth of the sack. A thin black tongue flicked forwards and tested the tile surface. Satisfied, the snake slithered forward. Pierre froze.

"Un serpent à sonnettes!"

"That's right. A rattlesnake. A Western Diamondback to be exact."

With a single sweeping motion of his hand, Dr. McElroy seized the back of the neck of the serpent and gripped it. With his other hand he stabilized the twisting torso. The snake was heavy-bodied and struggled, but McElroy prevailed. He smiled at Pierre.

"I used to milk these things. We had great hopes for the venom. We had a number of them in the lab. We don't need them anymore, but I've still got my touch."

He squeezed the head from the side exposing two curved fangs sheathed in shiny white tissue. Pierre drew back.

"Diable! I don't want to ... "

Dr. McElroy frowned at his reticence.

"You don't have to. It will be a simple injection. All you have to do is hold Hernandez. I'll hold the snake."

***

Cecilia assembled the folders from the first box. The Department of Justice, Civil Division, would want to know about the Medicare claims. Under the False Claims Act there could be a fine between $5,000 and $10,000 per false claim, plus triple penalties. She shook her head. That was just the beginning. The fake research involved an experimental drug, and the FDA would take note of that. However, if the correspondence was to be believed, the drug company had *not* used McElroy's trial in its request for New Drug Approval.

She was ready for the next box, but paused. The light inside the shed had grown dim. She lit the Coleman lantern. By its warm diffuse glow, she lowered the second box from its stack and placed it on the floor. Drawing forth several folders, she read diligently, but there was not much of obvious interest. She replaced the folders and considered which box to examine next.

She heard a sound outside the door. Someone was fumbling with the lock. She reached for her backpack, but realized that it was in the trunk of the car. She was unarmed. She turned.

A man stood in the doorway. He held a shotgun.

"What're ya doin' here missy? This here's private property."

The speaker cradled the shotgun. He was a scruffy individual with a sun-reddened face. Scraggly white hairs on his chin stood out against wrinkled wind-dried skin. Torn jeans were topped by a faded shirt. He appeared to be some sort of caretaker.

"I asked ya, missy. What're ya doin' here?"

As he spoke, the man's eyes took in the folders scattered on the floor. Cecilia found her voice.

"I was checking these records for Dr. McElroy."

"Who locked ya in then?"

That question stumped Cecilia. Where was Pierre? She did not want to say his name. She adlibbed

"Dr. McElroy. He wants the shed locked at all times."

"That's a fact. The Doctor's mighty 'ticular' bout this old shed."

Cecilia stood up with authority.

"I've got what he sent me for. Help me put this box back, and you can lock up after me."

"I dun know, I'd better ..."

But Cecilia acted. She refilled the second carton and restored that box to its position. Slipping the cloth hood into the first box, she signaled him to stack it on top. She put the critical files under her arm. She stepped outside and stood, waiting, for the caretaker to lock the door.

The caretaker, whose name was Darwin, hesitated. Leaning the shotgun against the door frame, he stooped over and picked up a tool box which he put in the shed. Then he lifted Cecilia's carton to the top of the stack. He stepped out, retrieved his gun, and snapped the padlock.

He turned to Cecilia, shaking his head.

"Is that yo' car up ta the cabin?"

She had to say yes.

"It's mine all right."

"Aint seed it a'fore."

"I'm new."

"The Doc's up at the cabin?"

"Yes."

Cecilia held her breath. Finally, Darwin nodded.

"I guess ya's OK. Y'aint the first pretty lady he's had up here."

He turned down a path that led downhill through the tall Apache pines behind the shed. He had a long stride. He quickly disappeared in the shadows beneath the branches. It was dusk, and the mountain air had cooled. Cecilia headed in the opposite direction, up towards the cabin.

***

She had taken only a few steps when she saw a man leave the cabin and run towards her. He was carrying something. In the dim light she could not make out his features. He appeared smaller than Pierre.

She dropped to the ground and hid behind a thick clump of bushes.

The man passed. In his hand was a can. She turned and watched him pile brush and branches up against the wooden shed, on all sides. It was almost dark and the shadowy figure worked fast. He jammed a stout branch against the shed door, sealing it shut. Then he unlocked the padlock and tossed it on the ground.

Cecilia stared, aghast, as the man splashed liquid from the can onto the branches. The man stepped away.

In seconds the shed was engulfed by crackling flames that stretched skyward towards the tops of the pines. Glowing fragments caught the fierce updraft, left the fiery mass, and sparkled high into the evening sky before dropping out of sight. The sounds of hissing needles and cracking and snapping branches punctuated the brilliant display. Shadowy pines illuminated by the furious fire stood dry and vulnerable to the flying embers.

The man jumped backwards, surprised by the rapidity with which the shed was enveloped. He stood there, a black silhouette against the raging flames.

For some moments he remained motionless. Then, still carrying the can, he ran up the trail past the junipers where Cecilia crouched. She heard a car start. Only when the sound of its motor faded down the mountain did she stand up to stare at the burning shed that would have been her funeral pyre. The flames were lower now, but still reached a nearby pine whose branches reddened and snapped, falling in a glowing shower to the ground.

A burst of color and heat marked the collapse of one wall of the shed. Fresh air rushed in and found stacked cartons, as yet unconsumed. Already glowing, these burst and exploded into flames that reached higher than before. Previously unreachable branches, already dried by the heat, crackled orange against the twilight.

She shuddered in horror. The fire had been intended for her. She thought of Joan of Arc, burned alive. *What a way to die.*

By a sheer effort of will, she forced her feet up the trail to the cabin.

***

Cecilia rounded the corner of the cabin. Her car was still there. *Gloria a Dios!*

Her keys were in the ignition. Turning to the trunk, she found her backpack and withdrew her Smith & Wesson from it. This in hand, she stepped towards the porch.

Inside the cabin was dark. She heard a whisper.

"Hernandez."

She looked towards the sound. Her eyes became accustomed to the dim light. A shadowy form lay on the floor. It was Pierre. He whispered again.

"Fais attention, le serpent!"

She understood to watch out for the snake. But where? She saw a shadowy form like a rope coiled in the corner. She pulled Pierre away from it. He was heavy. The snake did not move.

"What happened?"

She felt Pierre's forehead. He was feverish.

"He brought the snake for you. Bite you ... accident. I told him ... diable, go to hell. He threw the rattlesnake at me .. bit me ... Then he hit me with ... blacked out ... je ... pouvais rien faire ...my arm ... ."

Pierre's voice dropped off. Cecilia looked for the snake, but it had disappeared under a stuffed chair. Desperate, she scanned the dim room. She needed help, but the cabin had no electricity, no phone. She found Pierre's cell, but it was useless. Apparently no tower was in range.

She dragged Pierre through the door onto the porch and stopped, breathing heavily. Somehow she found strength to wrestle him into the front seat of the car. His 9 mm weapon fell onto the car floor. She stuck it in her pack.

By the light inside the car she examined Pierre's arm. It was swollen almost to the shoulder. She located the twin puncture wounds surrounded by dark and dying skin, already puffed and hard to the touch. She ripped a cloth and applied a tourniquet as high as she could on the arm. By such a means he had saved her. Could she save him?

She prayed. *Señor ten piedad de nosotros! Have mercy on us!*

She started the car down the mountain. She drove as fast as she could on the twisting gravel surface. Pierre did not move.

At last the road leveled. She was out of the mountains. Ahead on the right she saw lights. A house! They must have a phone, and ice to pack Pierre's arm. She pulled off the pavement onto a gravel drive and blowing her horn, drove to the front of the house.

***

******

Chapter 31
Saturday, December 30

Life as a bachelor was hard for Dr. Lawrence. Standing in his kitchen, he looked in disgust at the dirty dishes piled in the sink and on the adjacent counter. Thirsty, he rinsed a glass and filled it half with water. He wanted coffee, but the filter was filled with yesterday's grounds, black and dried, while the glass coffee pot was ringed with brown circular bands. Franklin snorted and left the room. Betty's work would wait for her until she came back.

Upstairs, in the master bedroom, life was no better. He searched five minutes for his wallet until he found it hidden in the folds of the bed sheets. The bed had not been made since Betty left. The final blow occurred when he opened the drawer for fresh undershorts. There was the note in Betty's neat hand, telling him how to turn on the washing machine. That note had been there yesterday, but he had forgotten to start the wash that she had pre-loaded for him.

The fact that he could not blame Betty for his predicament infuriated him. *Damn it woman. I told you this was a busy week. Mike and I have important work to do! You knew, but you went anyway*!

Dr. Lawrence, scientist, was too objective to let the loss of his creature comforts influence his judgment of his wife. Likewise, his objectivity did not allow him to blame Betty for the fact that her shape was not as stimulating as Sharon Husak's. Sharon was after all, much younger. But he did fault Betty for the sin of not supporting his career. Sharon would know better. She supported his work and was willing to learn.

Every scientist knows that the world is in a state of flux. People and things change. Betty had changed since he married her. He had changed too. As an objective scientist, he had to admit that he and Betty had both changed. That was a fact.

They could not *"not change."* He had grown well beyond the young man who had been infatuated with Betty!

Yes, this growth was an objective scientific fact. He was on the verge of a major medical discovery. One that could save the lives of thousands of women. Objectively, nothing must be allowed to threaten his research, not for his sake, but for the sake of thousands of people who would be helped, wives and daughters along with husbands and children!

Pushing the rumpled sheets aside, Franklin grabbed the day-old underwear and sat on the edge of the bed. His mind raced. The greatest threat to his research was loss of funding, and scandal would cause such a loss. At the least, scandal would stop future grant awards. Objectively, for the sake of research, he must avoid scandal and its consequences. Betty had pushed John. She was the cause of scandal!

He headed down to the kitchen. A cup of coffee could settle his thoughts, but the sight of the dried brown bands on the glass pot stopped him. He'd have to go out to buy a cup. Why had Betty left at this crucial time. She didn't give a damn!

The phone interrupted the objective scientific analysis of his relationship with his wife.

"Hello."

"Dr. Lawrence?"

"Yes."

"This is Agent Turner of the Park Police. We met before. Is Mrs. Lawrence there?"

"She's out of town until next week."

"Would you tell your wife I called and that I'd like an appointment with her as soon as possible. It's important."

"Is there anything I can do?"

"No thank you, Sir. Would you give Mrs. Lawrence the message?"

"I will."

"Thank you. Here's my number ..."

Dr. Lawrence hung up the phone and stood staring at the dirty dishes. A greasy saucer, stacked too high at a precarious tilt, fell to the floor and cracked. He picked up the pieces and threw them into the garbage. When an asset becomes a liability it is time to cut the losses and dump it.

Betty was no longer an asset. In fact, she was a liability.

Why had she gone to meet John? Stupid!

Triggered by this thought, potential newspaper headlines flashed before him.

SPOUSE SILENCES SCIENTIST'S ACCUSER
Slap on slippery slope nearly fatal.
Wife sent to do dirty work.
Eminent researcher implicated.
Fraud case re-opened.
Failed experiments were federally funded.

This was a can of worms he did not want to open. Perhaps he should dissociate himself from the cause? *Betty, you should have listened to me.*

Grim-faced, he slipped on his jacket and headed for the door. He needed that cup of coffee.

***

The bedroom was dark. Cecilia's mother awoke with a start and groped for the source of the noise. It was the phone. Groaning, she called her daughter.

"Cecilia, ... it's for you ..."

In her room, a weary Cecilia stirred and detached herself from her pillow. She struggled to clear her eyes, as she shuffled to the hallway.

"Hello?"

"'C,' it's me, Sam. ... Did I wake you?"

"Sam, do you know what time it is here? It's not even 6:00 yet."

277

"Sorry 'C,' I just got to the office, my Saturday shift, and ... I forgot about the time difference. Anyway, are you OK? You were supposed to call me yesterday."

Cecilia cleared her mind. Where should she start.

"I was in Benson, it's a town east of here. Lachance is in the hospital there. A rattlesnake, bite, but he's OK now."

"What!"

Cecilia recounted trailing Lachance from the clinic, the arranged phone calls, the hooded trip to the mountain cabin, the shed with the records, the fire. At that, Sam exploded.

"God 'C!' You could have been killed!"

He choked. With an effort he continued.

"Alone, no backup, you're lucky to be alive. Damn it 'C,' what were you thinking?"

He added lamely.

"... and you're on vacation."

Cecilia had no answer to his protestations. He was right, but she was right too. She continued her account, but when she described the false Medicare claims, he interposed.

"That's for the Department of Justice, Civil Division. The DOJ's Money and Finance lawyers will handle that. Look 'C,' could you see who burned the shed?"

"No, it had to be McElroy. Pierre said ..."

"It couldn't have been the caretaker?"

"No he was gone. Besides, there was a car. McElroy drove away."

"OK, so it *was* the bastard. Felony assault on a Federal officer, intent to kill. This is for the FBI. My God 'C!' You promised me you'd avoid the clinic!"

Sam choked, then continued.

"Don't do another thing till I call the boss. It's Saturday. He's home. I'll reach him and call you back. Stay put, for God's sake!"

"Sam, I promise I'll stay away from the clinic, but I have to drive back to Benson. I'll call you tonight."

"Cecilia!"

"I'll call you tonight."

She hung up. She felt bad for Sam. He was goodhearted, but she had to see Pierre.

Groaning, Cecilia slumped back to bed and buried her face in the pillow. She dozed.

When she awoke, the sun was bright. She ate. After her mother returned from shopping, Cecilia took the car and headed for Benson to see Pierre.

She had to do what she had to do.

***

Dr. McElroy, attired in a dark navy suit, sat in his office. Lights blinked on his phone console. He picked up. The voice was familiar.

"Doc?"

"This is Dr. McElroy"

"This here's Darwin. I was to thuh cabin t'day."

"Yes Darwin. What can I do for you?"

"There's been a fire up there. The shed burned. All gone, and all them boxes too. All burned."

Dr. McElroy had expected this call. It was Saturday and Darwin always checked the property on Saturday. Dr. McElroy wanted to act surprised at the news of the fire, and of the bodies; one charred body in the blackened remains of the shed, and the other swollen and dead of snakebite.

Darwin's voice filled the pause.

"I reckon she did it. Burned the shed I mean."

Dr. McElroy's surprise was not faked.

"She? ... What she? ... You mean the body?"

"What body? T'warn't no body! I mean thuh gal you locked in the shed. I let her out. T'was Thursday."

"You let her out?"

"Yup. Mighty pretty. Black hair. Mexican I reckon, but you knew that."

279

Hernandez! She wasn't in the shed. Dr. McElroy's facial muscles contorted. He loosened his collar and pushed his chair back from the desk.

"What were you doing there Thursday?"

"I missed last Saturday 'cause o' the holidays."

Dr. McElroy calmed himself. He had to find out about Pierre!

"Is the cabin OK?"

"Yup. It's fine. Only the shed and a coupl'ol' pines burned."

"You checked the cabin good?"

"Yup. Found a critter in it though. I got rid of him."

"What do you mean critter?"

"Big ol' rattler. I smashed him good. He won't bother nobody no more. Funny, a Diamond-Back. First of those I seed up in the mountains, they're usually down low in the desert."

"That's all?"

"That's it, Doc. Ya comin' up to see?"

"Yes. Thank you Darwin. I'll be up in a day or two."

Darwin hung up.

Dr. McElroy, sat motionless behind his desk, his mind racing and his hands quivering. *Where was that damned Hernandez? And where was Pierre?*

***

For a long time Dr. McElroy sat in silence. No bodies! What had happened? He could not afford to mope. He must act. He consulted a list of hospitals and clinics, and checked those closest to his cabin. He left the clinic and drove to a nearby supermarket. There he purchased a pre-pay cell phone. He would not use his own name, nor that of his clinic. The first three calls were uninformative. His fourth call was to a clinic in Benson, Arizona. He spoke with authority.

"This is Dr. Jones at the University Hospital here in Tucson. Did you have a patient admitted for snake bite in the last few days?"

"Let me check, Doctor."

"Thank you."

"Yes, we did have an admission for a snake bite. A male. ..."

"A Mr. Lejeune, Pierre Lejeune?"

"No, Doctor, I'm sorry, a Mr. Lachance."

Dr. McElroy did not reveal his excitement. He spoke smoothly.

"We have a project here at the university that studies the effects of cryotherapy in the treatment of poisonous bites, in addition to antivenin of course. We study not just reptilian bites, but scorpions, spiders, etc. Do you know if cryotherapy was used in this case?"

"I'm sorry Doctor, I don't have that information, but you could speak to the physician."

"That's not necessary. If I drove there today would I be able to speak to the patient? How is he doing?"

"I don't think that would be a problem. He's doing very well. If he continues at the present pace, he'll be discharged tomorrow or Monday, but he'll still be here today."

"Thank you very much. I'll drive over then. You are Miss? ..."

"Miss Robinson."

"Thank you Miss Robinson. Thanks very much."

Dr. McElroy whistled to himself as he drove back to the clinic. Down the hallway was his private laboratory. There on a table was a row of four glass-fronted cages. The fourth was empty, but the other three were occupied. Each held a diamondback rattlesnake.

Dr. McElroy fashioned a rubber diaphragm over a glass dish. He was out of practice. He had not done this in a long time and his hand shook. Still he was confident. He seized the first snake by the back of the neck. Mouth gaping, the exposed fangs pierced the diaphragm. Dr. McElroy applied pressure to the sides of the head. Drops of venom oozed down the side of the dish and collected at the bottom. There was lots of venom. The snake had not been "milked" in over a year. He dropped the snake back in its cage. He was glad that he had kept these "pets" as souvenirs of that defunct project.

When he finished milking the two remaining snakes, he collected the venom into a syringe. This he placed in his satchel. Going to the closet he removed a surgical gown and mask, and likewise placed them in the black satchel. He left the room.

He took the Mercedes to Benson.

***

After coffee, Dr. Lawrence drove to the university. He sat in his office, lost in thought. Then he picked up the phone and dialed. A voice answered.

"McSorley, Haslet and Wilson."

"Charles Haslet, please."

"Your name?"

"Dr. Lawrence."

"Thank you Dr. Lawrence. Just a moment please."

Dr. Lawrence drummed his fingers and waited. A cheerful voice came on the line.

"Franklin! How are you? And how's Betty?"

"Charley. That's why I'm calling. Fact is we're not doing well. Not at all."

"The hell you say. What's up?"

Dr. Lawrence's voice was strained. His own words appeared strange, as if spoken by someone else. Yet it was his voice.

"Betty and I don't see each other anymore. It's not working out. It's been like this a long time. I want a legal separation. Maybe a divorce."

"The hell you say. What does Betty think?"

"She doesn't know. Sari and Betty are in Arizona. She left against my wishes."

Charley's voice tailed off in shock.

"The hell you say."

"Damn it, Charley. Can't you say something besides 'the hell you say.'"

"Sorry Franklin, It's just that I'm in shock. I thought you and Betty had it all together. I didn't know, that's all. Are you sure you don't want time to think?"

"I want legal separation papers drawn up today."

"The hell ..."

Charley corrected himself in mid sentence.

"Look Franklin, I'm sorry. Divorces aren't my line. But there's a good lawyer in the firm who can help you, Jack Scully. I think he's here in the office today. Do you want me to get him on the line."

"Please."

"OK, hold on."

Dr. Lawrence waited once more. When, finally, Jack Scully Esq. came on the phone he was all business. He was busy on another case this weekend, but he would work Dr. Lawrence in, if he came over right away. Dr. Lawrence agreed.

As he left the Forster Building, Dr. Lawrence stopped at Dr. Santini's office. It was Saturday and Dr. Santini was absent of course, but as usual the secretary was there. He called to her.

"I'm going out. I'll be back in a couple of hours."

He made up his mind to divorce Betty. She would no longer drag him down. Her encounter with John Martin at Stony Man would not count against him!

***

Agent Turner stood outside room B326 at the Fairland University Hospital. He knocked and pushed the door open. Monique sat by the bed. She looked up. John, immobilized because of his leg, tightened his hand on Monique's. Agent Turner spoke.

"I didn't mean to surprise you. I'm Agent Turner of the Park Police. You're Dr. Martin, I'm sure. How are you Miss Laurier?"

Monique smiled at the agent. She sensed his change of attitude.

John let go her hand and fixed his eyes on Turner.

"Monique told me that you are investigating my fall at Stony Man."

"That's right, Dr. Martin. You gave us all quite a scare. I'm glad to see you looking better. You know, we all thought you were pushed. Do you want to comment on that?"

That question was a test. Neither Monique nor John knew that he had verified Mrs. Lawrence's presence on the mountain that near-fatal evening.

There was a long pause. Agent Turner was conscious of the long interval. Whatever John's answer, it would be prepared carefully. Monique felt John squeeze her hand.

The agent decided to intervene. If John wished to protect Mrs. Lawrence that was his business; however Turner wanted honest answers.

"I know Mrs. Lawrence was on the mountain with you. We have witnesses."

Monique sighed. John spoke.

"Yes, she was at Stony Man with me. We were talking."

"And?"

"It got heated. She was afraid I would make trouble for her husband, Dr. Lawrence."

"What happened then?"

"I said something. I'm not sure what any more, but she swung at me. It was slippery. She fell. I caught her."

"And then?"

"When I straightened up, some rock slipped under my foot. I couldn't catch myself."

"Did she push you?"

John had a vivid image of Mrs. Lawrence swinging at him. In all honesty, in the heat of the moment, it was like a push. But he had caught her. *After* that he had fallen. *What the hell.*

Suppose she did push at me. Poor Mrs. Lawrence. It's not important now.

He looked at Turner.

"No. I fell."

"Did she cause you to fall?"

John chose his words.

"Indirectly I guess, but she did not *cause* my fall. It was the slippery rock."

"Was anyone else present? Like Jeannine Ryan?"

"No and no. No one else was there."

Agent Turner was satisfied.

"Thanks very much Dr. Martin. I'm going to close the file on this accident. I'll see Mrs. Lawrence when she comes back to town, but I expect that to be a formality."

Agent Turner closed his notebook and prepared to leave. At the door, he turned.

"Dr. Martin, on a personal note, I think you are fortunate to have friends like Miss Laurier and Miss Ryan. I hope you appreciate them."

Looking at Monique, he added.

"Miss Laurier, please tell Miss Ryan that I admire her candor. Tell her I'm sorry that I misjudged her."

Agent Turner paused once more. He was at the boundary of professional standards, but his feelings forced him.

"Miss Laurier, Dr. Hartness appears to dislike Miss Ryan intensely. You might tell her that I think she should watch out for him. Tell her to be careful."

He turned to John one last time.

"Thanks for your time Dr. Martin. I hope you're out of that bed soon."

He left.

***

Back at the university, Dr. Lawrence felt a strange mixture of relief and satisfaction. His new lawyer, Jack Scully had agreed to call Betty in Tucson to inform her of Dr. Lawrence's intentions. The call was a courtesy. She would be served papers upon her return from Tucson.

Dr. Lawrence was relieved. Any publicity concerning Betty and John would refer to Betty as his "estranged" wife. He had protected his career.

The phone rang, and he picked up. He was happy to hear this voice.

"Dr. Lawrence, ... I mean, ... Franklin?"

"Yes Sharon. How are you?"

"Fine, Sir. My editor is sending me to Washington to get background for my story about you and the lab, and L-12."

Dr. Lawrence was exhilarated.

"Splendid Sharon. Your timing is perfect. When will you arrive?"

"I'm arriving Reagan National the day after New Year's. Tuesday, in the afternoon."

"Wonderful, we can have dinner together and get started right away!"

Sharon was surprised and pleased by Dr. Lawrence's enthusiasm. She needed his cooperation.

"That won't inconvenience you, Sir?"

"Franklin. Call me Franklin. Not at all. What hotel are you staying at?"

Sharon named a hotel near the university.

"Fine. I'll pick you up there Tuesday at 6:30. We can go to a French restaurant nearby. It'll be my treat. I look forward to seeing you!"

"Thank you, Franklin. I look forward to working with you, Sir."

Franklin winced at the last "Sir." It didn't matter. Sharon was coming. This was fate. He was sure of it. He wanted to tell her to wear her green suit. He decided not to.

"I'll go over your draft this weekend. By the way, the paper by Dr. Hartness and myself got favorable reviews. It's accepted for publication. It will be published."

He was loathe to describe the problems with his wife, but on Tuesday, he would use Betty's lack of understanding to obtain Sharon's sympathy. He needed consolation.

After Sharon hung up, he called Le Papillon for dinner reservations.

***

Cecilia drove east on Interstate 10 towards Benson and the clinic where Lachance was hospitalized. Pierre was the link between McElroy and the burnt shed. Alone, Cecilia could not confirm that McElroy had been at the cabin, much less the shed.

She drove faster than the speed limit. She approached an eighteen wheeler and signaled left to pass. From behind her, a Mercedes appeared, faster. She cut back behind the truck. Before she could catch her breath, the cream-colored car had passed both her and the truck. The Mercedes was traveling over ninety miles per hour.

She recalled Dr. McElroy's car, and the fallen boy, Pedro. That car had been a cream Mercedes. She increased her speed and passed the truck, but the Mercedes had disappeared.

Cecilia checked the gasoline gauge. It registered empty. She would have to stop for gas, and she was an hour from Benson.

***

Dr. McElroy parked two blocks from the clinic, and walked the remaining distance. His adrenaline was flowing, and he had just enough fear to maintain an awareness of the risks in what he was to do. Speaking to himself, he buoyed his own confidence, *All right Mackie, you've always been smarter than the others, and a hell of a lot more clever. This is no different. No dumb Quebecer is going to take down everything you've built up. You can do it. If anyone sees you, walk away and try later.*

He entered by a side door and slipped into the rest room. He emerged in a surgical robe, masked and capped.

It was lunch time. He passed the lunchroom and heard sounds of laughter and bits of animated conversation. He located Pierre's room and stepped inside.

287

Pierre's eyes were open. To inspire confidence, Dr. McElroy showed his patient the uplifted syringe and motioned him to silence. With an expert motion he vented the air bubbles through the vertical needle. He examined Pierre's arm. Blood vessels in the blackened necrotic tissue surrounding the bite had been destroyed, digested. He chose a spot near that area to insert the needle. He pushed the syringe.

Pierre drew back in agony, but supposed that the masked surgeon knew what he was doing. Dr. McElroy nodded to reassure him and left the room.

He exited as he had come, by the side door. Once outside he paused and removed his robe, but left the mask and surgical cap in place. He walked to his car. He did not remove the mask until he was back on Interstate 10.

***

Cecilia entered the clinic to find the staff in turmoil. The receptionist refused to let her see Pierre. Nurses ran back and forth. It was a half hour before the physician came to the lobby.

"Miss Hernandez, I don't know what happened. I've never seen anything like this. It's like a recurrence of the bite, but more powerful. It's venom all right, but I don't understand. We don't get that many snake bites, but it's never happened before. We've done all we can. It's the damnedest thing."

"May I see him?"

"He's unconscious, and it's not pretty."

"I'd still like to."

"Come with me. It can't hurt, there's nothing ..."

He didn't finish. Cecilia looked through the open door. Pierre's arm was blackened and twice its normal size. The doctor stepped past her into the room. The nurse shook her head. He turned back to Cecilia.

"He's gone."

***

******

Chapter 32
Tuesday, January 2

It was the most melancholic task Cecilia ever had performed. Pierre's mother, Lucille Lachance, had spent the New Year's weekend in the Laurentians. At last, this morning, Cecilia had reached her with the news of Pierre's death. The redemption Cecilia had experienced when she saved Pierre's life had disappeared with his death. All redeeming memories dissolved in Lucille's tears. Those tears increased as Cecilia talked to Lucille about her mother, Madame Gauthier. Cecilia had failed this family twice. Her French was not adequate to express her emotions.

Through her sobs, Lucille still managed to thank Cecilia.

"Je vous remercie d'avoir m'app ... encore ... merci. Thank you ... for calling."

Cecilia thought of Lucille's faithless husband. Too much sorrow for one woman. Was there a limit to her suffering?

Cecilia steeled herself for one more call, to Lise Jordan in Burlington.

After speaking to Lise, Cecilia could take no more. Her head ached and her shoulders were heavy. The rattlesnake had been meant for her, a natural "accident". Though she realized that Pierre had tried to play both sides, at the end, to save her, he had refused to go along with McElroy. Now he was dead.

She had not seen the driver of the Mercedes, but was sure it was that bastard McElroy. Somehow, he had killed Pierre.

She had to do something. She would call Sam. He would listen to her plaints.

***

"Miss Jones" was smiling. For the past two days she had felt her breast carefully. The lump was gone! She wanted to sing! Dr. Hermann appeared at the door. She stepped towards him.

"Good morning Doctor. It's gone! My cancer is gone!"

She was radiant and because of that all the more beautiful. She bared her breasts for his examination. Dr. Hermann was human, but he put aside all emotions. He could not be distracted. He decided to be honest with Miss Jones.

"Miss Jones, you can leave today if you like. You're fine."

"But what about the Tamoxifen, and weren't you going to use radiation? ... Dr. McElroy said ..."

Dr. Hermann was direct.

"Miss Jones, you are fine. There was no cancer. It was a cyst. There was no malignancy. You don't need an operation. You don't need further treatment. Your breasts are perfect."

She wanted to hug this wonderful man. Dr. Hermann took a step backwards.

"We can discharge you this morning."

She had a spring in her feet that she had not felt for weeks. Sideways she checked her bare breasts in the mirror. She turned back to Dr. Hermann. She caught his look and covered herself.

"Doctor, what can I do for you. How much do I owe you?"

"You've been here a week, but you could have been released earlier. The bill should be about $20,000, no more."

That was not a proper measure of her gratitude. She placed her hand on his shoulder and smiled up at him. She would not be undervalued.

"Nonsense. I insist on giving $500,000. Would that help?"

"But you've already given a million."

"And I was prepared to give another million. Believe me, I want to do this."

She knew what her health was worth!

"If you insist, we would be most grateful."

"Should I make it to the special account, like the first check?"

"What do you mean?"

"I made the first check to Dr. McElroy. He said it was a special account."

Dr. Hermann was accustomed to McElroy's dealings, but this went too far. He gritted his teeth, but did not reveal his concern.

"No. Just make it out to the *AMAH Clinic*. And we appreciate your generosity very much."

"Would you tell Rob I want him to start packing?"

"Certainly, and thanks again."

He permitted himself one personal remark. He meant it.

"You are beautiful."

She smiled at him. Then she bared her breasts and examined herself in the mirror.

He stared a moment, and then left. He wanted to see Dr. McElroy.

***

Dr. Hermann stepped into the corridor and almost collided with Dr. Wilson. She was a Ph. D. clinical psychologist who had several patients at the clinic. She was young, feminine, and always smiled. He grabbed her arm.

"What's the rush. How's your new patient?"

Dr. Wilson's new patient was Mattie Morton.

"She's doing fine. I've had several sessions with her and her mother together. I don't think she'll need to stay long. But I will have to see them both as outpatients. Look, I have to go."

"Can I talk to you later?"

She looked at her watch.

"Sure. I have a break in half an hour. But Jim, have you seen Dr. McElroy today?"

"Not yet. I'm looking for him too."

"See you in thirty minutes."

"Thanks."

Jim Hermann continued his search for Dr. McElroy.

***

Dr. McElroy was not to be found.

He was not in his office. Nor was he in the adjacent laboratory. Dr. Hermann stared. The laboratory was spotless.

In particular, the counter under the window was bare. The four cages were gone. *What did he do with the rattlesnakes?*

He mused aloud.

"It's about time. That project's been over more than a year."

"Jim, are you talking to yourself?"

Startled, he turned. It was Janice Wilson.

"I guess so. I still can't find Dr. McElroy."

"Me neither, but I'm on my break. Do you still want to talk?"

"You bet. You can tell me all about Eating Disorders."

They headed down the hall to the staff room.

***

When Dr. Wilson had informed Helen Morton that Mattie needed to be near the clinic for several months, Helen had acted immediately. Mattie was everything to her, and she had no worries about money. Helen rented a furnished home in the Santa Catalina foothills and invited Betty and Sari to stay with her. After Betty's traumatic conversation with Franklin's lawyer, she and Sari were happy to accept. In turn, Helen was grateful to Betty and Sari for their companionship for herself and Mattie.

Helen and Betty sipped afternoon iced tea. Sari sunbathed at the edge of the ceramic-lined pool.

Betty looked at her daughter.

"I hope she's warm enough?"

Helen smiled.

"I'm sure she is. This is not Maryland."

Betty wasn't so sure.

"Lots of people around here are wearing sweaters or windbreakers."

"Those are the natives. We Easterners are in shirtsleeves. Remember the weather we left back home. Sari's fine. Don't worry about her."

"Helen, thanks for having us. I don't know what I would have done. God, when that Scully lawyer called me, I couldn't think. ... All those years. ..."

"Honey, Honey. All men are like that. Franklin's as bad as Kenneth. No I take it back. I hope he's not as bad as that SOB. Look, Franklin doesn't know how lucky he was to have you. He's a rat. You're better off without ..."

Helen's voice trailed off, she resumed.

"He'll wise up in a few days, and when he comes crawling, you can give *him* the boot!"

***

The phone rang. Helen picked up.

"It's for you Betty."

"Mrs. Lawrence, this is Agent Turner of the Park Police."

Betty gasped. She could not speak.

"I don't want you to worry, M'am. John Martin has given a full statement of what happened on the mountain. M'am, I wish you had called right away, and not waited until you got to Luray, but I wanted you to know that I'm closing this file today. Dr. Martin says he fell, and I have to accept that. Are you there, M'am?"

"Yes, Mr. Turner, I'm here."

"I called your husband and told him too. He said you were staying in Tucson indefinitely. I hope that's not because of the accident."

"No Mr. Turner, my husband and I are having difficulties. Sari will be going to school here this semester."

"I'm sorry to hear that M'am, but next time call the authorities right away. Anyway, this case is closed now."

"Thank you Mr. Turner."

"Thank Dr. Martin. Good-bye M'am."

Betty hung up. She told Helen the whole story of her visit to Stony Man. She finished with Franklin's reaction, his anger.

Helen sat back in silence. Dr. Lawrence might be worse, even, than her ex.

Betty covered her face and sobbed. Helen rubbed her shoulders. Betty had come to Tucson to help Helen. Now their roles were reversed.

***

Next to the pool, Sari stretched out in the sun. Her stomach churned and her thoughts were in turmoil. *God, daddy, what did I do? I'm sorry. I know I've been a real pain. I'm really sorry!*

Mom is sorry too. Please. I can change, I won't get in the way anymore and I'll try to be good, and I won't bug you about designer jeans or anything else. I'm sorry I'm always in the way.

... But how could you hurt Mom like this! ... And what about me! We're a family aren't we? ... Don't you love me?

***

Betty lifted her head from her hands and stared out at her daughter. She already had a tan.

Oh to be young and unconcerned! At least Sari was OK. Thank God for that!

***

Dr. Lawrence met Sharon in the hotel lobby at 6:30 p.m. She shone in her green suit, and her greenish blue eyes sparkled. He smiled and took her hand.

The attentiveness of the great scientist flattered Sharon. She was a reporter, and far from naive, but she was delighted that a man of his knowledge and reputation wanted to impress her. He was distinguished, not bad looking at all. She returned his smile.

The restaurant, Le Papillon, was a short walk. It was already dark outside. The air was much warmer than in Chicago, and there was no cold, lake-spawned wind. She listened as Dr. Lawrence, "Franklin," outlined their schedule together for the next day. This was going to be a good story, an exclusive, with her byline.

The deferential Maître d' placed them at a secluded table. A candle was lit with a flourish, and the menus placed in front of them with the sweeping grace of a Baryshnikov.

Dr. Lawrence watched the candle's reflection in Sharon's eyes. The flickering flame brightened and shadowed her Slavic cheeks. She was stunning. Franklin thought of her article. She understood his science too! He was smitten. He wanted her.

"Sharon, they have wonderful smoked lobster. Would you like to try it?"

Sharon was game.

Dr. Lawrence ordered expertly.

"Le homard rôti et fumé dans la cheminée. Yes, two please, and a bottle of, let's see, a white burgundy would be nice, a Meursault. That looks like a good year."

He pointed to his selection. The waiter nodded approvingly.

Franklin smiled at Sharon. She returned his smile. She was glad he was paying. She had seen the prices on the menu.

***

Jeannine stumbled into the apartment, and deposited the heavy SAS software manuals on the floor. Her arms were stretched out of their sockets. She had toted them three blocks from the nearest parking space.

She had spent New Year's in Morgantown, West Virginia, with her mother and stepfather and this morning had returned straight to work at StatFind Associates. Finally she was home, exhausted.

Monique called from the kitchen.

"How was the trip. How's your mother?"

"She's fine but my *stepfather* is the same as ever."

Hearing Jeannine's pronunciation of "stepfather," Monique dropped that topic.

"OK, how was your first day at StatFind?"

Jeannine groaned.

"All computer, no math. I've got carpal tunnel syndrome!"

"And your boss?"

"Not bad, for a guy. He knows computers, but he's no mathematician."

From the kitchen, Monique spied a pile of books.

"What's all that stuff?"

"Their stat program is SAS. That's my homework. What's for supper?"

"I made tourtière."

"Great. Any apple pie left?"

"One piece, for you."

Monique turned to the stove, and called over her shoulder.

"John's doing great. He remembers everything. He wants to talk to you about Mike, and Agent Turner stopped by Saturday. He knew it was Mrs. Lawrence before John told him. He said the case is closed, an accident, and to say that he was sorry he suspected you.

"So he finally did his homework."

"Yes. And he also said to warn you about Mike Hartness."

"How does he know Mike?"

"I don't know, but he said be careful. He doesn't trust Mike But supper's on the table. Let's eat."

***

Mike Hartness walked up and down the B corridor of the third floor of Fairland University Hospital. The door to room B326 was shut. On his third pass, he paused and reached for the doorknob.

A voice stopped him. It was the blond nurse who spoke.

"Visiting hours are over."

"I'm looking for Dr. Martin."

"I'm sure he's asleep. I'm sorry but you'll have to leave."

"I just wanted to ask him a question."

"I'm sorry."

She walked back to the nurses' station. He followed. She reached for the phone.

"All right. All right. I'll leave."

Mike took the elevator to the lobby. He stepped into the night air, and pulled his jacket around him. A damp winter rain made him shiver. *What does John remember? No matter. He can't make Dr. Lawrence give him credit for L12. But what about that redhead Ryan? And why hadn't Turner called him for his statement?*

Drops on the branches overhead glistened in the lights of the passing traffic. Mike looked upwards. Lights shone from windows on all floors of the Main Med building. *Damn it. Researchers don't sleep enough.*

Across the street, a young couple, arms locked around each other, stepped out of Le Papillon. The man staggered, too much to drink. As the pretty woman steadied him, he embraced her. They stood by the entrance, bodies merged into a single shadow.

The scene made Mike think about Monique. His turn would come. He knew it.

As he started to walk away, a car illuminated the clinging couple. It was only for an instant, but that was enough. The sight of the man made his jaw drop.

The "young" man was Dr. Lawrence!

Mike froze. The couple, unaware of his presence, walked away arm in arm. They appeared oblivious to the light rain.

***

******

Chapter 33
Wednesday, January 3

Sharon Husak stretched her arms and yawned. Eyes closed, her head sank back into the pillow. Her ears buzzed. The effects of the wine and the after-meal cognac were still with her. She groped for her watch on the end table.

The sudden movement caused a sharp pain in her forehead. She shook her head and sat up. *What time is it?* She focused on the faint hands of her wristwatch. She needed a digital readout. It was 8:00. She had two hours before meeting Dr. Lawrence at 10:00.

Sharon stumbled to the shower. The cold water cleared her thoughts. She would be careful with alcohol around Franklin. She combed her hair and spoke to the mirror.

"At least you showed *some* sense when you didn't let him in the room. Sharon! What made you let that old guy paw you like that?"

The answer was simple. She was flattered that the eminent researcher found her attractive, and the alcohol and the ambiance of the expensive restaurant had helped. What had he said? He liked her *scientific mind*. She had a *deep understanding* of his research. Her article was *perceptive.* Sharon wanted to believe him, but she was determined not to let hormones drive their sessions. She had a series of articles to write.

Still, it didn't hurt to keep "Franklin" off balance.

With that thought, she stepped to the dresser and selected her tightest-fitting skirt, navy, to wear to his office. Then she rejected her flat shoes and chose heels instead. Although she could pass for a student, she chose to look older.

Sharon filled the hotel coffee maker and brewed a cup. She made it strong. She sat and sipped while she collected her notes. The phone rang.

"Sharon, this is Franklin. Did you sleep well?"

"Yes, I did. It was an elegant meal."

"Glad you liked it. Should I pick you up? We could have breakfast."

Sharon looked out the window at the clearing sky. She could walk to the university in ten minutes, and she had over an hour before their meeting. She wanted to be alone.

"Franklin, I'd like that, but I'm going over my notes, and I better get ready. I'm trying to learn as much as I can so I can ask you reasonable questions."

Franklin was disappointed.

"Of course. I'll see you at the lab at ten."

Sharon softened.

"Thanks for the wonderful dinner last night. I enjoyed it very much."

She was too honest to say more, but Franklin imagined that she had.

"Great, I'll see you at ten in my office."

She hung up and picked up the latest version of his manuscript. She had to cool Dr. Lawrence down, she wanted this story!

***

Sharon was deep into an article on cancer when she heard a knock. She was dressed except for her shoes. She left them on the floor and went to the door.

Through the peephole she could see a man. The distortion and haze caused by the fogged lens distorted his features.

"Who is it?"

"It's Dr. Hartness from the lab. I work with Dr. Lawrence."

Sharon loosened the chain and opened the door. She took a sharp breath. The man standing in front of her was tall and rather good looking. She smiled her approval and held out her hand.

"You're the other author of the L-12 paper."

"Right, I'm Mike. You're Sharon, right? I read your draft. It's great. Great job!"

"Come on in. I'm just boning up for my meeting with Dr. Lawrence. You must be grateful to work with him."

"I am. It's a privilege. Look, I know you're seeing the great man at ten, but would you like to have lunch with me at 12:30. There's a fun hang out, the Old Goose. I'll buy you a sandwich and a beer. I want you to see the *young* and *single* side of campus."

Sharon caught the emphasis and looked into Mike's eyes. The confidence she saw attracted her, and he *was* good looking.

"Sounds good to me. Dr. Lawrence is busy this afternoon anyway. Are heels OK?"

She indicated her shoes lying askew on the carpet.

"Sure. They're fine. Anything goes there, and I'll bring the latest draft of our article."

"Mike, are you an M. D. or a Ph. D.?"

"Ph. D., six years ago."

Sharon smiled. He wasn't a "doctor" doctor, but everything else was positive. She listened as Mike told her how to get from the Forster Building to the Old Goose.

***

Mike was pleased with himself and with Sharon, but he had another mission to perform. He left the hotel. His next stop was the Fairland University Hospital. At the nursing station on the third floor, no one stopped him. He entered room B326.

John Martin was in a chair next to the bed. The cast on his leg had been removed. Crutches leaned against the near wall.

"Hello Martin."

"Hartness, what are you doing here?"

"I'm doing you a favor. A letter for you came to the lab last Friday. Read it."

John took the envelope. It was from the Office of Research Integrity. It had been opened and resealed with tape.

He looked up and frowned. Mike laughed.

"That's right. I opened it by mistake. I read it! Now it's your turn. They're letting you off easy. You're only debarred for three years."

John removed the letter from the envelope and read.

December 27
John Martin, Ph. D.
Laboratory of Immunology
Fairland University School of Medicine
Washington DC
Dear Dr. Martin,
This is to inform you that the Office of Research Integrity has reviewed, and concurs with, the finding of the Fairland University School of Medicine that you committed research misconduct by fabricating radioactive counts for an experiment performed under grant R01 CA26B12-01 from the National Cancer Institute.
Accordingly the Secretary, Department of Health and Human Services, recommends that you
1. Be excluded from eligibility for all federal grants, contracts and cooperative agreements for three years.
2. Be excluded from service on Public Health Service advisory committees, boards or peer review committees for three years.
A notice of this finding will be published in the Federal Register.
If you choose to contest this finding and/or these actions, you must notify this office within thirty days of the receipt of this letter.
Sincerely,
Director,
Office of Research Integrity.

John 's face reddened.

Mike grinned.

"See Martin, you're finished. No one believed you or your stupid girl friends."

John reached for his crutches and struggled from the chair. He stood before Mike.

"You know damn well what you did."

"Sure. What's the harm in a little fake data when you're in a hurry?"

"Hartness, you're a disgrace. Get out of science."

"You've got it backwards. You're the one who's out. Be glad you're only debarred for three years."

The grin widened.

"I tried to do you a favor. I tried to get Dr. Lawrence to keep Monique in the lab. I wanted him to include Monique as an author, but she refused. Ask her. Dr. Lawrence *ordered* me to get all her data and notes. And as for your work, he made me write it up. He insisted that the cells belong to him. It's his grant, and his data. He and I have a paper accepted for publication. Hell, I wanted both you and Monique as authors, but he wouldn't have you."

"Mike looked up at the ceiling, as if thinking.

"Hell, I don't blame him. You were guilty of misconduct. Why would Lawrence want you on the paper. You're a screw-up. You're bad news."

Mike enjoyed mixing truth and falsehood. He continued.

"Take my advice, Martin. Pack up and leave. Forget biology. Forget research. You can't have a grant for three years, and after that you'll never get one. No one will touch you. If you try and fight Dr. Lawrence, he'll crush you, like he crushed that redhead of yours. That's right, Ryan is gone too. Dr. Lawrence killed her fellowship. She had to quit the Stat department. She and Monique are both out, and you're to blame. If they hadn't stuck up for you, they'd still be at the university."

He looked John in the eye.

"You know Martin, if you go quietly, maybe I could convince Dr. Lawrence to take Monique back. Unless I change his mind, Lawrence will see that she never gets another research job. Anywhere! Think about it."

"Hartness, Go to hell!"

"Ok. But Martin, you're finished! If Monique goes down with you that's your business."

Mike's lips curled into a sneer.

"But if you like the little bitch so much, why drag her down with you? Don't forget the world knows you're a scientific cheat!"

Mike spun about and left the room, leaving a frustrated John to ponder what he had heard.

***

In Tucson, Cecilia's mother and father were downstairs. She used the upstairs phone. There was no need to disturb her parents.

"Sam, I did everything you said. I gave the local FBI the records from the shed. They'll send them to the Department of Justice."

"What about Pierre's gun?"

"They checked it out. It's registered to the *AMAH Clinic*. He was in charge of security there, except he was Pierre 'Lejeune,' not 'Lachance.'"

"And the cabin?"

"McElroy owns it. That's how we found it. We went there yesterday.

"We?"

"Me and two FBI guys. The cabin had been cleaned. We couldn't find the snake."

Cecilia's thoughts drifted from the cabin to the charred remains of the shed and the scorched trunks of the nearby Apache pines. The shed's concrete slab floor had cracked under the intense heat. The branches that had extended above the shed had disappeared, vaporized. Their memory marked by short black stubs that protruded from the burned bark of the main trunks. *What if?*

She shuddered.

"Cecilia, are you there?"

"Sorry, Sam. I was just thinking."

304

"I don't suppose any records were left?"

"There was nothing like that. Everything burned. We found the padlock, but that was all. The autopsy showed that the cause of death was a snakebite. But Sam, don't worry about me. I'm flying back to Washington, *early*. I won't get in any more trouble!"

Sam was silent. She could not tell if she had calmed his concerns. He sighed.

"Bye 'C.'"

"Bye, Sam."

Numb and weary, Cecilia turned to her packing. Dr. Hermann had not returned her call. She did not care.

***

At the *AMAH Clinic*, Dr. Hermann stared in amazement at the mice. They were a tumor-receptive strain, and he had implanted tumors into them some time ago, planning to test A-11. When the L-12 became available, he had used that reagent instead. He was stunned that in the short length of time, less than a week, there was a clear response. Twelve mice, all with tumors decreasing in size! Where was McElroy? He had to see this!

He found the receptionist, Paula.

"Have you seen Dr. McElroy?"

"He's gone for a few days. He's in Mexico, at the hacienda. He might be back after the weekend."

Dr. Hermann needed to share the good news. If he couldn't find Dr. McElroy, he still could talk to the originator of L-12.

"Paula, get me the number of Dr. Lawrence, Fairland University Medical School, Washington, D. C. I need to talk to him."

***

Dr. Lawrence sat close to Sharon. Together they studied her draft. He let his hand slip to her thigh, but she stiffened. He withdrew. She pretended not to notice.

"Franklin, what about this paragraph. Is that accurate?"

"It's not bad, but I think you should explain '*Loss of Heterozygosity*' earlier, so the reader doesn't have to guess what it means."

He looked at Sharon out of the corner of his eye. She scratched corrections on her pad. She was all business this morning. Had she forgotten last night? Maybe she was shy?

The phone interrupted his thoughts.

"This is Dr. Lawrence."

"Dr. Lawrence, you don't know me. I'm Dr. Hermann, Jim Hermann at the *AMAH Clinic* in Tucson. I work with Dr. McElroy. I've got great news."

Dr. Hermann recounted the initial success with the L-12 *Phase I study.* Twelve of twelve tumors in mice showed signs of remission. In just a few days! Dr. Lawrence listened in amazement, but the source of his amazement was not L-12's success.

Sitting next to him, a shocked Sharon heard him scream.

"L-12! What are you doing with my reagent! Where did you get it? Who are you? Put McElroy on the line!"

A befuddled Hermann stammered.

"Mike Hartness sent it to us. I thought you knew."

At Dr. Lawrence's end of the line Sharon was treated to a string of expletives from the "great man." She sat silent at the tirade. On the other end of the line, Jim Hermann reached his limit. He hung up.

"Click!"

Startled, Dr. Lawrence stared at the dead instrument. Momentarily unaware of Sharon's existence, he sprang from his office. She heard him bellow in the corridor.

"Mike Hartness, where the hell are you? What have you done?"

***

The dress code at StatFind Associates was "computer-relax," and Jeannine fit right in. Her second day at work, she borrowed Monique's gray pullover and tied her hair at the back in a pony tail. What mattered at StatFind was production, not looks. For this, Jeannine was grateful.

She lost herself in the lines of SAS code that she deftly moved up and down the computer screen using the mouse. She heard Wayne's voice behind her and looked up.

"Jeannine, do you have the regression analyses yet?"

"Two more to go. If you wait a second, I'll give them to you."

Jeannine clicked on the icon of a man running, and the SAS log flashed on the screen in front of her. When it stopped moving, the output screen appeared. She clicked on the print icon, and turned to Wayne.

"They're printing at the station behind you. I want to make sure I did what you wanted."

Wayne was the director of the project. Jeannine had impressed him yesterday. He was more impressed today. He turned and scanned the output.

"This is what I want all right. Thanks."

Jeannine smiled. Wayne spoke.

"Look. It's obvious you know what you're doing. Could you suggest a better analysis? Particularly for the second variable."

Jeannine could.

"There's a better way. That relationship is nonlinear, and the variance changes as the X-value increases. Here's another analysis I did. I transformed the data first."

Wayne took in the results at a glance.

"That's much better. Thanks."

He disappeared into his office. Jeannine's thoughts turned back to John and Monique.

***

By the time Mike returned to the laboratory, Dr. Lawrence had left for his meeting. There was a note taped onto Mike's door. Mike read it. Dr. Lawrence was furious about L-12 and Dr.

McElroy! Mike re-taped the note to the door as if it were unread. Then he left the Forster building for the Old Goose.

The day was cool and clear. The morning clouds had dissipated. As he approached the Old Goose, Mike saw Sharon, coat unbuttoned, waiting outside in the cold air. She had come from Chicago. The balmy Washington winter did not challenge her. He shivered, but unbuttoned his own jacket to match hers. His voice was warm.

"Hi. I see you found it."

"Yes, you gave good directions."

Mike took Sharon's arm as they stepped through the door.

Sharon was not shy. Mike was young, available, and much more attractive then Franklin, and he was a co-author of the paper. He could help with her articles. They sat down. Mike spoke first.

"You want a beer?"

"Sharon thought of the night before.

"No thanks. A diet coke is fine."

Mike, too, thought of the night before, and Sharon and Franklin as they embraced in front of the restaurant. He smiled.

"Me too. We've got work to do."

He pulled out the draft of Sharon's article and a draft copy of the manuscript. He jumped right in.

"In this part of your article, I was the one that did the work. I think you should mention my name in that paragraph."

He paused, and continued smoothly.

"Let me tell you how research is done in a lab these days, who really does the work. It'll help you to know the ropes for other projects too."

Mike gave her his best smile. Sharon was not dumb, but like Monique at an earlier time, she was flattered by Mike's attentions, and he was more fun than Franklin!

***

Dr. Lawrence dragged himself up the stairs of the Forster Building. His back was sore from sitting all afternoon around a conference table.

"Damn it!"

When would Santini and Dean Hampton hold a *short* meeting. What a waste of time. At the third floor, he left the stairwell and limped into the lab. His note was still attached to Mike's door, just as he had left it. Where was Mike? He had some explaining to do. He went to his office and eased into the chair behind his desk. The time was 6:30! A whole afternoon had been wasted. He picked up the phone and called Le Papillon.

"Henri, Dr. Lawrence here. I'd like to reserve that same table for two. Yes tonight, at 8:00. Yes, that's the one. Thank you."

The dinner date was to be a surprise for Sharon. He thought of her tight-fitting skirt. Today when they had worked on her article, she had been all business. Tonight they could wine, dine and relax together. Dr. Lawrence kept a razor in his desk. He went to the sink and shaved, humming softly. He returned to his desk and called Sharon's room.

"Rring, ... Rring, ... Rring, ... Rring, ... Rring, ... Rring, ..."

It was quarter of seven. He waited for Sharon to pick up.

"Rring, ... Rring, ... Rring, ... Rring, ... Rring, ..."

There was no answer.

***

Home at last, Jeannine turned to the couch and collapsed. She shed her shoes, and extended her legs. Monique called to her.

"John's walking, he's got crutches."

Jeannine could use crutches herself.

"That sounds good. How is he?"

Monique ignored the question. She had news.

"Mike Hartness was at the hospital. He told John that his data and cells belonged to Dr. Lawrence, and that he tried to get John's name on the article as an author, and me too."

"Monique, Mike loves lying. John didn't believe any of that 'BS,' did he?"

"No, but he wants to get together with us. He got a letter from the ORI. He's debarred from grants for three years. They backed the university committee."

"That figures. I told you Delaney didn't care."

"Mike told John that if he left, Mike might convince Dr. Lawrence to take me back."

Monique's passivity in recounting Mike's deceits distressed Jeannine. She exploded.

"Monique! Stop it! You don't believe that. Get mad! Tell John that Hartness can go to hell. Nothing good for you or John will ever come from that animal! You know that, I know that, and John should know that."

"I know, I know, but how does such a bad person always win? John's career is over, maybe mine too. I can't understand Mike. He's from another world, one I can't live in."

Jeannine put her shoes back on. She hugged Monique.

"You're just too good for this world. Come on. Get your coat. We're going to McDonald's. My treat. Let's stuff ourselves with Big Macs and fries."

Monique forced a smile. She turned off the stove and went with Jeannine.

***

At 7:45 p.m., Dr. Lawrence tried Sharon's room for the last time.

"Rring, ... Rring, ... Rring, ... Rring, ... Rring, ... Rring, ..."

He hung up, disappointed and puzzled. Strange, where was Sharon? Whom did she know in Washington?

He headed for the restaurant to dine alone.

***

In Tucson, Cecilia was in her pajamas. She hugged her mother and father.

"Don't get up tomorrow. The cab will pick me up at 5:00. You need your sleep, and Mama, stop worrying about the plane. I fly all the time. Yo te amo!"

Upstairs, she buried her face in the pillow. Madame Gauthier was dead, and now Pierre. And where was McElroy? Had he won? Had he escaped the FBI?

***

A few miles away, in the dark of her room, Betty waited for daylight. *Franklin! My God! All these years. It wasn't supposed to turn out like this*. She sobbed. *Thank God for Helen!* Money was no object to her. Betty and Sari were welcome indefinitely.

Betty heard a noise in the adjacent room. She slipped out of bed. She held her breath and opened the bedroom door.

There stood Sari, red-eyed and shivering in the warm air.

No words.

They clutched each other and held on.

***

******

Chapter 34
Thursday, January 4

Sharon opened her eyes. The dark curtains over the hotel window were parted at the center so that a line of light split the shadowy room in two. Without turning her head, she felt the other side of the bed. Mike was not there.

Sharon's mind was clear. Neither she nor Mike had imbibed the night before. They had not needed alcohol. She raised her head. Mike, already dressed, sat at the table in the far corner. A small lamp illuminated his work. Doubtless, he was revising her article, adding his own name wherever Dr. Lawrence was mentioned. She would have to delete some of his insertions. She could not write "Dr. Hartness" into every paragraph.

Her instincts had been correct. Mike was more fun than Franklin, but there was a hardness about him that worried her. She knew that Mike wanted to use her, or rather her articles on L-12, for his own gain. She accepted that, because she wanted his scientific expertise to assure her articles were first class.

She would meet Franklin in two hours. She entered the shower. Done, she stepped back into the room wearing only a towel. Mike was too engrossed in his writing to notice.

Sharon slipped into her brown skirt and a simple white blouse. She turned towards Mike.

"You look pretty busy."

Mike did not look up.

"I am. Make me some coffee."

"No thanks. You're a big boy. Make your own coffee."

This time he looked up. Their eyes met. His were blank. In that instant Sharon knew that he was dangerous. Mike caught himself. He needed her publicity. He dropped his gaze to his feet and shuffled them. He looked up and smiled.

"I make strong coffee. How do you want yours? Black?"

He filled the coffee maker and switched it on. Then he stepped to Sharon, placed his hands on her hips and held her. His touch was soft and his smile was gentle.

"You're quite a woman Miss Husak."

Sharon succumbed.

"You're quite a man yourself, Dr. Hartness."

Mike pressed her against the wall and they embraced. Sharon, with both arms around his neck, twisted to see her watch. She would not miss her meeting at 10 o'clock.

***

At the *AMAH Clinic*, Paula stood by while Dr. Hermann spoke on the phone.

"Dr. McElroy. Where are you calling from. I can't hear you. This connection is bad."

Whatever Dr. McElroy's response, Dr. Hermann appeared satisfied. He continued.

"There's a lot to tell you. I told Miss Jones that she did not have cancer. I discharged her yesterday. Yes I told her the truth. She left a check for half a million, made out to the clinic. I need to find out about the first check. She said she made it out to you."

Dr. Hermann listened to the explanation, and then continued.

"OK, we'll talk about that later. L-12 is doing great. Yes, twelve for twelve in remission. What do you think of that? But I called Dr. Lawrence and he didn't know we had the reagent. I told him Mike Hartness sent it to us. He was upset. You have to talk to him, I can't. Yes, Mrs. Lawrence and her daughter are still here. They're staying with Mrs. Morton. No, I don't know for how long. Janice says Mattie is doing fine. Just a minute, Paula wants to talk to you."

Paula took the phone. It was Dr. Hermann's turn to hear one-side of a conversation.

"Dr. McElroy, this is Paula. Yes Sir. Fine, thank you. That FBI man called again. He wants to meet with you. He didn't say. Miss Hernandez? I called her parents' house like you said.

314

She's gone back east. Thank you, Doctor. I'll tell him. Here's Dr. Hermann."

Paula passed the phone back to Dr. Hermann. He spoke for a moment and hung up.

"Paula, call Janice and see if she can come to my lab. Thanks."

Dr. Hermann turned and walked away.

***

Mike enjoyed Sharon. He pulled her against him, tight.

"Rring, ... Rring, ... Rring, ..."

They tried to ignore the phone, but the ringing persisted.

"Rring, ... Rring, ... Rring, ... Rring, ..."

Sharon disengaged and smoothed her blouse. The phone rang one more time.

"Rring."

Sharon picked up.

"Yes?"

"Miss Husak, this is the front desk. Dr. Lawrence said to tell you he's on the way up."

"Thank you."

Before she could hang up, there was a knock on the door. She stared at Mike.

"It's Dr. Lawrence."

Mike paled and ducked into the bathroom. At the door, Sharon kept the chain fastened and spoke through the crack.

"Franklin. What are you doing here? It's early."

"Sharon. Let's have breakfast before we work. The hotel restaurant has great eggs Benedict. It'll give us a head start on the day."

"Wait a minute. I'll get my purse."

Sharon slipped on her shoes and straightened her hair. With a wave to Mike she left the room. She took Franklin's arm. He spoke.

"Where were you last night?"

315

"I stopped by the university library. I checked some of your articles. Why?"

"I just wondered. I missed you."

***

Mike waited a few minutes before leaving Sharon's room. Her room was on the sixth floor. He slipped out and went down the stairwell. His descent was rapid.

He hurried to the Forster building. As he passed the office, the secretary called to him.

"Mike, Dr. Lawrence was looking for you yesterday. He wants to see you."

Mike shrugged and continued past the office. Someday Santini's secretary would have to call him "Dr. Hartness."

He looked at his watch. Sharon was busy with "Franklin" until 4:30 that afternoon. Mike was to meet Sharon at the hotel after. Their evening was planned already.

Mike picked up his mail and left. He wanted to shower and shave before meeting Sharon.

***

Franklin had his own plans for Miss Husak. He proposed them over coffee.

"Sharon, your first article is nearly ready. We should relax. We could take the metro downtown to the National Gallery. I know a perfect place for lunch."

Franklin would make sure that lunch included a good wine. The wine at Le Papillon had produced its salutary effect on Sharon that first night.

Sharon's response sobered him.

"But I think we should work at your office. I need to get the feel for your workplace, the people around you, and all that. I need to experience what you feel day by day."

"We can do that this afternoon, after lunch."

She protested one last time, but Dr. Lawrence persisted.

"Nonsense. We'll have fun, and you'll love lunch!"

Sharon checked the time. It was 10:00 a.m. She must humor "Franklin." She prepared her excuse to return to the university after lunch. She was to meet Mike at 4:30.

They left the hotel. They walked to the metro. Dr. Lawrence squeezed her arm.

***

Jack Scully, the attorney, reached Dr. Lawrence's answering machine.

"Franklin, this is Jack Scully. Just a quick note. The time is 11:00 Thursday morning."

Jack cleared his throat. His tone was professional.

"About your wife staying in Tucson and keeping your daughter there I have a suggestion. The situation is that she's abandoned you, and taken your daughter from you. In other words, *she left you.* I suggest you call a locksmith to change the locks on your home."

Jack's secretary signaled him from the doorway. He had a meeting. He spoke rapidly.

"Meanwhile, Franklin, I'll check a few things here. So far, I don't see any problems. Call me when you get this message or if you have any questions. Bye."

Jack hung up. It had been a useful call. Any fraction of an hour was billed as a full hour.

***

Monique was waiting for Jeannine when she arrived home from StatFind.

"John's leaving research. He wants to take a job at some college in Pennsylvania."

Jeannine responded.

"I know the job. Before this mess with Mike, John received an offer from this college near Pittsburgh. He taught there when he finished his Ph. D. He liked them and they liked him. But there's no time for research. He was going to turn it down."

Monique had an answer.

"I know. Here's the draft from the computer."

She handed a paper to Jeannine who scanned John's text.

Thank you very much for your offer to join the biology faculty at Aquinas and Augustine College (AquA).

As you make clear, AquA is small and lacks the resources for a research program in modern biology. Each teacher has several courses a semester, including laboratories. Further, the excellence in teaching which you maintain requires that staff continually revise and adjust courses as new knowledge is accumulated. As you indicate, there is no time for research during the school year.

Since my teen years, I have wanted to be a research scientist. My life is immunological research. Therefore I regret that I cannot accept your position.

Jeannine looked up from her reading. Monique pressed a second paper into her hands.

"He wants us to replace the last paragraph with this."

I accept your offer and am available immediately. However, you may wish to withdraw this offer. Recently, I was found guilty of research misconduct and barred from receiving federal funds for research, including any salary from a research grant. I state that I am not guilty of this charge, but I do not have the money to fight this decision at this time. Accordingly, I am willing to teach full time. I will stress not only scientific facts, but also the commitment to truth.

If your offer is still open, I accept it.

Jeannine groaned and slammed the table with her fist.

"John will be out of research for good!"

"But what can he do? You went to the ORI. You talked to Dr. Delaney. He wouldn't do anything. I talked to the university committee. No one listened to us."

Jeannine pointed at Monique.

"I know, but damn it. Mike and Dr. Lawrence must not be allowed to win!"

But she capitulated. They could do nothing. John was right. There was no money for legal help.

"OK, Monique. I'll fix the letter tonight. You can have John sign it tomorrow."

But something more than a letter was on Monique's mind.

"John wonders why you haven't come. He wants to see you."

"You mean when you're with him he talks about me? Give me a break!"

Monique's voice fell to a whisper.

"Yes, but, I mean, you're so attractive, and ..."

"Monique, don't sell yourself short!"

Jeannine continued.

"Look, John and I can still be friends, but that's all. Stop worrying about me and him. He doesn't care about me. It's over. And he's damned lucky to have you!"

"Yes, but."

"No 'Buts!' 'Vive le Québec!' or something!"

Monique laughed. Jeannine had never tried French before.

***

Mike knocked on the hotel door. Sharon fell into his arms.

"It took a while to dump your mentor. I can't hurt his feelings. I need him for my article."

Mike smiled. He could help Sharon with science more than Dr. Lawrence, but "science" was not on his mind at the moment.

"Sharon, when's your next appointment with the great man?"

"Saturday morning, 11 o'clock."

"Look. I know this place on the Chesapeake Bay. You'll love it. We'll get a room and work on the articles there. Dr. Lawrence won't know where we are. We can watch the sailboats, maybe even a skipjack, lots of Canada geese and swans. I'll show you Blackwater Refuge. You'll have fun."

"You mean leave right now?"

"Sure."

"Should I check out? It's two nights. It will save the Express some money."

"Why not. Leave a message with the department to tell Dr. Lawrence that you'll meet him on Saturday. And leave the message at the hotel desk too."

Mike wrapped her in a last embrace. Then they left.

***

Dr. Lawrence called Sharon's hotel. He spluttered.

"What do you mean she checked out! She was supposed to meet me later this week."

"Excuse me, are you Dr. Lawrence?"

"Yes."

"Miss Husak left a note for you. Shall I read it or will you pick it up?"

"Please read it."

The clerk opened the envelope.

Franklin,

I'll be on the Eastern Shore tonight and tomorrow, but I'll be back Saturday to meet with you at 11 o'clock as scheduled. Thanks for the wonderful lunch.

Sharon

Dr. Lawrence hung up. If Sharon wasn't available, perhaps he and Mike could work together for a few hours. He called the university. The call switched to Dr. Santini's secretary.

"I'm sorry, Dr. Lawrence, Mike won't be back until Saturday. He's gone to the Eastern Shore. And a Miss Husak called. She confirmed your meeting, Saturday, 11:00 a.m."

Dr. Lawrence's mind raced. He must not rush to judgment. He put a handkerchief over his mouth and called the hotel. The same clerk answered. Dr. Lawrence spoke.

"This is Dr. Ames. I was to meet Dr. Hartness and Miss Husak at the hotel this afternoon."

"I'm sorry Dr. Ames, Miss Husak checked out an hour ago. A man she called 'Mike' was with her."

Dr. Lawrence clicked off.

He stood and bellowed like a bull elk.

"Mike! You traitor!"

The walls did not answer.

***

******

Chapter 35
Sunday, January 7

Sunday, Sharon's flight to Chicago was delayed for thirty minutes. She sat in the airport lounge with Franklin. He was silent, but appeared less tense than the day before. Sharon gave him a full-face smile.

"Thanks for driving me to the airport this morning."

Her gratitude was genuine. She had an early morning flight, and Franklin's thoughtfulness had spared her the worry about cabs and traffic. It was supposed to snow, but all she could see out the lounge window was a gray mist punctuated by crystalline sleet that melted as it hit the glass. Sharon tried again.

"Franklin, thanks."

She lowered her eyes. This time he responded.

"Sharon, I've been thinking about your articles. You've done a good job. You've got a good grasp of the science, and you're sensitive to my goals. You understand how I *feel* about this research."

His eyes sought hers. *Don't you know how I feel about you?* She did not look up. She was unsure what Franklin knew about her and Mike.

He frowned. She responded.

"I'm glad you like the articles. What about your latest paper with Dr. Hartness?"

"*My* paper should appear within three weeks. The editor isn't sure."

She caught the "my." *So you know about Mike and me.*

"Franklin, I faxed my editor the first article last night. It'll appear tomorrow. I'm sorry we missed this Sunday, but the second article should appear next Sunday."

As an antidote to the coolness, she reached across the table and squeezed his hand.

"You've been wonderful!"

She looked at her watch and jumped to her feet. She was unencumbered, her baggage was checked. She leaned over and kissed him full on the lips. For seconds, she let her moist lips linger. Then she pulled away.

Outside the crystalline sleet had turned into large white flakes. Sharon pointed.

"Look, it's snowing! Like the night we met in Chicago."

Before Franklin could rise to restrain her, she started away. She turned and blew him another kiss.

"Thanks for everything Franklin. Call me soon!"

Then she was gone.

Sharon hummed all the way to the Departure Gate. She had her by-line! Mike had been fun too. All told, a successful trip.

***

A pensive Franklin drove from the airport as the sun rose on the George Washington Parkway. He became Dr. Lawrence again. Still, if thoughts had color, his were "black." Mike had corrupted Sharon.

Snow accumulated on his windshield, and he increased the speed of the wipers. He thought about Mike. He had not seen him since leaving that note, and he had not confronted him about L-12. He must pay for that. And for Sharon! Mike was a traitor.

Franklin decided not to return to the empty house in Bethesda. Instead he headed for the office. Work would distract him. A frigid wind whipped the car as he crossed the Roosevelt Bridge, but his tires gripped the iced surface. He drove surely.

***

Monique awoke early. Jeannine was asleep. The early morning commute from downtown to Rockville had taken its toll. Monique slipped out without waking her.

Monique's plan was simple. She needed to remove John's belongings from the lab. Mike was never there early Sunday. This was the time.

She walked towards the Forster building. Monique was invigorated. The solid gray sky ahead and above, and the dense white flakes at eye level cheered her. Frosted breath extended in visible puffs from her lips. She enjoyed this too. The unrelenting cold reminded her of Montreal. She welcomed this shift to true cold from fickle wet and damp Washington. She pulled her hood over her face and walked steadily into the wind.

At the Forster building the unmarked snow on the steps indicated that no one had entered recently. She exhaled in relief. No Mike! She needed just a few minutes to remove John's belongings, and what was left of hers.

She stamped her boots in the foyer to shake off the snow, and started up the stairwell. Dr. Santini's doors were shut, and there were no lights in the hallway except for a lone fixture at the far end. At the door to the lab she paused and listened. There was no sound from within. She entered.

The sun, limited by the gray clouds and falling snow, cast eerie shadows around the desks and equipment. Monique left the lights off and quietly gathered her books and the remainder of John's notes.

As she turned to leave, she heard steps in the corridor. She flattened herself against the wall, in the shadows away from the door. It was Mike. He did not see her.

His hand reached for the light switch.

***

"Mike. Come to my office. I need to talk to you. Now!"

The angry voice came from behind him. Surprised, Mike backed into the hall in time to see Dr. Lawrence, shoulders whitened by clinging snow, disappear into his office.

There was snow on Mike's jacket too. He tossed it through the doorway onto a lab stool. He hurried down the hall to his mentor's office.

Monique trembled. Papers fell from her hands. She stuffed these into her sack. She could escape unnoticed. She stepped out, but paused. What were Mike and Dr. Lawrence doing here so early on Sunday? Why had they braved the snow to come in? All last night the newscasts had warned of this weather.

She slipped down the hallway towards Dr. Lawrence's office, her heart pounding. *Mon Dieu! What am I doing?* Jeannine would not believe her. The door to the office was cracked open. She lowered her sack to the floor and stood nervously behind the hall cabinet. She held her breath. She could hear everything.

***

Dr. Lawrence stood tall behind his desk. He looked over his half-frame reading glasses at Mike who stood motionless, head slightly bowed. Dr. Lawrence was angry about Sharon, but it was easier to talk about L-12.

"What the hell have you done. Who do you think you are Hartness, sending L-12 to Arizona. I can break your career. I can break you. Without me you're nothing. I'll give you thirty seconds to explain your actions."

Mike was grateful that Sharon's name had not been invoked. This would be easier than he had anticipated.

"Dr. Lawrence, I can explain why I sent L-12 to Dr. McElroy. First he's *your* friend and collaborator. Second, he was *my* mentor. He's the reason I'm here with you. Third, he was tooled up and ready for experiments with L-12. He had the mice with tumor transplants available. I'm sorry. Maybe it was poor judgment on my part, but I knew we could save ourselves a year if we joined forces. They have no rights to L-12, and it seemed to me that Dr. McElroy was doing you a favor. He *is* your friend and ..."

Mike sensed the tension easing. Dr. Lawrence's face was no longer flushed, and his shoulders relaxed. Filled with fresh confidence, Mike made a near-lethal slip.

"... and Sir, I'm sorry about Sharon, if I'd known that ..."

At the mention of Sharon, Franklin exploded.

"You insolent pup! If you'd known *what*? You *dare* to put yourself on a level with me! Leave Miss Husak out of this discussion! And don't you dare force yourself on her again. Dean Hampton will hear of your immoral behavior. Our collaboration is over! You stole L-12, and you tried to steal Miss Husak."

Franklin's eyes bulged with fury, but he paused for a breath as he realized that he had betrayed his own infatuation with Sharon. That increased his anger.

"Hartness, you're finished in immunology!"

Franklin paused. He lowered his eyes momentarily. He wanted to see Mike grovel. He looked up, glowering, eyes bulging, cheeks flushed, prepared to deliver the coup de grâce.

He stopped.

A different Mike stood in front of him. Mike was erect, shoulders back. He was smiling. The new Mike spoke in a low voice, but with menace.

"Sir, with all due respect, I am *not* leaving immunology, I *am* still your collaborator, and Miss Husak is free to sleep with a *younger* man *if she chooses*!"

Dr. Lawrence was stupefied. Over many years he had assiduously erected a structure of professorial superiority to govern relationships within his laboratory. Mike's words ignited that structure, and in just seconds, it was consumed to leave only a residue of dark smoke and bitter ashes. Dr. Lawrence's rage gave way to smoldering caution. Mike's words were preposterous, but his assured manner made the lab chief pause. What was Mike up to?

Mike filled the silence.

"It's in *all* our best interests to work with Dr. McElroy on L-12. He has the means and methods available to him that you lack. This is a great opportunity for *all* of us. Don't be narrow minded."

"As for Miss Husak, she means nothing to me. I don't find it hard to attract women."

For a brief second Mike thought of his failure with Monique, but the hesitation went unnoticed by the speechless Dr. Lawrence.

"Sir, if Sharon decides that it's for the best, I won't see her any more. But you should consider her feelings in the matter. No matter, Miss Husak is *not* important. What matters is *our* careers."

Dr. Lawrence found his voice. His throat scratched as he rasped.

"How dare you speak of *our* careers!"

"I do dare to speak of *our* careers. I hoped you wouldn't force the issue. But I see you are stubborn. Know this, *we* stand together or fall together."

"You bastard! What the hell do you mean?"

"Excuse me Sir, but profanity is *not* going to help. I mean that if I go down, I take you with me."

"Meaning?"

"I did all the work to prepare your last grant application. The one to the National Cancer Institute. The one for seven million dollars! You're the Principal Investigator on it."

"Yes, I am the PI, so what?"

"So *you* submitted *fabricated data* to the government in that grant! Have you heard of the False Claims Act. It's a federal offense."

"What do you mean, *fabricated* data?"

"It's clear enough. You wanted that grant application submitted ahead of Dr. Johnson's from Rochester. You told me to get the radioimmunoassay work done fast. You knew damned good and well there was no time. Who were you kidding? Yourself? So I did it for you, except I faked the data. I couldn't do the experiment. There was no time, and you knew it! The fake data went into the application."

Mike continued.

"A month later, when I actually did the experiment, it worked out like we thought it would. Meanwhile, you beat that ass Johnson to the punch. You got the grant. He was left out in the cold. By the time his application went in, you were already picked, and the Institute decided not to fund the same project twice. You get the money and he doesn't!"

"But Johnson wasn't ready to submit his application."

"That's right, but neither were you! We submitted faked data and we got the grant. The only problem is that we hadn't done the experiment. Your data weren't real."

"And no one knows?"

"No one except *me*, and now *you*. If you dare to go against me in any way at all, Everyone will know. I'll take you down. You're the PI, and you're responsible. I'll say you forced me to do it to beat Johnson. Everyone knows you'd do anything to beat him. Anything!"

Franklin sat down. His hands shook as he removed his half-frames. He looked up.

"But the data in the grant application haven't been published. It doesn't matter."

"It matters more! It's a false statement to the Feds for the purpose of getting money. It's a criminal offense. It's federal law, not just some stupid regulation. Don't listen to me. Read the False Claims Act. Check with your lawyer."

Mike was not done.

"You can't take any more bad publicity. You've already had one misconduct case in your lab, and your wife was with Martin when he was pushed or whatever."

Dr. Lawrence stared at him. Mike went on.

"That's right. I know about that too."

Dr. Lawrence spoke as if to himself.

"Mike, I can understand John Martin faking data, but you?"

Mike sneered.

"Don't whine. I did it for you. *You* got the funding support, *not* Dr. Johnson. You're on top! I can help you stay there, and so can Dr. McElroy. It will be worth your while! You will be glad we had this conversation."

Dr. Lawrence slumped forward, head in his hands. He was silent.

At last Mike backed off.

"I'm sorry it came to this Sir, but it's for the best. I have done, and will do, everything to support you. That even includes Miss Husak. See her all you want. I don't mind, and I don't care about your personal life. Just remember, her news articles are going to be first rate. Let's not alienate her."

With a wave of his hand, a despondent Franklin dismissed his protégé. Mike backed out of the room.

***

Monique saw that the conversation was over. She abandoned her sack and ran. Mike had a copy of the grant application in the lab. She had to find it. She tore through his papers. They scattered, falling to the floor. She picked one up. Not it. There, under the table. She had it!

***

Mike backed out of Dr. Lawrence's office. He saw the sack behind the cabinet. He recognized it instantly. *Monique!* His eyes brightened. *She's here*! Then his thoughts darkened. *But what did she hear*?

Dr. Lawrence's door had been ajar. Mike recalled how he had heard Dr. and Mrs. Lawrence. *You heard it all. Monique you are a clever little ....* The thought stayed unfinished. He heard footsteps down the hall, and looked up to see Monique's hood and jacket disappear into the stairwell. He did not call to her. Dr. Lawrence would hear.

Mike sprinted to the lab. His folders were strewn about the floor. *The grant application! Damn you Monique! You bitch!* He dashed to the window in time to see her, hood up, running through swirling flakes in the direction of the apartment. He grabbed his jacket and raced after her.

***

Monique ran the whole distance from the Forster building. The icy air in her lungs was like fire. She gasped with pain. When her legs would move no longer, she willed them to continue. She slipped on the icy sidewalk, but caught her balance. She stumbled up the steps to the apartment and called Jeannine. No answer. No Jeannine.

She collapsed inside the door. Her cheeks reddened and tingled as sensation returned in the warmth. She took deep breaths and loosened her coat at the front. She was too tired to remove it. The collar pushed tightly against her neck and made a seal that prevented air from reaching her back. Warm drips of perspiration ran down her lower back. At the same time cold melted snow chilled her ears and upper neck.

Still holding the precious grant application, she struggled to revive herself. She heard steps outside and looked up. The door was ajar! She had not locked it! She heard panting. It was Mike. He too was breathing hard.

"Monique, wait! ... I want to talk to you. ... Just talk."

She jumped upwards and threw the dead bolt. Just in time.

The handle rattled as pressure was applied from outside. Mike's shoulder slammed against the door, but the dead bolt held firm. Monique took the impact on her back. She dared not move. A small pool of melted snow formed at her feet.

"Monique, open the door! Damn it! Dr. Lawrence wants you back in the lab! Let me in. Let me help. You can have your job back. Dr. Lawrence will do whatever I say. I know you heard us."

She slumped to the wet floor. One hand clutched the now limp grant application. The other covered her mouth. The door shook once more as Mike slammed against it.

"All right. OK. Have it your way, but shut up about me and the grant. I'll deny everything. Dr. Lawrence will deny it. Nobody will believe you! Don't be a fool. You can't prove a thing. There's no computer program this time. I made those numbers up out of my head, by hand. Give it up!"

Silence.

"Come on Monique. This is foolish. I like you. Come back to the lab. You can have your project back, I'll help. Come back. Damn you! Be smart!"

More silence.

She heard steps, as if Mike were leaving. Was he faking again? She imagined hearing him breathing, still at the door.

But there was no sound. The passing minutes appeared as hours.

***

In a daze, Monique saw the handle turn. Had Mike found a key? She cringed.

The door opened. Red hair! Jeannine!

"Monique, what's wrong? What happened?"

Monique recounted Mike's assault on the door. Jeannine turned quickly and secured it.

Monique, pushed herself up.

"He told me that he and Dr. Lawrence would deny everything. That I couldn't prove anything."

"Deny what? What's going on?"

"Mike fabricated the data in the grant application to NIH."

Monique shed her jacket and recounted the events of the morning. She retrieved the wet papers from the floor.

"This is the application."

"Does it have the fake data?"

"They're in the appendix. That's why I needed Mike's copy. The NIH doesn't save appendices, they're too bulky."

Together they examined the damp document. One by one they peeled out the pages, spreading them out to dry.

Monique pointed.

"There. That's the appendix and those are Mike's RIA data. But this time he didn't use the computer to fake them."

Jeannine was glad Mike had not used the computer to fake his numbers. She dashed up the stairs to her computer and called Monique.

"Come up here. I want to show you something."

Monique arrived, breathless.

"Look at this graph."

"What's this"

"These are Maryland lottery numbers. I went on the internet to the *mdlottery.com* archives, and took the last two digits from each of 72 winning "Pick-3" Maryland Lottery numbers. This is the graph. The height of each bar represents how often each digit occurred in the winners."

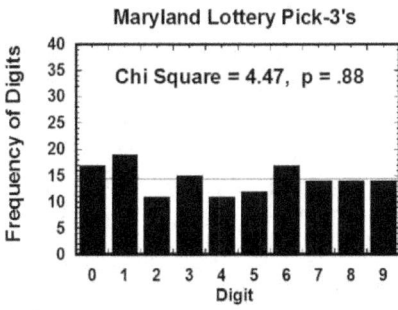

Maryland Lottery Pick-3's

Monique looked.

"So 17 of the digits were '0,' and 19 of them were '1.' So what?"

"The point is that for a lottery, the bars are mostly the same height, like boards in a fence. The fence is about the same height for all the digits meaning that the digits 0 to 9 occur pretty much equally, as they should in a 'fair' lottery. Otherwise, if there were favored digits, people would bet on numbers with those digits!"

"So?"

"So Mike was not as smart as he thought. We can check his digits for fairness."

"Why should they be fair?"

"Because rightmost digits can be random. Suppose your count is 9843. If you reran the sample through the gamma counter, you wouldn't get the same number again. Would you?"

"No, but you'd get close, like maybe, 9800 or 9900."

"Exactly. You would be close on the two leftmost digits, but you could not repeat the "43" on the end of 9843. Could you?"

Monique frowned.

"Of course not. This is biology. The counts aren't that accurate."

"That's the point. The rightmost digits don't reflect biology. You don't expect to repeat them. They can be random, or nearly so. Like numbers in a lottery."

Jeannine continued.

"When people cheat and fake numbers, they select the leftmost digits to give the results they want, but the rightmost digits don't matter, they are just 'fillers.' And the clincher is that often people unconsciously have favorite numbers, like *three* or *seven*. They are used too often, unlike a lottery. We are going to see if Mike unconsciously selected favorite digits."

Jeannine bent over the computer. She copied Mike's hand-faked counts into a file named "hand." She looked up.

"Monique, have you got any of your own experiments? We need real examples of numbers from the gamma counter."

Monique nodded and left. She returned with a notebook.

"Here, these are some real counts I recorded."

"Read them to me."

Monique read while Jeannine typed. She labeled the counts "cpm" for "counts per minute," and saved them in a file named "real" since Monique's counts were straight from the gamma counter. (The same counter Mike had pretended to use.)

Finally, Jeannine had Mike's fake data that John had copied from Dr. Lawrence's talk. She named its file "computer" since Mike had used the computer to fake those counts. She manipulated the three files "computer," "hand" and "real" into a single file, and clicked *Print*. The printer whirred and stopped.

Mike's Computer- faked Data			Mike's Hand-faked Data			Monique's Real Data		
cpm	cpm	cpm	cpm	cpm	cpm	cpm	cpm	cpm
9880	9843	9819	8172	8112	7621	7654	8350	8881
9509	9461	9485	7175	7635	7543	6446	4034	6491
9049	8922	8970	7120	7143	7179	3133	3831	3605
9878	9812	9860	8171	7715	8213	6314	1063	8801
9498	9482	9439	7210	7617	8101	4817	8488	7756
8745	8796	9018	6973	7432	8017	1250	3741	6835
9722	9859	9888	8317	7903	7557	9608	4319	7817
9298	9471	9336	7822	7327	7543	5976	2484	4372
8859	8970	9036	7292	7117	7137	4326	1491	3520
9875	9861	9580	7931	8021	7675	9222	1041	5549
9431	9491	9521	7512	7417	7612	7653	8141	3920
8979	9035	8941	7431	6876	7463	6977	3947	2683
9777	9654	9881	8213	7915	8001	6553	7798	8185
9339	9334	9646	8115	7731	7997	5231	4009	5641
8974	8996	9034	7872	7624	7713	2145	2664	2204
9789	9686	9781	7733	6817	7112	9380	8322	7549
9313	9530	9333	7251	6532	7035	7735	3838	7269
9049	8840	9076	6923	6471	6954	7174	2152	5434
9831	9790	9685	7613	8012	8171	7581	1023	7205
9347	9218	9428	7524	7812	8112	1502	7062	3948
9003	9069	8864	7130	7795	8025	1181	4882	3124
1002	9915	9861	8911	7812	7375	1034	5553	2841
9520	9380	9554	7347	7801	7291	8429	5238	2515
8953	8945	9031	7123	7713	7131	2395	2477	1726

Monique examined the numbers.

"They all look like pretty much the same, like RIA counts. So what's next?"

"I'm not done. I have to write some code to pick off the last two digits and make graphs and do some tests. It will take a few minutes. Maybe you can go down and fix us something to eat."

Monique went down to the kitchen. Soon the aroma of coffee wafted up the stairs. Jeannine turned back to the computer and typed vigorously.

**

Downstairs, Monique made sandwiches. Then she sat to wait. Minutes later, Jeannine, her face flushed, came down the stairs.

"We've got him! We've got that rat, Mike."

She grinned and put a sheet of paper on the kitchen table.

"Look at the graphs for the rightmost digits for your cpm's and Mike's computer-generated numbers. Both graphs have continuous fences with no gaps."

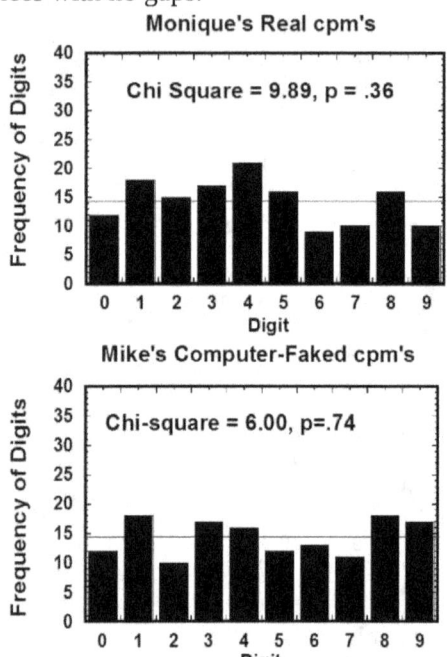

Monique's Real cpm's

Chi Square = 9.89, p = .36

Mike's Computer-Faked cpm's

Chi-square = 6.00, p=.74

Monique saw that her data had a pattern similar to the lottery digits, and that the same was true for Mike's computer-faked numbers. Both made regular fences. She looked up.

"My counts make a fence like the lottery. But what about Mike's? They're fake and they still look like a fence."

"They should. They're fake, but their digits should be like a lottery because they were generated randomly by the computer."

Jeannine put another sheet on the table.

"Now, look at these numbers Mike made up by hand."

Mike's Hand-Faked cpm's

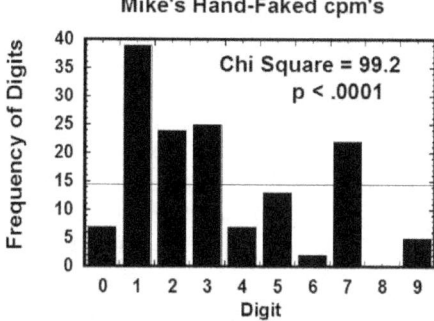

"They don't form a fence. There are 39 *ones* and no *eights*. The *one* is high and the *eight* is missing altogether. The bars are not even. The digits are not random!"

Jeannine pushed on.

"In Mike's hand-faked numbers there are too many low digits. He had an unconscious preference for the low digits, *one, two, three*. When he made up the numbers he favored them, and he favored *seven* too. There aren't enough of the others. That makes the bars ragged. And look at the Chi-Square test. The probability is way less than .05. His digits are *not* random."

Like many biologists, Monique knew the Chi Square test for randomness from genetics. A probability or "p-value" less than .05 indicated the digits were not random. Of the graphs, including the Lottery, only Mike's hand-faked "data" were not random.

Jeannine grinned. She put the sheets with the graphs aside, lifted her cup and drank. By now the coffee was cold, but no matter.

Monique laughed.

"Jeannine you're a real statistician. You convinced me. We can show that Mike faked the data in the appendix to the grant. But what made you think about lottery digits in the first place?"

"I read about this in a journal on research accountability. People have trouble making up random numbers. The terminal

335

digits don't have to be random, but they often are. That's why I wanted your real data for comparison."

She continued.

"Monique, tomorrow you can show the graphs to Marshall Hanes. This time he should listen to you."

"Do you think he will?"

"He should. First, *you heard* Mike say that he faked the data. Second, *we show* that the data don't behave like real counts."

Monique was silent. She hoped Jeannine was right.

***

******

Chapter 36
Monday, January 8

At the FBI field office in Tucson, the agent slammed down the phone and spoke to his partner.

"McElroy's secretary still doesn't know when he'll be back. She *thinks* tomorrow, but she's not sure."

His partner frowned.

"What about the coroner in Benson?"

"He double-checked for us. There's no doubt. Lachance died from a snakebite. It must have been a big snake. The venom was really potent!"

"What about Hernandez? Would a jury buy her story?"

"How would I know what a jury would do? But she has only Lachance's word, and he was a two-bit hood. Do you think he would have told her, that *he* was going to make the snake bite *her*? And who would believe Lachance over the good Doctor?"

"What about the shed?"

"So a shed burned, so what?"

"We've got to interview McElroy."

"Smart man."

The phone rang. He grabbed it in irritation, but grew silent. Face pale, he looked at his partner. His voice was low.

"José is dead, a car bomb in his driveway."

José was a newly-retired DEA agent who had worked the Mexican border for years. He was a friend.

"Are Maria and the kids OK?"

"Seems so. We're assigned to the case. We've got to get over there right away. Your guy McElroy will have to wait."

***

In Washington at the same time, a paralegal in the Department of Justice opened a package, the papers that Cecilia had taken from McElroy's shed. The paralegal studied them. They certainly seemed to indicate Medicare fraud. For her own edification, she pulled down a copy of the U. S. Code, Title 31, Money and Finance, and read briefly. Afterwards, she logged in the papers, and filed them.

The FBI agent in Tucson had included a brief note, saying that he would call soon with more information.

She looked at the mound of documents on her desk. It would be a week before she could clear those requests. There was already enough work. She decided to wait on the agent's call from Tucson.

***

Marshall Hanes sat in the provost's office and beamed as he read the Daily Express.

SCIENCE FROM A WOMAN'S PERSPECTIVE:
BREAST CANCER, A NEW HOPE
by Sharon Husak
<u>**You have cancer.**</u>
No phrase is more dreaded in this country today! There are many different kinds of cancer, and probably as many different causes, but cancer cells share a common characteristic. They multiply too much and spread themselves throughout the body. If they spread ("metastasize") from the original colony ("primary tumor") to form multiple colonies in other organs, there is often little hope for survival. ...

He focused on the end of the article.

By means of clever experimentation, Dr. Lawrence has established not only that protein L-12 binds to CA and disables it, but further that such action occurs even when protein CA is incorporated into cell membranes. In other words Dr. Lawrence's protein can stop growth in an existing cancer. Exciting? Yes it is!
<u>**Thank you Dr. Lawrence.**</u>
We women may soon be thanking Dr. Lawrence and his coworkers for our lives!

There was not a single mention of research fraud in the article. There was not even a hint of scandal The university's reputation was intact!

Marshall chuckled and rubbed his hands together. Now, the Provost would *have* to realize that he had done an excellent job. It was time for a promotion. No one else could have gotten that investigation completed so fast, and with only favorable publicity.

He heard a knock at the door. He looked up as the young woman entered. He knew the face. Damn! It was that Postdoc, Laurier, from Dr. Lawrence's laboratory. He did not want to talk to her. He forced a smile.

"Miss Laurier, come in. What can I do for you? I'm very busy at the moment."

Monique's voice was soft, but each word was distinct.

"Mr. Hanes, I wanted to talk to you about Dr. John Martin and Dr. Hartness and fake data. I have some graphs to show you."

Marshall Hanes folded the newspaper on his desk and put it to the side. Then he stood up and waved Monique to a chair. He looked at his watch.

"All right, Monique, I'll give you five minutes."

***

Jeannine left StatFind early. She could only tolerate so much staring at a computer monitor. Besides, she had loaded SAS on the computer at the apartment, and she could finish the computations there.

As she drove back to the apartment, she thought about a mathematical proof that she had wanted in her thesis. But now there was no thesis. Could she go to another university for her doctorate? Would she ever get back to mathematics?

Lost in these thoughts, the traffic irked her more than usual.

***

Franklin forced a smile into the phone.

"Sharon, your article is great. I've spent the morning giving out copies of the Express. Even Dean Hampton liked it. You did a great job. I was wondering. Could we get together next weekend? I could fly to Chicago."

As he said the words, he thought of Mike and Sharon together. He cleared his throat. At the other end of the line, Sharon felt the discomfort.

"You won't be mad will you? But, I can't. I'll be working on our second article with my editor. Maybe he'll let me come to Washington the week after."

Franklin thought.

... so you can see Mike too!

He held his tongue. Instead he murmured.

"That would be good."

Sharon realized he needed more.

"Franklin, I want to see you, and I'd like to spend some relax time with you, something will work out, I'm sure. I'll call later this week."

At least he had some hope.

"Sharon, the first article was great. If I can help any more on the next one, let me know."

***

Jeannine answered the knock on the apartment door. She peered through the peephole. It was John. She felt a rush of circulation to her head. Her face reddened. Her excitement surprised her.

John stepped into the apartment, leaned on his cane, and smiled.

Her stomach tightened. Memories! There, by the stairwell they had embraced that first night they had moved in together. Her eyes swept up the stairs, as she thought of the bedroom.

John's eyes followed her gaze, but before he could speak, she found her voice.

"Monique's not here. You look tired, do you want to sit down?"

The hoarseness in her voice did nothing for her confidence. She hastily pushed aside the pile of computer output on the sofa.

"Here, sit over here. It's good to see you out of the hospital. How do you feel?"

John shrugged his shoulders, and clumsily settled into the sofa, his bad leg extended stiffly in front of him. All the while, his eyes never left hers.

Now she really was uncomfortable. She tried again.

"Monique's not here. She won't be back until late afternoon. She went to the university, the Provost's Office, to see Marshall Hanes. I'm sorry."

Her thoughts were in turmoil. Once-dead emotions surged through her. She shook the hair from her eyes to steady herself.

It was a movement John had seen many times. He looked across the floor. There, as expected, were Jeannine's socks. How many evenings had he seen her throw shoes and socks across the room and then stretch her legs. Now his eyes dropped to her bare feet and then rose. He smiled, but it was strained. He could not voice his thoughts.

"Damn it John. Say something!"

He dropped his gaze. His voice was gentle.

"I knew Monique wasn't here. I wanted to see you."

It was Jeannine's turn to remain silent. She stared. He continued.

"I needed to be alone with you. I needed to see if ..."

His voice trailed.

"I mean I was hoping that you ..."

"Damn it John! Grow up! You're playing games."

John held out his hand, but Jeannine stepped back. He continued.

"No. I'm not playing games. When I saw you just now, I knew."

"What the hell did you know?"

"I knew that you still cared for me."

Jeannine backed farther. She spoke slowly.

"You took me by surprise, that's all. Whatever we had is over."

He interrupted.

"Is it? Be honest with yourself. Is it?"

Jeannine's analytical faculties strove for control.

"All right. Maybe it's not *completely* over. But it doesn't matter. It *is* over for us. I'm a woman, and for me love isn't just feelings and hormones. It's a decision. I know there's nothing left for us. Besides, Monique is my *friend*. We've become really close."

As she spoke, Jeannine saw lines in John's face that she had never seen before. He was weary. She continued.

"And you're damned lucky to have Monique. She worships you."

The evident pain in his eyes stopped her. He spoke slowly.

"I know. But your logic doesn't always work with people. You can't decide for me that I have to love Monique. I am not something you can just trade because it makes sense to you, because it fits one of your equations. I'm not up for auction. Damn it Jeannine, people don't work that way."

"Maybe people don't, but I do."

She continued.

"Look, I can see that you and I can't be under the same roof. I know half this apartment is yours, so I'll move out. I can get a place in Rockville near my work. You and Monique can live here, either apart or together. Whatever? You decide."

John's shoulders slumped noticeably.

"You won't have to move out. I'm not staying. I'm taking the job in Pittsburgh. It was settled this weekend."

Jeannine's tone altered.

"Oh John, you're leaving research. What about all your plans. You're a real scientist. You love truth. You can fight the damn university *and* the ORI. You're not guilty."

He shrugged.

"And I will fight them. But I've got to eat, same as you. You're not in research anymore yourself. What about your mathematics? You can't do that at StatFind."

"But I want to get back to mathematical statistics. My programming job is only temporary."

"Then think of my teaching job at *AquA* as the same thing, temporary. Maybe I can get back into research later."

"How are you going to do that if you don't appeal the university's finding?"

"Jeannine, I am going to appeal, but I have to grab this job while it's open. At least they trust me. They know me. I may not get another offer."

Jeannine nodded. She could appreciate his reasoning.

"What about Monique?"

"I like her a lot, a real lot. I think it can work out, but I just don't know. I wanted to know about us, about you. I wanted to see about you and me."

"John, don't do this. Too much has happened, and I can't think straight. I've just gotten over you. I'm not the same person I was last November. I'm different."

"But Jeannine."

"No! I can't expose myself to any more feelings, and you're different too. Whatever you do, don't hurt Monique."

"God knows I don't want to, but I had to see you alone first."

"When do you report to *AquA*?"

"This Wednesday. I was hoping I could stay here until then."

Jeannine stared at him.

"All right, but stay away from both of us while you're here. You're right about one thing, I still have my memories. I'm not up to having you and Monique upstairs in what used to be *our* bed. She is off limits while you're here."

"That's not an issue. Monique's a Catholic, a good one."

"I know Monique. It's not her, it's you I worry about. Promise me you'll leave her alone here. Promise me that!"

"I promise."

"All right then, you can have the sofa."

"Jeannine, thanks. And I still love the way you think."

"Damn it John, why couldn't you just be a rat, like Mike!"

***

The moment Monique came in the door, Jeannine spoke.

"John is here. He's eating supper with us."

Monique looked quizzically at her friend.

"Here? With you? Where is he?"

"He's upstairs."

Monique's foot was on the first step before Jeannine stopped her.

"Wait, did you see Marshall Hanes at the Provost's office today?"

Monique hesitated, she wanted to see John.

"He was there."

"Did you tell him about Mike's fake counts? Did you explain it to him?"

"I showed them to him, yes."

"What did he say?"

Monique fidgeted. Her mind was upstairs, but she answered.

"He said a lot of legal things. He talked about the Frye rule for scientific evidence, and then he talked about some Daubert ruling from the Supreme Court. He went on and on. Our statistics won't hold up. That's what he said."

There was a noise at the top of the stairs. Monique looked up. John stood on the highest step.

"Hi."

"Hi."

Jeannine persisted.

"Monique, didn't you tell Hanes what Mike told Dr. Lawrence?"

Monique lowered her eyes.

"I tried to, but he told me to stop slandering Dr. Lawrence and the university. He was angry. He said if I kept talking that way, the university would take legal action against me. He told me I was bad for science, and that people like me were against knowledge, against academic freedom. That I was ungrateful. He said to never come back!"

She turned to John.

"... and he said that you were a cheat and that you were finished in research, that you will never do research again."

John was silent. Jeannine started to erupt, but thought better of it. She returned to the kitchen to set the table. John followed her.

Monique stood alone with her thoughts. Then she, too, went into the kitchen.

***

That evening's meal was tense. Monique's eyes never lifted from her plate. John spoke only to ask for more spaghetti, while Jeannine, the cook and dishwasher, communicated through a loud clatter of clanging pots and rattling silverware.

Finally Jeannine turned from the sink. She had experienced enough awkwardness. She went upstairs for her scarf.

"You two have enough to talk about without me. I'll be back in a while."

When she came down, John and Monique were on the couch, engrossed in conversation. Jeannine slipped out into the chill evening.

***

Marshall Hanes arrived at home that night to a smiling wife who pressed a martini into his hand as she spoke.

"Honey, the six o'clock news had a spot on your Dr. Lawrence, and his cancer research at the university. It was good! I'm sure it will be on the eleven o'clock news. You can watch it then."

Marshall was excited. Sharon's article had been picked up by a major television network! Almost instantaneously he was concerned. He quickly queried his wife.

"Did they say anything about data fraud, or the Martin case?"

"No. Nothing about that. It was all about Dr. Lawrence and breast cancer, and the university. Oh! And I bought two more copies of the Express for you. Who is this Sharon Husak? Have you met her?"

Marshall sipped the martini and shook his head no. His wife kissed him on the cheek.

Later, when Marshall saw the eleven o'clock news, he was exultant. He had done a great job. The TV story was highly favorable for the university with no negative publicity. There was no hint of research misconduct in Dr. Lawrence's laboratory.

Surely now, more than ever, the provost would reward Marshall for his handling of the Martin case! Laurier, Ryan and John Martin were out of the picture!

***

It was dark when Franklin pulled into his driveway. He stepped to the door, the Express under his arm. He fumbled with his key, but the lock refused to turn.

"Damn it, why can't I get in!"

Then he remembered. The locks had been changed. He retrieved the new key and the lock turned easily. He opened the door. He was about to step in when he heard a step behind him. He peered back into the darkness.

"Who's there?"

His voice was unsteady, with a slight quaver. He spoke again, trying to force more assurance into his tone.

"Who's there?"

He was answered by a chuckle. A form stepped out of the shadows.

"Larry, it's me. Relax. It's OK."

"Mackie? What are you doing here? You gave me a start."

"Right. Sorry about that, but it's chilly out here, and it's starting to rain. I've been waiting for you. Invite me inside. I was in town, and thought I'd stop and see you."

Franklin was puzzled. The day had been long and difficult, and he was not in good humor.

"How did you get here? Where's your car?"

"Right there, on the street. It's a rental. Look, old buddy, can we go in now?"

Mackie pulled his arms together and shivered, as if to make the point.

"I guess so. Come on in."

Franklin started to explain that Betty was gone, but stopped. Of course, Mackie had seen Betty in Tucson. Maybe she wanted Mackie to influence the divorce settlement. If so, it would not work. Franklin compressed his lips into a thin line.

Mackie read his thoughts.

"No I'm not here to talk about Betty. That's your business old buddy, not mine."

"Then why are you here, to talk about *my* L-12."

Mackie was relieved.

"Not L-12 either! Look, Mike *assured* me that you had *asked* him to send the stuff to the clinic. If I had known you'd be upset, I would have called you right away. Anyway, I'm not here about L-12. It belongs to you as far as I am concerned."

They stepped into the kitchen alcove. The lights revealed a sink that was filled with clutter, but part of the breakfast table was clear. Mackie sat there and looked up at Franklin who stood silent, not sure what to say to his "friend."

Mackie seized the moment.

"I'm in a little trouble, and I'd like to stay here a few days, and I'd appreciate your not telling anyone I'm here. The clinic thinks I'm in Mexico."

Before Franklin could interrupt, Mackie conceived his lie.

"I'm 'undercover' you might say. I'm helping FBI agents in Tucson check on a Medicare fraud case."

"What in the world are you talking about?"

"It's pretty simple. Based on some cases they sent in, they think that either someone in the Department of Justice with Money and Finance enforcement is tampering with evidence, or maybe an FBI field agent in Tucson is doing it. Anyway, we at the clinic agreed to make up some documents to look like fraud. They sent them here from Tucson, and I'm here to follow up."

"Mackie, you're not making sense. What could you do that they can't?"

"I can't tell you. But if anyone calls you to find out where I am, even the FBI or DOJ, tell them you haven't seen me, and that you have no idea where I am. Can you do that for me old buddy?

Franklin shrugged in resignation.

"Mackie is this on the level. You can't be serious?"

"You bet I am, and I hope you'll help me by letting me stay here for a few days."

"Mackie, are you in trouble?"

"Of course not! What do you mean?"

"Betty didn't ask you to talk to me, did she?"

"I told you I'm not here for Betty. You know her better than that. I'm not here for her."

Franklin hesitated. He wanted to ask how Sari was, but he was irritated that Mackie should know anything about his family when he did not. He clamped his jaws together and nodded.

"OK, the spare room is at the top of the stairs to the left. It's a lot cleaner than mine. You can stay there. Don't mind me. There's a lot going on at work, and, you know about me and Betty."

"Thanks, old buddy. You won't regret this."

Mackie headed outside to retrieve his suitcase.

***

It was still daylight in Tucson. The private investigator finished addressing the envelope to *Dr. William McElroy, care of Dr. Franklin W. Lawrence, ... , Bethesda, MD.* He paused a moment, and added the words "Please Forward" at the lower left of the envelope. Then he studied his note.

> *My source says the FBI agents who wanted to see you are busy elsewhere. Very busy. There are no charges against you, and so far not even a hint of an investigation. Ditto for the locals at Benson.*
>
> *My source is totally reliable. You're OK here. You can come back anytime. If any investigation should start, I would know right away.*
>
> *Hernandez is back East. She's still on some sort of leave. Thanks for the cash. I need the money. Please send the next payment.*

He left the note unsigned and sealed it in an envelope.

***

A misty rain fell on Jeannine as she walked out of the apartment. She shivered, turned up the collar on her jacket, and walked randomly as her thoughts shifted back and forth from John, to herself, to Monique, and back to John. Likewise, the silhouettes of the trees changed with each gust of wind and produced shifting shadows with each passing car.

She had walked for five minutes, when in a rare moment, there was no traffic. At the same time the wind stopped. The distinct outlines of bare branches were framed, motionless, by the streetlight. Jeannine, too, stopped motionless on the dark sidewalk. Had she heard footsteps behind her?

She turned, but could see no one. The wind started anew, along with a fresh surge of traffic. The disturbed branches and the sporadic illumination from passing headlights made it difficult to focus. She resumed her pace. It was all confusing; John's leaving research, her loss of her fellowship, the momentary ambiguity about John and Monique, Monique's dismissal by Dr. Lawrence.

Finally, in spite of the rainy mist, her thoughts cleared, and the image of John faded. There was no going back. Whatever they once had was gone.

She felt the wet through her shoes and looked down. Her sneakers were soaked. But for the cold, she would have removed them. She quickened her pace and turned the corner.

The lights of a parked car blinded her.

***

Jeannine reversed her steps and walked back around the corner, but the car followed. It pulled alongside.

Her own Mazda!

Monique's face appeared through the driver's window.

"Jeannine. I was hoping you'd come this way. I came to get you. You're soaked. What are you doing? Get in."

Jeannine shook herself. Monique turned the heater on high.

"You had me worried. Why were you gone so long? Was it John and me?"

She continued without waiting for a response.

"John's leaving. He's not staying with us. He said you could have the computer. His van is loaded and he's heading for Pittsburgh tonight. He'll probably sleep at Breezewood."

Still no response. Monique whispered.

"Jeannine, later I may be going with him to Pittsburgh myself, would you mind? Are you all right with that?"

Jeannine stopped shivering.

"Monique, I'm happy for you and I'm OK, really. John's a good guy, but I just want you to be sure. I don't want to see you hurt. I'm really glad for both of you, if it works out."

The next words were addressed to the windshield.

"I lost a part of myself with him, but it's OK, and it's me, not John, that did it. It's my fault, not his. I just have to start over."

Monique reached over and squeezed Jeannine's hand. The heater's warm air flowed over her feet.

When they returned to the apartment, John was gone.

There was no note.

***

******

Chapter 37
Tuesday, January 9

The ringing in her ears continued as Jeannine struggled to wake herself. She sat up on the edge of the bed, but dizziness overtook her. She was stuffed and congested. She reached for a Kleenex. The ringing persisted. It was the phone.

Jeannine struggled down the stairs towards the irritating sound.

"Hello?"

"Monique?"

The accent was familiar.

"No, this is Jeannine. Can I help you?"

"Jeannine, this is Cecilia Hernandez."

"Cecilia, I thought you were in Tucson."

"I was, but I'm back in Bethesda. I'm at my cousins. I was hoping to see you and Monique. You sound different. Have you got a cold or is it the phone?"

"I'm under the weather. I think it's a cold."

"Could I stop by. I've got news."

"Excuse me Cecilia, somebody is at the door."

The "somebody" was Monique, burdened with groceries. Jeannine took the bags, and indicated the phone with a tilt of her head.

"It's Cecilia. Why don't you talk to her."

Monique picked up.

"This is Monique. I just got here. What's up?"

Jeannine headed for the kitchen and put the bags on the table. She shook her head, filled a glass with water and downed two aspirin. She took several Kleenex and tried to clear her sinuses. Then she slumped into the kitchen chair. She heard Monique hang up the phone.

Monique appeared in the archway.

"Cecilia wants to come by. She's got new information about Mike's mentor, McElroy. I told her two o'clock this afternoon. Is that OK?"

Jeannine groaned.

"I guess."

She stumbled back upstairs to bed.

***

Dr. McElroy awoke. Bright sunlight streamed through the parted curtains. He slipped to the window and looked out. The rental car was parked, undisturbed, by the curb. The house was silent. He looked down the hall. The door to Larry's bedroom was open, and the bed was empty. He went to the head of the stairs. Taped to the rail was a note along with a house key.

> *Mackie,*
>
> *I'm leaving for an early meeting. I have to see a lawyer in the Provost's office. His name is Hanes. If you need to reach me. I'll be in his office until about 11. After that, my office. The kitchen is empty. Give me more notice next time. I'll be back about five this afternoon.*
>
> *L.*

Dr. McElroy smiled. Dr. Lawrence had called him "Mackie," but had signed the note "L." Dr. Lawrence disliked his own nickname, "Larry," and was unwilling to acknowledge that epithet in writing. "L" could stand for "Lawrence" or "Larry."

Back in the bedroom, Mackie opened his briefcase. It was filled with bundles of currency. He reviewed his records. The transfer of funds to Switzerland had been successful. He was loaded. Next he checked his passport and his tickets, *Air France*, Dulles Airport to Charles DeGaulle Airport outside Paris, with connections to Geneva. If he could stay here one more night, everything would be fine. As for the *AMAH Clinic*, Dr. Hermann would manage in his absence.

Mackie was hungry. He left the house.

***

Cecilia, drove down River Road towards downtown. After thirty minutes of traffic, she pulled to the curb by Jeannine's apartment. Monique was at the door.

"Jeannine's not feeling well. She's upstairs. She'll be down soon."

Cecilia narrated her Tucson adventures, ending with Dr. McElroy's disappearance. Finally she added.

"I'm sure Mike Hartness is part of the Medicare fraud at the *AMAH Clinic*. I'm sure the fraud at Fairland is not the first time he has cheated. He's been with McElroy a long time. Maybe McElroy will contact him."

A disheveled Jeannine appeared. She interjected.

"Where's McElroy now?"

Cecilia looked up.

"No one knows. The best bet is in Mexico. I've tried to call the FBI in Tucson, but they're busy on another case."

At the mention of the FBI, Jeannine's eyebrows lifted. Cecilia quickly repeated what she had told Monique about her adventures in Tucson, and Pierre's death.

Jeannine commented.

"No wonder Mike is Mike, he had a good teacher."

Monique rose and paced. She stopped and turned back to the table. Fists clenched, She looked at her two friends.

"I couldn't sleep last night wondering what to do. About Dr. Lawrence, Mike, about John."

She glanced sideways at Jeannine before continuing.

"I want to be with John, and I think he loves me, but right now he can't fight the university, or Mike, or anyone. He needs the new job. Cecilia, is there any chance Bob Delaney might do something for us?"

Jeannine's eyebrows shot up. Cecilia responded.

"Bob's out of town on another case. A large clinical trial. He might be back next Monday, maybe not."

Jeannine tossed the hair from her eyes and looked away. It was Monique who spoke.

"I thought as much. There's no help there."

She held up a microcassette tape recorder. She stamped her foot.

"I've got to do something. I'm going to get Mike to admit he faked data. I'm going to get it on tape. He will brag to me about anything. I'll meet him and get him to talk."

Jeannine jumped up.

"Monique! How the hell are you going to do that? What are you thinking? Have you forgotten what Mike is like. He's a snake. It's not safe."

"With you and Cecilia helping me, I can pull it off. He's *too* sure of himself."

"He's got reason to be, so far everything he's done has paid off!"

A paper cup had fallen on the floor. Monique stamped it flat. Her hands waved a wide arc.

"This time he'll go too far. I can't let him get away with this and I won't let him blame John. John's ruined. The time to fight is now! Once I have the tape, Dr. Lawrence and Hanes will have to listen."

She turned to Cecilia.

"And ORI and your friend Bob too!"

For good measure she added.

"Mike will meet with me anywhere I want him to!"

Jeannine and Cecilia exchanged looks of alarm.

Monique set her hands on her hips.

"Don't look so miserable! Read Pascal's *Pensées*. They've got us by the throat, but they can't hold us down. This is going to work. I know it. It has to!"

***

Mike Hartness shuffled the papers on his desk. He had left several messages at the *AMAH Clinic* for Dr. McElroy, to no avail. *Where the hell are you? Why don't you call me?*

He had not wanted to blackmail Dr. Lawrence with the fabricated data in the grant application. His hand had been forced by the old fool's infatuation with Sharon. Monique had overheard. *Damn it. Now I've got to watch you and Lawrence both, along with Ryan!*

Mike wanted Monique on his side, in bed willingly, but through intimidation and fear if need be. With her silence, he would be secure. *Damn it Monique, come back to the lab. I'll help you, and show you some fun too.* He thought of Jeannine. *Monique, dump the redhead. She can't help you. She's a dumb mathematician. What does she know!*

Jeannine's shapely form flashed before him. *Hell, I'll teach you too, I'll handle you both!*

Earlier that morning Dr. Lawrence had greeted Mike in the usual manner. It was their first meeting since Sunday's Sharon showdown, and Dr. Lawrence had appeared normal. This reassured him, but ten minutes after the greeting, Dr. Lawrence had told the secretary he would be at Marshall Hanes' office. The thought of them together upset Mike.

That stuffed shirt bastard better not tell Hanes about me. I'll pull him down with me.

He stared out the window. The pane was cold, but not frigid. There were no clouds. The sky was clear. He thought of following Dr. Lawrence to Hanes' office, but the phone buzzed. Mike lifted the receiver. A familiar voice spoke rapidly.

"Go to 'our' phone. I'll call in five minutes."

It was Dr. McElroy. Mike donned his jacket and headed down the stairs.

***

The phone on his desk rang. Marshall Hanes picked up.

"Mr. Hanes, this is Dr. Hayman's secretary. Please hold for Dr. Hayman."

Marshall tapped his fingers. At the twelfth tap, Clay Hayman came on the line.

"Marshall, how are you? I saw Fairland University on TV last night. Congratulations! It was a good feature on Dr. Lawrence."

"I thought so. How's Health and Human Services?"

"That's what I'm calling about. How did your case with ORI go? Any problems?"

"No. The investigation is over, and the media didn't grab it. That's the good thing."

"I'm glad to hear it. I wanted to assure you that the Assistant Secretary is working on the ORI problem. We get complaints about them every day from the academic community."

Marshall thought of Monique.

"So far the only problems I've had have been with Postdocs who lost their jobs."

"That's typical. Look, if things work out here, I'll have news for you next week."

"What sort of news?"

"Good news for us, bad news for ORI. I'll explain later. This job is a rat race. I have to run. Congratulations on the TV spot."

The line went dead.

Marshall Hanes checked the time. He would have coffee before meeting Dr. Lawrence.

***

Marshall Hanes greeted Dr. Lawrence courteously. He knew that Dr. Lawrence did not like him. But today, Marshall sensed that a mutual enemy, Monique Laurier, might bring them together.

Dr. Lawrence did not sit down. Hanes did not force the issue. He began as cordially as he could, given the subject.

"I know it's preposterous, but Monique Laurier came to see me yesterday. She says that she heard Mike Hartness tell you that he'd faked data on your grant applications."

Dr. Lawrence's jaw dropped. *Monique knows!* Marshall Hanes interpreted the surprise as innocence.

"Like I said, I know it's preposterous. Just the sort of thing a fired malcontent would concoct, but I wanted to check with you. I showed her the door, of course."

356

Dr. Lawrence's eyes were glazed. Again Marshall filled the void.

"She showed me statistical data and graphs that she said proved the data were fabricated."

Dr. Lawrence thought to himself. *Ryan! You damned hellcat statistician!"*

Aloud he said.

"How could that prove anything?"

"Exactly! I told her that her arguments were useless, and that she had better not slander you or the university. Imagine coming here with such a story, just to spoil your success. That was a good Express article. I wanted you to know that I liked it."

Dr. Lawrence finally composed a full sentence, and more.

"Monique Laurier is bitter, first about John Martin whom she liked, and second about losing her job. It's a damn shame that she tried to implicate Mike. He's a fine researcher. As for me, my reputation is established. Her calumnies can't harm me, but I deeply resent this personal attack on Dr. Hartness, and by implication, on the university. There's this statistics student, or I should say ex- student, a Miss Ryan. She has been a terrible influence on Monique."

Marshall nodded. For the first time he appreciated Dr. Lawrence. Marshall was relieved. His judgment was supported. Laurier was nothing but a troublemaker.

He was validated. There would always be malcontents like Laurier and Ryan, ready to criticize any university decision.

Franklin sensed Marshall's approval.

"You know Marshall, ordinary people are only too ready to attack science in this country, but when a supposed scientist like Monique attacks science, it hurts. It's a betrayal. What she did in coming to you was reprehensible."

Marshall nodded twice, once for each point.

"Dr. Lawrence, if she harasses you in anyway, I'll threaten legal action. You must be free from mundane criticism. You're right. Research funds are hard to get these days. Science and academic freedom must be funded and protected."

Spontaneously, he added.

"Would you like to go to lunch, my treat, at the faculty club?"

Dr. Lawrence was touched. Hanes was on his side.

"Thank you, thanks very much. I'd like that."

They left the office together.

***

For January, the sky was bright,. Mike stood waiting in the sun for Dr. McElroy to call. Ten minutes passed. His sweater was too warm and he shuffled his feet impatiently. He glared at the pay phone. That instrument was not intimidated. It refused to ring.

He drew a deep breath, turned to go, and bumped into Dr. McElroy!

"Hello Mike."

"You're here!"

"So it seems. Let's talk in my car."

They crossed the street and got in. McElroy drove, circling the blocks.

Mike, what have you told Dr. Lawrence?"

"About *you*, nothing."

"And?"

"He was going to can me. I had to protect myself. I told him I knew that the data in his last grant application was faked."

Dr. McElroy raised his eyebrows.

"By him?"

"Well no. By someone else."

"You?"

"It was me. We had to beat Dr. Johnson."

"Anyone else know?

"A Postdoc named Monique Laurier. She heard us talking."

"Anyone else?"

358

"She has a roommate, a troublemaker, Jeannine Ryan. Maybe she told her. She probably did. Ryan's a pain."

Mike paused.

"Their apartment is in the next block."

Mike peered through the windshield. He distinguished two women standing on the sidewalk.

"That's them now. Up ahead, on the right. The redhead is Ryan."

A delivery truck double-parked and obscured their view. McElroy squeezed by, and then looked back. A woman with jet black hair had joined Jeannine and Monique.

Mike continued.

"Monique has the brown hair. I don't know the third one."

Mike was thrown off balance as the car accelerated suddenly. Dr. McElroy's face flushed.

"Hernandez, Mike. Her name is Hernandez."

***

McElroy turned the corner in the direction of Mike's lab.

"Mike, this could be trouble for you. Hernandez is a Fed. She was just in Tucson. She has nine lives. Those girls are up to something. If any of them contacts you, tell me right away. Find out what they want. That's all. If they ask about me, you heard I was in Mexico. Watch out for a trap, and whatever you do, keep your damn pants zippered. Hernandez would love to fry us both. And call me right away. We'll work out a plan."

McElroy dropped Mike at the Forster building. He frowned as he drove away. *Mike knows too much!*

***

As soon as Mike sat down in his office the phone rang. He picked up.

"Mike, it's Sharon. How did you like the article."

"Sharon, the article was terrific. You deleted my name several times, but that's OK. The article was good. When am I going to see you?"

"That's why I'm calling. Part II is running next Sunday. Now my editor wants me to do a third article, from the fraud and fabricated data angle. Could you help me?"

Mike bit his lip.

"Sure. But do you really want to play up that angle."

"It's not me, it's my editor, and I owe him. Is there a problem?"

"No. Of course not! But don't tell Dr. Lawrence. He's sensitive."

"That's why I called you. I didn't want him to know I was coming . Mike, could you pick me up at Reagan National tomorrow morning at ten?"

"Sure, as long as you keep tomorrow night free."

"It's a deal. And don't tell Dr. Lawrence."

No sooner had Mike put down the phone than it rang once more. This time he was truly excited!

"Monique!"

He strained to hear the softly spoken words.

"Mike, I need to meet you. Some place private where we can talk."

Mike grinned and leaned back in his chair.

"In my office?"

"Not there. Some place private, away from people. I could bring a lunch for both of us."

Mike was ecstatic, but he kept his voice level.

"I know a great spot where we won't be bothered."

***

******

Chapter 38
Wednesday, January 10

Jeannine paced the room and continued to protest.

"Monique, you can't be serious. You can't meet Mike alone at Great Falls Park. He'll rape you. What were you thinking? How will you hide the tape recorder when your clothes are stripped off. Are you forgetting who this guy is? What he is?"

She stopped pacing.

"This is ridiculous. You can't go!"

There was a stubborn streak in Monique that Jeannine had yet to experience. Monique's usually liquid brown pupils were rigid and contracted. They fixed Jeannine piercingly.

"You know Albert Camus, the existentialist?"

"What does he have to do with you?"

"In the book 'La Chute,' 'The Fall,' the character sees a young woman leaning over the railing of a bridge over the Seine. It's night. There's no one around. He hears a splash, and then hears cries for help, fading away. He does nothing. Then the cries cease. It's too late."

"Monique?"

"He did nothing. He did not dive in after her. That guilt goes with him the rest of his life. He was always afraid to cross a bridge at night. He couldn't live with himself. He despairs!"

"Monique, what are you talking about?"

"Don't you see? It's late. John's in the water. He's thrashing. He's even too proud to call for help, but I've got to jump in. I must try. I've got to meet Mike for John's sake!"

Monique dropped her gaze.

"Maybe it's even for my own sake. Maybe I want to be able to cross bridges with a clean conscience?"

"Monique, the point is that Mike has no conscience!"

"What Mike is has nothing to do with this. It's who John is, and who I am. Besides, I have you and Cecilia to back me up. He won't be able to hurt me."

Cecilia chimed in.

"Jeannine's right. It's too dangerous. You can't go through with this. What if something goes wrong? How will we get close enough to help?"

"Peu importe! Tant pis! I've got to do it! Will my friends be there? Oui? Ou non?"

Without waiting, Monique turned abruptly up the stairs.

Cecilia shook her head. Jeannine grimaced. They had until noon to dissuade her.

***

For the second straight day, Mackie slept late and awoke to bright sunlight streaming through the parted curtains. His host had left for the university long since.

Mackie looked at his watch. It was after ten o'clock. By now, Mike had picked up that reporter, Husak, at the airport.

He went downstairs to the kitchen and smiled at his handiwork. Yesterday he had cleared the counter and put the dishes away.

Soon the aroma of fresh-brewed coffee filled the kitchen. Mackie poured himself a cup and planned his day. His flight to Paris was not until seven in the evening. He would have lots of time to make the flight after meeting Mike at Great Falls.

Mike was to meet the Laurier woman at 1:00 p.m. at Great Falls, on the Virginia side. The accident would not take long. Afterwards, Mike would spend the evening with that Express reporter.

Mackie finished his cup and deliberately poured himself another. He contemplated the rising wisps of steam and savored the rich aroma. He raised the cup to his lips. The coffee was hot and delicious.

***

Dean Hampton was a distinguished academic with neatly trimmed silvery hair. This morning he appeared fresh and energetic as he entered the room. Without speaking, he let his eyes rest momentarily on each man seated at the conference table. Though no words were spoken, the brief glances were effective. Dr. Lawrence, Dr. Santini and Marshall Hanes each felt included and welcome.

The dean spoke first.

"Thanks for coming, gentleman. We all know why we're here, except for you, Franklin."

He turned and fixed Franklin with a penetrating stare. The dean relaxed. He smiled.

"Franklin, first I want to congratulate you on that Express article. It looks good, good for the university too. Was it accurate?"

Franklin nodded affirmatively and the dean continued.

"Fine. I thought as much."

He paused.

"Marshall Hanes and I had a chat yesterday afternoon, and we agreed you are the best person for this job. Here's the situation. We've been asked to contribute a position paper on research misconduct for the ethics committee of the Combined Medical Societies. It's quite an honor."

Another pause as he engaged Franklin's eyes once more.

"We think you are the perfect individual to prepare this paper. Chairperson Santini, Marshall and I would of course contribute, but given your experience with misconduct in this Martin affair, we think that you are the ideal individual to present the basic issues in depth. Would you consider doing this?

The dean turned to the others.

"I think I could find $4,000 dollars in my discretionary fund to partially compensate Dr. Lawrence for this task and the time he will lose from his research. Would you agree with such compensation?"

Both Hanes and Santini nodded in unison. Dean Hampton turned back to Franklin.

"There. It's done. All you have to do is accept. Your official title will be Chairman of the University Committee on Research Misconduct. Regard us as the members of your committee."

For the first time Dr. Lawrence smiled at his colleagues. He met the dean's gaze.

"I accept. I'm happy to give the university the benefit of my experience and knowledge."

At these words, Dr. Santini covered his mouth with a handkerchief as if stifling a cough. Marshall Hanes smiled. The dean reached across the table and shook Franklin's hand.

***

Mike was not in the lab. Dr. Lawrence sought out the department secretary. She was standing outside Dr. Santini's door. She spoke deferentially.

"I'm sorry Dr. Lawrence, I don't know where Mike Hartness is. I think he left the building. He's probably gone to the airport. He wanted me to see if a flight was on time."

"What flight was that?"

"A United flight from Chicago to National. I forget the number. It was due at 10 a. m. They said it would be on time."

"Are you sure it was from Chicago?"

"Yes. She looked at her watch. It should have arrived thirty minutes ago."

Chicago! Sharon! Sharon and Mike! A quiet fury seized Franklin. His muscles quivered. His face flushed. He wanted to smash something, anything, but he could not let the secretary see his rage. He turned to go.

The secretary spoke to his back.

"Dr. Lawrence, Dean Hampton left this envelope for you. It's your check."

He did not see her extended hand. He was afraid to reveal his anger. He mumbled.

"I'll pick it up later. Thanks."

He hurried out.

***

Betty Lawrence was tired. The flight from Tucson to Washington had been unusually turbulent, and the talkative man in the aisle seat had kept her from resting.

She paid the taxi, and stood before her home. Her home! She stared at the familiar doorway. She had expected to be overcome with emotion, sentiment, anger, anything. She felt nothing.

Numbly she saw the blue Buick parked in the driveway. There was that stupid license plate, LAB-DOC. Thank heaven the Buick's presence did not mean that Franklin was here. He usually took the Ford. Betty had no desire to see him. She was home to retrieve her grandmother's necklace and some of her belongings.

At the doorway, she fumbled with her key, but the lock would not turn. Frustrated, she stood indecisively on the step wondering what to do. The door opened from within.

"Betty?"

"Mackie!"

Their surprise was mutual.

"Betty, what are you doing here? I thought you were in Tucson!"

"I was about to say the same to you."

"Franklin is letting me stay here a few days."

"I'm here to pick up some of my things. Sari's with Helen and Mattie in Tucson. I'm going right back."

Betty pushed past him into the hallway, and smelled the freshly-brewed coffee. She stood in the kitchen, and absorbed the familiar sights in the subdued sunlight, the curved counter tops, her window curtains. She saw that the counters were clean and the sink was empty. She turned abruptly, smiling.

"Mackie, tell the truth. You cleaned the kitchen didn't you? I know Franklin, and I'm sure that ..."

365

Mackie smiled back. She remembered. So did he. For a brief moment, he was a young medical student again, intent on stealing his friend's girl.

"You're right. I cleaned it when I got here. It was filthy."

"And you made the coffee, right?"

"Right, do you want a cup?"

Without waiting for an answer, Mackie filled a cup for her and warmed up his own. They sat facing each other in silence, each looking back to those early years as students. Betty returned to the present.

"Mackie, where did I fail Franklin? Has he said anything to you?"

Mackie shook his head in denial.

For the briefest of moments he was seduced by her loneliness, years ago he had been fond of Betty. Now he felt his own loneliness. Betty was still attractive.

He cleared his head quickly. *Forget it, McElroy. You've got to get out of here and out of the damn country.* He glanced at his watch and then looked at his bag in the hallway.

Betty, ever sensitive, caught that glance and stared into her coffee.

Mackie arose, gathered some papers and stuffed them in his bag. Silent, he stood up and stepped to the hallway. She heard a murmured good-bye. Then the door shut.

She stared at her feet. An open envelope lay on the floor. It was addressed to Mackie care of Franklin. It had been mailed only two days ago. She read its contents.

My source says the FBI agents who wanted to see you are busy elsewhere. Very busy. There are no charges against you, and so far not even a hint of an investigation. Ditto for the locals at Benson.

My source is totally reliable. You're OK here. You can come back anytime. If any investigation should start, I would know right away.

Hernandez is back East. She's still on some sort of leave.

Betty was puzzled. She didn't recognize "Hernandez," but she saw the reference to "Benson." That was where the *AMAH Clinic*'s security officer had died. What trouble was Mackie in?

She went upstairs to find her jewelry. Their bedroom was a dark dreary mess. She needed sunlight. She stepped over dirty underwear, went to the window, and opened the curtains. There were two cars at the curb. By them, stood two men deep in discussion. The first was Mackie. The second was Mike Hartness. Mike stuffed something into the trunk of his car. Then he drove away. Mackie followed.

Betty was trusting by nature, but she did not like Mike. Mike and Mackie together could be bad news for Franklin. *You're not my problem any more!* But w*hy were they together?* She looked at the back of Mackie's envelope.

Mike will meet her at 1:00, Great Falls Park, Virginia.

Betty looked at her watch. *Forget Mike and Mackie! Forget Franklin! Forget them all!* She went up to her closet. She pulled out two suitcases and stuffed them with clothes.

***

Betty was in Sari's room, packing for her daughter when she heard a noise. A frowning Franklin stood in the doorway.

"You! What are you doing here? How did you get in?"

Betty realized then that her key was not defective, Franklin had changed the locks. He wanted her gone.

"I'm picking up my things. Isn't it obvious."

"What's obvious is that you shouldn't be here."

"This is my house too, have you forgotten already?"

"Where's Mackie?"

"Your friend is in big trouble. If you don't believe me look at the letter on the kitchen table. Go see for yourself."

Franklin stood stiffly. He refused to reveal emotion to Betty.

"You didn't answer. Where's Mackie? Or don't you know."

His tone implied that she never knew anything. Betty was beyond letting him bait her.

"I suppose with Mike. They drove away at the same time."

"Mike! You mean Mike Hartness?"

Franklin was irritated. Betty stayed calm.

"Who else?"

He's worried! In spite of everything, she tried to help.

"Mike is meeting some woman at Great Falls Park at one o'clock. Mackie wrote a note on his envelope, on the table."

Franklin gulped. He wanted to scream "traitor" and "Sharon," but he stiffened. He turned red and took several breaths. He squeezed the words through tight lips.

"Great Falls on the Virginia side?"

"Yes."

He spun about and stomped down the stairs. After some minutes she heard the front door slam. Then a car pulled away.

Betty went to the window. The Buick was in the driveway. Franklin had taken the Ford.

***

Betty closed Sari's suitcase. She slipped on jeans and sneakers and stood, relaxed and comfortable.

She went down to the kitchen. Mackie's letter was gone, but the house key he had borrowed was on the counter. Betty took it and left her outmoded key in its place. Then she loaded the suitcases into the Buick and headed for the Beltway.

Franklin was upset with Mike. Was he making trouble for Franklin? In spite of everything she still felt protective.

Maybe I'll go to Great Falls and find out!

***

Franklin left the house with a single thought, to drive straight to Great Falls and accost Mike. But once on the Beltway, he conceived a better plan. He would intercept Sharon at her hotel, before she left for the park. He left the Beltway, towards Canal Road. He would catch Sharon alone, without Mike.

At the hotel's main desk, he asked for Miss Husak. The clerk rang her room. Seconds seemed like minutes. He sweated. Had he missed her? The clerk turned back to him.

368

"She'll be right down."

He exhaled. He was in time. He went to the elevator doors. In only minutes, they opened and a jean-clad Sharon appeared. Her garb was relaxed, but her voice was strained.

"Franklin, how did you know I was here? I was going to call you. How are you? Did you get the extra copies of the article? I sent them two days ago. It's much warmer here. You call this winter? You look good. Where's your tie? What a nice shirt!"

In spite of himself, Franklin smiled. He checked his watch.

"Don't you have to meet someone?"

Sharon appeared puzzled.

"No, why do you ask?"

It was Franklin's turn for confusion.

"You're not going to Great Falls?"

"No. Where's that?"

"Is someone picking you up?"

"No. What do you mean?"

Now Sharon was puzzled. He must mean Mike, but that wasn't until tonight.

"Franklin, I don't know what you're talking about."

Franklin stared. She was not meeting Mike! He relaxed.

"Sharon, I wish you had let me know you were coming. Would you like lunch. There's a good Italian restaurant near here. They have great cannelloni and good Chianti."

Sharon thought of the reports and documents on research misconduct that were strewn about her room. She needed to study them, but they could wait. She would interview Franklin instead. But, she would skip the Chianti. Diet Coke was safer.

"Franklin that sounds good. Let's go."

She took his arm.

***

Monique came down the stairs. She had on a soft gray sweater that hung loosely about her waist. Her brown hair was fluffed off of her forehead. Her warm brown eyes advertised her vulnerability, but her mouth was set in a firm line. She was determined to get Mike to admit his crimes. She would tape them. Thus John would be exonerated.

The weather seemed to approve her mission. It was a warm sunny day for January.

Jeannine wore her faded *SKYLAND* sweatshirt. Her pony tail swung to and fro as she packed the basket of food. Mike liked roast beef sandwiches and brownies. Both were in the basket. Hopefully, Mike would talk while he ate.

Cecilia wore a denim skirt. Her new Lands' End jacket was unzipped. Her backpack contained a sweater along with her Smith & Wesson revolver, fully loaded. Her cousin had her phone, but no matter. Monique would not carry one. That would spook Mike.

There was no fancy plan. Monique was to drive Jeannine's Mazda. Cecilia would follow in her cousins' car with Jeannine hidden in back. Monique had the micro cassette recorder in a purse slung over her shoulder. She had practiced slipping her hand in and out to start and stop the recorder to record Mike. Cecilia was skeptical. This was amateur hour, but the plan was simple enough to work.

Still, Monique's detached air troubled both Cecilia and Jeannine. They decided to intervene the moment Monique appeared threatened, whether or not Mike's admissions were on tape. With that agreed, Monique got into the blue Mazda and pulled away from the curb. Cecilia and Jeannine followed.

The two-car caravan headed for the Beltway and Virginia.

***

Cecilia drove. Jeannine lay on the back seat, out of sight. They crossed the American Legion Bridge. As they turned onto the Georgetown Pike, a Volvo squeezed between them and the Mazda. Then a pickup truck forced itself in front of the Volvo. Now two vehicles separated them from Monique.

The Volvo slowed and Cecilia lost sight of the Mazda on the twisting roadway. Each time she rounded a curve, she expected to see Monique. Each time she was disappointed.

Finally, the road straightened and Cecilia saw the Mazda far ahead.

It turned into Great Falls Park.

***

Inside the park, Monique drove the Mazda slowly past the visitor center. She spotted Mike waving and pulled over.

He jumped in and pointed.

"Drive on down to the last lot. My car is there."

Monique looked in the rearview mirror. There was no sign of Cecilia. She hesitated. Mike stared, unsmiling.

"Well?"

Still no sign of Cecilia and Jeannine. *Where are you?*

Mike gestured again.

"My car is in the last lot. Get going."

Monique drove to the last parking area. Mike's was the only car, at the far end. She parked next to it and switched off the engine. Mike grabbed the picnic basket.

"You brought food. Good. I'm hungry.

Monique looked back. Still no sign of her friends.

Mike frowned.

Are you expecting someone?"

"No. No one."

The precious recorder was in her purse. She put the strap over her left shoulder, and locked the car.

Mike stared.

***

By the time Cecilia reached the park, there was a traffic jam at the entrance, caused by three vans filled with youths. The park ranger went into the gatehouse to use the phone. Finally, after much arm waving, the vans were allowed to enter.

Cecilia followed, only to be stopped once more. The three vans double-parked to discharge the students at the visitor's center. Her passage was blocked. She had to wait.

***

Dr. McElroy was at Great Falls to protect his own interest, Mike's silence. Seeing Hernandez, Monique and Jeannine together in Washington had unnerved him. He did not want to take chances. He would watch Mike's back. He hoped he was not needed.

He was under a willow oak near the Visitor's Center when Monique arrived and was joined by Mike. Some minutes later, the three vans of students had arrived at the entrance. He had watched, amused by the confusion over their entrance fee.

He turned to leave. Then he saw a woman driver stop at the ranger's kiosk.

Hernandez! Damn! But you're too late to help your friend!

McElroy moved to the other side of the tree and watched as Cecilia waited for the vans to unload before driving off. He walked along a shaded path under the trees and followed her. The successive parking areas terminated in a dead-end. Cecilia would have to park in one of them.

McElroy frowned. He was needed after all!

***

Mike took the picnic basket in one hand. With the other he seized Monique's wrist.

"Come on. There's a spot above the falls I want you to see."

Monique panicked. Where were Jeannine and Cecilia?

"Wait!"

Mike turned and stared. Monique tried to recover.

"Don't squeeze like that. It hurts."

Mike relaxed, but did not let go.

"Are you ready now?"

She nodded. They headed through the woods towards the river.

***

******

Chapter 39
Wednesday, January 10

Some thirteen miles upstream from the American Legion Bridge that carries the Capital Beltway across the Potomac River, the river cascades over a mass of ancient metamorphic rocks, dropping eighty feet in under a mile, to pour through a narrow channel known as Mather Gorge. The resulting falls, the Great Falls of the Potomac, were seen by John Smith in 1648. In 1785, George Washington, the first president of the Patowmack Company, saw the falls too, but as an obstacle to east-west commerce. His company started construction of a canal and locks so that boats and barges could skirt the falls.

At Seneca, Maryland, the Potomac river leaves the sedimentary rocks of the Leesburg Basin to cut through the metamorphic rocks of the Piedmont. Consequently, the nearest "workable" rocks to Great Falls are found upstream at Seneca. There the red "Seneca Sandstone," cut from a riverside quarry, was floated downstream to build the walls of the locks that skirt the falls.

Around the year 1797, an apprentice stone mason working in the quarry at Seneca, inadvertently fractured a block of red sandstone. In disgust, he grabbed one of the useless fragments and hurled it into the waters of the adjacent Potomac. Then he turned back to his work. The fragment settled, lifeless, on the river bottom, wedged against a branch whose protruding tips bent with the swirling current.

Partially buried in sediment and motionless, the rock remained in place until sometime after 1805, when after a winter of heavy snow, a swollen river dislodged the branch and projected the rock into a deeper channel. It had traveled all of four feet.

The rock was still in that spot in August, 1814, when the same stone mason refused to flee at the battle of Bladensburg,

Maryland, and was killed. A short time afterwards another surge of flood waters scoured the river, undercutting banks on the Maryland side and toppling sycamores, river birch, elms, box elders, and small paw paws into a brown foaming mixture of earth, water, twisting branches and tossing tree trunks. A large up-ended elm gouged the channel where the rock was half-buried, and it was shoveled up and wedged in the twisted labyrinth of the tree's roots. Thus transported, the rock floated over seven miles downriver, past Conn Island, to a point not far above the Great Falls. There the elm was caught in an eddy on the Virginia side of the river, and was buried in sediment.

Within a few years, the growing roots of paw paws, birch and box elders all found and embraced the sediments that contained the rock and the decaying elm beneath the surface. The young trees anchored the fresh bank.

Recurring floods eroded and redeposited sediment, but the buried rock, remained *in situ*, unmoved. It was unmoved in August, 1862 when the last of the stone mason's line, a grandson, was killed at second Bull Run. In fact, the rock stayed buried until June, 1922, when surging waters swept away the sediments where it had rested for over 100 years.

At that time, the roots of an upstart tree, a box elder just twenty years old, had twisted about and embraced the rock. Rock, roots, soil and box elder were swept towards the "falls," themselves completely submerged by the swollen currents. The waters raced above the inundated "falls," but the box elder was trapped in an eddy. Twisted and torn as it circled in the swirling foam, its soil-caked roots were washed clean. The rock, released from their grasp, dropped to the bottom and came to rest on a smooth rock surface in front of a crevice. That surface and crevice were formed in those resistant metamorphic rocks, metagraywacke and mica schist, that, when exposed, form the falls themselves.

When the waters subsided, the box elder was gone, but the fist-sized reddish sandstone fragment remained high above the falls, dry and exposed to the air. Only "great floods" that submerge the entire falls could reach it. But the crevice faced upstream, and even great floods merely swirled the sandstone fragment in the crevice without pushing it into the river. Each time the waters subsided and the falls reappeared, the rock settled once more at the base of the crevice.

It was still there on January 10 of this year.

***

Mike continued to hold Monique's wrist as he walked purposefully on a worn trail shaded by tall trees. The stagnant leaf-filled waters of the old canal were on his left. Above, dried oak leaves clung stubbornly to equally dry branches. Green thorny vines of smilax, stretching for sunlight, hung from the bare branches of small ashes, redbuds and paw paws, themselves shaded by the large tulip poplars and oaks. The pale bark of numerous sycamores shone through the shadows. Light patches of bare clay revealed the thinness of the soil, while patches of decaying leaves, collected in lower areas by the receding waters of the fluctuating river, darkened the floor of the floodplain forest.

Monique tried to relax, rather, to appear relaxed. Her purse was slung to her left. Her free hand slipped into it and pressed the recorder. Her fingers felt the slight vibration as it turned. It was working. She tried to suppress her excitement.

"Mike, why did you pick Fairland University. I mean, what made you pick Dr. Lawrence's lab for your work?"

She spoke easily despite the rapid pace. Mike glanced sideways. She was wearing the same gray pullover as the day he had grabbed her in the lab. He recalled her firm stomach. She looked great, and she was in superb physical condition. It was a shame she was the enemy.

"I don't know. Dr. McElroy I guess. I worked with him in Arizona."

"Did you fake data for him like you did for Dr. Lawrence?"

Mike paused. She was uneasy and needed to talk. Why not? He could talk freely. It was purgative. One should confess all one's lies to someone whose opinion was important. And Monique was a beautiful someone. Besides, she was to die. Whatever she learned would not matter.

"Sometimes, particularly for this one clinical 'trial,' but he didn't need my help, he was pretty good himself."

Inside her purse Monique's fingers felt the reassuring vibration of the recorder. Would it pick up Mike's voice? She shifted the strap so that the purse hung centrally. She prompted.

"What did you do?"

"I found people who had died, in the paper, the obituaries, the right age for our trial, and then I had this real slick way of getting their social security numbers. We had a completed trial in less than a month."

"Was that for the government?"

The recorder, now much closer to Mike, whirred away.

"It was for a drug company. Somehow they got wind that something was wrong. Seems they're pretty good at that, better than the Institutes of Health anyway. The company paid for the contract, but wouldn't use our 'data.' They cut Dr. McElroy off. Wouldn't fund the next phase."

"Is that why Dr. McElroy wrote such a good reference for you?"

"Partly."

Mike stopped walking and turned to Monique. He had never talked with anyone like this. It felt good. Maybe this was why Catholics went to confession. Besides, she would not be able to repeat his words. His grip slipped from her wrist to her hand.

They continued on the path.

"The real reason he helps me is that I know about the snake."

"The snake?"

"A rattlesnake, a Western Diamondback he kept in the lab for its venom. You see he was living with this girl, her name was Cynthia, my age actually, and very pretty, nice figure, brown hair, just like you. One day she tells him she's pregnant! Anyway she would not have an abortion, absolutely not! Pretty stupid really. So one evening they go for a walk in the desert and there's an accident. It's dusk, when the snakes are about, and she gets bitten and dies. Pretty convenient for the good doctor."

"But there was an autopsy, they knew she was pregnant?"

"Sure. But so what. The good doctor was distraught at the double deaths. He told everyone that damned snake ruined his future happiness, etc. etc. It was touching."

Mike chuckled.

"See, I saw the snake was missing from the lab before they left for their hike, and I saw him put the snake back when he returned."

"He left her in the desert?"

"No, she died in the car outside the clinic. It was late, and he waited before he called 911. We had antivenin in the lab too! But he waited to inject her too. He made sure it wasn't soon enough.

Anyway, ever since that time Dr. McElroy has been very nice to me. He's helped me a lot. I guess you could say I owe him. I know he owes me!"

Mike became silent.

***

The sun left the path as the trail entered the woods. There were large tulip poplars on all sides. Twisting up one tree was a knotted vine several inches in diameter with brownish "hairs" that clung to the trunk. It was dead, sawed at the base. Monique saw that it was poison ivy.

She tripped over a gnarled root that crossed the path, but steadied herself. A single hiker greeted them as he passed in the other direction. Now they were alone. She looked back. There was no sign of Jeannine or Cecilia.

Mike turned to her and smiled.

"We're alone. My spot is just ahead. This is going to be a great picnic."

Still smiling, he added.

"Funny, this is one of the few spots in the area where they still find Copperheads. Sometimes in January they find a warm rock and sun themselves, but don't worry, their bite usually isn't fatal, not like a Diamondback."

Monique shuddered and paled.

***

Jeannine and Cecilia found the empty Mazda parked next to Mike's car. They split up. Cecilia took the upstream trail towards Riverbend Park. Jeannine took the downstream trail towards the visitor's center.

The trail to the visitor's center was mostly empty. Of the few hikers, no one had seen a couple like Monique and Mike. At the center, a ranger was lecturing to a group of young people. There was no sign of Monique.

Jeannine debated whether to head back upriver to Cecilia, or to continue down towards the ruins of Matildaville. She sat at a nearby picnic table, face in her hands.

"Jeannine? Jeannine Ryan isn't it?"

She looked up.

"Mrs. Lawrence?"

"Why are you here? I heard you were in Arizona."

"I am. I came back for a few things. Right now I'm looking for Mike Hartness, and Franklin. And maybe Franklin's friend, Dr. McElroy, too."

Jeannine studied Mrs. Lawrence's eyes. Could she trust her?

"If he's here, it's to help that bastard Mike. It means that Monique Laurier is in trouble."

"Monique! Was she supposed to meet Mike?"

Jeannine outlined the whole scenario for Betty. The research cheating, McElroy's attempt to burn Cecilia, Monique's plan to trap Mike.

Betty absorbed everything.

"So 'Hernandez' is Cecilia That explains the letter I found this morning. Mackie is running from the FBI. We have to find Monique right away."

Jeannine stood up.

"We need luck. I don't think Mike will be down river. The ruins of Matildaville are not exciting. My guess is he'll be near the falls. I'm going that way. Come along if you want."

Betty rose to follow.

***

Mike led Monique across a small bridge over the old canal. Ahead, was a sign.

DANGER
HAZARDOUS AREA
STRONG CURRENTS
SLIPPERY ROCKS
NO SWIMMING

Mike veered off the path. He pulled her through the brush and small trees. They scrambled over and around several rock outcrops, and then started to descend. All the while Mike held her tightly.

Now they were in a secluded ravine, invisible to outsiders. On one slope tall tulip poplars reached skyward. On the other exposed rocks were visible among patches of scrubby Virginia pine, river birch and small oaks that formed a dense growth.

They started downwards.

The brush pressed their faces. Mike used the basket to push the piercing branches aside. One displaced branch snapped back against Monique's cheek. She winced, but was jerked forward as Mike clambered further downwards. She scrambled over sharp rocks and balanced herself with her free hand.

Suddenly Mike released his grip. He pushed forward through the thinning brush and stopped. Monique, too, stopped. She caught her breath. They were on a smooth stone ledge directly above the falls.

She looked down at the seething water. Beneath them was a raging flow that frothed and slapped the sides of a narrow channel. Ahead and to one side, was a whirling pool of brown foam, trapped in a circle of rocks. There floating sticks, foam, leaves and branches circled in rotating rings from whose margins branches and leaves occasionally escaped to immediately disappear in the rushing torrent.

Stretching across to cliffs on the Maryland side, masses of vertical gray rocks formed channels for water that cascaded and poured downwards. At the base of these cascades, Monique could see waves breaking backwards upstream. Objects trapped in that circular backflow would rotate indefinitely unless pushed by some sudden surge into the flowing channel.

Monique looked back upriver. Above the falls a Great Blue Heron stood motionless in the still water by the shore. The peace of that scene contrasted with the tumultuous rumbling that arose from the falling waters below.

The ledge darkened suddenly. She looked up anxiously. The sky was no longer blue, and gray clouds had formed overhead. One of them momentarily blocked the sun. She shivered.

She turned. Mike's eyes were not on the natural wonders around them. They were on her. His face softened.

"How do you like it?"

"It's ... spectacular."

He turned away. She slipped her hand into her purse and started the recorder.

"How did you find this spot, Mike?"

"It wasn't hard. Actually, we're not far from the observation rock. The park has a fence around that so you can look over, but they can't see us from there. You could get here from there too, but the park rangers don't allow that."

Monique looked over the edge of the precipice. She shuddered. Mike continued.

"They have lots of accidents here, over the years about seven people drown each year. The rocks are slippery when wet."

Monique looked up at the gray clouds, then down at her feet. Mike caught both glances.

"You're right. It might rain."

He added.

"The rock you're standing on is metagraywacke. It used to be sandstone before it was changed, 'metamorphosed' under pressure and heat. The rock behind me is schist. That shiny stuff in it is mica. These rocks were inter-layered shales and sandstones before they metamorphosed over 450 million years ago. Anyway, they're *solid* and they've been here a *long time*. They're not going to crumble into the river. That's all you need to know."

"How do they know the age?"

"They dated the mica in the schist, radioactive dating."

He put Monique's basket next to a crevice in the rock behind him.

"Enough talk. What's in the basket? I'm hungry. Let's eat."

Monique kneeled to open the basket. Her foot dislodged a rock bigger than a fist. It was red, granular and flat on one side, as if cut by human action.

Mike picked it up. He answered her unspoken question.

"This rock is different. It's sandstone, probably from Seneca. They used this kind of stone for the walls of the canal locks. It probably broke off one of the locks."

Mike started to pitch the rock into the torrent below, but put it down to take a sandwich from Monique.

"Roast beef! Great! Oomph!"

His words stopped at the first bite. He ate contentedly.

Monique knew she was on her own. Jeannine and Cecilia did not know where she was. She bit her lip.

"Mike, did you put those programs on John's computer? Is that what you were doing when I found you?"

Mike shrugged his shoulders. He talked between bites.

In the open purse, the tape recorder whirred.

***

Upriver from the falls, Cecilia paused under a box elder. Smaller paw paws, leafless, but with twigs ending in velvety brown buds, crowded about her. She pushed through their stems to reach the water's edge. A sign stood in front of her.

DANGER
SWIMMING, WADING AND
ALCOHOLIC BEVERAGES
PROHIBITED
TREACHEROUS WATERFALL
DOWNSTREAM

Here the river was wide, with a smooth surface. Scattered gray rocks protruded above the shallows. A kingfisher dove into the water and emerged with something shining in its beak. Closer in, a heron stood motionless, stalking its prey.

Cecilia pushed back through the paw paws to the path. She turned towards the falls. Through the trees to her right was the parking lot with the blue Mazda, and Mike's car. Neither had moved. There was no sign of Mike or Monique. She quickened her pace.

Something moved ahead of her. Through the bare branches, she saw a lone car in the next lot. A man stood by it. She peered under the branches. It was Dr. McElroy!

Chihuahua! This isn't Mexico. What's he doing here?

Before she could act, Dr. McElroy left the car and disappeared among the trees. There was no time to think. She followed.

***

Mike stopped talking. He regretted what he had to do. Those soft brown eyes and Monique's full form, only partially concealed in the folds of the gray pullover, weakened his resolve. He had talked for thirty minutes and had not held back. Now Monique knew all his misdeeds.

He stared at her.

How he wished those eyes would moisten out of desire for him. Did she avert her gaze because she was shy? Perhaps? He studied her face. No! He read fear, and though he could not admit it, hatred. She detested him.

But why was she pretending? She had made his favorite picnic! He put the last brownie in his mouth. Delicious. But why would she go to this trouble?

He saw her reach into her purse. Then he heard a sound.

"Click!"

That sound jarred him. It was man-made, out of tune with the natural sounds about them.

"What are you doing? What was that noise? What's in your purse?"

"What?"

"That noise. That click in your purse. What the hell are you up to?"

Monique stooped to put trash into the picnic basket. Mike seized the purse.

"A cassette! ... you little ... !"

He was strong. His first blow caught her on the cheek, forcing her backwards against the rock, one foot over the precipice. The picnic basket flew over the side, wafted for a moment in a current of air, and then fell into the roaring froth and disappeared.

He hit her again, this time above the eye. She spun dizzily and collapsed against the rock wall. A line of blood seeped from a cut on her face.

Mike leaned over her.

"Damn you! We could have had good times together. Why wouldn't you listen? Why do you make me do this?"

He hit her again. The blow fell on her left arm, numbing it. It hung loosely.

"Damn you! Answer me! Why?"

Her eyes glazed. She said nothing. He leaned over and looked into her face. One push, and it would be over.

***

Monique struggled to control her thoughts. She was on a ledge, or was she? ... Where were the falls? Which way? It was important to know ... or did it matter? *Seneca* ... *Metagraywacke ... John!*

She tried to move, but a sharp pain shot through her hip to her spine. Her thigh pressed something hard. The red rock! Her hand fumbled for it. She had it! She felt Mike's breath on her cheek. His eyes were empty and vacuous. She counted silently.

"*Un, ... deux, ...*"

She gathered all her energy for ... one ... swing.

"*et ...Trois!*"

She swung the rock. The roundhouse blow caught Mike on the temple.

"Crumph!"

His eyes glazed. He fell motionless. Monique too collapsed.

Minutes passed. She felt rain on her cheeks, and struggled erect. She stumbled across Mike's inert form, and fell to her knees. She sat up. She examined the rock in her hand. It was the fragment of red sandstone, the sole occupant of the ledge before their arrival.

The rock was redder now, with Mike's blood.

She did not know how the odd piece of sandstone had gotten on the ledge, but without it, her tortured remains would be twisting and tumbling in the turbulent waters below.

She hurled the rock out over the seething chasm. It bounced off an exposed boulder and disappeared into the current. Beyond sight, it tumbled to the bottom of the cascade and stopped, once again on its slow sporadic trip down the river.

***

Moments passed. Now Monique was fully conscious. She grabbed the purse with the precious cassette and looped it over her shoulder. Her left harm hung useless, but with her right, half-crawling, she pulled herself off the ledge up into the pines.

Behind her, she heard Mike stir.

***

Dr. McElroy walked purposefully. He had a specific direction in mind. Cecilia followed. She was sure that he would lead her to Mike and Monique. Ahead, two trees had fallen together to span the old canal. McElroy scrambled over them and disappeared into the shadows. She followed, but her foot slipped into the cold water. She crossed half wet.

At first, McElroy's path was marked by snapping twigs and shuffling leaves. Then the rain started, and she could no longer hear the doctor. She pressed forward.

The temperature fell with the rain, and clouds obscured the sun. The wet sock on her foot clung to cold skin, and the shoe squished. She stopped to listen for McElroy. All she heard was the wind in the tops of the trees, and a low murmuring that could be the falls.

Cecilia scrambled downwards. Her denim skirt caught in the branches of a scrubby pine. She pulled free, and found herself on the edge of a small alcove.

Four feet below was a ledge, smooth and worn. On it stood a lone man. Behind him was open space, sky and the distant Maryland shore.

The man looked up. A bloody face accentuated the hatred in his eyes. It was Mike!

"Diablo! What have you done with Monique? Where is she?"

A blow smashed her shoulder. Her spine twisted as the backpack was wrenched away. She turned and grabbed her assailant's shirt. It tore, but another blow landed on her head, and she fell forward. Her body landed on the ledge at Mike's feet.

Dr. McElroy, holding Cecilia's backpack, spoke.

"Hartness, try harder this time. Dump her over the falls. I'll find Laurier."

McElroy took Cecilia's revolver from the pack. He headed back through the brush.

Mike looked at the still form at his feet. He kicked it. There was no response.

***

Jeannine and Betty struggled through the undergrowth along a rocky ravine. A rumbling murmur of cascading water revealed that the falls were near. The gusting rain whipped their faces. The wet rock faces were too slippery to descend safely. They had to circle back.

Branches crackled and crashed in front of them. They stopped. Dr. McElroy, wild-eyed and shirt-torn broke forth from a cluster of Virginia pines. He pushed past, unseeing, and disappeared.

Betty climbed down through the opening from which McElroy had emerged. Jeannine followed. She spotted a green backpack at the base of a small birch. Cecilia's! She stopped to retrieve it. Ahead of her, she heard Betty shout.

"Mike Hartness. What are you doing? Stop!"

Mike stood at the edge of a precipice. Cecilia lay helpless, ready for a fatal push.

Mike turned, startled, at the authority in that voice.

"Mrs. Lawrence?"

Betty clambered towards him. Mike regained his senses, but he had gone too far to stop. He shouted back.

"Go to hell!"

Betty moved forward.

"You scum! You've caused enough trouble. Leave that girl alone!"

If there had been any doubt about Betty's intentions at Stony Man cliffs, there was none here. She shoved with all her strength.

Even so, Mike might have maintained his balance, but at that moment a dazed Cecilia struggled to rise. Unwittingly, she took a position like that of a school yard prankster kneeling behind the knees of the victim. Pushed backwards, Mike collapsed over her and flew off the ledge.

386

Launched, his hands and feet spread wide, flailing. He shrieked. His falling body rotated a half turn. Then mercifully his head smashed on a rock, the wailing stopped, and his lifeless form dissolved into the crushing torrent.

***

The momentum of her thrust carried Betty to the edge. Her feet flew from under her.

What seemed seconds to Jeannine was only an instant. In slow motion she recorded the pattern of arrows and half-moons on the soles of Betty's sneakers. She saw Cecilia's skirt disappear under Betty's torso. She saw arms reach towards the departing sneakers. She felt those arms pulled taut. A searing pain racked her shoulders. *Thank God*. They were her arms. Her grip on Betty's ankles held!

Jeannine's shoes slipped and gave ground, but one foot locked in a sharp indentation in the rock and she tugged Betty back from the precipice.

Then she reached for Cecilia.

All three women sat and stared. Numb, Betty wept into her open palms. Mechanically, Jeannine handed Cecilia her backpack. Cecilia shivered.

The bare rock offered no shelter. Rain soaked the ledge.

***

Cecilia struggled to her feet.

"Jeannine, I'm going after McElroy. You two find Monique. If she's dead, I'll ..."

"Cecilia, no. You're in no shape. Stay here!"

But Cecilia, pack over her shoulder, was gone.

Stumbling, Betty and Jeannine left the ledge. They fought through the dense brush.

Minutes later, they found Monique, collapsed, in a thicket of Virginia pines.

"Monique! Are you all right? Can you talk?"

Monique opened her good eye.

"Jeannine?"

"It's me. My God! Your face. We were afraid you went over the falls."

"Jeannine. Where's Mike?"

"Dead! In the falls."

Monique extended the purse with her recorder. Only when it was securely in Jeannine's grip did she relax. She laid back and tried to smile. Her head rolled towards Jeannine. Her voice was quiet but triumphant.

"Je l'ai! ... I got it! ... It's on the tape."

Then the one good eye closed.

They were soon surrounded by youths and park rangers. Betty talked to one of the rangers. Monique tried to sit up, but Jeannine restrained her. They waited for the ambulance.

***

******

Chapter 40
Wednesday, January 10

Cecilia's shoulder ached, but somehow she struggled up the rocks. The persistent rain soaked her so that both shoes squished wet. She remembered the dead trees over the canal. She was sure that McElroy would cross there. She wanted to head him off.

The pain in her shoulder helped her focus. She climbed upwards to level terrain. Here the trees were tall; tulip poplars, elms, sycamores. The high foliage sheltered the forest floor from the rain.

A dark form jumped in front of her. McElroy! His shirt was torn, his torso scratched red. His eyes shifted from side to side. He snarled.

"Hernandez! So you got away too, like Laurier! Damn Hartness, the idiot!"

Cecilia exhaled. Monique was alive, and she had the doctor in her hands. She felt in her pack for her revolver, but touched no metal. It was gone!

Still, she spoke with authority.

"Doctor, you're a murderer and a fraud. Come with me."

"With you? Why would I do that? Hernandez, you have no business with me. Why would you harass a reputable doctor?"

"Reputable? You tried to kill me! And more than once. You're no healer."

She continued.

"And you killed Pierre. I know it, and the FBI knows it."

"The FBI knows nothing. And Miss Hernandez, you're a killer. If it weren't for you Lachance would be alive, and his grandmother. Your meddling killed them."

He pointed with his left hand. His right remained behind his back.

"I know you're a *killer*. It's in your eyes. You'd like to kill me right now!"

Cecilia thought of Madame Gauthier's body and the horrible twisted angle of her neck. He was right. She wanted him dead! Where was her gun?

McElroy smiled. He had proved his superiority in reason, now he would prove it in action.

"See, I *was* right. You are *gun-crazy*. Pierre *told* me. Is *this* what you're looking for?"

From behind his back he produced Cecilia's own Smith & Wesson.

"You bitch. Of course I took the gun. I'm not stupid. No dumb girl with an accent is going to ruin *my* clinic, *my* work. You want to avenge the old woman because you are guilty. You are. She is dead because of you!"

"You're a loser Hernandez, a loser, and this time you lose for good."

He pointed the revolver at her.

She was unaware of his grimace. She was back in the cabin with Madame Gauthier and Red Sweater. Madame Gauthier's body and slippered feet flashed before her. There was a gun somewhere! Red Sweater faded and McElroy reappeared. Her own gun! Cecilia's field of vision narrowed, cone-like, so that all she saw was the aperture of the revolver pointed at her. The opening of the barrel widened as she focused on it.

Time was frozen. Every action slowed as her thoughts accelerated. McElroy would not know guns. His shot would probably jerk high and to his right. The bush to her right next to the sycamore! Down the hill! Now!

She made her decision as McElroy fired.

"Crack."

The gun jerked as predicted. The bullet passed above and to the left of a diving Cecilia. The sharp bare twigs tore at her face. She rolled through the piercing branches and sprang to her feet. She ran, putting the large sycamore between them.

"Crack, ... Crack."

Both shots scraped the sycamore. Down the hillside she slipped, stumbled and scraped, dislodging stones and snapping branches. Finally she paused, panting, behind a large tulip poplar. She breathed deeply and listened for signs of pursuit.

At the forest floor all was silence, but high above was a gentle whisking sound where the tips of the branches, far overhead, swept the sky. The winter woods were at peace. Overhead a squirrel chattered.

She peered around the tree.

"Crack."

The bark of the tree splintered above her head. Wood splinters flew, but she was not struck. She was wrong. McElroy could shoot after all.

She darted to the next tree.

"Crack."

She felt a tug on her arm as the bullet ripped her sleeve lengthwise and streaked her arm red. She glanced down. Another jacket was ruined, but the wound was only a graze.

The squirrel chattered again. Snapping twigs signaled McElroy's approach. Cecilia grabbed a branch the thickness of a walking cane and twisted it free. She was armed.

She stood in the open, a plain target to face her pursuer. Triumphant, McElroy lifted the revolver and aimed. He smiled.

"Good-bye Hernandez."

"Click."

Cecilia smiled in turn. She had counted the shots. Her "snubby" .38 had five chambers.

He hurled the gun at her. It glanced off her leg. He started towards her, but she stood her ground. He stopped. Deliberately, Cecilia retrieved the revolver and put it in her pack. Then she brandished her staff and charged.

McElroy was not a big man. His jaw slackened. He turned and fled up the hillside. The brush and trees obscured him from sight, but his path was signaled by branches that cracked as he crashed through the brush.

The adrenaline that had carried Cecilia waned. She stood exhausted. Her arms quivered and her shoulder ached. She could not run, but she forced her legs forwards.

Ahead, she heard water splash. McElroy had forded the canal on foot.

Her head was fuzzy. She tried to concentrate. The parking lot! McElroy would head for his car. She had to intercept him.

She came to the canal. Dead branches protruded from the water. Her first step sank through a false bottom of half-submerged leaves, a foot deeper than expected. Her next step was onto a protruding branch. It held. From it she could reach a submerged branch. She sloshed through the stagnant water. Her denim skirt was muddy and soaked through. Once out of the water, she shivered in the cold air.

The rain was irrelevant now. She squished along the path.

Ahead, she heard a car. She went through the woods towards the sound. She arrived at the edge of the lot to see a car speed away. Too late, McElroy was gone.

***

Dr. McElroy drove fast. He stopped near McLean. The gas station had a restroom with an outside door. He locked himself in and discarded his muddy clothes in the trash. He washed as best he could. He donned a clean shirt and casual slacks from his suitcase.

He filled the rental car with gas. There was no point in arguing with the clerk at the rental return counter. He started again for the airport.

His hands shook on the wheel. Hernandez was still a problem. Now he *had* to leave the country. No matter. Once overseas, he could plan his strategy at leisure. A good lawyer would demonstrate that hers was a personal vendetta, and an abuse of government power. She had harassed him, for personal reasons. Just a vendetta.

He congratulated himself. He was smarter than Hernandez. It was unthinkable that she could match wits with him. The bitch had been lucky to get this far.

He glanced at his briefcase. The case contained a hundred thousand dollars. It was not legal to carry that amount out the country, but no matter. Many times that amount awaited him in Switzerland.

It was after 4:00 p.m. His Air France flight was not until 7:00, but he had to return the rental car and submit to tedious airport security. The traffic thickened, then slowed to a crawl, and then stopped completely. An accident? He could not see ahead. He sweated.

Those three motionless minutes seemed like thirty. At last the cars inched forward. He reached the Dulles access road. The congestion disappeared and he regained speed.

***

At Dulles Airport, he returned the car with ease. He was early, and the line at Air France was not long. He showed his passport to the clerk. Her warm smile and the quickly-assigned window seat calmed him.

"Merci Monsieur. Thank you for choosing Air France."

He moved to the line at the security checkpoint. Five more minutes. Finally, he deposited his loose change in the basket and stepped through the metal detector. The door to a new life.

He was through when he heard the whining beep. He stopped, startled, but it was the woman behind him. The airport marshal was hand-scanning the woman's stylish metal belt.

His briefcase appeared on the conveyor. It emerged on its side, just as he had placed it. He grabbed the handle. Would the marshal find the money. He tried to appear calm. The marshal, a woman, appeared not to notice. She was busy with the woman with the metallic belt.

McElroy took a deep breath and stepped away. No one followed.

The airport shuttle led to the terminal and Gate 24. He stepped in and walked to the far end. There, he slumped onto a side seat. Both hands clasped the precious briefcase on his lap. He shut his eyes.

"Clump!"

He looked up. The shuttle had "docked". Passengers were unloading. He pushed out with the flow. Gate 24 was to the left. He walked purposely to the gate. His flight would not board for another twenty minutes.

He sat down, his briefcase on his lap, clutched by both hands. He leaned back and shut his eyes and let out a deep breath.

He was smarter than everyone else.

He had won!

***

The ambulance took Monique to Fairfax Hospital. She was examined and sedated. Cecilia and Jeannine returned to the apartment.

Cecilia slumped at the table. Once again McElroy had tried to kill her. Once again he had eluded her. Her ruined jacket lay on the floor. More evidence for her mother that Cecilia should leave law enforcement.

Jeannine read her thoughts.

"Think about this. Mike Hartness can't bother anyone anymore. He can't stalk Monique."

Jeannine rubbed Cecilia's shoulder as she talked.

"And Monique is OK. I never thought she'd tape Mike. And Mrs. Lawrence saved your life. You just never know."

Both fell silent.

***

Sam Jones was supposed to meet his wife at five, but he was still at the office. He was upset. He had to warn Cecilia. She might be in danger. How to reach her? She was somewhere in the Washington area. He called her cousin. She was not there.

That afternoon Sam had received the transcript of a wiretap from a DEA colleague. "The man," Tony Diorio, formerly of Burlington, was now in New York. The phone call had been made from someone in Tucson. Sam laid the paper on his desk, and read it one more time.

> *Diorio: **What the hell are you telling me?***
> *Voice: **I'm telling you I found Lachance. He called himself Lejeune. He was at the clinic with the good doctor.***
> *Diorio: **Where's my damned money?***
> *Voice: **Not with Lachance. He's dead. A couple of days ago.***
> *Diorio:[garbled] ...Where's the doctor? ... [garbled].*
> *Voice: **[garbled] ... Hernandez came to the clinic and he disappeared. She brought in the FBI. They think he's in Mexico, but he's in Washington. He's headed for Europe. [garbled] ... France ... [garbled]***
> *Diorio: **Did you say "Air France?"***
> *Voice: **That's right. [garbled] ... Hernandez ... [garbled]***
> *Diorio: **Where's that bitch?***
> *Voice: **She's in Washington, [garbled]***
> *Diorio: **OK, OK [garbled]. I'll handle her.***
> *That was all, except for a note added in his friend's hand:*
> *Sam, better give your partner a heads-up! This is all I got that concerns her.*

It was not just the contents that disturbed Sam. The phone call had been recorded on January 6, four days ago. Diorio might have acted already.

He fumbled with the papers on his desk. *Damn it. Where's that Ryan woman's phone number?*

He found a number with "J. Ryan" written above it

***

Jeannine answered the phone.

"Cecilia? She's right here, next to me."

She turned.

"It's for you. I think it's Sam."

"Hello, Sam. What's up?"

Sam relayed the information from the wiretap.

"Thanks Sam. Thanks for worrying about me, but there's nothing to worry about here. I'm fine. Don't worry so."

She lied. She did not want a lecture. Later, she would tell Sam of her last encounter with Dr. McElroy, but not now.

"No Sam, I'm fine. Just a little bruised from climbing on rocks. ... Right, a picnic. Thanks. Yes I'll keep you informed. ... Bye Sam, and thanks."

Cecilia immediately called U. S. Customs at Dulles Airport. A familiar voice answered.

"Barry! Cecilia Hernandez. Right, I met you at FLETC. Sam's fine. Look, I need you to find out if a 'Dr. McElroy,' ... that's right, ... 'Mc,' ... Right. Was he scheduled to fly Air France to Paris today? ... Right. ... Try and stop him. Call the Park Service. They'll tell you. I'm driving to the airport right now with a friend. ... OK, I'll meet you there. Thanks!"

Cecilia rubbed her shoulder and looked at Jeannine.

"McElroy's at Dulles airport. He may have left already."

Jeannine donned her jacket.

***

Dr. McElroy sat waiting at Gate 24. The steward had not yet called the flight.

There was a faint odor of garlic as a large man squeezed into the seat next to him. McElroy pressed the briefcase to his chest. The man's arms bulged over the arm rests. His eyes were shut.

Dr. McElroy got up. There was time for the bathroom before boarding. He stood at the basin and washed his hands. The door opened. He was relieved that it was not the garlicky neighbor. A man in a blue shirt passed him, stopped at the adjacent basin, and turned on the tap. The stranger spoke with a slight accent.

"Nice briefcase."

Dr. McElroy was in no mood for idle conversation. He ignored the comment and headed for the door. He pulled the handle. It would not yield. He pulled harder. For a brief moment the door cracked. He saw the shadow of a large man through the crack, and smelled a faint odor, garlic. Then the door pulled tight. He could not open it.

Dr. McElroy was trapped. He turned. The man with the blue shirt spoke.

"That's a nice briefcase, Dr. McElroy. Do you mind if I look at it."

McElroy's heart sank. He stammered.

"Who are you, FBI?"

The man in the blue shirt smiled. He extended his hand.

"May I look at the briefcase please? Or shall I call our friend in here?"

Dr. McElroy thought quickly. He handed over the briefcase.

"I can explain everything."

The polite man in the blue shirt placed the briefcase on the wash counter and opened it. When he saw the bundles of bills, he whistled.

"Doctor, do you know whose money this is?"

"It's mine."

"No Doctor, it's not yours. You stole Mr. Diorio's money. You shouldn't do that."

At the false accusation, a sense of righteousness momentarily overcame McElroy's fear.

"I never took any money from him!"

"It doesn't matter. Maybe you didn't. Maybe it was Lachance or maybe it was André. It doesn't matter. We want our money. You have money. You understand don't you, Doctor."

The man's smile turned into a frown.

"Doctor, you're leaving the country, aren't you?"

"Yes, but you can have the money. Take it. All of it. I have to go."

"Thank you doctor. I knew you would be reasonable, but there's one more thing."

Before Dr. McElroy could ask what that was, the overhead loudspeaker announced the boarding of the flight to Paris. Distracted, he looked up. He did not notice that the door to the restroom had opened. He was unaware that someone stood behind him.

Dr. McElroy saw the man with the blue shirt nod. He sensed a whiff of garlic. Then a strong arm seized him by the neck. He was powerless in that grip. He felt the start of a twisting movement. All went black.

***

The large man propped the body, the head at a bizarre angle because of the broken neck, on the toilet and then jammed the stall door shut.

The man in the blue shirt left with the briefcase. The large man stayed to wash his hands. Afterwards, he wiped the door handle with a paper towel, inside and out, all the while smiling. With no gun or knife because of the metal detectors, he had improvised. Now maybe the boss would forget Burlington, and they could concentrate on the Bronx again.

He left the restroom.

***

Barry, like Cecilia, a special agent with the United States Customs, met Cecilia and Jeannine near the Air France counter. He remembered "C" from their training at FLETC. Barry acknowledged Jeannine with a smile and turned back to "C."

"We checked with Air France. Your man checked in, but never boarded. The flight left twenty minutes ago. One of the marshals remembers a man who matched McElroy's description going through security. She describes him pretty well. We think it was McElroy. Nobody has seen him since. Ground security and marshals are alerted. We don't know why he didn't board the plane."

He turned away to talk into the two-way communicator. Then he turned back.

"The flight left from Gate 24. Mary Hunt is over there now. We can check with her. You remember Mary?"

Cecilia nodded.

They walked down the passage towards Gate 24. They passed a men's restroom, not the large kind with two-way traffic, but a small one with a single door. A mother standing by the door, called to her son.

"Johnny, aren't you done yet? Hurry."

Ahead, they saw Gate 24.

Behind them they heard a scream. Johnny, perhaps seven years old, clutched his mother hysterically.

They rushed back. The mother pulled Johnny aside as Cecilia and Barry entered.

The door of the stall hung on one hinge. A man's body slumped on the gray tile with his head and neck against the toilet, one arm in the bowl. The face was hidden.

Cecilia stepped into the stall and bent over. Barry raised his eyebrows in question. Cecilia nodded affirmatively.

"It's McElroy."

She stared. His neck made a bizarre angle with his body, the same angle that she had seen before, six weeks ago in Vermont, in Madame Gauthier's cabin. That angle and image had haunted Cecilia since. Now, as she looked at the dead doctor, the image of Madame Gauthier's body blurred with that of McElroy's motionless corpse.

For the first time in weeks, guilt and bitterness drained from Cecilia. She experienced peace, a peace that made no sense, but nonetheless stilled her anxieties. For the first time since Madame Gauthier's death, Cecilia felt forgiven. She realized that Madame Gauthier never had blamed her for the events in that northern cabin.

She stared at the body. She felt sorrow for that wasted life. There was no thought of vengeance achieved, only relief that

McElroy could no longer harm her or others. It was strange, as she stared at the twisted remains, she could no longer recall the image of the fallen Madame Gauthier.

Cecilia shut her eyes and asked God's mercy for Pierre, for Madame Gauthier, for herself, and for McElroy. She stepped from the stall and exhaled deeply. She turned towards the doorway.

There stood Jeannine waiting in silence. Together they stepped out of the now-crowded room.

The first person they called was Mrs. Lawrence.

***

******

Chapter 41
Thursday, January 11

The hotel curtains were drawn, but a ray split the curtains at the center and crossed Sharon's closed eyes. Startled, she awoke. Why hadn't Mike called? He had been so friendly at the airport. She had dumped Franklin in plenty of time for the evening rendezvous, but Mike had not come.

She sat up on the side of the bed. She was to meet Franklin at 9:00 a. m. She struggled towards the shower.

***

Sharon stood outside the door to Dr. Lawrence's office. She straightened her blouse, tucking it into an already tight skirt. She knocked and stepped in.

Dr. Lawrence appeared distracted.

"Sharon. Welcome. Have you seen Mike. He's not in yet."

"I haven't seen him since he dropped me at the hotel."

"Oh well. No matter."

He peered over his half-frame glasses.

"Sharon, I have been appointed Chairman of the University Committee on Misconduct in Science. I'm preparing a report. I have a draft for Dean Hampton tomorrow. It might help you with your own article. Of course, I'd be glad for comments."

The more-established researcher has no need of research misconduct, indeed the probability that such an individual would risk career and reputation by fabricating data is diminishingly small. On the other hand the least, most junior laboratory worker has the most to gain by taking short cuts, by substituting fake numbers from experiments not done for the hard-earned results of real work in the laboratory.

This scenario is confirmed in my own painful experience, where the most junior member of my laboratory, John Martin, blatantly fabricated experimental results rather than perform the time-consuming experiments. Of course he was discovered, and thanks to the prompt action of the university, he was found guilty of research misconduct.

"Franklin, do you think this is right? Don't you think an 'established' researcher might make a reputation on the basis of fraudulent data. Then he would be established. And why would he change his ways once he became established?"

Franklin's frown was a warning.

"Sharon, science is 'self-correcting' and such individuals would never obtain status."

Sharon thought of a deceased British psychologist who supposedly had fabricated an entire study. She wanted to ask Franklin whether the "correction" would occur before the person died. After all, misconduct findings against the dead were academic.

Before she could speak, Franklin continued.

"False results are detected when experiments are repeated."

This time she did not back off.

"But Franklin, what if the experiments are repeated too late to repair a person's reputation while they're alive? Or what if the conclusions are correct, even though based on fraudulent data. Repetition doesn't help there. Truth and falsity don't mix."

Franklin thought of Mike's confession. They had beaten Dr. Johnson to the grant based on Mike's fake data, but their conclusions were correct. His pause was fleeting.

"Sharon, sometimes they do. Lies can lead to the truth too. My ideas can be correct even without data to support them. Besides, data can be deficient, or poorly recorded. But what does it matter? If the conclusions are correct, then any misconduct in obtaining them was not serious. Maybe it isn't even misconduct."

His voice deepened.

"I'm a scientist. It's who I am, and who I become that counts. When you see my research, you see my life. You see change. You experience the search. I'm never satisfied. There's always more. It's the endeavor, the 'becoming' that counts."

She stayed silent before this nonsense. He interpreted that as admiration.

"Look at the next section for me. It gets to the heart of the matter."

Sharon took the text and read.

It is unfortunate that the new generation places much more emphasis on personal credit and self-gratification than the old. The discovery of scientific truth is not well-served by the emphasis on the personal. Scientific truth is impersonal, and the search for such truth should be objective. My generation knew this. Personal desire for credit and reputation was subordinate to a desire to further human knowledge. ...

She did not think that this text was consistent with his last revelation, but she skipped further. Franklin would not want to be reminded that hers was a different generation.

What the lay person fails to realize is that Science is self-correcting. Wrong results are automatically exposed by further research, and society is not harmed. It is not possible for fraud to damage the scientific endeavor. Those who would attack scientific honesty are untrained for, and unaware of, the complexity of scientific issues. They cannot presume to tell scientists how to behave.

Only scientists possess the knowledge needed to correct other scientists, and to preserve the academic freedom that is our heritage.

It is barely tolerable that government bureaucrats should control the flow of funds for research to the biomedical community. These mindless accountants must be held accountable themselves.

Scientists are truth seekers and are inherently truthful and trustworthy. In a free society, scientists themselves must be free to set and pursue their goals for the good and health of the nation.

Give us the money and leave us alone!

At the last sentence, she looked up.

"Give you the money and leave you alone?"

Franklin grinned and chuckled.

"Oh that! Of course I'll scratch that sentence before I send the draft to the dean."

Sharon smiled without conviction. It was an odd joke. Back at the hotel she had the data on NIH research grant expenditures. In 2000, the National Institutes of Health had spent almost 13 billion dollars for research and development. And it was increasing every year. That was a lot of money to be "left alone."

Before she could think of a suitable rejoinder, the phone jangled and Franklin picked up. A moment later, he turned to her.

"Sharon, there's been a horrible accident at Great Falls. Mike is dead."

Dr. Lawrence could not interpret Sharon's reaction. Her face, expressionless, told him nothing. She stood motionless for several seconds. Then she spun about and stepped out of the office. Only a few words reached his ears.

"... back to the hotel."

Then, silence. She was gone.

***

Franklin stared after her. His eyes wandered to the human genome chart on the wall. Mike had taped that chart to the wall for him a few months ago. Now he was dead, swept over the falls. His eyes returned to the empty doorway.

Shock gave way to relief. Mike was no longer a rival for Sharon's affection. The threat of blackmail was gone. No one would ever know about the fake data in the grant application. He collapsed into his chair. A few days ago, defeated, he had crumpled in this seat from Mike's brazen threats. Now, in the same position, he exhaled with relief.

Denial set in. His last meeting with Mike had been a total aberration. That was not the real Mike! Poor Mike. He had been jealous of his professor's status, of Sharon's obvious preference for the older man. More than likely, the story of the fake data in the grant application had been an invention, a ruse to stay his mentor's wrath. Given time Mike would have apologized, and retracted that absurd story of fabricated data. Mike was incapable of doing such a thing.

Dr. Lawrence sighed. Mike had been such a good worker: always the last to leave the laboratory at night, always the first to understand his mentor's reasoning, and to support it! Look at L-12, and before that, A-11. The loss of Mike was a blow to science! The university must recognize this. A memorial service! He needed to organize a memorial service. It would be in the auditorium at Main Med.

Dr. Lawrence stood up, his old-self restored. He must talk to Dr. Santini about the memorial service for Mike, immediately.

Besides, he had to obtain Santini's approval of the candidates he had chosen to interview for the vacant postdoctoral positions. The laboratory now had three rather than two vacancies. Speedy decisions were needed.

Franklin grabbed the job applications. Two of the choices appeared obvious. He glanced at the remainder and chose one more. Even Santini would understand the need to move fast on these appointments. The work must go on.

He left his office to find Santini.

***

In the hospital, Monique slept fitfully. Whenever she succeeded in dozing, the nurse woke her for medication, or blood pressure, or to check the bandage over her left eye, or whatever.

Monique turned. The pain in her left arm shrieked at her to stop. She lay motionless and rigid while the pain subsided. Slowly, she rolled until she rested on her right side. Her good eye closed, and her head sank into the pillow.

The pain pierced her head through the eye socket. She could hear the tumbling waters of the cataract below. Through the haze, she realized Mike had struck her. Her hand fumbled beneath her. She gripped something. The sandstone rock?

She awoke with a start. Daylight flooded the room. She focused her good eye. Were those flowers on the windowsill?

Her hand closed on something firm and warm. It was not the rock, but a hand. It squeezed. There was a face at the bedside.

"John!"

"Don't try to talk. Just listen, Jeannine told me everything. I drove down last night, as soon as I heard."

She started to roll over further, but winced. Her left arm forbade her to stir.

"Monique, don't move."

"I look a mess."

"What made you try such a crazy trick? You could have been killed. Never mind."

Her one good eye sought his. His eyes were moist, or was she seeing her own tears?

She felt his grip tighten. His voice softened.

"So this time it's me sitting here and you flat in the bed!"

"Until you go away, anyway."

He leaned over. His voice was a hoarse whisper.

"Monique, I'm not going away. I'll always be with you. If you'll have me?"

"If? Oh John!"

Happy tears flowed. Her eye closed and her head spun. But what about Jeannine? She felt John move aside. He still gripped her hand, but someone else stood by her. The nurse? She saw red hair. Not the nurse. She focused to see Jeannine's eyes, soft and moist. There was no hardness, only warmth.

"Monique, I'm so happy for you, for you both."

"Oh Jeannine. Merci."

***

******

Chapter 42
Monday, January 15

In Rockville, Clay Hayman looked up from his desk to see an unexpected visitor. There stood the Assistant Secretary for Health. Clay rose awkwardly.

The Assistant Secretary smiled.

"Clay thanks for coordinating the proposal to reorganize research misconduct investigations."

He extended his hand. Clay was pleased at the firm grip.

"Thank you, Sir."

"You did a fine job. The academic community will be pleased, so am I. The ORI will get my memo this morning by special messenger."

Clay swallowed. He spoke softly.

"So you took my advice about the ORI?"

"Yes. Their budget is reallocated away from investigations. We'll keep them to evaluate university investigations, and as a news service on misconduct for the academic community."

The Assistant Secretary started to the door, but turned.

"Clay, my government service is almost over, yours too. We can return to our universities holding our heads high as defenders of academic freedom."

A final nod and he was gone.

Alone, Clay sat silent. He thought back to the case he had investigated at his own university.

You ORI folks should have listened to me, instead of that dipsy graduate student, Sarah whoever.. You could have avoided this! Especially you Delaney! You took her side!

It was a simple matter of academic freedom.

No scientist would fake data. Nobody's faking data out there, or if they are, they are extremely rare. Anyway only scientific peers are qualified to investigate. The whole issue is exaggerated!

Clay smiled to himself. As always, for the good of science, he had been fair and impartial.

***

At Dr. Delaney's request, Marshall Hanes had obtained the conference room of the Medical Center Building, known as "Main Med," for their informal meeting. The dark stained table and large leather-upholstered seats, surveyed by the somber former deans in their portraits, established a serious atmosphere.

Marshall's expression matched those of the portraits. He had no smile.

"Dr. Delaney, I'm glad to meet you in person. It's always good to see the face that goes with a voice. I'm sorry that Dr. Lawrence could not be with us. He's busy preparing his remarks for the memorial service for Dr. Hartness. A great loss to the university. Tragic, he had such promise."

Marshall frowned when he recognized Jeannine. He nodded.

"Miss Ryan."

"Mr. Hanes."

Dr. Delaney intervened.

"Mr. Hanes, Miss Laurier is still in Fairfax Hospital, although she should be released today. Dr. Martin is assisting her, so he isn't here either. I would like you to meet Miss Hernandez. She is a special agent with the U. S. Customs."

Marshall's frown deepened.

"Please sit down. Dr. Delaney, what's this all about?"

Bob nodded to Jeannine. She produced her statistical "lottery" graphs of Mike's fake numbers and laid them on the table.

"Mr. Hanes, Monique Laurier discussed these graphs with you when she told you that Dr. Hartness told Dr. Lawrence about the fabricated data in their grant application."

"Statistics? They're worthless. Dr. Lawrence denies Mike said anything like that. This is a waste of time!"

Jeannine produced a small tape player and placed it on the table. The batteries were fresh. She pushed "play," and Mike's voice resonated through the room. At first, Marshall listened. Then he broke in.

"This proves nothing! How do I know that is Dr. Hartness' voice. You're slandering the dead!"

Cecilia pointed to markings on the microcassette.

"Miss Laurier recorded Mike before he attacked her. Miss Ryan and I marked the microcassette with our initials before she left. Those are our marks. Your Dr. Hartness tried to kill Monique and me. We are only alive today because he died. The tape is authentic all right, and you know it!"

"Why should the university believe you or Miss Laurier? We know she's biased. You must be too."

Dr. Delaney broke in.

"Mr. Hanes, besides the tape, you know that Miss Laurier testified to her belief that it was Mike who fabricated the data. You now have her testimony that she overheard Mike admit faking data to Dr. Lawrence."

"The data in the grant application have nothing to do with the Martin case! Besides, Dr. Lawrence denies any impropriety in the application. Am I going to believe your disgruntled Miss Laurier, or an established professor with an impeccable reputation!"

"But you heard the tape! Mike admitted he put the data on John's computer too! That admission *is* for the data you say John faked. And look at the other admissions on that tape. Surely?"

"*Mr.* Delaney. Everyone knows that Mike liked women. So he found a way to *seduce* Miss Laurier. Maybe he told her those things so she would let him! She was certainly leading him on. Entrapment! He told her what she expected to hear so he could make love to her. Besides, Miss Laurier and Miss Ryan have been trying to frame Dr. Hartness from the beginning."

409

"Mr. Hanes, perhaps *you* think that. Call Dr. Sadler and have her reconvene the university committee. See what *they* think!"

"Dr. Sadler is no longer in the area. She finished her detail at the National Science Foundation. It's my understanding that she is out of the country, doing research in France. She is not available."

"Find another Chairperson and reconvene!"

"You can't make me do that."

"No, but the ORI can."

"We'll see. I resent your implication that the university committee's work was flawed, and I deeply resent your impugning the character of a deceased researcher."

The final remark was too much for Jeannine. She snatched the tape player from the table and turned, pony-tail flying, out through the double doors. Cecilia followed.

Dr. Delaney spoke once more.

"You're being foolish Mr. Hanes. This is my case. The ORI has authority to make you redo the investigation."

Marshall's mouth twisted to a sneer.

"Do you? You'd better check with your office. *My* source at HHS tells me that you have nothing more to do with this case. You'd better see if you still have a job!"

Marshall turned to the wall and shut off the lights.

"Now excuse me. I have to attend the memorial service. Thank you for leaving."

Nonplused, Bob stepped out of the room. He located Jeannine and Cecilia in the foyer standing next to the potted Norfolk Pine. They left together in silence.

***

In the auditorium of the "Main Med" building, the memorial service started. Franklin stood stiffly at the podium. Betty sat in stunned silence at the back of the crowded auditorium. She once had loved the man who was speaking. Maybe she still did, but the inanities coming out of Franklin's mouth as he eulogized

Mike, the would-be murderer, shocked her. After a few minutes, she could stomach it no longer. She left, stepping over legs and brushing knees as she squeezed her way to the aisle.

An attractive young woman in a green suit sat at the end of the aisle. But for their difference in age, Betty could have been looking in a mirror. The expression of disgust on the young woman's face reflected Betty's perfectly.

Outside the auditorium, Betty consulted her watch. She still had two hours before meeting with agent Turner to give a statement on Mike's death. Odd that the Park Service had assigned Turner to this case too. She would finally see what he looked like. She did not expect any problems. With agent Turner's approval her flight back to Tucson was booked for this evening.

She crossed the street towards Le Papillon. Franklin often spoke of that restaurant. She had never eaten there. Today, she would!

***

Bob, Cecilia and Jeannine sat around a table at the Old Goose. It was the same table at which John had shown Jeannine the fake data and Mike's computer program. Jeannine recalled how John had struck the table for emphasis. She thought of the spilled coffee and her pink pullover, of seeing Mike and Monique enter together. It seemed so long ago. So much had happened since, in such a short time.

Cecilia turned to Delaney.

"Bob, I went to the Department of Justice last Friday. They're going after the *AMAH Clinic* under the False Claims Act. More to the point, they want Monique's tape. With Mike's admission on the tape, plus the documents I took from the shed. They think the case is a "slam dunk." They want to recover the Medicare payments from the clinic. Triple penalties! They should collect a bundle! Unless McElroy took it all."

She touched Bob's wrist.

"Anyway, the DOJ would like custody of the tape right away."

Bob shook his head.

"Not till I check with the office. Hanes said something funny after you left. He may know something about the ORI that I don't. I have to get back there."

Their sandwiches came. They ate in silence.

Jeannine kept her own melancholy counsel. She looked at her watch. The memorial service for Mike would be ending. That service disgusted her. The university had failed to reveal Mike's true character. Perhaps the DOJ would succeed.

***

Sharon was ambitious, but she detested dishonesty and fakery. At the podium, Franklin exhibited both. Her experiences with Mike had been informative as well as fun, but she had no illusions about his character. She had seen Mike when he was off guard. The person Franklin eulogized was not Mike.

Her disgust increased as Franklin droned on, extolling the non-existent virtues of his protégé. At least one other listener had experienced the same emotion. Sharon empathized with the evident distress of the woman who had brushed by her to leave early.

Sharon adjusted her skirt and refocused on the podium in time to hear Franklin.

"... Mike was the most generous, self-effacing person I have ever ... ."

Too much! She stood up and strode out. Whatever she thought about Mike, Franklin was an idiot!

The story on research misconduct would have to wait. She walked back to the hotel and packed.

She booked the first available flight to Chicago.

***

Bob Delaney arrived back at the office to a scene of turmoil. Clay Hayman had done his work well. The memo from the HHS had come down by messenger that morning.

412

In Bob's absence the ORI had held an emergency staff meeting. The investigative component of the ORI was severely curtailed. Several positions were abolished, including specifically Bob's. Effective immediately, he was re-assigned as a grants administrator, to an empty office with no grants to administer. The ORI's authority to review university investigations of misconduct was limited.

Marshall Hanes had been right. Bob was off the Martin case, or any other. Because the review of the Martin case had been completed, Martin was trapped in the transition. The best Martin could hope for was that his appeal to the Secretary (an *appeal* only that he be allowed *to appeal*) would be considered.

Bob Delaney called Cecilia.

"You've got to meet me at Chili's right away. It's across the Pike from White Flint towards Nicholson Lane. If you're quick, you'll get there before I'm totally drunk! And bring your cousin's car. You'll have to drive me home!"

***

The interview with Agent Turner, and Betty's formal statement, had not taken long. Now Betty stood alone in her former kitchen. The suffuse evening light cast the same shadows on the counter and table as they had during the years she and Franklin had been together. She called Tucson.

"Sari, Honey. How are you? ... Yes, I'm coming home. No Honey, Home *is* Tucson. We're staying."

She wanted to lie in answer to her daughter's next question, but instead she told the truth.

"No, Daddy did not say that he missed you, but he and I didn't see each other very long."

She switched the subject from Franklin.

"I'll be back on the next flight! Mattie's mom knows what time. I'm glad Mattie is doing better. That's great. Janice is a good doctor, I'm glad you like her. Bye Honey, see you soon. I love you."

Betty left the kitchen. She called the airport limousine service. She locked the outside door. She removed her suitcases from the trunk of the Buick and stood, waiting, in the driveway.

***

Jeannine was alone in the apartment. Monique was already on her way to Pittsburgh.

She went to the refrigerator and drew out a dish of cold pasta. It was in the Microwave when the phone rang.

"Miss Ryan?"

"Yes?"

"I got your name from Cecilia Hernandez. I'm an attorney with the Department of Justice. The DOJ's opening a case against the *AMAH Clinic*. Cecilia tells me you know about it."

"Yes?"

"We need a statistical expert to testify if we go to court. Cecilia says that you have experience with analyzing fake data."

"That's correct."

"Well the pay isn't much, but you should find the work interesting. You work in Rockville, at StatFind. Is that right?"

"That's right."

"Look, I could take you to lunch at Ambrosia tomorrow. My treat, if you're interested. We could discuss what's involved."

Jeannine hesitated. He interpreted the pause correctly.

"Call Cecilia and check me out. My name is Brian Daggett. I'm single, never married, and I'd like to meet you."

His voice had an Irish lilt. She was not ready for this.

"All right, Brian. I'll look at the case. But I won't meet you for lunch. We could meet at the university library at 4:00."

There was a pause on the other end.

"OK. Bring the graphs that Cecilia has been telling me about. The library, at 4:00."

Jeannine settled onto the sofa. She slipped off her tennis shoes and stretched her legs. Her feet, liberated, spread to a more natural shape. For a long time she sat staring at them.

Across the room, neatly laid across a chair, she saw her Page Premium jeans. Forget men! She carried the jeans to the kitchen and threw them in the garbage.

She took a statistics text from the kitchen table, sat down, and concentrated on the pages of mathematical equations.

***

In Tucson, the small woman stood, bent, staring at the lone Saguaro in the yard. In its shade a mesquite had sprouted.

What would happen to her daughter next? Dios mio! Next time might be the last!

The phone rang. She jumped at her daughter's voice.

"Mama, I'm OK. Don't worry. There's a chance I'll be assigned to Nogales in a year. As soon as I know, I'll call you! Yo te amo!"

There was a moment of silence and then …

"Mama, do you think you could buy me another Lands' End jacket?"

When she hung up the phone, Cecilia's mother went upstairs to the bedroom. There was a crucifix above the door. In the corner was a small table with a lit candle. Above it hung an image, Our Lady of Guadalupe. The small woman knelt down and prayed her thanks to another mother.

"Gracias nuestra Señora. Gracias por mi niña!"

***

When Franklin returned home that evening, the Buick was in the driveway, but there was no sign of Betty. He sat before the TV to relax. He had spent the afternoon with Dr. Santini, interviewing new postdocs to replace the lab's losses.

He dozed. The phone rang.

"Rrring."

He checked the ID. An Arizona area code. The number belonged to Helen Morton. Betty was staying with her. Betty must have taken an early flight back to Tucson.

Damn it. Leave me alone!

"Rrring."

415

Give up, woman!

"Rrring."

Talk to my lawyer, not me.

"Rrring."

Damn it, stop!

"Rrring, ... Rrring, ... Rrring."

Exasperated, he picked up and shouted.

"Stay out of my life. I never loved you. I never want to see you again!"

As his hand moved to smash the receiver onto its receptacle, a plaintive cry reached his ear.

"Daddy ... ?"

Sari! But it was too late. The phone crashed against its holder and the line was broken. For a brief moment he thought of calling back, but Betty might answer and lecture him about abandoning their daughter.

He turned to the TV and clicked it on.

***

Late that evening, John and Monique drove onto the Pennsylvania Turnpike at Breezewood, and headed west to Pittsburgh. Monique's head rested against the van's window, vibrating with the road. A small pillow dampened most of the vibrations. She slept peacefully.

John drove carefully as a sudden sense of responsibility overcame him. He gazed in awe at the sleeping form in the passenger seat. He didn't understand Monique's goodness, but he knew she was real, and that he loved her. He felt unworthy, and lucky.

John was not Catholic, but before leaving Washington he had called Father Hamilton, the dean at Aquinas and Augustine College, to reserve the college chapel for a March marriage.

He made a resolution to study French. He had to, if he wanted to understand his future in-laws!

***

******

Chapter 43
Epilogue

That March, Monique and John were married in Monroeville, Pennsylvania. A year later, their first child, a girl, was named Jeannine. Monique too, took a teaching position at *AquA*. Neither returned to research.

Jeannine finished her Ph. D. at another university in the Washington area.

Paul Pagé, the graduate student who had replaced Jeannine as Dr. Anderson's student, abruptly left statistics for pure mathematics. Two years later, Fairland University failed to grant Jack Anderson tenure.

Sharon Husak became a syndicated science columnist.

***

For two years, researchers at three universities wasted their time (and over ten million dollars from the National Institutes of Health) in studies of the structure of A-11 and its faked impact on breast cancer. Their results were negative and consequently never appeared in the scientific literature.

Dr. Hermann found serious toxic side effects with L-12 in animal models. L-12 was never used with human subjects.

The *AMAH Clinic* recovered from the pillaging of its funds by Dr. McElroy. It was able to settle its case with the Department of Justice for a large amount of money. A gift of several million dollars from an anonymous donor who had been healed of "cancer," helped the clinic to remain solvent.

Dr. Janice Wilson stayed with the clinic. She was widely recognized for her success in treating eating disorders.

***

Cecilia returned to her position in upstate New York and Vermont. She did not obtain an assignment to Nogales.

After his position at the ORI was abolished, Bob Delaney returned to university research on the west coast. His university colleagues never trusted him again.

Agent Turner remained with the National Park Service.

Soon after the events at Dulles Airport, Tony Diorio disappeared. Presumed dead, his body was never found.

Lise Jordan married. She and her husband moved to Sherbrooke, Québec.

Sam Jones retired to a farm near Plattsburgh. He never discovered the identity of the shadowy André.

Dr. Lawrence moved to a prestigious university in the Midwest to become Dean of the Faculty of Medicine there. Marshall Hanes moved with him as counsel.

The Lawrence Paradigm, "...that the established professor is innocent, and that the most junior postdoctoral fellow or graduate student (who stands to gain the most from research misconduct) is guilty," gained wide acceptance for cases of research misconduct with fraudulent data.

Betty stayed in Tucson where Sari and Mattie finished high school. Later, Sari attended the University of Arizona. She graduated without taking a single course in science or mathematics. She never visited her father.

***

******

Envoi
Summer
Some years later

The sun was high in the sky. The shadows hid directly under the trees, driven there by the hot rays. The grass was patched brown, but the child ran happily and freely, ignoring the heat. Her shoes crunched on the gravel of the playground. Laughing, she threw herself into her mother's arms.

The young mother looked into her daughter's brown eyes. In September she would be in the second grade. The mother smiled. On an impulse, she asked.

"Jeannie, do you know what 'cheating' is?"

"Sure Mom, if I copy Billy's homework and pretend I did it myself!"

"And that's wrong?"

"Sure. I didn't do the work and I say I did. It's not true. That's wrong."

"T'as raison, ma petite. You're right little one. It is wrong."

Monique smiled. Her daughter disengaged and ran towards the swing set.

***

******

About the Author

James E. Mosimann is a retired biostatistician who spent many years at the Computer Division of the National Institutes of Health. He has a Ph. D. in Zoology from the University of Michigan, and a Masters in Biostatistics from the Johns Hopkins University. After NIH, he joined the Office of Research Integrity of the Public Health Service, where he was a scientist-investigator for cases of research misconduct. He has numerous publications and one text. This is his first novel.

He and his wife, Barbara Jean, live in Virginia. They have eight children, all adult.

Author's Note

This book was a family project. Thanks to my wife for her support and to my adult children for their assistance: Tom's many hours of critical reading and editing significantly improved the manuscript, as did comments by Joseph, John, Theresa, Michelle, Mary and Madeleine. Finally Kateri, in addition to her comments, provided the cover graphics and design.

Thanks are due also to Ed Carroll and John Dahlberg for reading an early version of the manuscript.

Most of the locales in the story exist, however the road on the Vermont border with Canada and the ridge with the large pine were invented for the purpose of the narrative. Fairland University and its School of Medicine are imaginary institutions, as is the newspaper, The Chicago Daily Express.

Three more titles that follow Jeannine Ryan's career in numerical forensics will appear shortly:

The Assassin Chip,
The Prague Plot,
The Carolina Coup.